THE ROGUE OF THE SOUTH

The Elemental 6 Series Vol. 1

Karissa H. B.

Cover Artist: Youness Elh
Editor: Belle Manuel

ISBN: 979-8-9917700-0-2

This story is dedicated to every
Rue Kylexi of the world.
Those who survived the darkness
and wear their scars like armor.
You give others hope.

DISCLAIMER:

To those of us with soft, healing hearts:

This story is fiction, but that doesn't mean what Rue experiences isn't reality for some people, myself included.

This will be hard for some of you. There are real life issues in these pages that will be impossible for some people to handle. Everyone deals with trauma differently and everyone is deserving of their own healing timeline. If you have experienced abuse, rape, depression, or loss, this story might not be for you right now. Please protect your heart and proceed with caution. I've added a list of chapters dealing with these issues and others, tucking it away in the back of the book for those who need it. I highly recommend going through the list to give yourself peace of mind before reading on. The last thing I want is for you to be caught off guard and read something that spirals you into a dark place.

Please reach out to health care professionals or your local authorities if you find yourself in a situation where you need help, physically or mentally.

I want each of you to know that you are never alone. You are needed on this earth. Your choices matter. Your well-being matters. YOU, my love, matter.

ELEMENTAL MAGIC INDEX

Bright Magics: Naturally produced
Gifted by The Mother

AIR MAGIC:
Born from Aruelia, the Goddess of Air
Magic involving the use of air manipulation to move objects and control the winds. Derived through the inhale and exhale of the wielder's lungs. Physically collects in the palms and fingertips. Visually shown as a sparkling white mist. Can be suffocated by water magic.

FIRE MAGIC:
Born of Egan, the God of Fire
Magic involving the use of fire manipulation and the creation of flames. Derived through raising the temperature of the wielder's body. Physically collects along the arms and upper chest. Visually shown as orange ember covered skin with flames protruding out. Can be extinguished by water magic.

GROUND MAGIC:
Born of Doruk, The God of Ground
Magic involving the use of soil manipulation and the creation of flora. Derived through forming an orb of life in the wielder's hands or directly connecting with the ground. Physically collects in the fingertips. Visually shown as green fingertips growing flora. Can be killed off by both fire and ice magic.

WATER MAGIC:

Born of Cyra, the Goddess of Water

Magic involving the use of water manipulation and the control of the seas. Derived through the wielder's direct connection with water of any kind. Physically collects between flat palms. Visually shown as blue glowing runes covering the skin. Can be immobilized by ice magic.

ELECTRIC MAGIC:

Born of Titus, the God of Electricity

Magic involving the use of lightning manipulation and control over electrically charged objects. Derived through the wielder's ability to harness the energy of objects and one's own emotions. Physically collects up the arms, legs, and through the hair. Visually shown as purple electric currents coursing through the body. Can be neutralized by ground magic.

ICE MAGIC:

Born of Ira, the Goddess of Ice

Magic involving the use of ice manipulation and the creation of solid objects of ice. Derived through pulling magic from the chest of the wielder. Physically collects in the chest and hands. Visually shown as frost covered hands, pulling ice weapons from the chest. Can be melted by fire magic.

LIGHT MAGIC:

Born of Lilith, the Goddess of Light

Extinct magic involving the use of light manipulation and the creation of orbs of light. Derived through the connection of the mind and heart. Physically collects in the chest. Visually shown as a glow of yellow light projecting from the heart. Cannot be darkened by any other forms of bright magic.

Dark Magics: Synthetically produced
Created from the Void

SHADOW MAGIC:
Born of Lilith, the Goddess of Light
Dark magic involving the use of spell manipulation and the ability to drain other forms of magic. Derived by education only, cannot be passed down. Physically collects in the eyes and hands. Visually shown as black ooze seeping from the fingertips and tear ducts. At this time, it is unknown how this form of magic is destroyed.

*Wielders must use caution when learning dark magics. It is said to corrupt the body and mind. Leaving behind everlasting mental and physical effects.

Athinora's Visions of Awakening

In every lifetime there comes a seer who claims to predict the future. One such being who is connected to the universe themselves and holds the secrets of what is to come in their mind.

Athinora of the Northlands, the first recorded North Witch, was one such being. Forecasting ten chronological events that were to take place throughout our history:

1. ~~The first blooms will divide with the sunset.~~
2. ~~Light will leave the world for millennia.~~
3. ~~Shadows will seep up through the soil.~~
4. ~~Seasons will fail to coexist.~~
5. Frosted shadows will coat the future.
6. Her blend of Twin Light will yield hope.
7. A sacrifice of each soul will bring one from the roots.
8. The light will be found.
9. Shadows will fade without the help of man.
10. Those who survive will find awakening.

Unlike all others, Athinora has yet to be proven wrong.

It is now commonly known as The Prophecy of Salvation.

A Note From The Teller

Dear Traveler,

Purpose is a strange concept. One you cannot simply define in a sentence or two. Purpose is something told over a lifetime of happenings.

I'm going to tell you a story today. One about purpose yes, but also extraordinary sacrifices, and loss, and love, and hope, and death, and beauty, and everything that makes up a lifetime.

I'm going to tell you a story about a brave woman. One that her world tried to shatter, and crumble, yet she continued on.
This is part one of that story.

 With Love,
The Teller

CHAPTER

"MY name is Luna Quinn," she lies.

The security guard at the front entrance glances down at her outfit, lingering at her chest a moment too long, and then back up to her face, his Adam's apple bobbing from feelings of arousal. A loud thumping from his racing heart rings in her ears, like a siren of approval.

"Is there something wrong? Is it this dress?" she questions, rubbing a black painted fingernail slowly across the exposed part of her breast.

There is in fact something wrong with her dress. The invitation had specifically said *White Attire Only*. Her dress is black, and hardly a dress at all. It is mostly black tulle, covered in tiny golden stars sparkling in the light of the two moons. The only solid fabric is strategically sewn in to cover parts of her body the elder Highers might find offensive. With a plunging neckline, and exposed back, she knew she would be pushing the limits as to what would be deemed *appropriate* for this type of event.

She bats her lashes at him, waiting for his delayed response.

"Um, yes you… your body, I mean your dress is incredible. You… you just might get a lot of looks in there, miss." He stutters through the statement, as his skin turns an adorable shade of pink.

A bright, beautiful smile covers her face, and the lights of the building reflect off her eyes to give the illusion of them sparkling. Resting a hand on his massive bicep she laughs, "Well I hope they look; I spent a lot of money on this dress."

She pulls the sheer skirt to one side, exposing a slit that trails up her toned legs and connects to the bodice at her hip bone. She did look phenomenal; her curves were made for this dress, and she knew it. He checks out her body one more time, before glancing off into the distance at nothing in particular.

"So, is it all right if I go in now?" She leans in on her tiptoes, getting her red lips inches away from his face. "With this kind of attire, a girl can get a bit chilly. It's practically nothing," she purrs.

His Adam's apple moves once again when he clears his throat. "Um… Yeah. Yes, of course."

She gives him a wink as she pulls away, and leads herself into the main entrance, only turning around once to spot him staring at her. She gives him a small wave, which causes him to awkwardly turn away, running his fingers through his hair.

As soon as she turns back around, her sweet smile drops from her lips. "Men," she says under her breath.

Tonight's gala is being held in the Brighten Building in the High District, to honor the President of Currency for renewing his term for a fourth time. This was a common practice in

Alerious City. Those in charge, men from ages forty to death, would renew their seats of power year after year like clockwork.

The city operated in a state of dictatorship disguised as democracy. The Seven Presidents ruled over the people, and the people pretended to appreciate the Presidents.

They split their authority up over seven men, each specializing in one sector of the government. Currency, Justice, Environment, Technology, Unions, Religion, and one who was referred to as the Master President. He is seen as a peacekeeper, breaking ties on issues, and making sure one isn't overpowering the rest.

Every two years they renew their positions by holding elections in the High District only, leaving out the votes of everyone else, claiming those in the High District spoke for all the people.

If she is being honest, more work went into planning these Galas than the actual presidential races. The committees for these events would work for years on reserving the most prestigious venues, and import ship loads of goods from the fae countries on the mainland.

And somehow, a girl from the Low District found herself walking into one of these parties.

A small, older man, dressed in a white tailcoat suit that most likely dated back a century at least, escorts her to the entrance of the Grand Haul. During their short walk, she catches him calling her many foul words under his breath for her disrespect of the dress code. When she thanks him for chaperoning her down two hallways, he refuses to make eye contact, instead looking up at the ceiling and pointing to the curved staircase leading down into the madness.

Stepping out onto the marble tiles, she scans her surroundings, taking in the grandness of the space. Large white stone pillars line the circular room, accented with gaudy moldings and sparkling crystal sconces.

Above her hangs a large chandelier, imported from the Northlands, with twinkle lights connecting it to the bordering pillars. It is said to be made of petrified ice crystals from the Dioden Mountains. It's the pride and joy of the Brighten Building and was put in with a complete renovation four years ago.

On the ground below the steps, live jazz music is being played on a stage in the center of the room, echoing the sounds of saxophones and a grand piano. She can see the President of Currency talking to someone, and when his eyes meet hers, he stops mid handshake.

Her lips form a slight grin, and she looks back at her heels, trying to make the descent down the stairs as graceful as she can.

People are mingling. Drinking. Laughing. But most notably, almost everyone in this room is wearing white or a similar shade. Besides the few waitstaff passing around drinks and hors d'oeuvres, it's a sea of creamy fabrics.

Here goes nothing, she thinks to herself.

Walking through the crowd, she can see long glances from men as she passes. And can also feel the burning stares of their dates. Her skin grows hot with the tension, and her heart races a little bit faster. Whispers start to make their way into people's conversations around her.

"Who is that?"

"Didn't anyone tell that poor girl the dress code?"

"She must be from the Lower District with that type of disrespect for the Presidency."

"I'd like to see what's under that dress later."

She holds her head up high as she gives the other attendees a show. Swaying her hips a little extra, she makes her way over to the bar, sits down, and takes a deep breath.

"You look like you need a drink. What can I get you, miss?" the bartender asks in a very husky voice. He's tall and lean, but strong. Handsome. Rough looking, with shaved black hair and a trim beard. Tattoos shoot up his arms through his tight white button up shirt.

He leans over the bar towards her, close enough she can see a small scar across his nose, and the way his brown eyes almost look black in the golden lights of the ball room. He stares at her down the bridge of his nose with a smug look on his face.

"I'll have a Gin and Tonic, with lemon not lime," she winks, pulling out a tube of lipstick hiding in a small pocket of her dress to reapply.

"I can do that," he grins, "Do I get to know your name too?"

"Wow, straight forward for a bartender in the High District." She leans over the bar to grab an olive with a wooden toothpick. "Someone might be offended," popping the olive into her mouth. "You know how dreadfully prude Highers can be."

"And you're not a Higher, Beautiful?"

"Nope. Not interested. I'd rather be with the real people of this city, in the Low District. More exciting that way."

"Maybe you'll find something to make you stay up on this hill."

"I doubt it, honestly." A small smile forms across her lips which she tries to hide behind her hand on her chin.

"That's unfortunate." His voice comes out low and deeper than before, making her wet her lips.

Before she has a chance to respond to him, she feels a cold hand on her exposed back. It takes everything in her not to smack it away. A man comes around to her side and orders a scotch. He looks down at her chest, then to her eyes before saying, "And whatever this gorgeous thing wants." She can smell the alcohol on his breath already.

"You were just about to make me a Gin and Tonic, with lemon not lime, weren't you?" she says to the bartender, keeping her gaze on the man next to her.

A prick of a man who is now lowering his hand towards her ass. The audacity in him, someone who isn't even objectively attractive, to assume she would be okay with his hand placement. He is average looking at best. Grayish peppery hair, shaggy to cover up the fact that it's thinning. Medium built, standing around 5 '10", which is going to humble him as soon as she stands up to be eye level wearing heels.

His eyes are blue, and tired. Stress induced wrinkles frame his face. And for some reason, obviously not related to his hands on her body without her permission, she gets a bad feeling in her gut to flee.

"Hey there, Gorgeous," he leans in, "I'm Lex Macellarius, the President of—"

"Oh, I know who you are. It's an honor to meet you Mr. President of Currency. I'm Luna, Luna Quinn," she says in a voice a bit too high, reaching out her hand to shake his.

He returns the shake, kissing her hand with too much eye contact. "Well Miss Quinn, I must admit, that is some outfit you've got on. You sure know how to make an entrance, got a lot of people in here talking about you."

"That's so embarrassing, I'm sorry if I ruined your night. I think I missed the part of the invitation where it said white attire only," she says sheepishly, looking down to smooth out her dress, pulling one leg out of the tulle.

"Oh, don't you apologize, that dress was made for you. In fact, I think you need to buy it in every color."

She opens her mouth to make up something about the dress but gets interrupted by the bartender.

"Here you go, miss," he growls, all flirtation lost in his voice.

"Thank you." She flashes a small grin, and her eyes burn into his with untold lust. Turning back, she says, "So, Mr. President—"

"Please, just call me Lex. My friends call me Lex," he insists, moving his thumb up and down the small of her back.

She gives him a radiant smile. "Are we friends?"

"I'd like to be."

"Well, Lex, I've been dying to know, what made you run for President of Currency in the first place?" she questions, moving her hand to twirl a piece of her dark brown hair. She reaches for her drink and takes a few sips, waiting for his response.

"You know, I get that question a lot, and my answer is always the same. Money loves me!" He says this pointing to a banner on the wall with the same slogan on it.

Good Gods.

"I enjoy managing it and helping the community with trade, and I get to be a part of something that actually makes a difference."

Lex trails off into a thirty-minute monologue about the importance of the Presidency, and how without The Seven Presidents, the human territory would be destroyed by the monsters that live in the fae countries on the mainland.

She does her best to not roll her eyes while he goes on and on about how he single handedly conned the incompetent rulers of the East, West, and Northlands, bringing huge export deals to Alerious City and all of the people in the Southlands.

When he finishes explaining to her how he is the reason there is no coin conversion between the four nations, she moves her hand over his, giggling. "You're like a real-life hero!"

"Yeah, you could say that. Someday I plan on running for Master President, so I can oversee every aspect of our community. To really make sure we are doing the most good for the people," he responds in his most political voice.

She leans towards him, flipping her hair to one side and looking devastatingly interested in politics. "That's so noble of you."

"And what is it that you do, Miss Quinn? I'm not sure I've seen you at one of our galas before. I'm sure I would have remembered."

"Oh, I'm no one. I'm here on behalf of my boss, who's attending an event tonight. I clearly didn't get that many details considering what I showed up in."

"Really, who's your boss?" The ice clinks as he downs his third glass of scotch, sliding it across the bar and pointing to his empty cup for another.

"He works in real estate, owns a few places here and there. I just do the boring stuff like take care of the paperwork, follow up with his clients, and apparently cause problems at galas."

"The only problem I see is that we weren't introduced sooner."

She grins down at the floor. "I bet you have one of those fancy offices huh? Important meetings, and crucial decision making. Must be exciting." She makes a show of walking two fingers up his hand, before losing her balance on the stool and sliding to the side.

He reaches out an arm to catch her before she falls, and lets a giggle slip out of her lips.

"It's a good thing I was here to protect you, Miss Quinn. Gin and Tonics can catch up to you when you least expect it."

She wipes her long curls off her shoulder and whispers, "You have no idea," before finishing off her drink.

With a wicked grin, he leans in close, enough that she can smell his aftershave. "To answer your question, I do have a beautiful office. It's actually here in this very building."

"Oh my gods, really?" she says, a little too loud. She puts a hand over her mouth to stop herself from yelling further, and says, "Wow! You probably have such an incredible view of the city. That must be so nice."

"Do you want to go see it? I can give you a private tour?" His hand lowers to her ass, causing an unwanted chill to run down her spine

"I don't know. Don't you think they would notice if you were gone?"

"It's my party, Gorgeous. I can do whatever the hell I want."

She thinks for only a moment, running a hand down her dress. "Okay, if you think it will be all right. Just a quick one."

"Just a quick one," he says, squeezing her ass one more time. She lets out a surprised squeal and jumps down from her chair.

Grabbing her freshly poured drink, she winks at the bartender and gives him a devious smile. "Thanks for the drinks," she says before being escorted to the elevators.

On the top floor, Lex moves her through locked doors with his key. They pass a secretary desk with a **BETH FRANCIS-ASSISTANT TO THE PRESIDENT OF CURRENCY** name plate.

That poor woman must be a saint.

Lex Macellarius's office is spacious yet somehow feels small. It's filled with oversized leather furniture, a full bar, and at the end, a huge, dark, wooden desk overlooking the city. There is even a sliding glass door leading to a balcony. She realizes the man is most likely compensating for something. The number of plaques, awards, medals of honor, and photos he has of himself is astonishing.

"Wow!" she says, rushing over to the window. "This city is my favorite at night. The lights are so beautiful."

He walks up behind her and wraps his arms around her front, kissing her neck and removing a breast from the thin fabric to cup in his hand. "Yep, it's something else, isn't it?"

She manages to squirm away, tucking her breast back in place and moves over to a bookshelf behind one of the couches. She picks up a photo and gasps.

"Is this you with the Master President?" she questions.

"Yes, Robert and I go way back." He laughs and stalks towards her once more. "You want to know a secret?" he whispers the line into her ear, and his hot breath fills her senses with the smell of alcohol and bad decisions.

She turns to look at him with an excited grin plastered on her face. "Always!"

"Sometimes, Robby and I share the women we bed. If you're ever interested, the three of us could have a wild time together." Lex runs a hand down the bare skin of her front, causing her to want to curl away from his touch.

"That's if you boys could handle me," she purrs, bile filling her throat.

She shifts her way out of his grasp again and moves towards his desk, tossing miscellaneous paperwork and documents to the side. "Do you want me to make you another drink?" she says, plopping her butt on top of the wood and crossing her legs.

"I'll finish the one I've got. I want to remember every inch of you tomorrow, Miss Quinn," he says, downing the rest of his scotch in one, messy gulp.

Her eyes fall low with need, and a coy smile forms on her red lips, inviting him to have her. "Where do you want me?" she moans.

"I'm going to fuck you right there on my desk."

He strides towards her, tugging down the top of her dress, and starts to suck. Working his way from one breast to the other, to her neck, then finally to her lips. She grabs his hair and deepens their kiss, pulling him into her with all her strength.

She lets his hands explore her body like he owns her, while his lips stay locked on hers. They shift from her breasts towards her thighs, then gripping her ass and lifting her into his arms. Her legs instinctively wrap around his waist, and he flips them around with strength she didn't expect him to have. He dominates the encounter, taking the lead on how they move, running his hands up and down her body, forcing her to thrust herself against his pants.

"I like my women on top." He laughs. "That way I can watch…" He coughs, bringing a hand to his chest. "Watch…" He coughs a few more times into his hand, falling back on the desk.

Her drunken, doe eyed face shifts into something evil. She lets out a menacing laugh, in a voice that is lower than the sweet and innocent one she's been using all night.

"I'm sorry, I couldn't understand you?" she mocks, climbing off him and taking a few steps back to start readjusting her dress. "What was that, Lex? That way you can watch me ride your limp dick like it's the most amazing experience of my life? You know Lex, all you men are the same. All I had to do was put on this stupid dress and parade myself around like some prize. And it took you all of what, two seconds to find me at the bar and put your hands on me? Pathetic."

His eyes go wide, like he just saw the ghost of his first wife.

"What the fuck is going on?" he demands through a coughing fit. "What the hell did you do to me?" He is unable to get up. Unable to move his limbs. All he can do is choke on his words.

"Oh relax, Lex, all I did was poison you a little. It's this fun lipstick concoction I had made. It makes you go unconscious and paralyzed for about ten hours, I think. If anyone finds you, it will seem as though you had too much to drink. The poison in the lipstick reacts with all that alcohol you've been drinking tonight. See you add mint leaves to—"

She cuts herself off mid-sentence to examine him and grins, her golden irises sparkling in the lights of the city.

"Oh, that's not important. What is important, is the fact that you let me, a complete stranger, into your private office. That's bad business practice, Lex. Wouldn't want anyone finding out how easy it is to get in here."

She makes her way back and forth from one side of the window to the other. Talking to him as she watches the city below. "It really is a gorgeous view, isn't it?"

"What the fuck, Quinn. What do you want with me?" he asks through shaking breaths.

"Oh, and that's another thing," she admits, walking towards him again. "My name is not Luna Quinn. If you're smart, and I'm hoping you are, you won't investigate me any further. Or the next time I see you, I won't be able to let you live, Lex." She slaps him lightly on the cheek, then bursts into laughter. "Luna Quinn. It's the fakest sounding name, and you still fell for it. I was really rooting for you. You've got to start thinking with your brain and not your dick, Lex."

"Fuck you!"

"Yeah, I bet you wish you had the opportunity. I would have blown your fucking mind. But sadly, if my timing is right, which I know it is, our time together is almost over, Lex. Thanks for the wonderful evening, and the shitty company."

"Fucking bitch!"

Leaning against the desk next to him, she checks her nails as he falls into his ten hour deep sleep. After a few moments of blissful silence, she kicks his foot to see if there is a response.

Nothing.

She bends over his body and whispers, "The name is Rue Kylexi, you disgusting asshole, and I'm a Rogue."

Her lips meet his forehead, leaving a red lipstick stain with her conquest.

CHAPTER

RUE rushes to the office door and turns the lock, satisfied with the click that echoes around the space. She looks to the ceiling, praying to The Mother that no one will come looking for him within the next few minutes. Behind her, the room holds secrets needing to be uncovered.

Okay, here we go.

To his credit, Lex Macellarius's office is pretty tidy. His documents are all labeled and color coded. His file drawers are categorized by department. Even his bookshelves are alphabetized. Everything labeled in a pretty, cursive handwriting. His assistant's work, she assumes.

"I guarantee he doesn't pay her enough to do this shit," she mumbles to herself.

The desk, now a bit disheveled from their encounter and still holding a passed out President, is her first stop. She grabs a stack of miscellaneous papers and reads through them, looking for anything regarding business with the fae countries.

Her boss had asked her to take anything related to tax write-offs happening within the last four years that involved the mainland. When asked for more information on what he was looking for, she was told to *figure it out*, so somehow, she needs to find the right needle in the needle stack.

Breaking the silence, Lex snores so loud it could wake the dead, and Rue drops the stack of papers on the floor. Instead of picking them up, she leaves them and moves on with her search.

The bookshelves aren't much help either, the displays only hold his accomplishments. Glass trophies, medals of honor, and wooden plaques for his work in connecting the Southlands to the rest of the world sprinkle the shelves with his ego.

Pictures of himself shaking hands with other politicians and local celebrities line the glass shelves. The smiles that don't meet their eyes tells Rue everything she needs to know about how exciting it is to be in politics. Artificial happiness is not something she strives for in this short life of hers, but that's not a thought she has time to analyze right now.

In the cabinets under the open shelves, she pulls out binders full of laws and regulations for the Southlands. Boring legal jargon patronizing the citizens are typed out front and back for hundreds of pages of pure, sleep induced madness. Not a single thing here has to do with what she needs. Nothing.

Or maybe something.

She spots a loose file folder haphazardly wedged in between one of the binders and the wood of the cabinet. The shade of blue strikes her as strange considering all the binders and files in this office are white. With a light tug, she pulls the folder out to read.

Inside is a chaotic mix of newspaper clippings, scrap papers with dates and times, and a list of names with random numbers next to them. A yellow piece of paper with the words *The Organization* written in blue ink is stapled to the inside fold. It's circled a few times with question marks and underlines around it. Rue's eyes fall to the newspaper clippings, and she starts reading about the rising number of Lowers going missing in the middle of the night.

What the fuck?

Rue has heard about an influx of people going missing, but it's so common in the Low District she didn't think anything of it. People disappear all the time, but no one usually reports it because nine times out of ten it involves the crime syndicates, which have people turning the other way.

Before she can look too much into the rest of the file, she hears the ding of the elevator. Her mind clears away any useless questions, and she tries to give herself tunnel vision for the task at hand. Tax documents.

Swiftly, she places the blue file back in the cabinet and moves to the drawers across the room. She scans over the labels for anything remotely related. *Bingo!* There is a whole file drawer labeled *Tax Office- Authorized Personnel Only*.

"It can't be this simple," she breathes.

It isn't. The drawer is locked.

She spins around on her heels and heads straight for the desk. Lex lies limp on the top of it still, snoring and making an aggravating whistling sound through his nose.

Rue's heart starts to race as the time ticks on. The thrill of being caught engulfs her in its twisted grasp, adrenaline pumping through her veins. She has always found that being in foreign places, with a limited amount of time to complete tasks, is somewhat of a fun game for her. It reminds her she's still alive.

She opens drawers with such force, the objects inside shift. Finally in the middle drawer she finds a set of silver keys. Grabbing them, she races back to the file cabinet. One key after another gets pushed into the lock with no avail. After the fifth and final key she tries doesn't work, she runs over to the desk one more time, trying to find something, anything, to get this damn drawer open.

The rest of the desk doesn't leave anything helpful in its contents, so she searches the obnoxious man on top of it. In Lex's pockets she pulls out some random tissues (attempts not to gag), his key for the office, and his wallet. Inside the leather she finds three gold coins and gasps, "Holy shit!"

Tossing the rest of his personal things in the drawers of the desk, she stuffs the three gold coils into her dress. Even if she doesn't find the files her boss is looking for, that gold alone was worth the nasty make out with Lex Macellarius.

Rue is running out of options, and mostly time.

"Shit, I really didn't want to do this but whatever," she says as she pulls two bobby pins out of her hair, bending them into makeshift lock picking tools. She lowers herself to her knees and a brunette curl falls into her face. She swipes it away as she takes a deep inhale, and picks the lock, praying to all the Gods it works this time.

Suddenly, the office door rattles, and Rue immediately stills. Her hands start to shake for the first time this evening.

"Boss, you in there?" a voice calls from the other side of the door. Rue can make out three different male voices and one female.

"I have a key in my desk," she hears the woman say. It must be Beth.

Rue gulps. She has approximately two minutes maybe, before this whole thing goes to shit. Returning her focus back on the lock, Rue jiggles the pins around a little bit longer before hearing a click.

She is so distracted by the door, she isn't sure if the noise came from it, or the drawer she is currently breaking into. Lucky for her, it pulls open silently and Rue is in.

"Mr. President? Are you all right in there?" she hears Beth ask.

Her heart feels like it might fly out of her chest at any moment. She looks down in the long file drawers and skims through the labels of assorted files. Nothing is jumping out to her as important.

"Boss, we're coming in. If you got a lady friend in there, it's time to finish up. You got your speech soon," one of the men yells.

Rue looks towards the door with a little spark in her eye. She takes a deep inhale and lets it out in the direction of the office door, then turns back to the files.

Gods be on my side today.

The door rattles once more, then there is a popping sound of it being unlocked.

"Mr. President, make sure you're decent," Beth pleads quietly. The door shakes but doesn't open, which makes them jerk it more violently.

One of the men grunts, "What the hell, it's stuck."

All three of the men outside the door are now pounding on it, pushing their whole body weights against the wood, but it won't budge. One of them decides to start kicking it when Beth yells, "What are you doing? That is an imported Northlands wooden door, it is practically priceless!"

"What else would you have us do?"

"I… I'm not sure, just try not to break anything," she says, clearly irritated by the men's little regard for the craftsmanship.

One of the men takes another shot at the door, taking a few steps back he rushes towards it, pushing with his shoulder. As if someone opened it at that exact moment, he bursts through with ease, falling to the floor with the impact.

"Oh my gods, Mr. President!" Beth screams, running towards her boss. The men search the room for any sign of tampering, but nothing seems out of place, other than the fact that the President of Currency is passed out on the desk with his pants around his ankles.

"Go down to the haul, Beth, you don't need to see this. Tell everyone there has been an emergency. Tell them something came up with the President, and we need to reschedule his acceptance speeches."

"What do I tell them when they ask what's wrong?" she asks through short breaths, her hand to her heart.

"I don't give a shit, make something up! Just don't say he's passed out drunk after fucking a random woman in his private office. The two of you, go look for that girl in the black dress."

Outside, to the right of the balcony, Rue clings to the stone building. Balancing herself on the eight inch cornice, her dress and hair blows in the wild gusts of wind. In her hand, she grips onto a file folder she hopes is significant.

Her breath is jagged as she blows in and out trying to figure out her plan. She can't very well go back in the way she came; Lex is sure to have constant monitoring now that they've found him. The way she sees it she has two options, climb her way to the roof somehow, or fall to her death, and the latter doesn't sound as exciting.

Faint sounds of clinic emergency trucks fill the white noise of the city, a bad omen she hopes isn't for her. With a quick peek down to the ground, she can see a few security guards on their communicators running around the building. Thankfully they don't notice the mysterious woman in the black dress scaling the wall.

She turns her head to the right, causing her hair to blow in her face, but she can still make out a metal drainpipe on the corner of the building. "Fuck," she whispers, looking out onto the High District below and trembling as she starts to move.

Side stepping along the ledge, Rue makes her way to the pipe, keeping her eyes on the reflection of the city lights off the bay. Soon her hand is grasping the cold metal, and she gulps, not ready to make a move yet. Taking as many deep breaths as she can to calm her racing heart, she tries to hype herself up. She's scaled buildings before, there's nothing to it. *Right? Right,* she tells herself. As long as she ends up on the roof instead of the pavement below, it's a win.

With her free hand, Rue bunches up the skirt of her dress, and tucks it around her body, creating more mobility for her legs. Balancing on one foot she removes her heel, then the other.

"Damn, I really liked these," she admits tossing her shoes to the ground below.

She looks to the pipe and gives it a pull, praying to the Gods it can hold her body weight. With one swift movement, she wraps herself around it and begins to scale the side of the tallest building in the High District.

"Okay. This is fine. I'm fine," she lies, biting down on the file folder in her teeth.

As she climbs, a powerful rush of wind pushes her towards the roof. Her feet grip around the pipe allowing her arms to reach higher. With each inch she lifts, her confidence grows.

Soon she is at the top and uses the decorative cornice to hoist herself up and over the ledge. Rolling over onto her back to reach the stable ground of the roof, she finally exhales. The wind howls around her as she stares up at the night sky. Or at least a sky, it has more of a brown hue from the city lights and smog.

She turns her head to scan her surroundings and notices a pile of vomit, and two rats eating a dead pigeon. Pinching the bridge of her nose, she closes her eyes.

"This city is disgusting."

Rue fidgets with her key as she opens the door to her studio apartment. You could compare it to a shoe box, just big enough for her bed and a few other pieces of furniture. A small, wooden table she found on the side of the road sits by the entrance. An old dresser and pink chair that were left from the old tenant are placed in a windowed corner of the room.

The apartment has a kitchen, if you want to call it that, with a sink (doesn't work 98% of the time), a cook top that only has one degree (lava), and a fridge that only keeps things slightly cooler than room temperature.

She saunters in, tosses the file on her mattress, and makes her way around the room, stepping over piles of clothes and miscellaneous things scattered all around. She takes a quick look out the window, getting a not so charming view of the Low District.

Scrap metal and wood snake up the sides of buildings keeping them together. Power lines crisscross from rooftop to rooftop, connecting everyone to a grid that doesn't work. Lights flicker across this part of the city as if on purpose.

At her dresser, Rue rips off what is left of her dress. After jumping across rooftops, getting it snagged onto every rough edge of stone in the city, and having a tussle with a pesky chain linked fence, she never wants to see it again.

The three gold coins and the red lipstick fall to the floor, and she places them on top of her dresser. The poisonous lipstick goes into a little basket of makeup she keeps for *special events*, and she pulls out a box from her top drawer for the gold. Inside she keeps one of her biggest secrets.

From the outside, the wooden box looks like any other jewelry box. The top is hand painted with a forest full of animals Rue has only ever seen in daydreams. The border is covered in every color of flower imaginable. A rainbow of life she wishes to see with her own eyes. She has been keeping spare change in this box for years in the hopes of using it to escape this island prison someday, and travel to the mainland.

Rue has never felt like this place was home. Yes, it's the only place she knows, but her soul has been pulling her across the sea since she realized a different world was waiting on its shores.

It's been a slow process, but her savings are almost enough to give her a fresh start. Almost. Unfortunately, Rue has a problem of helping those who cannot help themselves. Coming from nothing, gives you a very different perspective on what it means to survive. It often leaves Rue in a fight with her moral compass and her job, taking from the Highers she is hired to con and giving a majority of her earnings to the Lowers she cares about.

For now, she leaves the coins on top of the box, wanting to go over the totals after she showers and collects herself. She desperately needs to wash off today's disgust.

Rue walks naked to her bathroom and turns on the shower faucet. "Mother and Gods, please let me have hot water tonight," she begs.

While the water heats up, she takes a second to look in the mirror. Slowly she pulls at the dark, nappy curls, and removes the wig she's been wearing tonight, revealing her nappy, auburn red hair underneath. She runs her hands a few times through it before slowly, achingly getting into the shower, letting the mildly warm water soothe her sore muscles in a few moments of bliss before it turns to cold. After a few minutes of washing up, she pulls the curtain back, wraps herself into a towel, and steps out onto the cold tile floor.

She wipes the steam off the mirror and stares at her reflection. Makeup has smeared under her eyes. She has the beginnings of a hickey on her neck from Lex, right above her scar. Rue's eyes linger on the scar for a moment. She moves her fingers over the long, raised line that runs across the side of her neck and drifts back to the day she got it. It sends a chill down her spine. She blinks her way back to reality before losing herself in a memory she doesn't have time to analyze. She grabs a hand towel to clean the black from her eyes, and the remainder of the lipstick from her lips.

There is a creak on the floor coming from the other room that breaks the silence. Rue turns her head an inch to listen for another sound. It's quiet, but she can make out the shallow breaths of one person, a man. Her hand grips tighter on the tower. She takes a deep breath in, channeling all her confidence back up to the surface.

CHAPTER

"DID you come here just to spy on me in the shower? You should have joined me," she says seductively with a sly smile.

As if on cue, a sigh comes from beyond the door frame to the bathroom. In the reflection of the mirror, she can see a man step out, holding the brunette wig in his hands. She lets out a breathy laugh and continues to wipe away her makeup.

"You'd think you'd know where all the creaks are in the floor by now."

He laughs too. "You know, I prefer your red hair over this. It's too ordinary," he comments, tossing the wig to the ground.

"You seemed to like it when you were pouring me drinks tonight. Thanks for keeping mine virgins by the way. How was my performance? I'd say it was one of my best."

She turns around to look face to face with Diego Metus, the bartender, her boss, leaning in the door frame. Rue's eyes run from the tattooed arm muscles strained across his chest, to his smug smile, and ending on his eyes that look like drops of midnight. He stares her down past the bridge of his nose, scanning every inch of her. The act sends chills down her arms.

"Luna Quinn, huh? Interesting name choice," he jokes.

"Yeah, you know, your first pet's name and the street you grew up on, or something like that."

"I'm pretty sure that's supposed to be your stripper's name."

"Oh, it's basically the same thing." She shrugs, moving an arm up and down her cold shoulder muscles. "Anyway, I didn't even have to make up an excuse at the door, that poor kid let me walk right in once I gave him a little twirl."

She pauses a moment, looking at the green tile of the shower, then asks, "How do you do it?"

"Do what?" One of his eyebrows raises.

"Go to those events, and be with those people, while the rest of the city slowly dies from their living conditions? I have done more jobs in the High District than I can count, and it still upsets me."

The wealth in Alerious City has always been extremely skewed. The land on the island was divided up between the High District, and the Low District. The Highers were blessed with things like fresh water, air purifiers, and real food imported from the fae lands. While the Lowers suffer in the slums, drinking water collected from the rain, eating processed meal bags, and living like rats. Simply surviving until death takes them to the meadow.

The island was manmade centuries ago, to protect the humans from the fae folk with elemental powers on the mainland. It was promised to those that made the journey to be an even playing field, and a place for humans to prosper at their own rate, with their own technologies. Fast forward to today, it's a lopsided, hostile environment for most of the citizens who still live here. The purpose has been lost somewhere in the modernization.

The humans still trade with the rest of the world, exporting manufactured copper and bronze, mechanical parts, and products produced from factories. 90% of the Southland's space is made into factories, Alerious City being the only livable place on the entire island. Other than exports to and from, no one leaves the island in fear of being killed by those with powers.

Diego looks at Rue for a long moment before answering, as if the truth and what she wants to hear are not the same thing.

"It's not my job to be upset, Beautiful. It's not my job to try and make sure everyone is happy. The Seven Presidents need the districts at war. They need the chaos, so the people think they need the Presidents."

"It's just, I was standing in this guy's office, which could fit about four of my apartments in it by the way, and he starts bragging about being buddies with the Master President. Talking about the three of us having a threesome." She looks down and shakes her head. "All I could think about was how many people could stay warm in this office. And at that point my blood was boiling so intensely that I *wanted* to poison him, I *wanted* to see him suffer and be scared. Because that man deserved it. They all do."

Diego clears his throat. "That asshole didn't deserve to lay a finger on you."

"Funny, because that's why you hired me for the job isn't it?" she mocks, crossing her arms over her towel and leans on the sink. "Honestly, that was the easiest part of the night. Macellarius was total trash. I had hardly walked into the room before he had his hands on my tits."

He stalks towards Rue, lifting her chin with his finger to look at the marks on her neck. He palms the back of her head, jerking her towards him. Rue winces for a split second, then focuses her eyes on his, looking up at him down the bridge of her nose, mimicking his favorite stance.

"What did you let him do to you?"

She blinks a few times. *Let?* "I did what I had to do," she whispers.

"Did you let him fuck you?"

"Eww, no. It didn't get that far. I hardly touched him." Rue gulps and moves her eyes to focus once more on the emerald tile. *Did you let him?* Like she had a choice.

"He fucked you, didn't he?" he questions, tightening his grip on her neck. His question comes out more like a statement, like he was in the room and saw it with his own two eyes.

"No! I swear. I went in, kissed him, he passed out on the desk, and that was it. He didn't do anything I couldn't handle."

"Good girl," he growls slowly, loosening his hand around her neck and sinking his face into the side of it. His hand moves into her wet hair, the other lifts her towel and grabs her ass. "Because you are mine, and I don't like to share."

Ironic, considering that's mostly what her job entails, being used by men to con them into what he wants her to take.

Diego may be Rue's boss, but they share a connection closer than most. The two of them dance around a relationship based on passion, and lustful rage. Healthy? Absolutely not. But it doesn't stop Rue from wanting to be with him, wanting his hands on her body. He is her addiction, like a drug her body can't function without.

Rue clears her throat, and starts to breathe heavily, not sure from lust or fear. He is always so intense after a con, something about the deception and lies makes him so desperate for her.

"I got the file you asked for. At least I think I got it. It wasn't easy to find when I didn't have much to go off of."

He pulls her head back with a fist full of hair, stares her down with his endlessly dark eyes, and whispers, "You better hope you got it, or we might have a problem, Beautiful."

Her gut instinct stirs. "I did my best. I had to escape through the balcony. I scaled the fucking building to get to the roof for Gods' sake. I could be dead."

"That's not my problem."

Excuse me?

"Well, fuck you!" she yells, pushing him off of her. She moves her hand to slap him, but he catches it midair, squeezing her wrist until she winces. Hot rage starts to make its way into her gut. She attempts to jerk out of his grip, but he doesn't let her go.

"Fuck me? Oh, not yet, Beautiful. First, you're going to tell me what else you found in his office."

She throws him a confused look. "What are you talking about? You told me to find tax files on international trade deals. That's exactly what I did."

"True, but that's not all you found now, was it?" He whispers the last few words, stepping towards her once more, making his chest brush up against her own.

Was he talking about the file, with the missing people, she thinks to herself.

Before she can answer, he reaches into the pocket of his jeans, pulling out the three gold coins. Gold is not common in the Southlands, reserved only for the Presidents, and the Highers who have the most connections to the Presidents. These three little coins added up to more money than Rue made in a year.

Shit!

"That's not mine," she says, not breaking eye contact with him, lifting her chin up to meet his. Challenging him.

"You're right. Because it's mine," he snaps. "I didn't think we kept secrets from each other, Rue. We're a team, and teams share. But since you tried to lie to me, this is mine now."

"I didn't want it anyway, as you can see, I'm already living in luxury." Her arms reach out around the tiny apartment, reminding him of the cracks in the walls and leaking roof tiles that surround him.

He glares for a second, breathing in deep and pressing his hands into the delicate skin of her neck. Rue's breath becomes short. Her heart rate accelerates, yet she keeps her eyes on him, showing no pain in his touch.

Then, talking himself off the ledge, his intense look fades away. The anger in his eyes clears to their normal dark chocolate color, as if he just reminded himself she was supposed to mean more to him than his other employees.

A flash of regret washes over his features. He brushes a lock of hair away from her face and lets his hand linger on her chin. "I'm sorry, I don't want to fight. You know you don't have to live like this. Stay with me. Live with me, where you can be safe and taken care of."

What is safe?

"And give all this up, no. Like I said at the bar, I'm a Lower. I don't belong up on that hill."

"You belong with me, let me take care of you," he says as he gives her a soft kiss on her lips.

"You might have missed it through your annoying man rage earlier, but I scaled a building thirty stories in the air tonight and made it back in one piece, in a dress. I can take care of myself thank you very much," she smirks. He lets out a low, sinister groan.

"Speaking of that dress."

"Yeah, you liked it?" she purrs.

Rue has seen this time and time again. Anger then lust. Like the two sides of a coin that never quite stop spinning. Over and over their relationship circles between those two emotions. It used to bother her, but as sick as it is, she finds comfort in knowing his anger eventually becomes some form of love.

Toxic, this is so toxic.

He closes his eyes, rests his forehead on hers, and breathes, "I wanted to jump over the bar and fuck you right there in that dress." He takes a deep inhale of her scent and grabs her face with his hands. "I wanted to rip it off of you and show everyone there how I can make you moan."

Toxic. That is all this is.

Rue's stare softens and something hot begins to build between her legs. "Oh, all those dreadfully prude Highers would have loved that."

Fuck it.

Without another word, Diego pulls the towel off Rue, leaving her naked body exposed to him. In the same breath, she frantically moves her hands to his jeans and loosens his belt. He grabs her hair on the back of her head and pulls her in for a kiss. The deep, lust filled kiss sends sparks shimmering down her body, exploding as she opens her mouth for him to explore.

Rue's breaths become short and heavy, she moves her hand up and down the outside of his pants, feeling his already hard cock push against the fabric.

"Someone is excited," she giggles.

A small whine pulls from her mouth with the sudden feel of his hands on her breasts, rubbing her nipples between his fingers in circular motions. They harden instantly with his touch. She works one of her hands on his zipper, keeping the other against the length of him. The moment they are undone, she moves to her knees and slowly, achingly pulls his erection from his briefs.

Rue looks up at Diego, biting her bottom lip, waiting for him to make the first move.

He grips the back of her head, holding a fistful of hair as he takes his cock in his hand and strokes a few times. Rue instinctively licks her lips at the movement, watching as precum forms on the tip of him.

He moves himself up to her soft lips, letting her lick the tip once before pushing it into her mouth. She moans as the length of him fills her throat, twitching as she sucks. She takes every inch of him as he thrusts himself in and out of her mouth.

Rue's free hand moves in between her own legs, working herself up so she's ready for him.

Diego's eyes roll back and eventually close as his head tips up.

"That's it, baby, take it."

Rue loosens her mouth to let him get deeper into her throat while tears fall from her eyes from the pressure, frantically wanting to be the reason for his pleasure. Their movements are always frenzied, quick, hard, and so desperate one might think this was their last day on Ethos. The passion radiates off their bodies, both doing anything the other asks of them, in the hopes of being the one they need the most. Two shapes determined to connect into one.

He leans his body over her, resting an arm on the bathroom sink. The muscles in his biceps tense, like he is trying to restrain himself from losing all control. Their eyes connect, dark and deep with need, before he closes his to moan her name.

She takes him out of her mouth just long enough to whisper, "Hope you can forgive me for earlier."

"Fuck," he growls.

She giggles devilishly, and continues her motion, using her hand to squeeze the base of him. His long shaft pulses in her mouth as her tongue works its magic. His breath is short and jagged while she sucks. She can feel the tremble in his legs from the sensation, and revels in the power of knowing that is because of her. She is the one who can make this tough, guarded man weak under her touch.

She stops to look up at him, knowing exactly what he needs from her, and smiles. "Take me to bed."

Diego's eyes turn black, and without a word he lifts her off the floor, but instead of taking her to her mattress, he sits her on the edge of the bathroom sink. She lets out a small whimper when the cold tile hits her ass. He grabs her face and kisses her, opening his mouth for hers.

His hand moves down her front, stopping at her full breasts a moment, before lowering in between her legs. She moves her hips to meet his hand, spreading her thighs for him.

Opening her with his two fingers, he groans, "You're so wet for me, baby." He moves his fingers out, then back into her, repeating the motion over and over again while his thumb plays with her clit. The sounds that leave her body are intoxicating.

Slowly, he moves his lips to her neck, kissing her over top of the hickeys she has from Lex, sucking them and nibbling on the tender skin. Her arms start to shake from the delicious pressure of his fingers, and she grips the porcelain sink with more force, causing her knuckles to whiten.

Diego moves to her ear and whispers, "When you look in the mirror tomorrow…" She closes her eyes from the sensation building in her core, letting out some breathy noises. He continues, "I want you to know those marks are mine. You are mine. No one else's."

He moves his mouth over her nipple and sucks hard, pumping her with his fingers faster now.

"Diego," she breathes. "Please. Take me to bed. Now." Her body is on fire from his touch. The need for him to be inside of her is mind bending.

"Tell me whose you are, Beautiful," he orders in that husky, sexy tone he always uses to make her melt into a puddle. "Tell me who you belong to, so I can show you what you mean to me."

She gazes at him with heavy eyes, panting from the pressure that is about to burst out of her. "I'm yours."

"That's it, baby. Tell me again, and I'll give you everything you want."

Fuck!

"Yours!" she yells. "I'm yours." Rue is almost over the edge. She might not make it another second let alone to her bed. The need to release this glorious pressure is overwhelming.

"Yes, you fucking are," he growls, picking her up off the counter and walking her to the bed, where he indeed gives her everything she wants and more.

An hour later, the two of them lay twisted in the sheets of her mattress. Rue rests her head on Diego's tanned, bare chest. She lazily runs a finger over one of the tattoos on his shoulder. A roaring lion, with smoke swirling around it is inked into his skin. Her fingers move over the outline of an M, the same design as the ring he wears on his pointer finger. She traces down to another one on this bicep, a small set of numerals in the ancient language of the Gods, spelling out the date his father was murdered.

She was with him that day, sat with him as he stared into the void after his father's assassination, while the pains of the needle sank into his skin. She looks to her own bicep, finding her own tattoo to match. Under the words *Extraordinary Sacrifices*, is the date of her own parents passing, or what she had figured it to be. They sat together in that tattoo house, holding each other's hands as they got branded with the mark of being an orphan. Both of them silently grieving parents and a life they wish had been different.

Watching someone you care about go through grief is hard enough, but watching someone grieve a person who destroyed your own life is a pain far more terrifying. Allowing him to be angry and hide his sadness for someone Rue has only ever known as a monster, changed the way she looked at Diego.

She lay there, allowing her thoughts to drift to the night she met Diego's father. Manny Metus.

Twelve years ago, a cocky, starving sixteen-year-old Rue attempted to steal food and any coins she could find from a restaurant in the High District. She broke the lock on the back door and snuck in through the employee entrance, searching the pantry for anything left from the day before. What she didn't realize was that she was stealing from the most feared crime boss in the entire city. He was in charge of the Smoke Runners, a crime syndicate of assassins and thieves that would work in the night, doing whatever Manny wanted, to whoever Manny wanted. Stealing from rival club owners, burning down business of people that betrayed him, and most commonly "taking care of" anyone he felt didn't serve a purpose anymore.

The night he found her in his restaurant's kitchen, will forever be one of the worst moments of Rue's life. She was just a child. A starving child from the Low District.

Instead of letting her live, which would have been an easy thing to do, just giving her a few pieces of bread and a coin to go home, he decided to make an example out of her. He needed to show the rest of the crew what it meant to take what belonged to Manny Metus.

After stripping her down to her underwear, chaining her up against a wall, and whipping her with a belt, he explained to the rest that no one takes what is his. He proceeded to beat and humiliate Rue for three days. She took it all. She had no choice. It was either take the pain, take the torture, or let him win. And Rue could never let him win.

On the fourth day, Manny held an execution. Rue lifted her head high when he pulled out his knife. She did not falter when he scraped the cold blade over her chest. She did not even blink when he made a cut around the side of her neck and watched as she slowly bled.

She was prepared to die. She prayed in her head. She called to the Gods to take her to her parents. To free her and let her walk in the meadow. They did not listen to her pleas.

With everyone around, Manny stood in front of Rue. She looked up at him with the golds of her eyes glowing in hatred. She threw him a wicked, powerful smile and whispered the two words she believes saved her life that day, "I win."

Rue would die with dignity. She would not beg for her life. She would not apologize for stealing from him. She would not let his methods of torture break her. In return showing everyone else that they too could withstand him, and break from his control.

Manny cleared his throat and stood there assessing the situation. He looked around at the puzzled faces of everyone in the room. His crew, *his people,* sat there watching a sixteen year old girl stand up to a man that was known for being untouchable. After a split second of panic, he stared back down at her and changed his plans.

Manny pointed his knife at his seventeen-year-old son, demanding he kill the girl, as a way of initiation into the Smoke Runners. Diego, being the charming and conniving asshole he was, took the opportunity to convince his father to save her. Claiming that they could use her. The girl that would not be broken.

Manny demanded that if she was to live, *Diego* would be the one to train her. And if she was to mess up, *Diego* would be the one to take care of her. She was his responsibility, and if she was going to live, she must pay with her freedom.

Diego nursed her back to health and taught her everything he knew about the life she now was a part of. She was given a number barcode tattoo on her forearm, a way to tell whose crew she belonged to. She was further stripped of her dignity when they strapped her down, and forced her to receive a hysterectomy, making it impossible for her to have children in the future.

They gave her no purpose, just a name, Ghost. She would be nothing but a good little soldier for an army she didn't enlist in.

Rue would forever be branded. She was no longer a woman; she was no longer anything. She was only a Smoke Runner.

Her mind blinks back into her studio, eyes connecting with Diego's. He runs his hand through her hair, gazing down at her with tired eyes and the tiniest of grins on his face.

"Where did you just go? I can see your mind wandering in your eyes."

"Do you ever miss him? Your father?"

Sighing heavily, he simply says, "No."

"Was he ever good?"

Rue knew the answer before she even asked. Manny Metus was anything but good. In a family that passed down trauma and abuse like recipes, Manny was known for being one of the worst. Her mind wanders once more to him, and the things she knows to be true. One story sticks out to her among the thousand others.

When Diego was only six, he and his mother were caught trying to flee to the fae countries for a better life. She was executed by his father in front of Diego. Then, Manny proceeded to make his child clean up the mess.

Rue tugs Diego a little tighter at the thought. A helpless child, begging for someone to care for them, but finding that they are alone in the world. The two of them shared the same spirit, they understand each other's struggles more than anyone. She knows his tics, his goals, even the feelings he doesn't dare share with those he surrounds himself with. An unbreakable pair trying their best to survive side by side.

She looks up at him, holding on so he remembers he is safe with her.

With a slow rub on her cheek, he pulls her up to let his lips meet her forehead. "No Rue, he was never a good man. Not a single day. But the one good thing he did was bring me you."

CHAPTER

RUE'S eyes focus on the water stain on the ceiling above her head, rubbing her fingers over the tattoo on her chest. Four small X marks run downwards in between her breasts. The four days she was tortured. The fourth X is done in white ink, representing the day she was given another life. Her fingers brush over the marks abstractedly while her mind wanders to her Smoke Runner job a few hours ago.

"I lost you again, didn't I?" Diego moves his lips to her neck, kissing her back into her reality.

"What? No, I'm just tired. Long night." She turns her head to meet his, wrapping her body around his torso.

Images of the blue folder pop into her consciousness. The words *The Organization* float across her mind, adding questions to her ever growing list of unknowns about the world. The newspaper clippings fill her with images of those currently missing from the Low District. Times and dates for unknown events are scattered around her brain trying to connect to each other.

It's too strange not to question further. She may not have heard of this group herself, but what's the purpose of having a crime boss boyfriend if not to ask questions about shady deals in the city.

"Hey," she lifts her head, resting herself on her forearm. "Do you know anything about people going missing, like more than normal? Or something called the Organization?"

"Not that I can think of, why? Who needs to know? Where did you hear that?" His brows lower causing his eyes to darken from the shadow of his lashes.

"It's just something I've been hearing whispers about in the district, wondering how serious it is," she lies.

"I don't know anything, but I can look into it if you want."

"Thanks. It's not important, just curious." The golds of her eyes start to sparkle with need again, and she leans down to rest her body on top of his, kissing him once more. He pulls her in with his hands on her face, breathing her in, and rolls them both over so he's on top of her now.

"I'll let you sleep. I have to go." He leans in to kiss her gently on the forehead.

She wraps her arms around his neck. "Please stay."

"You know I can't, Beautiful." Diego pulls her off himself and stands up, leaving Rue cold with goosebumps from the chill of the apartment air. "Besides," he laughs, zipping up his jeans. "I'm not sleeping anywhere that looks like this."

She throws a pillow at him, hitting the back of his head. *Like this*, like he isn't the one that pays her. Like he isn't aware of how little she makes.

"Asshole," she says in a playful tone, hiding the sting.

"I mean it wouldn't kill you to clean up your shit. How do you find anything in here?"

"Clean and organized means things are easy to steal."

"Come on, your fucking mattress is on the floor, Rue. You have clothes and shit all over. This place isn't one I'd call comfortable."

"Okay, rude! I've been a little busy scaling buildings and taking men down with poisonous lipstick. I'm so sorry my Low District ass is damaging your spectacular reputation of being a High District prick. Maybe if I could get a raise for my hard work, you wouldn't have to fuck the poor girl in her tiny apartment."

Oops. Too far.

Before she can find words, he looks down at her and shakes his head in annoyance. "It doesn't work that way, Rue."

"Yes, actually it can. It can work however you want it to, Diego. You can be your own person; you are not your father. The business can run however you want it to." She glances up to study his face, but he turns to look out the window. The muscles in his jaw clench and she notices his knuckles turning white. His heart is beating so loud she can hear it ringing in her ears.

Rue's body goes cold, and her pulse accelerates. She focuses her attention on the now very interesting folds of her sheets, centering her mind to be cold and calculated. Mixing personal and professional has never been something Diego has loved about their relationship. It has always led to arguments or silent treatments, like he doesn't know how to blend the two together.

"I don't know what you want me to say." He wipes his hands over his face, and points at Rue. "You know, I've risked a lot for you. I've put up with a lot of shit for you and gambled my own life to keep you safe. But I have a legacy to live up to. An image of what everyone expects me to be. I can't just let it all go for some bitch I'm fucking!"

There it is.

The imaginary line dividing up her lover and her boss, shatters beneath her feet. She doesn't respond for a few moments, trying to compose herself enough to hide the hurt in her voice. Then, with a burst of bravery, she sneers, "Oh, I'm aware. Sorry, I just figured since he has been *dead* for four years, you'd have the balls to be a decent man."

"I'm not in the business of being a decent man, Rue. We've been over this millions of times. Our life isn't some fucking fairytale. Whatever you have to tell yourself to spin this so you feel better, is your business. But I can't just go around making exceptions and giving more money to a girl whose biggest asset to the team is her tits." He laughs at her, pacing back and forth around the room. "Do you hear yourself? Do you have any idea how that would look? Did you think for one second how that would affect me and the trust the rest of the team has in me. It would expose us within minutes. So, before you go puffing out your chest, acting like you have it all figured out, why don't you for once think about someone other than yourself."

The pressure in Rue's head is about to pop. Her hands shake by her sides, but she doesn't show him her weakness. Her eyes stay focused on the patchwork quilt draping over her lap, drawing imaginary patterns over the seams to keep her mind composed and the tingling feeling in her palms from exploding outward.

Without making eye contact, Diego storms towards the front door. On the way, he grabs the file from Macellarius's office and says, "I got to go. Here is the agreed upon bronze for your job tonight." He slams the coin on her entry table, rattling the keys on top of it. "Clean up your fucking apartment, Rue."

The force of the door closing shakes her entire studio, Rue's eyes close with the impact.

She is alone once more.

She watches him from the window as he storms out of the building, kicking over a trash bin, releasing a rat back into the streets along with a pile of garbage. She can see him take a few deep breaths through his hands before a cenzium vehicle is pulling up on the curb. He jumps in and it rushes away into the night. Leaving the street behind like it means nothing. Like she means nothing.

For a man worried about anonymity and keeping their relationship private, he sure flaunts his status of being a Higher by getting picked up in a car. Driving vehicles powered by cenzium fuel, which is only produced on the mainland, is the equivalent of holding a neon sign that says *rob me, I have money.*

Rue turns around to examine the aftermath of whatever the hell just happened. She's still naked. She's cold. Tired. Starving. And by herself. The silence fills her ears as it bites at her iron heart.

During his fast and aggressive exit, Diego forgot his sweatshirt. Rue pulls it over her body, instantly breathing in his scent. Sandalwood.

She moves to her dresser and opens the top drawer, searching for shorts. The cotton ones she puts on are swallowed up by the oversized sweatshirt. On the bottom of the drawer, she pulls at the seam, peeling back the contact paper. Underneath it, rests an envelope and she places it in her front pocket.

Drifting into her bathroom, Rue finds a hair tie and twists her auburn hair into a bun on top of her head. She pulls off the mirror hanging over the sink, and gently places it on top of the towel still at her feet from Diego. In its place, resting in a carved-out hole in the side of the brick wall, is a raw opal stone on a simple silver chain hanging in secret. Rue stares at it as it hides from the rest of the Southlands.

Slowly she removes it from the wall and clasps it around her neck. Not wanting to risk anyone seeing this priceless item, she chooses to tuck it safely under her sweatshirt. The cold of the stone hums against her skin, waking her up, tingling the back of her neck.

In the kitchen, she finds a bottle of wine she snagged the last time she was in the High District. She searches through her meal bags, pulling out one that makes pasta.

Meal bags are the Southlands solution for feeding the poor. The island cannot produce its own food naturally, so it is either imported from the fae mainland, or created synthetically in a factory for cheap. Their solution to the human population not going extinct, meal bags. Brown, plastic pouches of food like mush, that do nothing for your taste buds, are unfortunately the only source of nutrients people get.

Food in hand, Rue leaves her apartment. She takes the steps up two more floors to the roof. The top of her building is dark, but the lights shining from the High District in the distance leave a hazy glow that mimics moonlight. A soft breeze floods around her, causing her to shiver into her clothes. She steps towards the edge, where she has a folding chair set up, facing the view. The chair creaks as she sits down, and Rue brings her knees up to her chest.

In the darkness of the night, you can really visualize the wealth gap of Alerious City. The outskirts are filled with factories and smokestacks of chemicals pumping into the sky. As a barrier to shield the Highers from the industrial life outside their walls, the city built the Low District. Think of it as a fence keeping out unwanted life.

The Falls (the borough Rue lives in), and twenty other boroughs create the Low District. Broken down apartment complexes, abandoned shop fronts, and makeshift bridges going from one building to the next cover the stone prison of an island. Nothing is sound or safe when it comes to the Low District. The original buildings are reinforced with recycled materials tossed out from the High District. Trash fills the streets and mixes with the toxic smelling steam rising from the sewers to create an incredibly undesirable aroma.

Rooftops, and skywalks are the safest way of transportation throughout the district. Train cars carry people through the streets if you can afford it, if not you are forced to walk. Running water is not common, most people relying on rainwater to drink and bathe. Electricity is scarce, and those hooked up to the grid, lose power at least a few times a week. It is not an easy life, but one that people have adapted to.

Past the Lowers, sits the High District on top of a hill made of white stone, casting its shadow at those beneath them. It is surrounded by a large limestone wall. A beautiful, modern looking suburb of the city stands tall amongst the decay and chaos of the Low District. The artistically built structures hum with lights, and comforts, and hopes, and dreams.

The Highers have air purifiers, which make it possible for them to grow some fresh food. They have water treatment systems that take the water from the surrounding ocean and decontaminate it, making it safe to drink. They have parties, galas, and celebrations for accomplishments and technological advancements. They have freedom, while the Lowers only have survival.

Every political race is won by those who promise the same opportunities for the Lowers. Year after year those promises are left to float away into the wind, leaving the people on this side of the wall with outreached hands full of nothing.

Rue's head lays back, resting on the chair, and her eyes shift to the sky. Every night she searches through the smog and light pollution to find stars hidden like buried treasure. She can't even remember the last time she saw one, or the real night sky for that matter. Somewhere past the clouds are two moons, one big and white, and a smaller blue one. There are constellations amongst the millions of stars and other galaxies that tell stories of the past, but she has never seen it. Yet each night, she searches, looking for something to connect her with this world.

Being on this roof, with the wind around her makes her wish to fly in the sky, feel the rush of air blow past her as she soars above the clouds to see what is beyond them.

She tries to look past the clouds tonight but does so with no avail. Her face goes slack, and her eyes shut, hands automatically moving to her neck to run the opal stone between her fingers, letting it warm with her touch.

Breathe in. Breathe out.

"Gods, what am I doing?" she moans to herself. "What the actual fuck?"

She shouldn't have challenged Diego tonight. She knew she should have just left it alone. It would have made things so much easier for her moving forward. Now, she'll probably get low paying jobs, and smaller paychecks for a few weeks as a twisted punishment for calling him out.

"I need you mom… I need you. I don't know what I'm supposed to be doing. I'm just lost here." She speaks to the sky as if it will answer back. The wind picks up again, causing loose hairs to blow across her face.

Rue looks down to her sweatshirt, the warm black fabric hugs her as she tucks her knees inside of it, rolling up the sleeves that are too long so she can use her hands. She reaches into the pocket and pulls out the envelope. The paper is worn and discolored, crumbling from years of opening and refolding.

The letter illuminates in the lights of the city. She takes a swig of wine straight from the bottle before reading.

> *My Darling Aruelia,*
>
> *I am writing this letter to you in the hopes that someday, you can find forgiveness in your heart for what I have done. My only purpose in this life was to keep you safe, and I have failed. I failed you. I have failed my magic. I have failed your father. And I have failed this great nation we call home. The north will be a safe haven once more, but right now, it is not that simple. Which is why you had to leave.*
>
> *Lord Magnus, my husband, is the Lord of the North as of this letter. He is a man of great power, and a dark heart. I was sold to him to be his wife, so his heirs would stay strong of northern blood. Unfortunately, he was not my twin light. Your real father was.*
>
> *I met your father a few years ago, he was contracted to work for my husband from the human lands. Fae and Humans were forbidden to be together, but when you find your twin light, there is not much the Gods can do to keep you apart. It is a beautiful thing to find your partner, and it's something I hope you can experience some day.*
>
> *Your father and I tried to keep our love a secret for as long as we could. But when you were born, and your red hair started to grow, there was no denying you were not Magnus's daughter. You look just like your father, Aruelia. His hair, his golden brown eyes, even the tiny freckles on your cheeks. My little red fox.*
>
> *Magnus grew angry, and I knew there wasn't much time. He took the life of your father, told the whole castle that he was a traitor,*

and made me watch. A small piece of my heart died that day with him. He was kind, and good, and everything Magnus could never be. I knew you were next, then he would kill me too. So, on your fourth name day, I made the impossible decision to send you away to the human country, where no one would look for you. Where you would be safe, even if that meant separated from me. This is my greatest regret. But sometimes you must make extraordinary sacrifices for the ones you love.

I unfortunately will not be there to witness your successes firsthand. Your failures. Your love. Your bravery and courage. But just know I am always with you. When you feel the cool breeze on a warm day. When you feel the wind pulling you. The smell of pine that comes off the ocean. Know that it is me, my darling. You will always have me watching over you.

The pendant you wear was mine. The opal was passed down from generation to generation of women in our lineage. It was my job to teach you about its origin, but we were never blessed with time. Keep it safe. It is a part of me, and you, and every woman before us.

We should have had a lifetime together, Aruelia. I should have been the one to teach you about all the power you hold. You were born of true love, and that makes your powers stronger than most, even if your father was human. You have the power of the north in your blood. Air and Ice flow through your veins. Use them. Nurture them. Teach yourself, because I know you're capable.

When you feel that invisible tug towards something, follow it. Your magic will call to you. When you need it most, it will support you. All you need to give it in return is hope. And trust in yourself. Please hold on to your intuition, it will keep you safe. Hold on to your kindness, it will keep you grounded. And most importantly hold on to your determination, it will keep you going after you've been knocked down.

You are brave. You are strong. You are smart. And you are loved more than you will ever know. I hope you can understand, this is not an easy decision for me. This is excruciating. It is not the outcome I want, but there is no other way. We will not see each other again in this life I am afraid, but I will wait. I will wait in that meadow as long as it takes.

I am going to leave you with this. Your name is Aruelia Kylexi. You are named after the Goddess of Air, Aruelia. The bravest, most powerful of all the Gods. She led the people into the light and fought off the shadows. She cared about others. She stood up for those that could not bear their own weight. When we named you, your father and I knew you'd do the same someday. Be the light, my love. Shine true and strong. Have faith in yourself. Show this world what it means to be good. You are good.

My devotion to you will never falter. I would give up all my powers, if it meant you were safe.

You are my brave little fox.

And now I need you to be brave without me.

I love you more than life itself,
  Your Mother

A lone tear starts to stream down Rue's face, but she quickly blinks it away. Not today. She will not cry today. She will be brave.

It's all she has left of her mother, this letter and the necklace. No memories, or images she can hold on to in her head. Just these two objects. This small piece of who she really is. Aruelia Kylexi, Half Fae of the Northlands.

With her eyes fixed on the last few lines of the letter, Rue moves her hand to her ears, and she can feel the invisible points.

They will start to reappear to the naked eye soon, an elixir's power starting to wear off.

She looks out onto the only home she has ever known. One that does not belong to her. A foreign place, whose people are fearful of "monsters" like her, those gifted with the elemental powers of natural magic.

She would be sentenced to death if the wrong person found out. But what the humans didn't understand was that there were always fae folk amongst them hiding in plain sight. There were souls who left the mainland for adventure, or a fresh start, or to hide like her. Sadly, like most tragedies, the fae folk found a new home in a place as toxic as the void. A place that is filled with corruption and darkness and run by people in power that only make decisions to benefit their own wallets, instead of the citizens.

Rue closes her eyes, squeezing them shut to concentrate on her mother's face. Trying to add features to a blurred figure she has never been able to remember. She tries to imagine her hair, and if it was long or short. She wonders what color her eyes were, and if she smelled like the winter. She thinks about what it would have been like growing up in a castle on a mountain side, running through forests of pine trees, and chasing rabbits through the snow. She dreams about the possibility of having siblings, playing games, and exchanging gifts on holidays.

"He will pay for what he did to the both of you. I won't let your death be for nothing. I just have to get off this rock," she whispers into the air.

Rue lowers her chin to rest on her knees as an unseasonably warm breeze washes over her. She smiles into the fabric thinking back to the wind pulling her to the roof of the Brighten Building. "Thank you for being with me today."

She points her fingers at the meal bag leaning on the edge of the building. Suddenly, her eyes begin to glow and sparkles dance in their coloring. White, cloudy, glitter emerges from her palms, flooding down to her fingertips. It floats gently towards her dinner, and without moving, the sparkles lift the bag and begin opening its contents. Rue focuses her energy on her magic and prepares her packaged meal of pasta like mush. Her deep breaths in and out fuel her power with every bit of oxygen.

After a few hours of playing with her magic, rereading her letter three more times, and choking down the pasta (which got easier the more wine she drank), Rue stands to leave her safe rooftop. She will worry about the Organization, her parents' killer, leaving this island, and just how generally fucked her life is another day.

CHAPTER 5

… Something is not as it seems…

… This isn't home…

… I look down at my trembling hands and can see the blood starting to harden. White sparkles are floating off them like steam. I lift my linen dress and can see that I'm barefoot. My feet are covered in blood and dirt. I'm standing on what I believe to be pine needles, but I can't feel anything.

My eyes trail upward, and I can see the forest glowing ahead of me. Trees I have never seen before in person. Different shapes, and colors. Some deep greens with tiny pin like needles, some large and fragile, so bright they almost look yellow. Beams of light casts shadows over the tree branches like beacons, showing me which direction to take.

A force is pulling me towards the glow. "Go to her. You must find her. Find the Light," a calm voice whispers. As if tied to an invisible rope, my body steps forward. I search the forest around me. Trees sway as the winds start to push me onward.

I'm shoving branches out of the way as I search for the source of the light. I can see a clearing a few feet ahead and work my way through the brush. I step out into a golden meadow. The sun warms my face. A monarch butterfly flutters past my view, and I follow it through the tall grass. It perches itself on a white rock, and begins to move its wings back and forth, as if to say hello.

The cracking of a branch is coming from beyond the stone, stopping me from touching the butterfly. I take my focus off of it and can see the shadow of an animal disappear into the trees ahead. Something about it makes my soul curious.

"Go to her. You must find her," the voice reminds me.

I start to run. Using the wind to propel myself forward through the swaying field. This forest is different. Dark. Cold. Blue instead of the warm golden light of before. I want to go back. This isn't right. My heart starts to race. The trees rustle in front of me. The creature is close. I can feel it and the invisible string drags me towards the noise.

The bushes in front of me have thorns. My hands are bright red from the blood. Scratches go up my arms. I feel nothing. My heart races faster and I can hear it in my ears.

"Go! Go, my little fox." The voice sounds panicked. I'm panicked.

I ignore the blood dripping down my arms onto my dress and begin pulling branches back to get through. Further and further I step into the forest. Deeper into the darkness around me. I'm shaking from the cold. My mind is telling me to turn around. Everything in me wants to go back to the meadow. Back where it's warm. And safe.

My whole body now has the sparkly cloud swirling around it. I'm shivering and I don't know if it's fear, or the cold, or both.

I step out behind a thorn bush and can see the creature at last. A small little fox, with golden honey eyes, sits on a path of more pine needles, just looking up at me. This little creature doesn't need to be here. We don't need to be here. We need to go back. We need to go back to the warm sunny stone and stay with the butterfly.

I reach down to pick her up and as soon as my hand touches her fur, she turns stark white. Before I have time to question what just happened, my arms start to turn blue. My breath is now a cold mist blowing out of my lungs. I lift my hand to examine it, but I can't move. I'm frozen. My skin starts to frost over. I'm so cold. I'm scared. I feel my lungs freezing from within.

…I feel…

… Oh gods I might…

… I feel like I might…

CHAPTER

RUE sits on the train car with her face in the paper, not for the joy of reading, but simply to make sure no one will talk to her. She scans an article about three fae that were found dead in an alley not far from her apartment. They had been brutally slashed with a knife and their ear points cut off. The article was praising the Presidents and their Marshals for keeping the city streets clean.

Sadly, this type of story wasn't front page news; it was tucked away where they hoped no one would read about it. Fae were killed all the time in the Southlands. These three victims made the total for the month over twenty. People feared them so much, they turned to violence more often than not. The irrational fear of those with magic always confused Rue. Not once has there been a news story about fae folk becoming violent with a human, yet each and every one of them are convinced fae folk are the enemy.

Her eyes lift off the words on the page to see an ad stuck to the side of the train car explaining if you see something, say something, and a communicator code to call the local Marshal branch when dealing with "monsters." Rue sits, tapping her foot to an imaginary beat, laughing to herself.

If these idiots only knew who was on this train car with them. They'd shit themselves.

She despised taking the train. For one, it smelled like dirty feet. It's also bumpy, crowded, sticky, and for some reason gives people the courage to talk to strangers. Even if those strangers are putting out all the tell-tale signs of someone who does *not* want to be bothered.

Rue has her sunglasses on, a newspaper open, and she has perfected a facial expression that could only be described as, talk to me and I'll kill you. Yet, this crazy, old woman next to her thought it would be a great idea to tell the tale of when she used to sell hair accessories, knitted exclusively out of her cat's fur. She would spin the hair into yarn (as one obviously does in this line of work) and create headbands and clips out of it. She proceeds to tell her that after her cat died, she had a dream about said cat's spirit, telling her to stop the business or it will haunt her for the rest of her days.

She's in the middle of explaining how difficult it is to spin cat hair when Rue finally turns to glare at her. She pulls her purple shades down towards her nose and snaps, "Ma'am, if you say one more word about cat hair, I think I might just die and haunt you myself. For the love of the Gods, leave me alone."

Without giving the woman a chance to respond, Rue stands up and moves towards the front of the train car.

By the front row of seats, Rue's eyes lock on a young woman clutching her purse, she can hear the woman's heart rate ringing in her ears. The hairs on Rue's neck stand up as her gut screams to investigate. An older man is holding onto the grab rail, leaning over the girl with one of his hands on her shoulder. His slimy fingers creep up her neck and palms her cheek, making her wince and close her eyes.

Rue watches in shock, peeling her eyes away just long enough to see the passengers around the girl ignoring the situation. They turn their eyes to stare out the windows and maneuver their bodies away from the scene.

What heroes.

Rue's senses intensify. Slowly, her hand leaves her pocket, trying to calm the pulsing sensation wanting to burst out and throw the man across the room. She does her best to stay calm and conjure her magic without wandering eyes. If she breathes slow enough, the magic will happen without the normal glittery cloud. She just needs to focus.

She wanders towards them, looking around like she is trying to find another spot to sit. She grabs the rail behind him and can hear the one-sided conversation.

"Come on pretty girl, let me show ya a good time. Don't pretend you didn't wear that outfit for attention, you knew what you were doin'," he nags.

Barf.

As if out of nowhere, a gust of wind slams against the train car, causing it to jerk to the side. The man's head crashes into the side of the car, and Rue tumbles on top of him. She maneuvers her hand into his pocket on the impact, picking his wallet. Once the car settles, the man lifts himself up and cups his forehead which is now bleeding.

"Fuckin hell," he yells.

"Oh, shit. You better go see if they have a med kit or something to get that cleaned up. Gods, that came out of nowhere," she says, sitting down next to the woman. "You shouldn't have been so close to the side of the train; they do get pretty bumpy sometimes." After noticing Rue snickering, the man storms off.

"Are you okay? I saw him hovering like an ass," she asks the young woman. "I was coming over here to say something, but The Mother had other plans apparently."

"Yeah, I'm… I'm okay. He just wouldn't take no for an answer."

"I'm sorry no one stepped in sooner."

The train is full of cowards.

Rue casually opens the wallet she just snagged, hiding the act in her own bag, looking to see what's of value. There are a few copper and one bronze. She tosses the wallet under her seat and pretends to pick up the bronze coin off the floor.

"Oh, you must have dropped this," she says handing the coin to the woman.

Her brows furrow. "That's not mine," she admits.

"Huh, I wonder if it was the asshole's?" She pauses a moment looking over the coin, like she doesn't already know what to do with it. "Take it. He owes you one." She gives the woman a genuine smile, dropping the bronze into her hand.

Over the loudspeaker, the operator announces a stop in West Harbor, although the reliability of the dated speaker makes it come out more like *Est Rbor*. Luckily, Rue understands and gets to her feet to leave before the woman can question her further about the coin.

She steps off the repulsive train and lands smack dab in the middle of one of the busiest boroughs in the Low District. Unfortunately, the number of people walking the streets does not correlate with its charms and beauty. While it is on the coast, so there is a breeze off the ocean, it has a constant fishy odor due to the fish markets in town.

Yes, fish, the only natural food source the Lowers have at their disposal. Most of the community in the Low District are from fisherman families. It's considered an honor to be a fisherman to the people. It allows the community to be self-sufficient and support their families without the control of the High District. The Highers refuse to fish due to the nature of the job. Too messy. Too smelly. Too much *actual* hard labor.

The cobblestone streets around her are full of vendors selling everything from clothes, food, fabrics, and even basic weapons. The buildings are constructed from wood and bricks. Some utilize materials from the landfill for repairs and look like they could collapse at any moment. Ropes draped with today's wash hang out windows connecting one building to the next. Rusty awnings cover balconies from the apartments on top of shops. A hum of voices fill Rue's ears, making it hard for her to pinpoint who is saying what, even with her fae hearing.

As she walks down the main market street, she lifts a crusty piece of bread from a vendor who is busy arguing about prices to another patron. A wafting stale smell fills her nose when she breaks it in half, placing one piece in her bag, the other she begins to eat herself. Not the best baked good she's had, but calories nevertheless.

The busyness of the morning calms Rue, allowing her to blend into the background of people's morning routines. She weaves in and out of people wandering from vendor to vendor and laughs when she sees a small child sneaking food from a cart selling "genuine" mainland jams and jellies.

Ahead of her, she can see a crowd forming around a man standing on a wooden bench. He is preaching the use of citizen vigilantes to get the growing number of fae folk down to zero. Claiming they are contaminating the city and are responsible for the rising number of kidnappings in the area. That perks Rue's interest, *kidnappings*, it couldn't be a coincidence.

She slides into the crowd, listening to him spit his ideas at others.

"'See something, say something' has always been our motto in this town. But that is not working in this day and age. The government is tricking all of us into believing they will rescue us. They want us to rely on them, when we are the ones with the power. We are the one on the street with the most to lose. So, I say fuck 'see something, say something!' We demand action! We demand justice! From now on I say if we see something, we do something."

Rue's eyes flicker over the crowd, people are nodding in approval. Some are whispering their agreement with their neighbors. A few start to clap. She spots a swift blur of black coming towards the crowd, Marshals, and that's when Rue realizes it's time to leave the situation.

She backs up slowly, taking another bite of her bread, and shifts her focus to a vendor selling recycled linens. She can hear the uproar as the marshals defuse the situation, the man on the crate is being escorted away from the scene. She rolls her eyes listening to him yell out that it's time for the people to take over control.

"They are slowly killing us all!" he screams as he's being taken away down a back alley. Rue shakes her head, knowing that he will never be seen again. She wants to feel bad for him, he was arguing the truth, but if you are willing to publicly talk down to the government, you better be willing to die on that hill.

Hushed mumbles of people agreeing with his statements surround Rue as she walks farther into West Harbor. The idea of vigilantes running around trying to be heroes causes a tightness to sting in her chest. Hopefully, people won't start putting themselves in dangerous situations, because she can guarantee if the fae folk are cornered, they won't go down without a fight. The ignorance of humans to assume they could win that type of fight is what worries her the most. But all she can do at this very moment is wipe away her concern for others and focus on herself.

She passes a corner store that sells Meal Bags and miscellaneous items. Generals, which is what the community calls them, are spread throughout the district for the convenience of the citizens. They are funded by the government and are there to provide basic resources to the people. Things are marked with low prices, making it easy to afford for even the poorest of souls. However, as wonderful as it sounds on paper, it is rare that things are stocked to their capacity, making it difficult to get what you *actually* need.

The shop owner, Fiona, is outside sweeping the stones when Rue walks by.

"You're not going to say hi," she jokes in her comfortingly, dreamy voice.

Rue stops in her tracks, opening her mouth to say something sarcastic, but thinks against it. Slowly she turns to face her, giving a small grin when their eyes meet. Fiona is a short woman, warm ivory skin, long gray hair, kind eyes, and wrinkles on her face from a long life.

What the people around them don't realize, is that their beloved store owner Fiona, is a Druid. A shapeshifter, who can turn into the form of any living being, originally from the Eastlands. Druid's powers are a type of ground magic and originate from Doruk, the God of the Ground. She swam herself across the ocean to find a better life after her wife died over one hundred years ago.

Every few decades, she changes her name and shapeshifts into another form to continue helping in the shop. Rue has only ever known her as Fiona, her friend, someone who helped raise her as a child.

"Hi Fi," Rue smiles.

"What? Didn't think I would recognize you? Our big hot shot working in the High District," she laughs, moving in for a warm embrace. "We miss you, Honey."

"I know. I know. I'm just busy. Working a lot at the restaurant. You know how it is." Rue uses the lie of working at a restaurant in the High District to cover up the fact that she is a Rogue. It is the easiest way to explain her odd hours of working nights and weekends, and the stream of money she gives back to the ones she cares about. It also keeps them in the dark if ever questioned about her. She is a ghost, even to those who know her best.

"She's been worried about you, you know," Fiona says so only Rue can hear.

"I know. She always has. I'm on my way to see her now."

"You better apologize for last time. She worries it's her fault you don't come around anymore. Thinks you don't want her to be a part of your life. You and I both know that's not true, but she forgets what it's like to be young."

"I know, I'm sorry." Rue looks to her feet, and something pulls on the iron stone where her heart should be.

"It's not me you need to say sorry to." Fiona grabs Rue's face with both hands, warming her cheeks from the early spring chill. Her eyes dart around her features, as if to examine her for marks or bruises. "She just wants you to have the best life possible. We all do."

Rue pulls her face out of Fiona's grip and rolls her eyes. Wanting to change the subject immediately she asks, "How's the shop?"

"Oh, you know, never enough. I had to start rationing people to only buy one meal bag per person per day. It's not gone over well."

"Anything I can do?" Rue tilts her head, lowering her eyebrows.

"Not unless you can convince the government to send us the supplies we desperately need."

"I'm sorry. I wish it was easier."

Fiona looks off towards her shop and says, "It's the way it's always been. Lucky for us, Lowers are a scrappy bunch."

"Any news in the borough? How's everyone doing?"

Fiona pauses a moment wanting to say something but stops herself, looking around them worried. Little alarms go off in Rue's mind, something is off.

"We're good. Charlie was able to get his ankle looked at. Finny has been helping at the docks to make some extra money."

Rue perks up, "How is Finny?" She hasn't seen the little guy in years, although she supposes he's not little anymore considering he's old enough to work on the docks.

"He's doing really well. Staying out of trouble, which I'm grateful for."

"Good. I miss him."

Fiona's face warms with the hint of a smile, then slowly it drops into a frown. Rue can't help herself and asks, "What's really going on, Fi? What is it you're not telling me?"

"There have been some rumors floating around the neighborhood."

"What do you mean by rumors?" Rue crosses her arms and lowers her head towards Fiona.

"Some people have been going missing."

The kidnappings.

Trying to keep her composure and not seem too interested Rue says, "I did hear about that, do you know anything? Strange really."

"All I know is that every so often, a new missing person flier goes up in my shop. Always someone young and strong, which doesn't make sense. It's made some of us come to the conclusion it might be a group of kidnappers, not just one individual."

A flash of blue in the form of a folder pops into her head. "Have you heard anyone mention a group called the Organization?"

She thinks for a moment before answering. "No, I haven't, but I'll keep my ears open. I was thinking of shifting and going on a little eavesdropping mission."

Rue's jaw drops, "Um, no. You do not need to be doing that. Let someone else handle this. Just focus on keeping you and especially Finny safe." Fiona doesn't answer right away, causing Rue to say, "I'm serious."

"I guess you're right."

"Please just be careful, okay?" Rue smiles and gives Fiona one more hug.

"You too, Honey. Tell Olympia I said hi."

Rue lets out a giggle under her breath, "Why don't you make her dinner and tell her yourself?" She has always poked fun at Fiona's admiration of Olympia for years. The two of them have always been close. When Rue was younger, she had always hoped they'd end up together and raise her as their own.

"Oh, you!" Fiona taps her broom on Rue's head playfully. "Go. Go. She'll be excited to see you."

Rue waves her off as she turns to head towards Olympia's shop. Around the corner, along a coast lined street, there is a line of artisan shops. Little makeshift store fronts fill the side of the street with vendors trying to sell their creations. Some have homemade soaps and bath products, driftwood furniture, even a sweet old woman who sells instruments she makes out of recycled items she finds in the landfill. This is by far Rue's favorite part of the city.

She walks past the soap lady and kneels in front of an elderly man sitting on the side of the street.

"Hey Charlie! I hear you got your ankle looked at. I'm so glad. You got to stop dancing with all those young ladies," she teases.

"Oh, you know me, Rue Girl. Can't keep the ladies away. Why, you just dropped by to see me, and I didn't even have to pray to the Gods," he jokes, laughing with his hand on his stomach.

Charlie is probably over ninety years old, but no one knows for sure. He forgot his own age years ago and hasn't been able to remember since. His wrinkles are deep, and his skin is burnt from the sun. His white hair is a dirty mess on his head, and she can tell he's been sleeping outside again.

"Charlie, why aren't you staying with Olympia or Fiona? They both have the space and could use someone to talk to. You'd be helping them out if you stayed with them."

"No Ma'am. The streets are my home, those are my people living in these apartments. Who's going to look out for the neighborhood if I'm cooped up inside some stuffy box?" His gravelly voice rings in her ears with his stubbornness.

Rue knows not to argue. Charlie has been a resident of this street for as long as she can remember. She used to run up and down the cobblestone, having him time her when she was little. She would bring her lunches out and share with him on days she noticed him looking too thin.

"Hey, I got something for you," she says, taking the bread out of her pack.

"Oh, you don't have to do that. I'm doing just fine."

"Nope, I insist. I couldn't finish it. Take it, it's yours." She hands him the bread, so he doesn't have to get up off his blanket. He nods and takes a small bite. Rue stands up, brushing off her fishnet tights, and looks down at Charlie with a smile. "Hey, be careful out here, okay. People are being taken left and right and I don't want anything happening to my favorite guy."

"Oh, they ain't coming for me. They know they'd get messed up if they did."

"That's what I like to hear." She giggles, and heads down towards the shop, leaving Charlie with a nod and a wave.

Moon Child Apothecary is tucked away into an alcove on the end of Artisan Row. A small brick storefront with two floors of apartments on top. The wind chimes on the door jingles as it closes behind Rue on the way in. Recycled Wood cabinets are stocked with crystals, tarot cards, books, natural supplements, and little bottles filled with essential oils from the mainland. Plants fill empty spaces, creating a cozy yet chaotic feel to the shop. A familiar aroma of jasmine and bergamot fill her with a sense of calm.

She steps past a younger man looking at a book called *Crystals of the Westlands* and makes her way to the front desk.

Behind the wooden desk stands Olympia Tutrice, an older woman, with sepia toned skin that glows bronze in the light coming in through the windows. Her springing curls are turning gray with age and hold their shape in an Afro on top of her head. Olympia has her signature wildflowers tucked into her hair, making it look like she is growing them right from her roots. She is talking to another customer, so Rue wanders to a table of dried herbs observing their conversation.

Olympia's soft spoken, deep voice soothes her into a state of nostalgia. She watches as she talks with her hands and comforts the woman with a rub on her back. There are some capsules in her hand in a small glass jar that she hands over to the woman, who gives Olympia a hug of appreciation in return. The woman pulls some coins out of her pocket, but Olympia shakes her head, pushing the coins back to the woman.

While most people see Olympia's shop and are awed at the fact that she can grow so many different plants in a harsh environment like the Low District, Rue knows the real reason she has such a green thumb. Olympia is a Nymph. A type of fairy that originates from the Eastlands.

She has ground magic, making it so she can grow almost anything in any environment. After traveling to the human lands years ago, she saw the opportunity to help those who were missing the nutrients of fresh foods in their diets. She opened her shop up and has been selling her own products ever since.

Rue owes her life to Olympia. After her mother had placed four-year-old Rue on a cargo ship and sent her off to the Southlands, Olympia had found her washed ashore. The ship had capsized off the coast in a storm, and Rue had been thrown into the sea. Olympia had been tending to an oak tree she was attempting to grow, when she noticed Rue's tiny little body lying limp on the shore.

Olympia liked to say The Mother let the tree grow so she could be there to rescue Rue. An act of fate.

Rue woke up three days later in Olympia's apartment with no memory. Her only clue to her past came from the letter Olympia had salvaged in Rue's pocket, and the opal necklace around her neck. To this day, Rue believes it was actually her mother's spirit that brought them together. A protector when her mother could no longer be one.

Rue grew up running around this shop. She slept in a bed just up the steps for many years, but things were not always perfect. Olympia was not Rue's mother, and Rue made sure she knew that. The angst of being a teenager and dealing with no memories of her true parents took a toll on Rue. Still trying to come to terms with having to hide who she is her whole life, she lashed out. Often. Pulling the rage that sat below the surface of her emotions and expressing it in violent ways.

Her powers didn't start to show until she was about twelve. She had grown up with Olympia teaching her about all the fae creatures, their lands, and all seven types of bright magic. She even taught Rue about the dangers of shadow magic. What she could not teach her, was how to harness her air powers. Only another air magic wielder could do that. So, Rue was forced to teach herself, or abandon her power, but that came at a cost.

Rue was a little over fourteen when she came home one day after getting into a fight. Someone had called her a mistake, that her parents didn't want her, and that's why Olympia had to adopt her as her granddaughter. Rue came home sobbing and trembling from anger. Olympia had tried to comfort her, but Rue couldn't see past her rage. Without thinking, Rue threw Olympia across the shop using her magic, breaking Olympia's arm, and knocking her unconscious.

She left that day, deciding it would be safer for everyone if she was on her own. But no matter how many days or months or even years went between visits, Olympia would always welcome Rue back as if no time had passed at all.

"Can I help you?" a soft, angelic voice came from behind Rue. She turned to gaze into Olympia's olive green eyes.

"Hey Oly," she says, smirking at her.

"As I live and breathe. Come back for more… Oils again?" she asks, raising a brow at Rue. Suddenly she felt eight again and was just found red handed looking at potions she wasn't supposed to.

"Sorry, I need them for something, and it can't wait." Rue says it casually, looking over to the customer watching this interaction. "Can we talk upstairs?"

"Promise not to leave through the window this time?"

Rue nods, thinking back to the last time she was here. Her cheeks flush with embarrassment.

Olympia looks at her a moment, puckering her lips, before turning to the woman watching them. "Rose, could you watch the store for a moment. My granddaughter and I need to have a little chat about respecting your elders."

Rose agrees, and Olympia motions for Rue to follow her up the steps. "This way."

"Yes, Ma'am."

She tries to shake off the feeling like she's about to be grounded at the age of twenty eight.

CHAPTER

OLYMPIA rents the apartment on the second floor. It's a small space, but bigger than Rue's current apartment. Two tiny bedrooms, a U-shaped kitchen, a bathroom made of miscellaneous tiles, and a small living room make up the space. The living room, which is used for Olympia's experiments, is filled with glass cabinets of random bottles, and herbs in pots. All used to mix concoctions for fae folk.

To all the Lowers, Olympia is just another shop owner, while very eclectic in style and business, normal to the human eye. To the fae living in the Low District, Olympia is responsible for keeping them hidden. She specializes in potions and elixirs to hide features that would alarm humans. Features like odd colored skin, animal-like eyes, and pointed ears are among the things she can glamour away. She has mixtures for individual issues and sells/barters them from her apartment on the side.

Last time Rue was here, Olympia found her escaping through the window, stealing a pack of Ear Elixirs. In her defense, it was three in the morning, and she didn't want to wake her up. She had just got word of an underground poker game she needed to infiltrate and was out of her own supply at home. Rue glances to the window, then her eyes lower to the yellow and blue tiles under her boots.

Olympia moves a chair out at her kitchen table and motions for Rue to follow. "Sit down, Honey Bee. I'll make you some tea."

"No, I'm fine. I just came for some elixirs… and to pay you for what I took last time," she says apologetically.

Olympia ignores her decline of the tea and continues pulling out cups and her kettle. "I don't want your money. I guess I should just be grateful you came in through the front door instead of the window this time, huh?"

The guilt bubbles over in its imaginary pot, this is not how she wanted this to go. "I'm sorry about that, Oly. I just… I had a shift at the restaurant last minute and needed some extra doses. I'll pay you for it, I promise."

Olympia turns around abruptly in the middle of filling her kettle with a glass jar of filtered rain water. "Rue, it's not about the money. It's about you not being honest with me, ever. You and I both know you don't work at a restaurant. We both know you continue to put your life in danger and get yourself into situations that could expose who you are," she says sharply. Her concerned eyes rip through Rue like acid. "I have lost too many friends to the Marshals. They will kill you, Rue. No questions asked or back talk needed. Fae in this country need to lie low. That is why I do what I do. To help us blend in. Not so you can go be some vigilante running through the streets."

Rue glances down at her hands, and picks at her black nail polish. "I'm doing what I have to do, okay? And that's all I can tell you. I need you to trust me and believe that I know how to keep myself safe. It's better for you if you don't know any more than that. I promise, I am capable of taking care of myself. I've been doing that for a long time." Rue's eyes bore into Olympia's, pleading, "Promise."

Olympia takes a second to think, puckering her lips, and nods in defeat. She turns to continue making tea. "Chamomile or mint?" she murmurs.

Rue blinks a few times trying to make sure her answer actually satisfied Olympia's concern. She doesn't blame her for being upset. She realizes she would be just as protective of her own child.

"Um, either is fine. Thank you."

A few moments later she answers, "I'll make mint, that was always your favorite. When you were little, you used to always ask me to put mint in everything. *Oly, I want mint in my pancakes. Oly, I want mint in my sandwich.*" She starts to laugh to herself. "And no matter how many times I told you mint didn't belong in those things, you would look at me with those big golden eyes, and I would do it. Then we would both laugh when it turned out absolutely horrendous."

The tension building in Rue's shoulders starts to fade. That was one of Rue's favorite things about Olympia, she never held a grudge for long. She understood why people act the way they do, and didn't hold it against anyone. She would simply say her peace, then move on to happier things. She was always there to listen and give advice if you asked. And if you messed up, she would be there telling you it's going to be all right.

Rue starts to giggle. "Oh, I know. Remember the mint potatoes. I snuck in when you weren't looking, and we served them when everyone was over for Winter Solstice? What a mess."

"Yes, and you tried to convince us that one year old baby Finny did it. Yes, that's my Honey Bee, always one to have an idea and run with it no matter the outcome." Olympia turns around with two mugs of tea, setting one in front of Rue then one for herself before turning back to the counter and grabbing small dishes from a cupboard.

Rue watches as she pulls together some sort of snack for the both of them, cutting into a homemade loaf of bread she had cooling on the counter and adding some preserves from a jar by the sink.

Olympia sits down across from Rue at the table, sliding the toast in front of her.

The wonky cup and matching plate make her smile, but she tries to hide it. It's a set she made for Olympia when she was only six. The sides of the dish are warped, and the handle of the mug has been glued back multiple times, but somehow it still holds liquid. The terrible yellow glaze is haphazardly slopped over the red clay. Rue was so proud of this mug when she made it and gave it to Olympia on her name day.

"You better eat something; please tell me you aren't living off those foul Meal Bags. That is not food, Honey Bee, no matter how many times those Presidents scream at us they are."

"I'm surviving just fine," Rue says, looking down at the floating bundle of mint leaves tied together in her cup. "And thank you." She searches for a feeling of hunger, but right now with everything she needs to figure out, food is the last thing on her mind. She runs her finger over the rim of the mug, steam lifting into her face. A sigh comes out without warning, like she's been holding it for decades and is finally allowed to lower her walls.

"Why don't you just tell me why you're really here. Let's start there."

"I need more Ear Elixirs, that's all," she lies.

"Now I may be old, but I know you. And I know when you're lying to me. What else?"

Rue takes a minute, contemplating whether or not she should get Olympia involved in whatever this is. "There have been some kidnappings in the district, I'm sure you've heard about them. I was working a few nights ago, and came across some info I think is important. I haven't been able to stop thinking about it, and the risks it puts you and our people in. I just came by to see if you've heard whispers, like from your clients or anything."

Olympia eyes search Rue for the truth while she sips her tea. She places her cup on the table and interlocks her fingers before answering. "There has been talk of a slew of kidnappings. I don't know all the details, but I know some. People are worried, they aren't acting like it, but the energy has shifted. I can feel it. My crystals and plants are acting out. The ground is starting to crack, and I'm not sure the community is ready for what's to come. This is something dark I'm afraid."

That sounds… ominous.

"Has anyone ever mentioned a group called the Organization?" Rue asks, leaning forward across the table. Her eyes go wide with a rush of hope for information. Olympia is tuned in to all the happenings of the Low District due to her work with potion making and herbal healing. If there are even the smallest whispers, she knows about it.

Olympia leans back in her chair, her narrowing eyes fixed on Rue. "Yes. I know who they are. How do you know who they are? How mixed into this are you, Aruelia? Because what I know is enough to make me stop asking questions."

"My gut is telling me they are the ones responsible. I also have this idea in my head that Highers might be involved, because according to every report I've seen only Lowers are taken. If this was a High District issue too, it would be all over the news. Right now, it's nothing but silence and that makes me more concerned about it being covered up. But other than hunches, I have nothing concrete."

"I don't like that you are involved in this."

"I'm not officially involved, I'm just curious," she clarifies, raising her hands. "I haven't been able to stop thinking about it for weeks. I just want to understand what's going on in my city. I don't like that innocent people are being ripped from their homes."

Olympia nods apprehensively. "What I've heard is not much. Your instincts were right, I can confirm the group is called the Organization. I can't tell you who I got the info from for their own safety. I know they are taking men mostly, but there are some reports of women who have been taken as well. They always attack at night. Always in a group. Always in the Low District."

Rue tilts her head and asks, "Anything else, anything solid?"

"Yes, and this is when I need you to promise me, you'll keep yourself safe."

Rue's brows lower and she swallows. "Yeah promise, what is it?"

"Now this is just rumors, but my source is reliable. There are whispers that the group meets at Lucky Clover. Now, I don't know when or where exactly they meet, but it's a start."

Rue's expression drops from her face. The Lucky Clover Casino is run by a rival of Diego and his family in the High District. Notorious for hosting poker games and parties for the mob elite. The kind of place Rue would never leave alive if someone found her snooping.

"Oh, Gods," Rue whispers under her breath, running her hands through her hair. She unconsciously pulls on the tiny braid she keeps in the back of her head, twisting it between her fingers while she thinks.

"One more thing, and I'm not sure how it's all connected yet, but there is a woman. She's been helping people escape the city. Apparently, she has a way to get people to the mainland. She's been using it to help fae for years, but recently she has been offering her services to the humans too."

"What's her name? How can I get in contact with her?"

Olympia shrugs. "I only know her by the name The Blue Lady. Nothing else. I've never met her, it's just what I've overheard."

"Well shit, that's not useful," Rue says under her breath.

"Sorry, that is all I know unfortunately."

"No, thank you Oly, you've been so helpful." Rue grabs her hand from across the table and squeezes gently, rubbing her thumb over Olympia's knuckles. "I know I don't say it but I really do lo… appreciate you." The word almost slips from Rue's lips without her realizing it.

That four-letter word is not one she says to anyone. If this life has taught her anything, it's that there is no safe place to keep love. Rue doesn't need to say it to Olympia for her to understand. She knows. She has to know.

Olympia smiles, squeezing Rue's hand right back. "You know you don't have to be a stranger. You don't have to sneak in and out the kitchen window to avoid me. You can come by. For dinner, or tea, or just to say hello. I miss you around here, Honey Bee. You bring so much life and hope with you wherever you go, you make us all want to be better when you're around us."

What a beautiful lie.

"I wish I could." She looks down at her lap, smoothing out the fringe from her jean shorts. "But the more time I spend here, the more danger you get put in. And I couldn't live with myself if something happened to you. You're too important to this community. To me."

"You sneaky little fox, always getting into trouble. I was so much like you when I was your age, believe it or not. Did I ever tell you the story of why I came to this godsforsaken city?" Olympia asks, trying to change the subject once again.

Rue rolls her eyes and lets out a huff. "Yes, only about a thousand times. You were tasked with a mission to find answers. Sent to the Southlands to find a way to unite the realm. Blah, blah, blah. Only to find a new purpose and reason to stay. Blah, blah, blah."

"Oh you! Let an old woman amuse herself once in a while."

"I do, the other one thousand times I've heard that story."

After the laughter dies, the two sit there staring at each other for a moment, Rue opens her mouth to say something but decides against it. Olympia draws back her hands, slapping them on the table and causing the spoons to rattle in their cups.

"Enough of this sad stuff, you came here for Ear Elixirs, so let's get you some," she says with a grin. Without another word, she scoots out of her chair and motions for Rue to follow her into the living room.

In the corner, Olympia has a metal desk covered in empty bottles, a notebook for her recipes, and an assortment of ingredients from all over the world. She always reminded Rue of a wizard or witch, like the ones she would tell Rue about when she was younger, beings who roamed long ago. Rue knew it was all folklore, but she liked to pretend Olympia was a secret witch and she was her helper. Olympia would catch Rue mixing potions on her own and have to repeat the dangers of mixing the wrong things together. She even went as far as to show her how things can explode when not properly combined. Little did she know, Rue would grow up to use those skills to her advantage in the Smoke Runners.

Rue was decent at potions, but nowhere near as exceptional as Olympia. She didn't even need to measure anymore for her concoctions. She could tell by her eyes what ingredients were in a potion and if the amounts were off. Those who wielded ground magic were often connected to nature on a deeper level, but Olympia was one with it.

She would always say the plants she used in her experiments would talk to her. She would go on and on about being able to stick her hand in dirt, and the right ingredient for a new elixir would sprout. She often would use her knowledge to create rubs and salves for those in need. The work of a healer intertwined into her world as a ground magic nymph.

Olympia was the one who created the poisonous lipstick for Rue. She came to her with the idea a few years ago, claiming she wanted to feel safe walking home at night, and Olympia had six different shades prepared within a day.

"Okay, Ear Elixirs. How many do you need?" Olympia says, pulling out some small pink tubes from a drawer. "A few days' worth? A month?"

"How long will these ones last?"

"After taking the vial, you should have round ears for seven days."

"Probably a few months' supply. I don't know when I'll get back here again," Rue suggests.

The look of disappointment washes over Olympia's face before she can compose herself. All the progress they made at the table is thrown away as Rue steps back behind her invisible walls.

It's the way it has to be.

"Sure, just be careful. Remember you can overdo it. Make sure your ears change back fully before drinking another." She wraps up a bundle of the glittery tubes, rolling them into a navy cloth, and hands them to Rue.

She thanks her, bringing Olympia in for a hug. A warm hand runs up and down her back in a familiar way, letting a little more tension leave her shoulders. Before letting go of their embrace Olympia asks, "Any news on finding someone who knew your father? Is that what is bothering you?"

Rue backs away, eyes lowered. She hasn't even thought about her dad for weeks, focusing all her brain power on trying to make sense of this kidnapping mess in her free time. "Nope, still nothing. Everyone with my last name has either died or gone missing. No one can ever give me any info on who the Kylexi's were or where they lived. Every time I think I found something; it turns into a dead end."

Olympia runs a finger over Rue's tiny braid, playing with it in her hand. She looks her in the eyes and breathes, "Don't worry yourself on who you are related to. You are Aruelia Kylexi. You are brave, and independent, and smart. The answers will come, when the time is right. The Mother has a way of showing you what you need when you least expect it."

Rue huffs and says, "Yeah, I know. I just can't understand why he was in the North. What was he doing working for him? It doesn't make any sense to me. That's the farthest you could go from the Southlands, and I can't wrap my head around what he was running from. I don't know how to let it go."

"And you don't have to, but you can't let the what ifs stop you from moving forward. What has happened, as tragic as it is, has happened. You can try and make sense of it, but you cannot change the outcome."

Rue's grin doesn't meet her eyes. She looks off towards the glass shelves trying to compose herself.

Olympia tilts her head and says, "There is something else isn't there, Honey Bee? Come on, you can tell me."

Rue instinctively starts to rub her hand on her forearm to calm herself. "Yeah, I started having the fox dreams again."

Olympia exhales deeply and says, "Okay, how far did you get?"

Her memories think back to the little fox in the woods, the ice, and the feeling of being frozen to death. Goosebumps cover her, almost as if she is freezing now. "I touched the fox, she turned white, and I turned into some sort of icicle. It was like I froze in place. And then when I woke up, I was screaming and cold, and my lips were blue. It was like it was real."

"Did you hear the voice this time?"

"Yeah, I did. It told me to find *her*. Find the light. I figured it meant the fox."

Rue has seen foxes in her dreams her whole life. When she was a child, they were innocent. The fox would show up to play with her or lead her to adventures. Once her powers came in, they turned dark, like she was losing control of her mind. They led her to death more times than not, generally following the same pattern through the woods.

After one too many nights waking up in a panic from watching herself die, Rue looked to healers to help her contain the thoughts. She took vials of mysterious liquids. Tried hypnotherapy by a man with electricity magic. She even got a tattoo of a fox on her ribs made from the ink of a poisonous squid. The artist said it would harness the evil spirits inside of her and contain it like a dream catcher. Obviously, none of those things actually worked.

Olympia is silent for a few moments, trying to make sense of the words. Then she says, "Like I've explained to you before, the fox is your spirit. Every fae folk has one. It is a way for The Mother to guide us through our lives. Do not be afraid of what it is trying to show you, Honey Bee. Many of us have our spirit come to us in dreams. There is nothing to fear."

"It just seems like my spirit is the reason I die every time."

"It could mean anything."

"Easy for you to say, you have a delicate little butterfly as your spirit."

Olympia shakes her head, snickering. "I wouldn't worry about it too much." She pauses, looking down at Rue's clothes with a scrunched face. "Your only concern should be staying warm in this outfit."

Well, there goes that tender moment.

Rue is taken back. "Ha! My outfit? What the hell is wrong with my outfit?" She has on jean shorts over her fishnet tights, an old t-shirt, and a flannel wrapped around her waist. "I look cute! This is what people wear in this century."

Olympia shakes her head, "Well, it's not what I would choose."

"Olympia you are over five hundred years old, I'm about to be twenty nine. I pray to the Gods you don't choose to wear what I wear."

Rue moves her hands towards her flannel, unwrapping it, and putting it on properly. "Is that better?" she mocks, doing a little twirl.

"Can I give you one of my sweaters to put on? There are just… crazy people in this city, and I don't want anyone taking advantage of you, thinking you're *someone* you are not."

Oh, the irony.

Rue lifts her hand over her face, laughing in disbelief and jokes, "Okay, I'm leaving. I'm not going to sit here and be called a prostitute, which is a perfectly acceptable profession nowadays, by someone who only wears linen pants and sweaters that could fit three people in them."

She grabs her bag from the kitchen table, stuffs the Ear Elixirs in the main pocket, and throws it over her shoulder.

"It's because I love you, you know," Olympia says in the doorway of the kitchen. "I'll let you know if I hear anything more about the Organization. Just promise me you will be safe. Don't get yourself involved in something that doesn't concern you. And promise you'll come back sooner rather than in months from now. At least let me see you on your name day."

As Rue opens the door to leave, she calls out behind her, "Yeah, yeah. I promise."

"And come in through the door next time, windows are off limits now."

Rue is half way down the stairs when she yells up, "I will, promise! And I'll make sure to wear a trench coat so everyone knows my whoring days are over."

CHAPTER

RUSHING back down the steps into Moon Child Apothecary, Rue nods at Rose who is still sitting behind the desk. The man who was reading about crystals is now flipping through a book about the Northlands Flora and Fauna. She didn't pay attention to him before, but she notices him glancing up at her from across the store. His piercing pale, blue eyes look at her through his lashes. They immediately shift down when he sees her staring back and his jaw clenches.

She makes her way through the shop, weaving in and out of people. Her gaze stays on him so she can meet his eyes once more before she leaves. His hands stick out to her, large and strong, covered in rings, with veins running up his forearms. She has a moment of weakness and the primal urge to have those hands around her throat takes over. A lock of blonde hair falls over an eye as he reads, and she can see his jaw tick as if it's taking everything in him not to look at her.

On her way past him they lock eyes, she winks and flashes him her flirtiest smile. Instead of the normal reaction she gets from men, he just glares at her and looks away, like she's growing warts on her face like a witch.

Well, I'm humbled.

Brushing off the awkward interaction as an off day, Rue saunters down a few streets into the fish market. She decides to grab something fresh for dinner using the few coins she picked off the asshole on the train.

The market is in the center of West Harbor, making it one of the most crowded (and loud) places in this borough. There are men tossing fish off carts and onto display cases. People are yelling out what species of fish are on sale. Individuals are wandering from stall to stall, purchasing what they can for the week. The smell is almost unbearable, but Rue has no choice. If she wants to eat something real and not produced in a lab, this is the place to get it.

As she walks through the market, a blip of something in her chest guides her through the stalls, a feeling she gets randomly and likes to think of it as her sixth sense. It's like a tug from a tether around her chest, pointing her in the right direction for what she needs. Although sometimes it pulls her to the sea so maybe her sixth sense is hanging on by tape and a prayer.

She walks up to one of the stalls on the edge of the market, and the blip turns to something warmer in her gut.

This is the one.

A giant of a man with a curly bun of black hair flings large fish into the front bins for sale, wiping their guts on his cargo pants before walking around to the back of the counter. He flips a knife in his hand and begins gutting more fish for the customers of the day.

She approaches the counter, having no clue what she plans to buy. An older man, with white hair coming out of his knit cap, greets her with a warm grin and a nod.

"What can I get for you today, kiddo?" he asks in a gravelly voice, wiping his hands on his once clean apron.

Rue glances in the case, not sure what slab of meat is what fish. "Um… What can you give me for three coppers?"

The man's eyes widen. "Well, young lady, that could get you a whole lot of fish! Why, you could get a whole halibut filet, or three cod filets, or two pounds of mackerel. What'll it be?"

"Hmm, which would you recommend? Honestly, I don't know much about fish."

"I'd pick the halibut; I caught it myself this morning. A real beaut of a fish. Fry this baby up with some oil and a little seasoning and you got yourself a meal!"

"Sounds perfect. I'll take it." She hands him the three coppers and places a fourth on the counter in front of her, flashing the man a bright smile.

After wrapping up the filet in paper, he hands it over with enthusiasm. "Thank you kindly, kiddo."

Rue places it in her bag and waves in thanks, turning to look out into the crowd. She is looking for the quickest route to escape the madness when her eyes lock on the icy blues of another. It's the man from Moon Child, his face forming a hostile glare. Then, as if vanishing into thin air, he's gone. Disappearing into the crowd.

Rue blinks a few times, questioning if she just saw him for real or if her mind is playing tricks on her. Maybe the fish smell is getting to her. The hairs on her neck stand up when a voice deep within her yells *Go! Now!*

Without overthinking she leaves the market and heads down towards the train stop to take her back to the Falls, walking as quickly as she can. Her mind sifts through scenarios as to why he had that nasty look on his face. She glances back behind her a few times, reminding herself he isn't following her, and slows to a normal step.

The train isn't due to arrive for another few minutes, so she takes a seat against a stone fence, and focuses her mind on the sounds around her. Listening for anyone in distress, or someone with an accelerated heart rate. She can hear a woman arguing with her partner about who will watch the kids tonight. Another person is singing off key, which is causing the elder next to them to start breathing heavily with irritation.

To the left she can hear a teenager yell, "Watch it, Dude!" which catches her interest. She leans past the others on the bench and can see Blue Eyes pushing the young girl out of the way, scanning the crowd in front of him. She realizes this is no longer a coincidence. This man is looking for someone. For her.

His eyes meet hers and he starts moving faster, pushing people out of the way. Her first instinct is to stay and fight, ask him what he wants with her, probably kick him in the balls for being an ass. However, this side of the street is too busy for a fight, and she doesn't need more eyes on her, the girl that is supposed to be a ghost.

Without another thought Rue stands up, grabs her bag, and throws it over her shoulders. She books it down the cobblestone, making sure to maneuver her way through the crowd as quietly as possible as to not cause a scene. She looks back only once, to see him lock eyes on her a few paces behind. His mouth forms an eerie, thrilled grin, which Rue is sure will haunt her dreams. He continues to shove people out of the way to reach her. Jogging turns into sprinting.

Luckily, Rue knows these streets. She prays to the Gods that Blue Eyes doesn't. Her chest is on fire from running, weaving in and out of side streets and alleyways. She does her best to make it through the borough, hoping to lose him in the chaos of the busy sidewalks.

Don't look back, only forward.

If there is even the slightest chance, he is catching up to her, she needs to draw him away from bystanders. Get him somewhere less popular so she can properly confront him if need be. So she can figure out what the fuck he is following her for.

She guides herself to the boat docks, less populated, more alleys to wait out her stalker. Zigzagging her way to some empty streets, Rue attempts to find a place to get to higher ground. There is an abandoned building a few streets away that has an old fire escape leading to the roof that would be perfect.

She takes one last glance behind her and can see only garbage blowing in the wind. Slowing her pace, Rue bends at her hips to rest her hands on her knees to catch her breath. Combat boots and fishnets were not made to run gracefully through city streets. She feels more like a clunky toddler learning to walk than someone who has had an embarrassingly high number of hours training in awareness survival and surveillance.

Realizing she lost him; she takes it as a win. No need to confront someone who can't keep up.

What an amateur.

She walks a few feet towards an alleyway to cut over into the next street. Surveying the block behind her once more for good measure. Still nothing.

As she turns the corner, her body slams into the stone wall. Two ice blue eyes engulf her in their fury.

Fuck!

He pushes her into the rock with his forearm on her neck, holding her body up against his, lifting her off the ground. His touch is freezing cold, almost to the point of burning.

Her breath is quick, and jagged, overwhelmed from the pressure of his arm. She starts to choke, and her hands shake as he pushes his against her exposed wrist. Coughing, she tries to center herself.

"Fuck you!" she tries to scream. Her eyes squeeze shut, and she uses her knee to ram into his balls. Hitting her mark with such force, he lets go of her, sinking his body to the ground with a guttural moan. Her boot connects with his face, and she shoves him to his back. She makes it a few paces away before falling on her backside, gasping for air.

Rubbing her neck, she tries to compose her thoughts. "And to think I thought you were following me because you liked me. I'm hurt, Blue Eyes."

She hunches forward, resting her hands on her knees, while her anger builds in her chest. How could she have been so stupid? "What do you want? Who sent you?"

Not a single word escapes his lips as he wipes away blood across his face. His eyes are full of darkness and hatred, jumping to his feet and pulling out a knife with one swift movement, as if it was part of his training.

Rue shoots out her hands in front of her. "Listen. Listen! You don't want to do this. You do not want me as an enemy."

He disregards her plea, and charges at her, knife pointed in between her eyes. She has no weapon. No line of defense. She darts her eyes to her left, grabs a rusty pipe, and uses it to stop his blow. Crossing it over her body within a second of death. She locks her arms straight out, to keep him from crushing her into the pavement. The blade is inches away from her neck, shaking in his hand as he pushes towards her. Rue channels her powers instinctively, white sparks rage in her irises.

His face goes pale, eyes wide, and she uses that moment of weakness to drive her boot into his shin. Pushing him back with a gust of air swirling around them. His body slams into the stone across the alley.

She gets to her feet, leaning on the wall, still out of breath and feeling lightheaded from the magic surge. "Listen, you fucking dickhead! Tell me who the hell is behind this *pathetic* attempt at killing me." Sweat trickles down her neck.

He stands, eyes turning evil with fury. He lashes towards her, knife once again at her throat. She rolls her body out of the way as his blade stabs the wooden wall with a thud. His eyes dart to her, he tries to pull the knife from the wood, but it's stuck.

The knife is stuck!

One more try.

Now's her chance. She elbows him in the nose, causing him to tumble backwards. She steps back and anchors herself with her knees. He lunges towards her, getting one good punch in before she drops to the ground. Rue can feel her heartbeat in her ears, and blood starts to slide down her nose and onto her lip. She spits red, a copper taste filling her mouth.

"Okay, now you've really pissed me off!" she shouts, eyes turning white instead of their usual golden brown.

She stands up with the help from a gust of wind, arms leaving a white cloud in her wake. Her hands shake with rage, and with her eyes fixed on him she tilts her head, revealing red teeth with a sinister smile.

Her hands shoot out in his direction, causing a burst of air to push him up against the stone. Squeezing his neck with her powers, she lifts him up the wall. He starts kicking his feet frantically, gasping for air. Her eyes continue to spark white.

The power flowing through her veins steals her blood and replaces it with something dark, allowing it to feed off his pain.

"Who the fuck sent you? WHO?" she screams.

He doesn't answer and she tighteners her magical grip on his neck. Dirt and debris swirl in the air from the force of her powers. It is as if a tornado is forming in this very alleyway.

"WHO?" Her voice is hoarse and foreign. The outlines of Rue's vision are beginning to turn as black as the void.

He's choking for air while she moves closer and closer to him. He begins thrashing in her restraint. A sudden pain hits the back of her neck, and it's enough for her to lose her connection with her magic, as if to tell her to calm down. She allows him to drop to the ground, panting for breaths with his hands over his throat.

Rue's eyes clear with the disconnect to her magic, calming her breathing and blinking away the black dots in her vision. Her hands rest by her sides, still shaking from the adrenaline. Residual power sparks through her veins. It feels good, letting the power flow through her, reminding her how much of a force she truly is.

He slumps to the ground, almost lifeless, and she squats down to get on his level.

"I'm going to give you one last chance to tell me who you are. Who sent you to follow me?" she demands.

With his head leaning back on the stone wall, he pants through coughs. He meets her stare with heavy eyes and smiles.

A whisper leaves his lips, and Rue is frozen in time. "The Organization will always prevail. All the lands will be clean soon."

With her focus on his smiling face and an unfamiliar accent she doesn't recognize, Rue doesn't see the pill he pulls out of his pocket. Before she can stop him, he throws it into his mouth and bites down hard.

"No! No, no, no." She reaches her hands out to try and stop the inevitable.

The capsule explodes, making him foam at the mouth from the poison within it. He chokes on his own spit for a few seconds before blood runs from his nose and eyes. His body convulses in his last few moments in this world. Blue Eyes eventually stills, slumped over into the abandoned alleyway.

Rue sits there in disbelief, hands shaking out in front of her. Her eyes search his features for any sign of life before falling backwards, moving her hands to cover her mouth and stop her from screaming. She can't look away.

His skin pales and foam drips from his mouth onto his shirt. The veins that run up his arms take the shade of a deep purple, pooling under the skin with death running through them. The Organization. He was with the Organization. And he was tracking her. Her, a random woman who knew absolutely nothing concrete about them. She was no threat. She was no one.

Rue runs her hands through her hair, eyes still fixed on his, the blue in them turning to the gray of the sky with red bleeding out. It was as if his spirit was still in him, staring back at her.

She finally inhales sharply, realizing how exposed she is in the middle of an alley with a dead man. Someone could see her. Someone could have already seen her. She needs to be careful where she travels to, and who she visits.

Visits! Olympia!

Did he know she would be in the shop? Was he there waiting for her to show up? Unless it wasn't a targeted attack, and he thought she would be weak against him.

Her mind spins as she tries to answer impossible questions. She gets to her feet and paces back and forth a few times trying to figure out what to do. When she lifts her arm above her head she is brutally reminded of the bruising on her ribs from his beating. She runs to her pack and opens the zipper to find the fish filet squished into a fish mush and tosses it out into the street. In a small pouch in the side pocket, she pulls out a blue vial of liquid healing potion, and tips it back into her mouth. The effects work almost immediately to heal all her internal bruising. She thanks the Gods her injuries weren't more severe, or this would have been like hoping a bandage could stop the bleeding of a severed limb.

Her steps echo off the surrounding buildings as she walks up to the wood wall and pulls out the knife that was intended for her throat. The weight of the blade sits heavy in her hands, and in the light, she can make out some sort of inscription on the side. The symbols look ancient, in a language she doesn't understand. She tosses it into her bag for a closer inspection later.

Rue's focus drifts back to him, and the illusion of him following her with his eyes sends shivers down her spine.

He's gone. It's over.

The foam isn't dissipating as fast as she would think a poison would. It piques her interest in a sadistic way. What was it made of? Could she replicate it?

She walks over to him, and squats down to be face to face with this mystery man who wanted her dead. Still holding on to the empty vial of healing potion, she reaches forward with it and fills it back up with the residue of the poison. After the cork is back on, she places it in her bag, making sure to not get any of the soapy liquid on her own skin.

Her eyes move to the pockets of his jeans. She rushes towards his body and digs through them to see if there is anything of value or some clue as to why he chose her.

In the first pocket she pulls out a toothpick, and some lint. The next has a copper coin and a crumpled yellow paper. Rue jumps to her feet, tossing the trash aside. She pockets the coin and unfolds the scrap paper to reveal the words she is dreading.

Her full name, Rue Kylexi, is written in blue pen on the inside. Goosebumps form on her arms and she loses the ability to breathe.

Minutes go by. Rue doesn't move, she would look frozen if not for her trembling fingers. She doesn't look away from his face. Inside her mind is an uncontrollable fire of questions. How did he find her? Or knew who she was? Who put the hit out on her?

Her mind replays his last and only words to her. *All the lands will be clean soon.* His voice scratches her eardrums. The lands. Did he mean the Southlands? Or all four lands? Her gut was telling her the latter. Her gut was actually screaming at her to leave this alone, to walk away and let someone else handle it. But she can't, this is now her problem whether she likes it or not. Someone wanted her dead. For reasons she doesn't understand. And her top priority is now to find them before they have a chance to try again.

Rue's mind is scrambled. She needs to get somewhere where she can focus. Somewhere the air is clear. Where his corpse isn't watching her.

When she feels confident enough, she peers out of the alleyway to check for innocent bystanders. The docks are empty, thankfully. She turns back to the body of Blue Eyes and points her hands towards him. With quivering fingers, Rue inhales deeply. On the exhale her magic grows. The white sparkles ignite around her palms, with every breath she grows calmer, and more controlled. Her magic flows out of her hands and wraps around his slack body with a glittery mist. She pulls as hard as she can, dragging him across the wooded dock, and into the water. The sea creatures that inhabit the bay should be fast enough to take care of his body before anyone notices.

She runs back and forth with handfuls of water to wash away the blood from their encounter, tossing her smashed dinner into the bay so nothing can be traced back to her.

Watching his flesh being torn apart by fish, Rue can't help but feel uneasy. This is bigger than a few kidnappings. This is something someone doesn't want to stop doing, and they are willing to kill anyone who gets in their way. She needs to talk this through with someone she can trust.

Diego.

She needs Diego.

CHAPTER

THE sky has turned blood orange by the time Rue walks up to the front steps of Sinners, Diego's luxury strip club in the High District. The white stone has a red glow due to the spotlights, a stark contrast to the surrounding buildings. Rue can already hear the bass of the music from outside.

She took a quick trip home to change before sneaking over the wall into the High District. It would be a death sentence to show up to Sinner out of her Smoke Runners uniform. She did her best to clean herself up, pulling back her hair into a high pony, and cleaning off the blood from her hands. In a last minute decision, she decides to leave her bloody lip and black eye exposed for dramatic effect. Hoping to bring home her point about the severity of this issue.

"Hey, Ghost," a beefy guy at the door greets her.

She looks up from her hood and without any emotion demands, "Franky, I need to speak to Diego."

"Shit, girl. What the fuck did you get into?" he jokes, motioning to the bruises on her face.

"Minor scratches. An absolute *thumb* of a man thought he could jump me in an alley," she looks down at her nails and grins. "So, I killed him." A flash of two dead blue eyes stares back at her in her mind.

"Fuck, you okay?" He rests his hands on her shoulders and lowers his head to her level, searching her features for more cuts and bruises.

"It was nothing, I'm fine," she lies. She shrugs his hands off her and steps back.

"Anything you need me to clean up?"

Rue looks up at him, face blank and says, "I took care of it myself."

She has a role to play as Ghost, the nickname given to her because of her ability to blend in and disappear without a trace. Show no emotions. Let no one in. Put up iron walls to guard anything that makes her human. That way no one could get to her, no one could break the girl that would not be broken.

It was easier that way. Things happen in this line of work, and if she didn't make friends, she wouldn't be upset when they ended up dead. It was also a smart tactic to keep the crew safe when one of them was being questioned. It's hard to rat someone out when you don't know their true identity.

No one else in the Smoke Runners knew Rue's real name, other than Diego. Besides him and Franky, she didn't know anyone else either. Although Franky was just the bouncer to the club, he wasn't actually a Runner, but he held many secrets for Diego and his crew. She knew he was someone she could trust with the information of her attack.

"Franky, I really need to talk to him. It's important."

"Sure thing, he's up in his office. Just don't tell him I let you in the front door looking like that."

Rue nods and without another word she swings the doors open to Sinners. The music is blasting when she enters the main stage area, and the lights give the whole room a dark red glow. There are spotlights on dancers on the stage, and plush, red velvet sofas that border the edge.

The bar to the right goes down the length of the room, with lines of alcohol bottles glowing on the glass shelves. The smell of coconut oil, and alcohol fill her nose. Her eyes move to the back of the building, to a set of steps going up to the private rooms, and a hallway that leads to Diego's office.

Luckily it is still early in the evening, so most of the booths and tables are empty as she walks through. Rue pulls her hood lower over her face, trying not to draw attention to her injuries, and gives a quick nod to the bartender as she walks past.

She is almost to the steps when some drunk idiot slurs, "When can I have a private room with this tight ass." A sting of pain shoots up her back when he slaps her behind.

She stops mid stride. Her hands form fists by her sides, her heartbeat a siren ringing in her ears. Rue spins around on her heels and within seconds has the man in her grasp, pushing his face against the bar with her palm. Grabbing a fist full of his shirt, she leans forward getting inches from his face and sneers, "If you touch me, or another woman in this building again, I will cut off your micro penis and feed it to the sharks in the bay. Do you hear me?"

"You fucking psychopath!" he stutters.

"The word you're searching for is innovative." Rue gets closer, opens her mouth to threaten him again when she gets interrupted.

"Ghost!" someone growls over the music from the second-floor railing. She looks up to see Diego, burning her with his eyes.

She sighs and hisses to the man, "You got really lucky tonight," shoving him into the bar before walking away.

"GHOST!" Diego yells again.

Rue holds her head high as she saunters up the steps, swaying her hips a little to the music. Her eyes narrow, covered by the shadow of her hood, and she welcomes the bite from her nails digging into her palms.

At the top of the steps, Diego stands with his hands in his pockets. His stare is deadly. The muscles of his jaw move as he grinds his teeth.

Two other Smoke Runners stand behind him. They work on rotation, protecting Diego at all times. Each Runner has a specific skill set, Rue's started as her ability to pickpocket and break into any lock, but soon she was promoted to using other assets, her body and charm to swindle weak people of power.

Arrow, the tall skinny guy to Diego's left, can shoot a moving target 200 yards away with his bow without looking. And Delta to his right, a shorter woman who never showed her face behind a mask, knows all the pressure points of the human body. She can kill someone with one touch.

Rue does her best to ignore the thoughts in her head about her abilities being inferior to the other members of her group. She swats away the idea that she's a glorified whore for Diego to use to get what he wants. She isn't oblivious to how she looks to the others though, she hears their whispers when they think she isn't listening.

Rue walks straight up to Diego, getting inches away. "We need to talk, now."

His eyes show nothing as to how he's really feeling. "What do you think you're doing right now?" he says in a hushed tone for only her to hear.

"It's about the Organization," she whispers as she pulls away her hood, revealing her black eye and bloodied lip. Diego's eyes dart around her face in confusion. He looks away to think for a split second, then jerks his head in the direction of his office.

"Wait out here. No one gets in until I'm finished dealing with this," he commands the two Runners. Arrow scoffs at the idea, which makes Diego glare at him and ask, "Something you need to say, Arrow?"

He clears his throat and stands up taller, looking out onto the growing crowd. He gives a small shake of his head, not daring to speak to his boss in a negative tone. Diego grabs Rue's arm and pulls her, squeezing her bicep tight.

As she walks past the other Runners, Rue smiles and winks at Arrow. The two have never gotten along. When Rue was first introduced into the Smoke Runners, Arrow had asked her out multiple times and she would laugh in his face with each attempt. After admitting defeat, he changed his attitude to attack her often and raise questions about her lack of skills to the other Runners. As soon as Diego took over for Manny, and became Arrow's boss, he grew jealous of the two of them spending so much time together. He is now the loudest when it comes to gossip about Rue and Diego's relationship, which the two have denied for years, claiming it is strictly professional.

The hallway is dimly lit by red pendant lights. At the end is a frosted glass door, with a red neon sign over top. It reads *We're All Sinners Here* with flames coming off the sides.

He opens the door and throws her in, turning around to slam it behind them. Rue winces with the blow, but quickly recovers to her normal, unbothered state. She makes her way over to his desk in the middle of the room and sits on top of the dark wood. The music sound is muffled, and she can finally hear herself think for the first time.

His office isn't the largest, but big enough to fit all twenty of the Smoke Runners at one time. The lights are dim, just like the rest of the club. A red velvet couch that matches the ones downstairs sits in the corner with a pole for his own private shows. Bookshelves with red under lighting line the walls. The hue makes Rue want to change her hair color, and never see red again.

"What the hell? You didn't have to throw me so hard!" she protests.

"Have you lost your damn mind? Why the fuck would you walk in here looking like that?" he demands. He turns to lock the door.

Rue doesn't respond, just rolls her eyes. The man secretly runs most of this city, yet he hates attention to be drawn to himself.

Diego is facing the door still when he says, "Who did that to you? Whoever it is…" He trails off to breathe in all his anger. She can see his hands forming fists against the glass. "Whoever that mother fucker is won't live to see the sunrise tomorrow."

"Someone from the Organization followed me today, tried to jump me in an alley by the docks, but I took care of it."

He turns around and looks her down the bridge of his nose, narrowing his eyes like he's trying to tell if she is lying or not. "Did you leave a trace?"

Rue's eyes meet his. She shakes her head, "No. I'm not stupid. I threw him into the bay. The fish will get him before anyone comes looking for him." She leaves out the part about throwing him in using her magic. "I'm fine by the way," she adds just to be an ass.

She can see the pain in his eyes even though he won't admit it's killing him she was hurt. He clenches his jaw, then slowly moves over to her, spreading her legs where she sits on the desk so he can stand in between them. Diego moves his thumb softly over her busted lip, red from dried blood. His eyes search her face, lifting her chin and moving around her head to check for more marks.

He leans in, kissing her neck. "You all right?" he breathes in a soft, husky tone.

"Yeah, I'm really okay," she lies again, brushing the image of foam dripping from his mouth out of her mind. "Just came to see if you had any leads, or anything else. I know the last time we talked about it; our conversation ended kind of abruptly. I was hoping we could share info; I'll tell you mine if you tell me yours," she purrs, cocking her head to the side, leaning into him.

"Actually, there is something I've been meaning to tell you," he says, pushing away from her to sit down in his leather chair. In the middle drawer of his desk, he pulls out a file folder and slaps it down in the middle of them.

Rue hops down and leans over the desk towards Diego. "And this is?" she questions.

"All I know about the Organization."

"It's a little light," she mocks, opening the file.

"Yeah, that's the problem. They are good. Too good. None of my contacts know anything about them." He pauses like he is about to reconsider his next words. "Here's the thing, Rue, I've been working on this for weeks now. I have a small team working solely on this, yet we have nothing. This group is causing a decline in clients at our locations in the Low District and it's becoming more than a nuisance. Someone was taken right in front of one of our clubs, and let's just say it's been bad for business. People are afraid, thinking they are going to be taken or some shit. I'm losing serious coin over this fucking mess."

Rue stands up straight. "Wait, stop there. A team? Without me? What the fuck?" Something sharp scrapes the sides of her stomach, she swallows down her hurt. He looks at her with a death glare, letting her know she is about to cross a line. She doesn't care and spits, "When was I gonna be filled in?"

Through gritted teeth he says, "When the time was right. I didn't want to put you in danger."

Rue snorts, slamming her hands back on the desk, "Oh really? You know when a great time would have been, when I asked you about it. Remember? Right in between you fucking me and reminded me I was yours. Oh, that's right, you were too busy trying to leave my shitty apartment."

She lets out an exaggerated sigh, she couldn't believe this. If she had known Diego had people looking into this, she wouldn't have been so careless about traveling to see Olympia. She would have known to travel at night. She would have never been in West Harbor, let alone in Moon Child.

There was one thing she learned in the last twelve years of being a Smoke Runner, it was whoever you're looking into, most likely is looking into you. Information travels fast in this city. Contacts you thought you could trust, end up being a traitor for a few more coins given to them by your enemy.

Diego stands up, mimicking Rue's position against the desk. Their faces are inches apart. "Don't push me. I'm your boss, not the other way around. You do what I fucking tell you, when I tell you to do it. And when I tell you I kept you from something to protect you, I damn well mean it," he threatens. His eyes look almost black with anger.

She scowls at him, and challenges, "So are you going to tell me what you know now, or are we going to sit here and bicker? Because I have a lot more shit I could be doing with my time. I came here to work with you, not be scolded over something *you* failed to mention until now. I'm involved whether you want me to be or not."

Her eyes plead with him to let her in. "They have my name Diego, my real name. It was on a piece of paper he had in his pocket. What I can't understand is why? Why attack me and try to kill me, when most people are being kidnapped. Why send only one man after me, when the others are being taken by a group. The MO doesn't add up."

She stops talking for a second to clear her head of the dark poison in Blue Eyes' veins after he died. "I think this may be a lot bigger than you think. The guy who came after me, stalked me through all of West Harbor. He said..." she moves her hands into fists to stop them from shaking and swallows. "He said..." Rue shakes her head, replaying his words over and over again in her mind.

"What happened out there, Rue? You've seen death before, it's nothing new. Why are you being so dramatic over this one man?"

She looks at him with wide eyes and continues, "This wasn't just a death, this was a promise that it would never end. The man poisoned himself in front of me instead of admitting who he was working for. He chose a violent death, instead of surrender. His only words to me were, the Organization will always prevail. All the lands will be clean soon."

Diego licks and bites his lip while he thinks. "You're sure he said *all* the lands?"

She nods and admits, "I don't know if I'll ever forget those words. You should have seen him. It was like he was possessed. I think this might be bigger than just the Southlands."

He leans back to sit in his chair, moves a hand over his mouth while he studies her. "I don't like that they know who you are."

"I don't either, but there's nothing we can do at this point. Let me in. Let me help you. Let me be an asset. Getting information is what I'm good at," she begs.

He thinks for what feels like hours before demanding, "I'll let you in, but promise me you'll stay with me. If they know who you are, they probably know where you live. Those fuckers won't make it two feet into my building. You'll be safe there with me." He swallows before admitting, "I can't lose you."

Her heart sinks and she rolls her eyes. She hates that idea. Not only does she love her tiny little apartment, her freedom, and the people she lives around, the idea of living in the High District makes her want to puke.

"You know how I feel about this damn hill," she mentions, looking at him with empty eyes. "Don't make me do that?" Her voice is only a whisper in the wind. As much as it will kill her inside, she knows he won't budge. Diego has been trying to get her to move in with him ever since he took over after his father's passing, and she walked herself into this one.

He stands up and walks towards her, pushing a loose lock of hair behind her ear. "It's my only condition. Agree and I'll tell you everything I know. This can be your only project if you want it to be. But you have to say yes. It's the only way I can promise you're safe." Leaning down, he brushes his lips against hers before kissing her like it's the only way he can get oxygen. They pull apart and he leans his forehead on hers. She warms with the touch of his thumbs on her cheeks soothing her bruised skin.

"Let me take care of you, Rue." The soft desperation in his voice makes her quiver under him.

"Two seconds ago, you were yelling at me, saying I'm the boss, not the other way around," she says in a mocking voice, snickering up into his eyes.

He smiles and laughs through his nose. In the same mocking tone, he says, "So, do what I tell you, when I tell you to do it, smartass."

She loves his smile; it doesn't come out often anymore. Her heart races a little knowing she is the reason for it. She loves happy Diego. His smile reminds her of when they were teens, sneaking into shops in the High District, pocketing money or goods, then going to hand it out to Lowers. Balancing the scale of rich and poor, one coin at a time.

Rue tugs lazily at the chain he wears around his neck, reminiscing about getting it for him after their first job together. He hasn't taken it off since. They had perfected their con, Rue would be the distraction, and Diego would lift what he wanted. Most of the time she would charm the shop owner into telling her about an item, batting her lashes and leaning her chest over the counter.

Meanwhile, Diego would sneak into the back and pocket whatever he could. When he was done, he'd come rescue her using their code words. She would ask, "Did you find what you were looking for?" and he would answer "No, unfortunately."

The two of them felt invincible, like they could do anything and never get caught. They planned on traveling the world, pickpocketing their way through. Stealing from the corrupt and giving to those who had nothing. They were going to run away. Run away and be happy.

Rue sometimes believed Diego was her twin light. A bond as strong as a twin light cannot easily be broken. It is thought to be a force so permanent it's been written into the history of someone's soul from the beginning of time. A feeling of knowing in your bones you've loved this person in every lifetime.

She imagined the moment the lights would flicker on, the two of them connecting forever.

She only knows folktales about twin lights, how the two souls will search for their match above all other things. Changing one's fate to find the other half of their golden burst of light. A light so strong it can't even be extinguished in death.

She wondered if she would someday have that with Diego, their meeting all those years ago did feel like a weird twist of fate. Maybe, maybe not.

Her parents shared that bond, she knew it was possible to find each other. Humans so rarely experienced it, most people assumed they were immune to the power. But she always had faith. If her human father could find his light, why couldn't she?

She had always pictured her future with him. That is until Diego's dad was murdered four years ago, and the business was given to him to run. It changed him, made him cold. Distant. And as much as she wanted to believe he would stay the same, she would never have that carefree version of him again.

Happy and energetic Diego, with his brave spirit. Her heart, hidden under layers of iron, ached for that back. She wanted so badly to make him happy, to bring back the man she once knew. Maybe moving in with him wouldn't be so bad. Maybe it would give her time with that version of him again.

Rue looks up at him, putting her arms around his neck. He wraps his around her waist and starts swaying back and forth like they are slow dancing. With a weak smirk, she says,

"Maybe… living somewhere with actual hot water and a fridge that works wouldn't be so bad."

"And my mattress isn't on the floor."

She huffs a laugh, "Leave my mattress out of this."

"So, what'll it be? Me and you? We doing this?"

This is a bad idea.

She looks into his eyes, the golds of her irises sparkling with hope. With a deep breath in, she makes a deal with the devil, signing away her independence. "We can try, but just until this whole thing blows over, okay?"

His smile beams across his face when he says, "Okay."

"And let me help you with this. Let me be involved."

A second of hesitation crosses his eyes. "You got it, Beautiful." Diego kisses her deep and slow, letting them melt into each other. His hands move up her body, weaving through her hair. She wants so badly to lose herself in him, let him take her here and now, but she needs answers first. She can't waste time.

She pulls away long enough to purr, "Hey, boss?"

"Hmm," is all he can say, trying to continue their kiss.

"You might want to stop kissing your employee in the office. I think it might be some sort of HR violation." Her grin shows all her teeth, and she brushes her lips against his.

"Let's see someone try and tell me what I can and cannot do in my office." His low and husky voice against her skin shoots straight between her thighs.

"We have work to do. Plus, you know I'm yours when we get *home.*"

His eyes open to look at her, the words catching him off guard. "Oh, it's *our* home now."

"Listen, I'm testing it out. You want me to move in with you or not? Because I have no problems fighting people off in my shoe box apartment in the Falls."

"Gods, you're something else, Ghost."

"Oh, now I'm just Ghost."

He chuckles and leans towards her again, "This is the office after all."

"Fair enough." She studies every part of his face, his tanned complexion, his dark eyes, that facial hair she loves so much, the dimple that peeks out when he's smiling big enough. She never wants to forget this face. This Diego makes her feel safe.

Rue lets out a long exhale before insisting, "Now can we please share our info and figure out next steps?"

"Of course," he says, kissing her forehead. Diego moves away from Rue, leaving her feeling cold and exposed again. "Why don't you start by telling me what the hell happened today."

Rue moves to a leather chair across from the desk. She sits down with her legs crossed and starts to explain the chain of events from the day. She goes over the fight first, getting it out of the way and allowing him to calm down knowing she handled it like he would have. She talks briefly about talking to her contact in West Harbor, leaving out details about who it is, and how she got some information about where the Organization meets. She pauses to look at her hands, playing with her nails.

"Where do they meet, Rue?" he asks when she goes quiet.

"The Lucky Clover," she admits, looking at him with worried eyes. Diego detests the family that runs The Lucky Clover Casino. The Finnegan's have been this family's rival for longer than she's been alive.

A few decades ago, one of the Finnegan son's and his crew blew up a restaurant owned by the Metus family, with Diego's grandparents inside. The men involved were sent to prison, where some were killed, others still rot there to this day. The two families have been trying to eliminate the other ever since.

"Fucking figures, Finnegan would be the one to take innocent lives." While all the crime families in the city actively try to take out one another, there is an understanding that innocent lives are left out of dealings. If the community can't trust the families, their power is lost.

"Now, I don't know if they are the ones involved, but the group is at least meeting at their casino. So, I feel like that would be a good place to start. See if we can sneak into a meeting, or at least see who's there."

Diego's mind runs rapidly with possibilities, she can see it in his eyes. He moves his hands together and twists his M ring between his fingers. On his exhale he asks, "What else you got?"

"Not really anything, rumors about how they attack in groups like a pack. Taking young people. Happens at night. The basics everyone knows."

"It's about the same I have. The crew has been profiling all the people confirmed to have been taken, and their families. Here is a list so far." He hands her the folder with the list of those kidnapped. It's long, about forty or fifty names. "I agree, we need to get into Clover without being detected. Is that something you feel confident doing alone? They'd never let me set foot in there."

"Yes, absolutely. It's what I'm best at. What other Runners are involved? Maybe I could go with one of them as backup."

"No!" he bites back at her. "Sorry no, we can't have anyone else knowing you're involved. They already know who you are, I don't need the rest of my crew outed as well. Besides, two or more of you running around would look too suspicious. You're going to have to do this on your own, okay?"

Rue looks up but doesn't reach his eyes.

Alone. Always alone.

"Yeah, I can handle that."

He nods his head, "I would give it a few days before you stake it out. They are going to be wondering what happened to the guy you killed and come looking for you. Just stay at my place until it calms down. Don't tell anyone what you're doing. And make sure you come straight to me if you find anything. I'm here for you if you need me. Anything at all."

"Sounds good," she answers. "I have a few more contacts in the city I'd like to talk to before I go to Clover anyway."

A few moments go by in silence. She whispers, "I guess I need to go pack my stuff, huh." She looks at him under her lashes and smiles. Her heart turns to butterflies with the thought of staying with him and waking up warm against his chest.

"You wanna grab dinner or something after you settle in, that Westlands place you love?"

Her smile widens and she says softly, "How about I make you dinner as a thank you?"

"I think I'm going to like this arrangement," he jokes, running a thumb across his bottom lip.

"Yeah, well don't get used to it. I know one recipe and it's only mediocre."

"Nothing you do is mediocre, Beautiful." His eyes burn through her with need. She winks, then stands to walk away, swaying her hips for his enjoyment.

When she opens the door and is about to walk out, he orders her to stop, "Ghost!" His dry and authoritative tone is back.

Rue turns to look at him, all the warmth gone in her face, back to the characters they play around the others. "Yes, Boss?"

"You're off this project the moment you do anything stupid."

A second of a smile washes over her face that only he can see before she replies, "That would be unfortunate."

CHAPTER

RAIN is washing away the smell of trash as Rue walks down the street. Her mind calms with the sound of pitter-patter of water against the cobblestone. The sky is full of gray, angry clouds, but it makes her feel at peace. The city is so quiet when it rains. It is Rue's favorite. She has space to breathe.

After living in the High District with Diego the past three weeks, Rue is glad to be back with the Lowers.

The move went about as well as her gut thought it would. Diego's loft was nice, but it felt cold. The furniture was dark, and sharp. She didn't feel like she could relax there. On top of the decor, he had 24/7 surveillance in the form of bodyguards at the door, not allowing her to leave, or anyone other than Diego to enter. She tried having conversations with them, hoping to befriend one and talk them into letting her leave, but other than a smile from one, they were immovable statues.

Diego promised her it was for her own protection after her attack, but she felt like a prisoner, like she was suffocating in the loneliness. Her hopes of using this time to spend with him were quickly squashed into the dark wood floorboards with the rest of her sanity.

The first night was pure magic. He had a bubble bath waiting for Rue when she arrived, and after she soaked, he surprised her with a candlelit dinner of salmon and scallops. He took her to bed, and they made love for what felt like hours, falling asleep together wrapped in his sheets.

The next morning, she woke up to a note saying he'd be back late, and to take this time to relax. The note came with books to read and a list of places she could order food from.

Nights two through seven were the same, romantic evenings followed by morning love notes and things to keep her occupied.

On day eight, she started working on deciphering the language on the knife from Blue Eyes, using books Diego had on ancient civilizations, but came up with nothing solid as to where it came from. At the same time Diego was becoming paranoid, doing hourly sweeps of the apartment, questioning neighbors, claiming he found people snooping around at her old apartment building.

Days nine to fifteen she did her best to stay busy and not think about the world outside the walls of his apartment. When she did see Diego, she would try to talk about the job and her ideas, but he would change the subject or simply start kissing her to stop her from talking. She spent her time alone looking into what components could be used to make the poison, and when she didn't have those answers, her mind started to shift.

At this point the bodyguards outside the door were no longer allowed to talk with her. Her positive outlook on her situation came crashing down, the realization she was thrown away and left to go mad in an expensively decorated cell.

The past week has been spent alone. Diego wouldn't come home until well into the night after she had passed out waiting for him. He would sneak out before she woke up, or some nights he wouldn't come home at all. The notes stopped. The love stopped. She felt her mind starting to slip away.

So, this morning she snuck out. She told herself it was to get back to work, and she used that as a reason to leave. He couldn't argue with that, they agreed this was her only project, and she wasn't going to finish the mission sitting in a loft. Diego may have been trying to keep her safe, but that didn't mean she would spend the rest of her life inside a high rise. After the guards did their hourly sweep of the space, she slipped out the bathroom skylight and climbed down the fire escape.

As soon as she scaled the wall back into the Low District, she felt a rush of oxygen go into her lungs. Like somehow, the smog and smell of death was cleaner than the purified air of the High District.

A puddle splashes under her boots as she walks across the street to a vendor selling coffee and baked goods. "Can I get a coffee and bagel," she asked the man behind the counter.

"Sure thing, miss, that'll be two copper," he says in a gruff voice.

She keeps her head low under the shadow of her hood when handing him the coins. Her wounds from the alley fight had healed completely at this point, but she isn't going to risk showing her face to anyone she didn't already know. In the past few weeks of her being locked away, over thirty more Lowers have gone missing. On top of that, a dozen more fae folk had been found and killed in the streets all in the same fashion, knife wounds and ear points cut off.

This is not a time to be careless. Every move she makes needs to be calculated and planned out in her mind to keep herself safe, and well as her informants.

She takes a few side streets then turns to follow an old familiar dirt path. It leads to one of the largest homeless communities in all of the Low District, located under one of the bridges to the High Wall.

Rue spent a few years living here when she was a teen, in between staying with Olympia and becoming a Smoke Runner. She has always been pulled to protect them, when the system has failed them so miserably. She remembers the feeling of living outside in the elements, scraping by with nothing while the High District looms over you. But the people here have always pulled through. They care about one another, and look out for their friends, keeping each other safe is a top priority. And to Rue's benefit, they also have some of the best intel she has ever received.

Walking through the tents, she keeps her head low. Although she lived here, she is now an outsider prowling around.

A few feet ahead she can see a young child, probably about four or five, sitting against a cement pillar. Her hands are shaking and all she has on is a thin, tattered blanket. In her arms is a shabby, old stuff bunny. Heat floods Rue's heart when she looks into her eyes. Scared and about to cry.

Alone.

Without thinking, Rue pulls a few loose coins out of her bag and kneels down to give them to the little girl.

"Where's your mama, sweetie?" she asked in a soft voice, a pitch higher than normal. A tight grin crosses her lips.

The little girl looks up through her lashes as she speaks. "My mama's not here anymore, but my daddy will be right back. He went down there to get some food from Miss Kennedy."

"Oh, I know her. She is the sweetest."

"Yeah, she's really nice, she always gives me cookies."

"That's the best!" Rue's smile grows. "I like your bunny. You know I used to have a stuffy too. He helped me when I was scared, he was a little red fox named Phoenix."

The little girl starts to giggle as her walls come down, causing her shaking body to relax under the blanket. "Phoenix? Like the fire people?"

Rue smiles at her word choice for Phoenix Shifters, fae with strong enough fire power to grow wings made of flames.

"Exactly like the fire people. My Grandma Oly told me stories about them when I was itty bitty like you. I named him Phoenix so he could keep me warm at night. And you want to know a secret?"

The young girl's head nods rapidly. Her eyes fix on Rue like she might tell her the secrets to the universe.

"He had powers, and he did keep me warm. All I had to do was tell him I believed in him, and he would warm me up all night long." The magic in the child's eyes repairs a crack in Rue's iron heart. "You know, I used to live here too, and when I was too cold from the wind or the rain, I would hug Phoenix, and he would keep me safe. I bet your bunny would do the same for you if you told him you believed in him."

Her innocent face fills with wonder. She looks at her bunny and breathes into its ear, "I believe in you."

"Now give him a big hug and he'll start working."

She squeezes the little rabbit tight, and then her eyes dart to Rue, "It's working."

"See! I told you. You must have some strong magic in your heart." Rue holds out her hand with the coins. "I have something for you, okay? Do you think you could hold on to this and give it to your daddy when he gets back?" She slowly hands the little girl the coins, helping her close them in a fist. The girl nods, smiling at Rue.

"Perfect! Thank you, I knew I could trust you. Make sure to keep your bunny close and take care of your Daddy, okay? They both need someone strong and brave like you."

Rue pats the bunny on its head before standing up. She gives the little girl a wink and waves her goodbye, as her lungs fill with silent rage. No child should have to be living under a bridge while those with money stand over the edge looking down at her, like she's some sort of caged animal.

Towards the end of the row of tents, near a large pile of scrap, sits a tent made from wooden pallets and a blue tarp. Rue walks up to the entrance cautiously, her boots squishing in the mud. She clears her throat loud enough for the person inside to hear her, then laughs at herself. Of course he can hear her, he's an elf.

"I brought you breakfast," she calls into the dark tent. "And a coffee."

From the inside she can hear a scratchy voice say, "That ain't no real coffee, that's a pathetic attempt created out of a lab."

"Well, if you don't want it, I'll happily drink it," she threatens.

Without another word the tarp door flings open, a short, hunched over man emerges. His skin is tanned from the sun, his wrinkles are defined, and his face looks as though it's withering away from the elements. His salt and pepper beard is unkempt, matching the hair on top of his head. His ocean blue eyes peer up at her, with dark circles around them from lack of decent sleep.

"No, I'll take it!" he quickly replies, snatching the cup out of her hands. She laughs, handing him the bagel bag as well.

"What, you want me to thank you or somethin'?" he jokes.

"That'd be nice." Rue stands with her hands on her hips smirking at him.

He takes a sip from the cup and looks up at her, the lines around his eyes wrinkle. "Ahh, that's delicious."

"No, it's not," she grins.

"No. It's terrible actually." He lets out a hoarse laugh which turns into a cough. The two stand there for a moment before he says, "Hi, Red."

"Hi, Issak."

Rue has known Issak since she was a teenager, living in this very community. He actually saved her life once, when she was fourteen. Rue had been trying to teach herself magic, working in an alley on the outskirts of town.

She was working through a maneuver to move some boxes from one side to the other, pulling all her strength into her move. She was so focused on her hand movements and connecting with the cardboard, she didn't notice who was walking up behind her.

Some older kids saw her channeling her magic and decided to take it upon themselves to take care of her. Magic, to the humans understanding, is dangerous, and therefore has been illegal in the Southlands since its conception. Humans are expected to report magical use to the Marshals and let them handle the punishments. These kids had other plans. They were much bigger and stronger than her, so she had little chance in escaping their grasps.

She was on the ground, being kicked and beaten to death, when the next thing she knew Issak was there, picking her up into his arms and scaring the boys away with his enraged appearance.

He sat her up against the bricks and hovered his hands over her body. Her vision was blurred from the trauma to her head, but she remembers the warmth filling her lungs. It was like being kissed by the sun. Suddenly she could breathe again, and her head didn't throb, and she could see.

Issak was a healer and had electric magic. However, his electricity powers were minimal, the most he could do was produce a spark. Not all fae folk could harness their magic at the same intensities. The closer one was to the original god or goddess in lineage, the stronger their powers could be.

At a young age Issak knew he still wanted to be helpful despite his lack of natural powers, so he taught himself how to be a healer, a type of bright magic that could be learned by any fae folk. He traveled the realm, helping who he could.

When he had seen all walks of life on the mainland, he moved to the Southlands for a new start, hoping he could help those in the poor communities. He was right, Issak is the homeless community's healer now. They keep his identity safe, and he heals who he can.

"So, what ya comin' around here for?" he asks, taking a bite of the bagel.

"I need some questions answered about people going missing. There is a group called the Organization. Any whispers?"

He looks towards the other tents, lets out a sigh and answers, "It's tragic, people being ripped from their families like that. How you roped into this, Red?" He looks at her with narrowed eyes.

"It's affecting my boss's business, and I'm trying to see who's involved. Trying to keep it on the low, we don't want to tip off anyone that we're looking into it." She does her best to seem unfazed by the issue at hand. Keeping her voice even and casual, her mind plays the image of Blue Eyes slumped over, dead in the alley.

Issak doesn't say a word, instead he looks around, then nods his head in the direction of a path leading past the scrap pile. He motions for her to follow as he starts to hobble through the mud. The rain has lightened up, but still comes down around them. Her flannel becomes heavy from the water drops, causing goosebumps to form on her arms and legs as the cold mist of the day begs her to turn back, to leave this alone.

She focuses her mind on the here and now. Listening to the silence of the rain and sounds of puddles under her shoes. Her curiosity outlasts her survival instincts.

"I need to show you something," he says nervously. His eyes are on edge, and he keeps looking over his shoulder, which sends alarm bells to her ears.

"Issak what is it?" Rue has never seen him like this before, so frantic and unsure.

"You'll see."

He brings her to an underpass of another section of the bridge. They walk down the darkened tunnel, passing trash and debris. Water drops fall from above due to cracks in the concrete. In front of a section of graffiti on the wall his legs stop, staring down at some words. "Take a look, this tag is poppin' up all over the city."

Rue turns her focus from Issak's concerned expression to read what he is pointing at. The hairs on her neck stand up, and a prick of pain brushes her skin at the nape of her neck. She moves a hand to cover her lips, and squats down to get eye level with the words she's been hearing in her dreams for weeks.

There, in spray paint the color of blood, reads **THE ORGANIZATION WILL ALWAYS PREVAIL- ALL THE LANDS WILL BE CLEAN SOON.** Circling the graffiti are missing person fliers with red X marks over the victims faces.

Minutes go by before Rue moves. Her mind fills with visions of the body in the alley. His angry blue eyes, and the pure hatred that filled them. His smile when he knew he was about to die for his cause. His only words to her. A challenge. A dare to make a move against the Organization.

"Who else has seen this?" she asks, forming her hands into fists against her knees so they don't shake.

"Sadly, anyone who walks by really. People are scared, Red. They don't feel safe."

"They should be scared," she admits under her breath. "A few weeks ago, I was attacked in an alley by a man. His only words to me were those written on that wall."

Issak looks to her for confirmation. His expression changes from fear, to confusion, back to fear as he thinks in his head. He rubs a hand over his matted beard and says, "I don't know much, Red. But what I can tell you is that this isn't going to be simple. I've seen them, listened to them speak to each other."

She cuts him off there and gasps. "Wait, you've seen them?"

"I have. These guys know what they are doing. They have lists. Plans in place for who their next targets are. I heard them mention labor barracks on the mainland. They kept mentioning someone higher up but would only address them as *Him*. I didn't catch a name."

"How did they not see you?"

"You'd be surprised how much people are willing to admit, when they think you're passed out drunk on the street." He tries to laugh but it falls flat. "Anyways, I got a hunch about the fae dyin' too. I'm convinced it's all connected. I don't have any proof or a concrete idea, but my gut is telling me it's all the same."

"What makes you think that?" Rue crosses her arms and moves in closer to Issak.

"Every time a human gets taken, fae are being hunted in the same neighborhood. It's like clockwork if you know what to look for."

He takes a second to pull a flier off the wall. "These are our people, Red." He points at the woman's face plastered on the paper. "They are taking out people, like they're animals. Collecting them for slaughter. I've lived in this city for half a century, and this has never been a problem. Something in the air doesn't smell right, and I'm afraid of what's to come."

"I know. Me too." Rue's eyes trace the tag. Reading over the words again and again. "Did you get a chance to see any of their features? Could you tell if they were male or female voices?"

"They sounded like a strange mix of both. I didn't see anything unfortunately, but…" His voice trails off and he shifts his weight around, avoiding her eyes.

"Spit it out. Tell me what you're thinking," she demands.

"There's someone who might know more about them," he says as if she's supposed to know who he's referring to.

"Who?"

"He goes by Guy. No one knows his real name. He was found a few days ago. Mumblin' to himself about his daughter being taken by masked men."

"Take me to see him. I need to talk to him."

"You can't, you… He…"

"I need to speak with him. He's my only lead." He hesitates and stares back towards the camp. Rue continues, "I need to know what I'm up against. At this point I don't give a fuck what my boss wants, I need to figure this out for me, Issak. They had *my* name. They wanted *me*. I need to know why."

Reluctantly he nods. "Okay, Red. But I have to warn you, he isn't all there mentally. His daughter being gone broke him in a way none of us can repair."

"I understand, if I don't get anything, it's okay. But I need to try."

Issak starts to walk back towards the camp, motioning for Rue to follow him. They pass his tent and then a few others before he leads her down another path away from the bulk of the group. Sheltered from the rain, under an old car port, sits a red tent.

They approach slowly. Issak puts his hand out towards Rue, signaling her to stop and wait. He looks back, gives her a tight nod, and enters. She can't make out what is being said over the wind and rain, but she can hear Issak try and talk to Guy. Muffled voices grow silent.

Rue starts to think this might be a dead end. What is this man going to tell her, a random woman he's never seen before asking about his daughter? If anything, it might cause him more pain, asking questions about something so traumatic. But she has so many questions. She has this itch she can't scratch to know everything there is to know about these demons.

She's lost in her own head, staring out into an industrial field of muddy dirt and old metal parts, when Issak emerges from the tent. He jerks his head for her to come in. Rue exhales slowly, attempting to calm her heart.

Inside Issak leads her to a man at the end of his rope. Guy, big and burly with a wiry blonde beard, rests on a tiny stool with his hands over his face. He has on pajama pants with a windbreaker and no shoes, like he left in the middle of the night in a hurry. His skin and clothes are covered in dirt, and there is an odd mix of smells in the air. Rosemary and sweat.

Rue approaches them cautiously so as to not intimidate Guy. She kneels in front of him and places her hands on her thighs. Guy doesn't move his hands off his face, trying to hide the streaks of water trickling down through the dirt that has started to take over.

Another crack forms on her heart, thinking about making him relive this horrendous situation.

After a moment of only the rain filling the sounds of the tent, she speaks in a soft tone. "Hi Guy, my name is Rue. Whenever you're ready, I'd like to talk about what happened to your daughter. See if I can help."

She can hear his heart slow. His hands lower from his face, revealing bloodshot eyes and silent tears. As their eyes meet, Rue smiles gently. He does not return the gesture; he simply stares into her. His gaze is haunting. Like there is no longer a person behind his eyes. He is just a shell.

She tries to continue the conversation, even if it's only one sided. "You look hungry. Is there anything we can get you to eat?" He doesn't respond, only looks towards the ground. "Issak, do you think you could go find him something to eat? Maybe something warm to drink as well?" Issak nods before heading out into the rain.

Rue listens for his footsteps to disappear before speaking again. She pulls a hand to her chest and tells him, "I am so sorry this has happened to you and your daughter. I was also attacked recently by them, and I'm now looking into the Organization and who is behind it. Any information you could share with me would be greatly appreciated, but I understand if it's too hard to speak about. I know what it's like to have loved ones taken from you."

He looks back up at her and whispers, "Who was taken from you?"

A simple question really. Something she should easily be able to answer after all this time. Yet, Rue can't make herself say it. Her eyes flicker towards the ground before taking a deep breath in, pulling all her courage up to the surface.

"My parents, right after my fourth name day. I know what can happen to your spirit when you blame yourself. Run through scenarios in your mind about how it could be different. What you could have done to change the outcome. I know how dark it gets."

Silent moments go by before he asks, "How do you get over it?"

Rue looks at her hands, not wanting to admit the truth. "You'll be the first to know when I figure it out." He nods his head. "But what we can do now, is try and find out what is happening, and try to save others from being taken from their loved ones. I will do everything in my power to find your daughter, but I don't have a lot of information right now. As far as I know, you and I are the only ones who've survived attacks. I need you to tell me what you can remember from that night."

Guy rubs a hand over his beard. He opens his mouth like he is about to speak but gets interrupted by Issak returning with a plate of food and a cup of coffee. "I hope you like jam and crackers, that's all I could scrounge up. I did manage to get some coffee though. Here ya go," he says handing the plate to Guy. He thanks him with a nod before taking a sip.

Rue can see his shoulder relax to his sides. She takes that as an opportunity to ask, "Why don't you start by telling me your daughter's name?"

His eyes fill with tears and whispers, "Annie. My sweet Annie Bananie. You're probably not much older than her. She is so full of life, kind, everyone that knows her loves her." His voice breaks, causing a tear to fall from his face and land on his plate.

"Guy, I need to know what happened to the two of you."

He closes his eyes and shakes his head in protest, begging her to end this conversation. "I can't."

She reaches out her hand, gently grabbing his, and squeezes. "I know it seems impossible right now, but do this for her. She still needs you."

Waterfalls pour out of his eyes. His body starts to shake with every sob, and he folds over crying into Rue's hand. She doesn't let go.

"I wish they had taken me. Not her. She has so much life left to live." He lifts his head to meet hers, sniffling in between words. "She is starting this group to teach teens in our neighborhood how to use metal and make things to sell. That's what we do, we're metalworkers. We scrap things from the dump, rework them, and sell them around town. One night..." He trails off, wiping tears from his cheeks. "One night, we were coming back from picking, and this cenzium van pulls up next to us on the street. Before I had time to think, five or six people came jumping out, grabbing her. They took her. Took her right out of my hands. I couldn't protect her."

Rue buds in with another question. "Do you know for sure how many there were? Were they all men, or did you hear feminine voices as well?"

Guy is trembling, he closes his eyes and with every ounce of composure he has left says, "I don't remember for sure, but more than I could fight off. Their voices were all muffled, or maybe it was only one person talking, they all sounded the same. It was mostly grunts when they were trying to grab her. They ripped her from me. They pulled her away and she was gone.

They beat me with the metal we collected and left me for dead. Driving off with her screaming for me. Her voice haunts me every night."

Rue's heart is in the ground, as soft as she can she asks, "Did you get a good look at any of their faces?"

"No," he mumbles, shaking his head. "They all had on black sweatshirts and these white masks. I couldn't see anything."

Rue sits back, letting everything he just said sink in. This attack was so different from her own. This isn't making sense.

Rue ponders her intel before asking her last question. "Did any of the attackers have knives?"

Guy looks confused. "No."

Rue gazes around the tent, rubbing her thumb nail over her bottom lip while she thinks. "Thank you for sharing all of this with me. I'm going to do everything in my power to help find Annie." Guy's head lowers, he nods as a thank you.

She points to Issak, "If you think of anything else, let Issak know. He knows how to get in contact with me. Even if you think it's a small detail, please share. It could be more important than you realize."

Without another word, Rue stands up, brushes off her jeans, and leaves the tent. Issak follows, looking at her like she just became a shapeshifter. As they start walking back through the rain he presses, "How the hell did you get him to talk to you?"

Rue turns to him, brows furrowed, "What do you mean?"

"We haven't been able to get him to say one word to any of us. And here you come makin' him sing like a songbird."

"I just explained that I knew how he felt. To lose someone and feel like it's your fault. Keep an eye on him Issak, I've seen those eyes before. The look of being lost, not believing there is hope. He needs to be reminded to hold on. If he starts to slip, just tell him to try one more time. One more day."

Issak's tattered tent flaps are blowing in the wind when they reach it. The chill of the spring storm has everything covered in a cold, damp layer of misery. Flashbacks to when she lived in this community flood her memory. Being exposed to the elements, people fighting over spots with the most sun, or the most cover, or arguing about who gets the old mattress dumped in the landfill. The panic of the unknown. These people don't deserve this, no one does.

"I have something else for you," Rue adds as she pulls a sack out of her bag. She glances at Issak with a small grin, tugging his hand to place the pouch in it. "For a new tent."

Issak glares with confusion, his eyes double in size when he opens to find coins.

"You are going to take this," she demands. "It's fifty copper. You need a new tent, Issak, no more of this shredded tarp. Hell, go get an actual place to stay for a few nights. But this," she pulls at the strings of frayed plastic, "This isn't safe."

"I don't need it. I need to stay hidden in the trash. You can't listen in if you're not in the shadows, I've always told you that. But my friends will surely love the donations to their tents." He grins wide, pats her on the shoulder, and hides the bag under his mattress.

"You're too good for this world, Red. I know you do a damn good job at hiding the fact that you care, but let someone else worry for a change. Stay safe out there. No more men in alleys, I don't want to have to save you again."

Rue lets out a laugh, ignoring the compliment. "You too. Thanks for today. And hey, you get any intel just leave the mark like normal. I'm not staying at my place right now, but I'll check it every few days."

"Red rock on the kitchen window, you got it."

Rue's eyes peer into his. "Issak, I'm serious about being safe. You need to warn everyone about how serious this is. Make sure everyone stays in at night, and I would set up some sort of watch. We still don't know how they are choosing their marks. Until we do, watch out for our people." She motions her hands around the camp. "You may have magic, but they don't."

"What did I just say about worrying about others? Careful there, someone might notice you aren't made of stone." When she doesn't say anything, he adds, "I know. I know, Red. I'll do my best."

Rue leaves his tent, stepping around mud and sighing as she adds more questions to her list of unknowns.

CHAPTER

THE sun is setting behind the few clouds left from the storm. Rue sits on top of the bathroom skylight, trying to open the latch as quietly as she can. The glass lifts with a click, and she tosses her bag down onto the bathroom tile, landing silently on a pile of towels she set out earlier. Her arms are on fire as she hangs from the ledge of the window, trying to land as light and noiseless as she can. Her boots hang from her neck, tied together by the laces. Her socks land on a rug, and she takes the impact in her knees.

Without moving, she slows her own breathing and listens beyond the bathroom door, trying to hear heartbeats or voices from outside Diego's bedroom. Just one echoes in her ears, calm and slow.

Diego should be home in a few hours, so she does her best to move about like she's been here all day. Grabbing one of his white t-shirts from a drawer, she puts it on and lets it hang to her thighs. She tosses her damp clothes into a pile in the bathroom, layering the used towels on top. Before leaving she twists her damp hair into a bun, and shuffles things around the room, making it seem as though she's been reading and working out all day.

At the door, she inhales deep and cracks her neck, forcing her facial expression to be blank and bored before turning the knob.

The moment she opens the door, she is taken back at the sight. The entire main living space is in disarray, like someone came through and sacked the place looking for something. Or someone. There is broken glass from a bottle smashed against the wall. The furniture is all turned over and thrown around the room. Papers, and mail are spread out on the floor. Anger. Anger happened here.

Her panic subsides when she gets a rush of sandalwood through her nose. The hairs on her neck stand, but not from fear, from the realization that this is self-inflicted destruction. Rue scoffs, lifts her head high and walks into the kitchen. If he wants to destroy all of his own possessions, that is not her problem.

Strutting past him like he isn't in the room, Rue starts to open cabinets pretending to be looking for something. She does her best to hide the grin on her lips, biting down on the inside of her cheek, knowing her escape today proves to him he cannot force her to stay here.

Diego sits on the center island, fingers interlaced in front of him. He tilts his head and glares at her down the bridge of his nose. A move he often uses as a nonverbal way of saying he is pissed at her. His eyes have the power to make shit happen, forcing deathly stares at people until they give in. But not her.

It no longer scares her. His tricks are not worth the time trying to decipher what she did wrong. Refusing to turn towards him she hums while she moves around the kitchen, if he wants her to acknowledge him, he's going to have to work for it.

He is treating her like one of the kidnapped victims in this godsforsaken apartment, and it's him who put her here. He is the one who needs to apologize, the one who needs to explain himself. She has been trying to do nothing but listen, and sit, and wait for an imaginary partnership to handle the devastation happening outside these walls.

Rue has done nothing wrong by leaving, she would have used the door if she was *allowed*.

She is not a prisoner. She will never be a prisoner.

Her leaving is the only chance she has at getting more information for *his* mission. Which they agreed to work on together. So, she will let him stew in her silence, not cave into his game of chess. He will not win this time. No breaking.

Today will not be the day that she allows a pathetically over protective man to intimidate her into submission.

Rue walks over to an upper cabinet, grabs a stemless glass and an open bottle of wine. She pulls the cork out with her teeth and shoots it out of her mouth onto the counter. While pouring her drink, she hums a random melody loudly enough for him to hear, acting as though it's any other day in her pretty cage.

She can feel him studying her from behind, and her mind is melting from the pressure of it. It feels like two knives scraping down her back. Her fingers turn to ice while the blood inside her body starts to boil over, but she will not allow him to see her weakness. She will not give him a show of rage this time. She can't. She must stay strong.

I can't.

She is ice and fire at the same time. Rue hates that somehow, he always manages to give her this reaction. He just sits and watches his prey wreck herself in front of him. Like her body is incapable of choosing a side. Fight or flight. Safe or dangerous. Good or evil.

Rue has watched Diego use psychological tactics on people before, he has mastered the art of being the good marshal and the bad marshal all at the same time. She needs to be stronger to withstand him when he's mad. She needs to predict his attacks before they come, whether that is verbal or physical. When she masters that, she can be the one in control, or at least put up a good fight. She has found in the past that letting him win and submitting to his wants is sometimes the only way to keep the peace.

But this is not one of those times. Or is it?

Gods, he makes me question every fucking thing.

No, it is not one of those times. He tried to keep her from the outside world. He left guards at the door so she physically couldn't leave. Whether it's out of fear of losing her or a desire for control, the why doesn't matter. What she does know is that she will not let him get to her. She will continue leaving one way or another, because she is her own. Her mind and body and soul belong to her, even if he believes otherwise.

Rue takes a large gulp of wine and lets out an exaggerated exhale. Her fingertips begin to shake with the internal rage rising in her stomach. She grabs the bottle again, and pours another full cup into her glass, before lifting to put it back into the cabinet. As she arches on her toes, she extends her body enough so the t-shirt rises above the bottom part of her ass. Her lips twitch up knowing he can never resist looking. He isn't the only one with moves. She has tactics of her own she can shell out to get to him.

She hears him clear his throat before he threatens, "Did you think I wouldn't notice you sneaking out? How stupid do you think I am?"

Rue doesn't respond, only takes another sip of wine while internally she is begging herself not to explode.

He repeats the question, this time a little louder. "How fucking stupid do you think I am, Ghost?"

Oh, I'm Ghost now.

A laugh escapes her lips while she takes another big swig of wine, which causes Diego to slam a fist into the marble counters.

"Fuck Ghost, why do you have to be so difficult?"

Do not respond. Don't do it.

"Answer me dammit."

Fuck this shit.

"I wouldn't have to sneak out if those fucking buffalo at the door would let me leave!" she yells into the cabinets, refusing to look at him.

"They're just following orders," he says through gritted teeth.

"And whose order is that?" She spins around to look him dead in the eye. "Because last time I checked, I was still a free woman. This whole arrangement was agreed on only because you promised me, I could help you with this issue. Not sit in this dark apartment, alone." She can feel her arms trembling as ice cold fury starts to build. Her heart is racing in her ears, and she pushes her feelings back down into the depths of her soul. She needs to stay calm if she is going to get to him. She has to show him he can't aggravate her, and she's currently failing. Getting under her skin is his second favorite thing to do, only behind fucking her.

Shit, stop!

This is not the time to be thinking about fucking Diego.

"If you really cared about me or the Smoke Runners, you'd fucking listen to what I'm asking of you. Rue, you're my number one priority. I can't just sit back and watch you run around the city unprotected."

She laughs at his pathetic reasoning. "You've been *watching* me run around the city unprotected for years! I have been surviving on my own since I was fourteen. I don't need protection," she yells, pressing a hand to her chest.

Diego stands up, saunters towards her and stops within inches of her face. Rue's body stiffens, she refuses to make eye contact, looking out the window across the room instead.

His eyes narrow and he spits, "See that's where you're wrong, Ghost. *I* saved you. *I* kept you alive when everyone else wanted you dead. And this is how you repay me, by sneaking around behind my back?"

His hands move down her forearms, causing the hairs on her body to stand up. He moves his mouth to her ear and whispers, "No, Beautiful. You did not survive on your own. Everything you are is because of me." His tone goes deep with the last word.

Rue's heart is about to rip from her chest, and there is now blood in her mouth from biting down on her cheek. Her hands form fists, and she is squeezing the wine glass so tightly it might break. That feeling comes back up to the surface, crashing into her mind like tidal waves of seething rampage. Internally she is screaming.

"Who do you think you are?" he questions.

She won't grant him the low blow of getting to her with a few words. She turns her head to glare at him. She hates him right now, this isn't her Diego, this is the worst part of him. She studies his eyes, dark and empty, full of betrayal. She needs to take back the power.

"I could kick you in the balls and drop you to your knees in front of me right now. I'd be careful about what you say next," she sneers.

"Then do it. Show me how tough you can be." He jerks her leg in between his own, pushing her thigh against his cock.

Rue's chest rises and falls against his, and she is sick with herself for proving he has an effect on her heart rate.

She doesn't move.

"That's right, you can't. You're fucking weak. You need me. I could throw your ass out in the rain right now if I wanted to. Let them take you. Fuck you. Kill you. You're disposable, Ghost. You do not and will not have any power over me."

Rue shakes her head and with all the bravery she can collect says, "You're really proving your father right, aren't you?" A menacing laugh leaves her lips like poison. "He would be so proud. Controlling women. Locking them away. Taking away their freedom. It's like looking in a mirror, I bet. Like father, like son."

That hits his deepest nerve. His breath quickens, within a second his hands are locked around her throat, pushing her back over the counter top. "I am nothing like him," he shouts. She drops her wine glass, causing it to shatter against the wood floors. He doesn't even flinch. She is on her toes now, desperately trying to gain back control. His fingers are crushing her.

"Get your hands off me," Rue calls out, stern and direct, yet her voice breaks.

Diego shakes her and screams, "Who the fuck do you think you're talking to? Do you think I want to be this way? I have no fucking choice, Ghost! I am in charge of everything. Everyone! It's not my fault you can't fucking listen. I am holding everything together and it's killing me."

Rue's act falls, her face slacks. She went too far. She knows what she needs to do, and it takes ripping a small piece of herself off to do it.

Her face is blank, made of stone. She moves a hand over his, trying to pry it off her neck. She doesn't break eye contact. Pleading she says, "Diego! Come back to me. You're not Manny. I didn't mean it."

His grip lightens slightly, and she can finally inhale. She moves her hands to push on his chest and begs, "Let go of me. Let's talk this out. Let me go."

Diego is gone, his anger takes control, and he screams at her, "I am not him!"

Rue doesn't respond, only begs to find him again with her eyes. She does not look away. He will come back, he always does. She fucked up, she knows it. Bringing up Manny was one move too far. His eyes flutter away, under his breath he murmurs, "I'm not him."

She needs to salvage this, calm him down in a way that she can make it out of this. In a soft voice Rue repeats herself, "Let go of me. Let's talk this out. Let me go." She just needs to stay strong for a few more moments. She closes her eyes and reminds herself of their teen years. Happy Diego. Carefree, brave Diego. Her Diego.

Visions of his sweet face, while they ran through the streets of the Low District fill her mind. His laughter as they stole money from some stranger in the market. She can feel the sun on her face as they get chased by a crooked shop owner on the coast. The smells. The sounds. Him. She thinks of nothing but him. Her brain fills with picture after picture of their life. Happy thoughts. Only happy thoughts.

Diego will come back to me.

He will.

As if he has the same memories, Diego's grip on her fades. The cold of the apartment air hits her as he sinks to his knees. Rue finally opens her eyes, lets out a deep breath, and moves her hands to her neck. Her skin is hot and hurts to touch. Diego sits with his head leaning on her legs.

Shit.

What has she done?

So fucking stupid. So reckless.

As much as she hates aggressive Diego, pitiful Diego is much worse. The man has been through and seen so much in his twenty nine years and she feels sick to be contributing to his pain. Why does she constantly do this? Why does she continue to make problems for herself?

"Fuck," she whispers, almost silently.

She lowers herself down in front of him, wrapping her arms around his neck and straddling him in his lap. She whispers one more time, "Let's talk this out." Her forehead meets his, and she can hear his racing heart echo in her brain.

"I'm sorry," he whispers regretfully.

Rue is taken back. He's apologizing? That is… different.

"Fuck," he growls, punching a fist at the cabinets they are leaning up against. Rue jumps, then tightens her hold on him.

She kisses his forehead and admits, "I know. I'm sorry too."

He looks at her, eyes bloodshot and she realizes he's been crying. "Rue, I'm so sorry. You are all I have left, the Runners are just my job, you…" He moves his hands to her face, pulling a loose wisp of hair away from her eyes. "You're mine. You are everything to me. I can't lose you, and today… today I thought I did. I lost it. I thought I lost you, and if I don't have you, there's nothing good left of me."

She softens her gaze and says, "Diego I was gone for a few hours. That's all. I came back. I'm sitting right in front of you, safe."

"But what if you don't come back next time? He wanted you, Rue. They know you. My girl. They want *my* girl, and I hate it. It's eating me away. I will do anything to keep you with me. Even if that means keeping you here until I figure out what to do."

"You know I can't just sit here and wait this out. It's not who I am. I need to be in the streets, with the people. With the Lowers. Not here. I'm not some trophy you can keep on a shelf." She motions around the room, at the dark gray interior. The cold walls, and stone, and brick, and emptiness.

"I like being with you. And having dinner with you. And you keeping me warm at night. But you're never here. I'm alone. I'm not doing anything useful. I need to talk to people, and research, and uncover bits until I have the whole picture of something. I can't sit idle."

He looks away from her, clenching his jaw.

"Today when I left, I felt alive again. I felt like I could breathe for the first time in weeks. I learned something useful, and I was excited to come back and tell you. That's what I should be doing. Finding answers, sneaking in the shadows, using the few gifts I have. Diego, you can't lock me away. I can't survive like that."

He looks at Rue with tired eyes, rubbing a thumb across her bottom lip. "I know. I'm sorry, just sometimes I get so mad when you don't fill me in on your plans."

"You weren't here! How was I supposed to communicate when I was alone?"

"I know. I know." He pauses for a moment, running a hand over his shaved head. "Starting tomorrow the guys will let you leave whenever you want, if you promise to let me know where you're going. I just want to know where you are. That way if anything happens, I'll know where to find you. I won't be able to do this without you."

"Thank you," she whispers and hugs him tight, letting her head sink into the crook of his neck. All the confessions catch her off guard. She wonders if he truly means it. "I know how to take care of myself, you know."

Diego kisses her shoulder, and squeezes her tighter, holding on to her like she's the only life raft in the middle of an endless ocean. His heart rings in her ears. She's engulfed by his presence, by his smell, his warmth, it's intoxicating. As desperately as she wants to stay mad at him, her body betrays her in this moment.

Having him this close does something to her, like a magical pull towards him. She naturally latches on to him because he cares, he doesn't know how to express it, and she can't deny it's toxic, but she wants to be important to him. She wants to kiss him. She knows she shouldn't. She knows any third party would question her sanity, but she can't stop the feeling of needing to be the reason for his happiness. He is her weakness; one she's never been able to conquer.

His voice brings her back to the dark kitchen floors. "I know you can take care of yourself, Beautiful." He kisses her again on her neck. "I don't know what I'd do without you. I love you so much, Rue. I can't imagine my life without you. I need you to be safe and stay safe. You're all I have. You. It's always just been you." His voice trails off and she can feel every beat of his heart. "You are everything that is important to me."

Rue inhales deeply. This is who she wants to be with, this is the man she knows in her soul he can be. But him wanting to be better, and actually becoming a better man to her, are two completely different things.

She doesn't need someone to protect her. She needs an equal, someone to show up when she needs it, and stand by her side when she wants to handle things on her own. Not someone who blames her for things getting hard. Someone who destroys his own home to relieve his anxiety.

She doesn't want some powerful, enraged crime boss trying to prove he's enough of an alpha for the job. She wants Diego. This one. The one that's sitting on the floor with her in his arms. The one with his face in her neck while he plays with her hair and rubs her back.

She wants for once in her life, for something to be easy. For someone that wants to be with her, no strings attached. No limits. No excuses. No guilt. She wants that with him.

Now if only we can stay like this.

Rue leans her head back, breaking their relaxed rhythm of holding each other. Her eyes are soft, and she moves close to kiss him. His hand on her back pulls on her bun, leaning her face up so he can suck on her neck. He pulls her towards him, getting as much of her as he can like this is their last moment together. He lowers his other hand to her ass and squeezes, which sends a shock of heat between her legs.

She hadn't noticed while they were fighting, but she was wet. And while she knows in her mind this is a sick reaction to getting choked and yelled at, she wants to fuck him and make all their rage melt away. She wants to throw away all the anger and hurt, and just get lost in each other. Let their bodies do what they do best and ignore all the red flags catching fire in the corner of their relationship. She needs euphoria, even if it's only for a moment.

It's her last tactic. The final card to play to win the game.

Sex calms him down. It calms both of them down in a way nothing else does. She knows it isn't healthy, but it's all she has. This relationship that pulls them to extremes, and leaves her wondering if love is real, is the only thing she has accepted as part of her life.

Are all relationships this fucked up?

She is exposed to him, having only his t-shirt on. The only fabric keeping her from rubbing herself on his cock is the cotton of his sweats.

Without another thought, she starts to rub her wetness on him, begging for him to make another move. Begging for more, for a sign he wants her too. She's desperate to know he needs her like she needs him. A sign this is truly real.

He moves his other hand to her ass, lifting her slightly as she moves herself back and forth, feeling his hardness grow under her. She glides a hand down, trying to free him from his pants but he swats her away.

She pulls back from his lips enough to purr, "Let me in. Let me show you how sorry I am." He doesn't respond, just pulls her back in, exploring her mouth with his tongue. She tries one more time, slowly moving a hand over his sweats, sticking two fingers in the elastic before he swats her away again.

"Come on, let me give you what you want," she breathes into his ear, nipping at it as she does. She can feel him getting harder underneath her.

He lets out a moan that is almost silent, but she catches it. She giggles and moves her lips to his neck, kissing and licking all his favorite spots. This is going to work; it will fix all the fucked up shit they both do to each other. It has to.

Please work.

He pulls her face to his lips and kisses her again, just once, before pushing her face away with his palm. His eyes go dark, but not with anger or need, with something she can't place. A dirty look that has her desperate to understand it.

"Let me have you," she demands in a voice filled with lust.

"No," he says simply. His mouth twitches to the side into a smirk.

Rue pushes herself back against the cabinet, puzzled at his answer. Her eyes narrow and she snaps, "Why the fuck not?" His body goes rigid, and he stares at her down the bridge of his nose again.

Shit.

He lets out a low husky laugh and says, "Because fucking me is a privilege, and you haven't been very good today. You can't seem to get it through your pretty little head that I'm in charge."

"What?" she breathes, utterly shocked at his change in demeanor.

"You deny me what I ask of you, and I'll deny you what you want from me. I'll let you leave tomorrow, but your actions have consequences, Ghost. You went behind my back. You did this to yourself. I would do anything to make you happy, but I need to see you do the same for me. Respect. That's all I want. Until you can show me that, you can stay in the guest room."

Rue lets out an audible sigh, searching his face for a tell that this is a joke. This has to be a joke. He was just confessing his love for her a second ago, practically in tears like a fucking baby.

"Really?" she asks. "No sex because I left the house one time."

"No sex because I need to know I can trust you again. I need to see some change in you that shows me, you love and respect me as much as I do you. Simple as that. You can't just throw yourself at me and expect me to forgive everything. I have made so many sacrifices for you, and now I want to see you do the same."

Check mate. He got his prey. The mouse fell for the trap once again.

Rue doesn't answer. She just sits in the silence staring into his eyes. They are blank, no emotions she can grab onto. Like he just turned off how he feels once he realized he got what he wanted.

Rue bites her bottom lip and looks down at the wet spot on his pants, suddenly embarrassed that she let her cards show. Embarrassed that she was played by him so easily. She can feel her cheeks turning red. He didn't even have to try, she folded at the first sign of vulnerability on his part.

Gods, so fucking stupid.

He grabs her by the chin and forces her to look at him. His eyes. His stupid eyes, so dark and angry. She sees Manny whether she wants to or not.

In a low voice, he says, "Doesn't feel good, does it? Now you know how I feel every time you betray me." He pauses to look around, focusing on the mess the broken wine glass made next to them. "I'm going to bed, clean this fucking mess up."

Without another word, Diego lifts Rue's legs off himself, and stands. He readjusts his hard bulge before stepping over the broken glass and walking into his room. The echo of the door slamming shut makes Rue wince. She closes her eyes, leaning her back against the cabinet.

Fuck, what a shit show.

She looks off into the room, staring at the mess he made just hours ago because of his fury with her. Who is she kidding? Her Diego is long gone, and there may be glimpses of him, moments he lets his emotions out, but he will always be the man his father created. There is no going back.

What has her life come to? She is sitting on the kitchen floor, surrounded by broken glass and red wine, locked in an apartment that's not hers, with a man she isn't sure knows what love truly is for how often he throws the word around.

She has no one to talk to, because the people she wants to tell can't know about her job, and the people that know about her job can't know about her relationship with Diego. What an absolute fucking mess. She moves her hand to her face and sits with her thoughts.

Alone once again.

She's beginning to get used to it at this point. Hoping and praying to the Gods that someone would be in her corner is just fairytales now. Make believe. Because why would someone care about her? The orphan. The girl whose parents sent her away instead of fighting to be with her. The disappointment. The problem. Rue can feel the water coming to the surface in her eyes and pushes it back down into its locked, wooden box.

No! No, no, no. No pity parties today. Lock up that stone in your chest godsdammit. You had your moment of weakness, time to pull yourself together. You won't be broken. You will not. Be. Broken.

Rue sits in the kitchen watching the sky as it changes from orange to brown with the night, as more rain falls. She watches the water drops slide down the glass windows. Like the clouds are crying for her, so she doesn't have to. Her eyes shift to the skylights, where a rat outside goes from one to the other, looking for a way in.

It's safer outside, little guy. Once you get in, there is no escape.

Minutes go by before she moves, and even then, it's only to readjust her legs. She pulls her knees towards her chest, and hugs herself tight, trying to warm her practically naked body. She isn't ready for the cold sheets of the guest room bed just yet, so the wood floors will do for now.

The silence of the night is peaceful in a way, like none of the last hour actually happened. Her ears focus on the rain hitting the glass, when a blinding bolt of purple lightning brightens the room. The sounds of thunder fill the space, causing Rue to close her eyes and enjoy the music of the night. The pattern continues, light then boom, light then boom as if the Gods are sending out a signal. The rhythm of the sounds echo in her ears in the most beautiful melody.

She smiles, thanks the Gods for keeping her company, and rubs her legs to warm up. She lets her mind drift, thinking about her mother and father, about Olympia, about the little girl under the bridge. People need her in the Low District. They need her to be strong. They need her to be brave, and smart, and purposeful in her actions.

She needs to get to the bottom of this chaotic situation in the city, so no more humans are taken from their families. With that solved, she realizes it might be time to go. Screw saving enough money, she is scrappy enough to make it on her own on the mainland. The need to get off this rock is increasing by the day.

She accepts the fact that she won't be able to do any of that if she is busy worrying about getting under Diego's skin. Or just getting under him for that matter.

This isn't about him; this is about her people. She has to stop with the betrayals. The sneaking around. He is not her lover or her friend. He is just her boss in this, and one with connections she doesn't possess. Money. Resources. Power she doesn't hold in this city.

Rue sits thinking about her options moving forward while she looks out into the muddy sky, lightning in the distance still keeping her company. With another boom, she centers herself, repeating the words from her mother's letters.

Please hold on to your intuition, it will keep you safe. Hold on to your kindness, it will keep you grounded. And most importantly, hold on to your determination, it will keep you going after you've been knocked down.

She smiles, tilting her head back against the wood of the cabinet. She will hold on. She will continue to play her part, act as the character she needs to be in the moment. But, in the back of her mind, that little voice will always remind her of her true self, the girl that will not be broken.

Let's try one more time.

CHAPTER

…The meadow….

… The butterfly and the voice…

I step out behind a thorn bush and can see the creature at last. A small little fox, with golden honey eyes, sits on a path of more pine needles. Just looking up at me. This little creature doesn't need to be here. We don't need to be here. We need to go back.

I reach down to pick her up and as soon as my hand touches her fur, she turns stark white. Before I have time to question what just happened, my arms start to turn blue. My breath is now a cold mist blowing out of my lungs. I lift my hand to examine it, but I can't move. I'm frozen. My skin starts to frost over. I'm so cold. I'm scared. I feel my lungs freezing from within.

As if out of nowhere, fire forms in my heart, expanding through my body like I'm being burned alive. No, not burned alive, brought back to life. The flames rush through my veins like someone just poured cenzium fuel into them. I lift my head towards the sky as the uncontrollable power rushes over me. Each breath comes out as a hot steam.

I look down at my hands and they are mine again. No blue. No ice. No death. I am not dead.

Ahead of me on the path is the fox, now white. The land around me is white as well, and full of snow. The tree branches, once covered in green a minute ago, lay bare, snow piled on top of them. The forest has become a snowy wonderland, so beautiful and majestic. Yet, I still feel uneasy.

I take a step towards the fox. Looking down to see the snow melt around my footprints. With each step, wildflowers grow around my feet, as if my footsteps are bringing back the spring. My toes are dirty from the muddy ground underneath. My dress now shredded. The linen charred and swaying in the cold wind. Hot embers still holding on to the fabric.

"Go! You must find her," the familiar voice echoes in my ear. More panic in it than I've ever heard. I step. And step again. Making my way through the snow. Staring at the fox who is perched on top of a snowy hill. Head tilted. Blending into the surrounding, except for her eyes, which burn the color of a golden flame. The flames dance with excitement as I get closer and closer.

The higher I climb, the more the fox moves in place. She sways her tail, and paws at the ground, like she's dancing. As if to say, this is the right way. I'm feet away when she looks behind her. I use her distracted glance as a chance to pick her up and get her out of here.

With mere inches between my hands and her little body, she bolts away, down the path further towards a waterfall. The water rages behind the fox in a way that doesn't feel safe. Chunks of ice break off, crashing into the rocks below the falls. The remaining pieces rush down the river out of sight.

Her quick movement takes me off guard. I fall into the snow, which melts as I land, causing me to lay directly into the mud. I don't move. I sit and watch as she does her little dance again by the water, like she wants me to follow her.

"Go!" the voice yells again. "Get to her, now. Go to the light!"

The fox's movements become still. She lowers her head, and her ears are pinned back. Her tail wraps around her as she backs up. She opens her mouth to yip and call out, but no sound comes out. She tries again and still nothing.

She's only steps away from the rushing water, and I try to stand to get to her, but I can't move. My dress is snagged on something. I call out in her direction, begging her not to move, but my voice is silenced by the wind. Without looking away from her, I pull on the fabric, hoping to set myself free from whatever is keeping me from her. When nothing works, I turn to see what it is, and my lungs collapse within. I can't breathe any longer.

Towering above me, with his boot on my dress, is Blue Eyes. His knife in hand, and an evil smile across his face. In the shadow of the light behind him, all I can see clearly is his eyes. His eyes aren't just blue, they are glowing. Seething with hatred. They are light and dark at the same time.

"Run! Gods, run, Aruelia!" the voice demands. I pull at my dress, trying to rip it away from his boot, doing anything I can to get free. I can't get free. Gods I'll never be free. My heart is beating out of my chest. I try to use my powers, but no air is coming out of my mouth. My hands can't move to manipulate the oxygen around me, which feels like it is disappearing by the second.

The fox, the little fox, my mind cannot stop thinking about keeping her safe. Keeping her away from this demon of a man. Something in me tells me she's next.

"Find the light! Go to the light!" The voice is yelling in my head, but I can't focus on it. I just see those eyes. Those are not the light; they are something much darker. Not the eyes of a human, or a fae creature. They shine light blue but are somehow shadows. Nothing but shadows.

Suddenly I'm pinned down, ice wrapped around my hands like a pair of handcuffs. He laughs, a slow, deep, gravelly laugh. The voice doesn't match the man from the alley, but it's familiar. A voice of a man I know, but don't.

Black smoke starts radiating from him, engulfing the two of us within it. A tornado of darkness swirls around us as he stands above me. The shadow of Blue Eyes looks at his knife. He runs a finger over the blade, which is dripping a crimson liquid. I taste blood in my mouth.

Oh, Gods, I'm choking on it.

I'm drowning in it.

My lungs are full of red death as he watches me.

…My vision starts to go, coming in and out of focus…

…I choke on my own blood…

…He raises his blade into the air, and drives it into…

CHAPTER

THE morning sun begs to reach past the clouds while Rue walks the coast lined street. Artisan Row is practically empty, reminders of the storm last night still around as shop owners clean up debris and fallen goods.

The warm spring air flows through her, embracing her every step with a hug, smelling of salt water and the slightest hint of pine. She thinks of her mother and a flash of a smile grazes her lips, pausing a second to welcome her into her thoughts, hugging back.

She leans over the railing overlooking the ocean. The warm colors of the sky swirl around, mixing together like watercolors. Pinks, oranges, and purples that linger from the sunrise are painted on the clouds and melt into the blueish gray of the day. The ocean water glitters with happiness as it dances, crashing into the shoreline. Unfortunately, the beauty ends there.

The first ten feet or so of ocean water is full of litter, tumbling through the waves as it crashes into the stones on the beach. Trash, debris, and dead fish are washed ashore, making row after row of oily garbage as the tide goes out. It makes Rue sick. Everything people touch becomes robbed of its beauty. It's purity. The ocean can't even have a peaceful morning without suffocating due to human interaction.

She wonders what The Mother would think if she descended onto this man-made dump of an island. How would she feel when she saw her creations dying at the hands of another? How would she react to the fact that there is so much pollution in the air and soil, that life can't grow naturally? What would she say when she saw the mountain of trash piling up in the lower west corner of the island? Would she be proud? Would she call this way of living *revolutionary*, like the Seven Presidents preach in the news?

I doubt it.

While progress is essential for human survival, doing so in a way that eliminates the environment you are trying to survive in is pointless. Humans can try to replace nature with machines, but in the end, the only thing they are accomplishing is their own demise.

However, somewhere deep in Rue's soul, an ounce of hope still burns. Hope that the mainland is different. Hope that she came from a place where her kind lived amongst the natural world, not in spite of it.

Rue fills her lungs with oxygen, ignoring the smell of dead fish that slaps her as she inhales. She lets the overwhelm leave her mind. She is just one person, and in her eyes one person is not enough to save the world. So, she will continue on, doing her best and not thinking about the future of her home. She has learned over the years to not allow these types of thoughts to stay, sweeping them out the front door of her mind. If she lets them stay too long, she knows she will go mad. Helplessness is a terrifying feeling.

She watches some sea birds fly along the coast, stamping black shadows into the pastel colored sky. A small blip of feeling in her gut is begging her to leave, pulling her tether towards the ocean like it is where her soul is meant to be.

Maybe someday, but not today.

Her eyes take in the horizon one last time before walking towards Moon Child. She hops over a puddle and does a quick survey of her surroundings. Her plan is to use this ungodly hour to her advantage. Hoping it will be easier to spot things, or people out of place if there are less to keep track of. Other than a few shop owners, the streets are practically abandoned so far.

Posters and fliers of missing people are starting to take over storefront windows, covering the streets with depressing wallpaper. Rue takes note of the large government propaganda displays portraying the Low District as some sort of war zone. Claiming they have everything under control, and the phrase **SEE SOMETHING, SAY SOMETHING** plastered over images of fae in handcuffs. Another one has a group of citizens hugging masked Marshals with the words **PROTECT THE PEOPLE, BECOME A MARSHAL TODAY.**

The one that makes Rue stop moving, is a poster with Lex Macellarius shaking hands with a homeless man, the words **HERE TO SERVE** happily spread across the top. What catches her eye isn't the human scum that is Lex Macellarius, it's the dripping red handprint over his face that reads **OUR BLOOD IS ON YOUR HANDS.**

The energy of the Low District is shifting. People are no longer waiting for someone else to save them. They have every right to be angry and have decided amongst themselves that they will take matters of safety into their own hands. In other circumstances, she would be proud of the humans for protecting themselves, unfortunately their deep-rooted fear of fae folk means she, along with many others, are in more danger than normal. All she can hope for now is that fae folk are focused on safety as well.

She continues her walk back through her childhood neighborhood, trying to keep her head down so no extra attention is drawn to her. These are her people, but with everything going on she doesn't know who she can trust.

Rue makes a sharp turn into the alcove Moon Child is in, and gets forced back, falling on her ass from a brick wall… no, not a brick wall, a person.

"Oh Gods! I'm so sorry!" a hoarse voice apologizes, grabbing her hands to lift her back to her feet.

She tugs herself out of his grip with force. "Watch it you fu—" Rue stops mid-sentence. "Finny?"

The boy standing in front of her, who now looks like a full-grown adult man, used to be like a little brother to her. Finny. *The Artisan Row Baby.* He was named that after being left on Fiona's doorstep as an infant. The whole community raised him, but Fiona took on the most responsibility. He grew up with her as his mother, officially adopting him when he was three.

Rue hasn't seen Finny in years, the last time he was probably eleven or twelve, and a little scrawny thing. Chasing girls and getting in trouble with the marshals for tagging bridges with graffiti. Olympia and Fiona had begged her to come back home and talk to him about the path he was going down, ironically following in her footsteps.

Now, standing in front of her is a six foot, scruffy looking man. Still skinny, but with wide shoulders and more toned muscles from hard labor. His hair is still as messy as she remembers, a black mop on his head. His normally olive skin is tanned deeper from the sun.

"Hey, dude," he laughs, running a hand through his hair.

"Hey yourself," she says, a smile growing wide across her face. "How are you? Fi told me you got a second job down at the docks! Good for you."

"Yep, she won't admit it, but we needed the extra money. With the supplies from the government being so scarce lately, we haven't had much profit. I started helpin' out on the docks for some of the older captains who can't haul as much to the market anymore. They pay me decent, and the hours aren't bad, just early mornin's." His eyes fill with pride as he speaks, silver sparkles dancing in his iron colored irises.

"Good, I'm glad she has you to help. Gods, it's been so long. How old are you now?"

"I'm sixteen almost seventeen," he says, running a hand through his hair again like somehow, it's an embarrassing fact.

He towers over her now, but she can't help but still view him like the little boy she used to protect. Her mind flashes to all the afternoons she would watch him while their parents worked. The two were inseparable, Rue taking him under her wing like a little brother. Two orphans, who found a home amongst the Lowers. Even after she left to live on her own, she would come back to see him, help teach him how to survive in the city. Since the first day she held him as a baby, she has felt drawn to keep him safe.

"Well, I'm happy I ran into you, did you just come from Olympia's?" she asks, pointing to the shop feet away.

"Um, no… I mean yeah, she was helpin' me with somethin'," he says, glancing back at the door, once again pulling his hand through his hair.

"Oh, yeah?"

"Nothin' major, just some questions I had." He pauses for a second, staring at the ground before continuing. "Anyway, I got to go help Mom open up. It was good seein' you, Rue." He smiles and awkwardly goes in for a hug, hesitating for a split second before committing fully.

Rue doesn't have time to stop his arms before they are around her. She's stiff for a minute, then relaxes letting the warmth of him calm her muscles.

Finny always ran hot, his hugs were like infernos taking over the space around them with warmth, the smell of citrus and a hint of campfire clinging to her senses. She never understood why he smelled like that; always like he had just spent the week sitting in front of a fire without a shower.

A laugh comes out of her, before she hugs him back. "I miss you, kid," she whispers. "Come see me sometime, okay? I can sneak us into the High District, you'll hate it. But at least we can make fun of it together and swipe some good food."

He laughs and mumbles something in agreement. A thought pops into Rue's head. She pulls away from him and asks, "Hey, have you heard anything about the people going missing? You're being careful right?"

He takes a step back, lowers his head and rubs a hand on his forehead. "Yeah, I know about them. I'm pretty sure they took my friend a few weeks ago, he's missin'. They are some serious mother fuckers, Rue. Their tags are goin' up all over the city, no one sees who's doin' it."

"Got any info you can share?" she asks, grasping for anything at this point.

"All I know is to stay off the streets at night. They stay away from the roof systems it seems, so if you're plannin' on coming back to see Oly or whatever, I'd take those. I've been tryin' to keep my head down, not get into trouble. I just stay with Mom at night, I'm not gettin' taken."

"Good, she needs you." She takes a step forward to place a hand on his shoulder. "Just promise me you'll watch your back and listen to your gut. If a situation seems sketchy, just remember all the ways I taught you to stay in the shadows. The Organization is good, but us street kids are better."

"Don't worry about me, I had the toughest kid as a big sister. She kicked my ass until I learned how to fight back."

Rue laughs, stands on her toes to ruffle his thick black locks. "Tell your mom I said hi, okay?"

"I will." He lifts his chin in a nod and starts down the cobblestone towards the General.

Rue waits, leaning on the brick of the building watching him leave. A pull in her gut screams at her to protect him. Keep him close, make sure nothing happens to him. Her magic stirring below the surface on its own accord.

Guilt fills her as she stares at his long frame. She hasn't seen him in over four years and it's her fault. After Diego took over the business in the wake of his father's passing, she got in deeper with the Smoke Runners. She had to leave the rest of her life behind, which meant leaving Finny. He was just a kid, and his best friend/ older sister left with no warning. Rue lowers her head with that thought. Abandonment is something the two of them bonded over, and without thinking about the impact she had on him, she had just left.

She has always felt such an innate maternal instinct to watch over him. The only person she's ever felt that for. She never put on a show for him. No mask of what she thinks he wants or needs to hear. Just the truth, sharing what she knows about how to survive in this cold world. Striving to make him tough, and smart, and pushing him to be confident in his decisions. Trying her best, even at a young age, to help him succeed.

Rue realizes how much she's missed him and smirks, knowing he turned out okay.

Once he's down the road, she can see him turn into the corner store. Her heart, that she didn't realize was racing, calms. Exhaling, she turns towards Moon Child, a familiar feeling of worry washes over her now that he's out of her sight. Something she hasn't felt in years.

Weird.

She shakes it away focusing on her task at hand, somehow getting the most intuitive woman in all of the Southlands to help break down the suicide poison, without her knowing where it came from.

The happy little chime sings as Rue opens the door, disrupting the silence of the shop. The morning light is causing tiny specs of dust to glow as they float through the air. The shelves are overflowing with items, making the space seem even more claustrophobic with spiritual knick-knacks.

Rue can smell the sweet aroma of jasmine and bergamot as she walks past displays. She relishes in the stillness of the shop, no patrons roam the shelves, which reassures her that no one will be listening to their conversation.

"Olympia?" Rue calls out. "Olympia, it's Rue."

She takes a few steps further into the store. A creaking sound comes from the wooden steps in the back, and she calls out a third time. "Olympia? You here?"

"Back here, Honey Bee!" she can hear faintly from behind the desk.

She steps her way through the shop, strategically contorting her body so as to not knock anything over with her bag. "Store is getting a bit full isn't it," she jokes as she approaches, leaning over the checkout desk.

Olympia comes around the corner of the steps, holding up the tapestry that usually hangs from the wall behind the desk. She shuffles over to the hooks and tries to lift it high enough to clip into place with no avail. Height has never been Olympia's strength with her five-foot frame. Rue laughs, watching her struggle to reach, and removes her bag to help.

"You need me to get that?" she jokes.

Olympia turns to glare at her, eyes barely popping up over the fabric. She huffs and admits, "Well, clearly I can't do it myself, and I don't feel like going to get a chair."

"I'm getting you a stool and platform shoes for Winter Solstice this year," Rue laughs.

"Aruelia, will you just come here and help me," Olympia says in a stern tone.

"Yes Ma'am." Rue stands up straight with a solute against her forehead. Taking the tapestry from Olympia's hands, she reaches up with ease, attaching the metal rings to the hooks. "Why was it down anyway, you never take it down?"

"Oh, you know. I needed to clean it, and there were some snags I've been meaning to mend."

Rue smooths out the fabric, allowing it to hang freely from the wall. She takes a step back to admire it, smiling at the beautiful work of art that has hung in this exact spot all her life.

A golden tree, with roots coming out the bottom, shines in the light of the day. A depiction of the world map, and color coordinated borders to represent the different countries lie within the trunk and branches.

Olympia stands a foot behind Rue, smiling at her as she appreciates one of her most prized possessions. "Do you remember the story of Ethos? Or would you like a little refresher?"

Rue lets out a breathy laugh through her nose. "Do I have a choice? I'm guessing you're going to tell me anyway."

Olympia has always been a history buff. She could talk about the history of Ethos until she passed out from lack of oxygen. So, because of her constant history lessons growing up, Rue also knew a lot about the world's history, although she has always thought that Olympia stretched the truth quite often.

Olympia chuckles. "It's always good to be reminded of where you come from. It's important! The Tree of Life has all the answers you will ever need weaved into it. Never forget that, Honey Bee."

Rue looks back towards her and smiles. Olympia continues, making her way next to Rue and pulling her close. "It all started with The Mother, a spiritual entity who traveled through space and time trying to find somewhere to plant her roots and live out her days. She found a floating rock that had the potential for life, so she claimed it as her own. Naming it?"

"Ethos," Rue buts in, refraining from using jazz hands with her answer.

"Ethos." She smiles, shaking Rue lightly. "The Mother spent time creating a beautiful environment, but she got lonely by herself, so she created seven other beings to help take care of the planet."

"The Seven Gods," Rue says without being asked.

"Correct! And when creating them, she offered up a little of her power, Bright Magic, to create theirs. Weaving her own spirit into each of them. Egan, God of Fire. Doruk, God of Ground. Cyra, Goddess of Water. Titus, God of Electricity. Ira,

Goddess of Ice. Lilith, Goddess of Light." Olympia explains this, pointing to the colored symbols stitched into the roots of the tree. She pauses to turn Rue towards her, hands still on her shoulders. "And Aruelia, Goddess of?" She stops so Rue can answer.

Rue lets out a huff, rolling her eyes. "Aruelia, Goddess of Air."

Olympia's bright smile beams across her face. "Right! Goddess of Air. Your birth name was given to you as a permanent reminder of where you come from. I'm sure your mother knew you would do great things."

Rue rolls her eyes again, feeling the heaviness of that opinion. "Clearly she was wrong, my life is in shambles." She laughs to cover up the unhealed ache of loss. Rue focuses on the tapestry, trying to force her feelings deep down into her soul where they need to stay.

"Oh, that's where you're wrong," Olympia says, moving Rue to meet her eyes again and tapping her cheeks with her palms.

"I'm only half fae though, nothing special."

Olympia sighs. "Honey Bee, I can't wait to see the day you change your mind about that. You are special, more than you know, but that is for another day."

Rue's eyes narrow, but before she has time to disagree, Olympia is turning her to look at the fabric again. "Now where was I?"

"The Gods and Goddesses," Rue chimes, in an annoyed voice.

"Yes, yes! You see, after the Seven Gods were created, Ethos thrived. Eventually other beings sought refuge on the planet. Some like the Northern Witches, which were the first to arrive." She points to the tapestry. Up in the north west corner of the map sits the Dioden Mountains surrounded by a forest of pine trees.

"These special witches had powers of their own unlike the elemental ones of the Gods and Goddesses, passed down from mothers to daughters, but we can go deeper into that another time. Then came the Merfolk," she says, pointing to the Brine Isles. "And then eventually everyone else. Nymphs, Druids, Orcs, Elves, Electrokinetics, Phoenix Shifters, Dwarfs, Humans, and so many others."

Her hand tapped the map on the tapestry over and over again, like she was placing the groups of people into the world herself.

"The original Gods welcomed them, finding their twin lights within other beings, and passing down their magic from generation to generation," she says, pointing to the branches of the tree expanding over the world.

"All the original Gods except for Lilith. She did not agree with muddying the bloodlines of magic. She was caught by The Mother trying to destroy all other life using the first recorded Shadow Magic, and she was trapped in Hell's void at the center of the world for all eternity as punishment."

"How?" Rue whispers, interrupting Olympia's impromptu history lesson.

"How what?"

"How did The Mother trap Lilith and her darkness in the void?"

Rue thought about the story of Lilith more than she would like to admit. She always wondered how someone created out of love and light turned out to be filled with darkness, and often worried that the same could happen to her. Deep within her core, she questioned if she is more connected to Lilith than Aruelia when she finds herself fighting to push down her own darkness. Trying to look at herself in the mirror after completing a job for Diego or witnessing death and feeling nothing, it constantly leaves her with anxious thoughts about her true nature.

There has to be more to her than the persistent struggle between good and evil within her mind.

"No one knows for sure about how she did it," Olympia says in a calm voice, bringing Rue back to the present moment. "Some prophecies state that only light magic can chase away shadow magic, because it was the origin of Lilith's power. Some say there is another light being still alive today, when some are convinced, it was a North Witch. Others think The Mother herself used the last of her magic to stop Lilith. It's one of the many mysteries of our world."

"And what do you think?" Rue asks, glancing at Olympia.

She opens her mouth to speak but hesitates. Olympia's green eyes meet hers and she smiles weakly. "You know what I think? I think this is enough history for one day. Come with me, I've been working on something for you."

She pulls Rue by the arm, linking it with her own, and tugs her towards the steps. As they walk up, Rue glances back at the tapestry, thinking to herself how humans fit into the history of the world.

Why were they sent to live on a useless, lifeless island, when the rest of the world thrived on the mainland?

What was so bad on the other side of the ocean?

And why did the blip in her gut sometimes remind her she longed to be there?

CHAPTER

THE door to Olympia's apartment opens with a creak. Inside Rue is greeted with an overwhelming floral smell, making her stop in the doorway. Her eyes race across the room in a frenzy, every empty surface is full of flowers. Every color, every variety. Her apartment has taken the shape of a flower field, and not in a good promised-to-stay-under-the-radar kind of way.

"Um… Care to explain whatever the hell this is?" Rue asks, arms gesturing around the chaos.

Olympia enters the apartment like this is a completely normal situation, making Rue question if she ingested some rancid potions in the last few hours to make her hallucinate the mess. The Mother herself must have thrown up into the room to produce this many blooms.

With the confidence of a high elf, Olympia walks swiftly through a handmade narrow path on the floor through the pots.

The leaning towers of plants, waiting to become an avalanche with a soft breeze, take up the rest of the space. They continue up to the table which is full of pot after pot of bright colors, soil from plants pouring out onto the kitchen floor. Buckets of dirt and gardening tools rest in every square inch of space.

"Oly, what the fuck?"

"Oh, language please," Olympia answers, waving her hands as she disappears behind a wall of vines and into the living room.

"You starting some sort of underground, black market, flower business or something? What's with all the blooms?"

She turns in a frazzled gaze, almost knocking over a pot of pink flora on a side table but catches it mid wobble. "Well, if you must know, I'm experimenting with something I think is going to be revolutionary in the field of natural medicine."

"Is it how long it takes to get spring allergies? Because I can confirm this amount does the trick. I've been standing here for two seconds and can already feel my eyes itching."

Olympia laughs. "No, Honey Bee, I've already proven that decades ago, and it's six minutes after being exposed to the allergen, remember that."

"I wouldn't dare to forget it." Rue's brows lower and she rubs her forehead with her fingers, letting out an exhausted sigh. "Now what's really going on?"

"I have a hunch."

"A hunch? All of this—" Rue lowers her voice and clears her throat. "All of this madness is because of a hunch?" She pinches the bridge of her nose. "Oly, if the wrong person sees this apartment, they will know you're not human! No one can grow this much without being fae and using magic in the soil. Not to mention, most of these I've never seen before adding to the fact that *you are fae!* You know more than most that we've been killed for a lot less."

Olympia squints up from the flowers she is clearing off the desk in the living room. Placing a ceramic pot on her hip she huffs, "If my research is correct, ingesting a specific mixture of petals can counteract a poisoning. Erasing all of it, or at least most of it, out of one's bloodstream. If it's achievable, think of the possibilities to help people. Chemical exposures. Eating unidentified foods out of desperation. Children getting into products they shouldn't."

Ingesting too much lipstick poison when trying to… get to know someone.

"So," she pauses to study the mess, "how did this all start?"

Olympia doesn't answer. She walks back into the kitchen, placing the pot from her hip on the countertop and squishing it into the already overflowing spot. Rue watches as she nudges all the plants closer together away from the edge, and starts petting some magenta, pom-pom looking flower.

"You need a minute alone?" Rue jokes. "Because I can come back." Olympia ignores her jab and mumbles something that sounds like mathematical formulas under her breath. "Oly! Are you even hearing me?"

Without so much as a glance, Olympia picks up the pot with the pom-pom flowers. They bob up and down on their vine-like stems that have been braided together, allowing the puffs of petals on the end to drop down similar to lilies of the valley. With closer inspection, Rue can see little pollen filled anthers extending out mixed into the petals. It's so dainty and beautiful. She has never seen anything like it, and growing up with Olympia that's saying something.

"This right here is an Arching Touch Me Not. I created the seeds from a dream I had the other night. Isn't it marvelous?"

This is not the first time Olympia has taken her magic too far and transformed her living space into a greenhouse. Her dreams, unlike Rue's, come to her with gifts, and ideas on ways to save humanity and fae alike. Her butterfly spirit leads her to new creations, which turns into experiments and random hypotheses about future species of flora. It's a revolving door of ideas and executions until she creates what she believes The Mother has sent her to figure out. She has been known to throw all logic of self-preservation out the window and fixate on a hypothesis until its complete.

"You made that… from a dream?" she responds, moving towards Olympia and the pom-poms. Her fingers trail over the skinny purple petals that make up the round shape. It feels like feathers under her touch.

Olympia grabs Rue's hand, holding it flat between her palms. "That's what Nymphs do, Honey Bee. You know that. Creating species from memories or my dreams is who I am. Experimenting with different soils and fertilizers until I get the right formula fills my soul with life. Why should I shy away from my gift?"

"Because it could be the reason they *kill* you!" she says, pain in her voice as she pulls her hand out of Olympia's grip. "You have to be more careful than this, especially right now with how things are going out there." Rue points out the window, which currently has a dark green vine trying to escape through a crack in the glass. "If one single person has suspicion and acts on it, the Marshals can just storm right in. Fae have no voice here. We have no say in how our punishments turn out. They hear fae and can only see us as monsters."

"Well, I'm not going to change the essence of who I am just to hide and cower in these four walls. This country, the Southlands, was created in the name of peace. A way for the humans to live and prosper without the threats that face them on the other side of that sea! My research is not a threat. Everything I am doing is to help."

"They don't care."

"In all my years, my research has done nothing but give humans more time. I have been down here for decades helping those who have been provided nothing. Meanwhile the humans hiding away up on that hill have taken, and taken, and taken. Laughing at their galas, and restaurants, and shopping plazas, while the other half of the city fight over bread, and shelter. Tell me, who are the real monsters? Because it certainly isn't me and my plants."

Rue tilts her head, staring into Olympia's green eyes. She is right, the Highers have always held all the cards when it comes to the structure of the Southlands. They hold out the invisible carrot for the Lowers to fight over, while they bet on who will come out on top. Empty promises of jobs, and healthcare, and security are what they preach repeatedly, yet nothing productive comes of it. If anything, it divides the two districts even further.

When Rue doesn't answer, Olympia continues, "Let them take me, I'd like to see them try. I'm almost six hundred years old for Gods' sake. They aren't worried about my old bag of bones."

Rue lets out a breathy huff and rubs her hand on her forehead. "Oly, they don't give a shit who you are, or how much you do for this community. They don't even care about this community. You are fae. They are not. That makes you a threat, end of story."

Olympia turns to look at her plants, running her finger over the edge of one almost as if to tell it everything will be okay. Her intense look fades into something on the verge of exhaustion. "Yes, well," she pauses. "When did you become the parent?"

"I'm not trying to tell you what to do," Rue says. "I'm trying to keep you around, so this community has at least one person looking out for them. They need you. I need you. And you growing a flower forest in your kitchen is just putting you at a higher risk. In the nicest way possible I am begging you to be subtle because this… this is not subtle."

Olympia, still not looking at Rue, says in a soft voice, "This is going to work. I know it will."

"I'm not saying it won't or that you need to quit your research, you just need to find a better way to go about it. You don't know who you can trust right now, the Organization is gaining momentum, and they aren't going to stop. I have a contact that helped me work out that the fae killings are connected, we don't know how exactly, but it's all starting to fall into place which is terrifying. It's incredible how much you care, it really is, but it's not going to matter if you're dead."

"That is a morbid way of looking at the world," Olympia says, face painted in worry.

Rue lowers her eyes to the ground, brushing her boot against a ceramic pot of yellow flowers. "Yeah, well that's the world we are forced to live in."

"Have I not taught you to look for hope? Search for the good? We can be the good."

"You taught me to listen to my gut, and my gut is very clearly screaming at me to see that this district is becoming hostile to our kind."

Olympia lets out a long breath and turns towards the living room, stepping over pots as she makes her way through the maze. With her back to Rue she calls out, "Well I didn't bring you up here to lecture me about things I'm already aware of. I have some new items for you. I think you'll like them."

Remembering why she came to the shop in the first place, Rue drops her bag from her shoulder and takes out the sample of poison from her fight with Blue Eyes. As her fingers grip the small vial, flashes of his ice cold stare come into view. His words. The dark tone of his voice when he knew he was about to take his last breath. The smell of coppery blood and fish from the bay fill her mind like she is back on the docks. The poison dripping from his mouth, as his dead eyes crumble her walls of confidence, leave goosebumps in their wake. Her hands start to tremble, frozen in a time loop of watching death take place.

"Aruelia!" Olympia yells, pulling her out of her spiral. "Hurry up now."

"Yes, Ma'am. Sorry."

Following Olympia's foot placements, Rue delicately steps around flowers and into the living room. She lifts a pot on the armrest of the couch and sits down, holding the plant in her lap. A sweet, citrusy smell coming from the orange petals under her chin welcomes her back into the present.

She looks around at the flower forest in front of her, wondering if the plants can be seen from the kitchen window, and makes a mental note to check from the outside after she leaves. She balances the plant in one arm and points her fingers at the window, letting out a long exhale through her mouth. Her hand sparkles as her white cloudy magic takes the breath with it to draw the curtains closed.

Better to be safe than sorry.

"That wasn't necessary. The plants need that sun, and I only have the one window," Olympia complains with her back still towards Rue, rummaging through her desk for something. She can feel Olympia rolling her eyes without needing to see it and lets out the tiniest of laughs.

Memories of being a kid and trying to sneak around Olympia flood Rue's mind, washing away any visions of death that were there before. Somehow, she was never able to get away with anything, convinced as a kid the woman had a second pair of eyes in the back of her head.

Rue's gaze wanders around the space, lingering at spots where memories hold a sacred place within her soul. The kitchen table where they would cook what food they had for their friends. The door to the tiny bathroom where Olympia used to measure Rue and Finny's heights as they grew. The fireplace that never worked properly, and how they would light candles to act as a fire, to keep them warm when the power would go out.

The two of them would cuddle on the couch, and Olympia would tell Rue stories of the mainland. She would point to the family crest that hung above the mantle, a golden stag with leaves hanging from its antlers, and explain that the vines and runes surrounding it protected the family's lineage as brave warriors of the forest. She would share her family's purpose to protect the peace of the woods. Rue would often wonder if her own family had a crest, and what her purpose was supposed to be.

"The gold of the stag represents generosity and wisdom, and the green that surrounds it shows the abundance we offer to the world. The vines tracing the border show we are strong and connected to the planet. This crest is yours too now, Honey Bee, you are my family just as much as those who

share my blood," she would say to her, braiding small pieces of Rue's hair while her little frame would sit in Olympia's lap.

The same symbol is now inked into Rue and Olympia's right shoulder.

She would tell Rue tales of her childhood growing up in the Eastlands and share stories of others throughout history. Tales of brave travelers, who would fight creatures in the forest. Tribes of mermaids living off the coast, hiding their cities from the rest of the population. Witches who guarded mysterious temples that held all the secrets of the world. Stories of love, and friendship, and hope.

An unconscious smile forms on Rue's lips. A rare warmth fills her lungs with the reminder that it wasn't all bad. Her life wasn't all darkness, there was light too, even if it was long gone. Rue can hold on to these memories. Keep them deep within herself and picture the joy she once had. The joy that was given because of Olympia.

"Aruelia!" Olympia yells. "Honestly? And you say I'm the daydreamer."

"What?" Rue snaps back to reality once again, almost dropping the pot in her hands.

"I asked what you had in your hand, in that bottle. Would you like to share? Or am I to guess?"

Her hand tightens around the bottle instinctively, pulling it up to her face. The mixture of ingredients Rue has been trying to deconstruct for weeks taunts her in the glass, swirling around in a pearlescent liquid.

"I need help breaking down this poison. I can't tell you where it came from, or why I have it. Just know that it's extremely toxic, and I need the results as soon as you can. I tried to decipher it myself, but my limited knowledge of Mainland plants has made it a bitch to figure out. I also don't have the same access to books and resources as you do without raising suspicion."

Olympia narrows her eyes at Rue in a very obvious I-don't-like-this-one-bit-but-I'll-help sort of way, taking the vial out of her hand and holding it up to the lamp light. "How far did you get in the formula?"

"All I was able to understand was traces of Spittlebug larvae, and Jimsom Weed. But there must be more to it, those two things alone wouldn't cause the effects this did."

Hesitantly, Olympia asks, "And what would those effects be?"

Rue looks to her, shaking her head the smallest bit, begging her with her eyes not to ask any more questions.

"This is information I need so I know what I'm looking at, was it used for life or for death?"

"Death." The word leaves Rue's lips like a forbidden whisper, and the sight of Blue Eyes plays over again in her mind.

"I have one more question, then I will shut my mouth, and we can move on to the new items I have for you."

"Okay."

"Was this intended to be given to you?"

His blue eyes blind her in the alley. She didn't see the capsule. She could have stopped it. Could have asked more questions. The pop of the capsule in between his teeth. Life drains from his eyes. His soul sinks down to the void. Foam drips down his chin and onto his shirt.

"No, it was used as self-harm."

"Oh, Aruelia, what have you gotten yourself into?" Olympia's deep voice echoes in her mind, attempting to comfort her thoughts. "Are you okay? Was it a friend of yours?"

"I'm okay. I didn't know them. I just need to know where it comes from so I can figure out how this person got their hands on it." Olympia looks at her like she doesn't believe a word she just said. "I'm fine. Really, I am," she lies.

"I'll see what I can do. I can already tell it's not synthetic, this is from real flora and fauna, so it wasn't created in the Southlands."

"That's what I figured too."

When Olympia doesn't answer, Rue asks, "You said you had something for me?"

Olympia holds up the vial one last time before placing it in the front pocket of her corduroy jumper. She brushes off her hands as if the ingredients linger on her skin. With a light tone that doesn't match their depressing conversation she asks, "Right, do you have room in your bag for a few explosives?" Their eyes meet and Olympia gives Rue a casual look, like that question is indeed a normal one.

Rue almost falls off the chair.

"Explosives? What do I need explosives for?"

Turning back to her unorganized desk, Olympia shuffles through drawers of miscellaneous containers. "Honey Bee, you said it yourself, it's not safe out there. I kept thinking about you defending yourself after our last visit and since you won't actually tell me what you do for a living, I had to guess on what you would need," she says, extending her hands out, cupping three tiny blush compacts.

"Exploding makeup?" Rue says with a smirk. "I love it. Pairs perfectly with my poisonous lipstick." She places the pot on the ground in front of her, then reaches out a hand, grabbing the compacts with excitement. She readjusts on the armrest and goes to open the small round container.

"STOP!" Olympia yells, launching herself towards Rue, grabbing the compact out of her hands. "You open this and tiny shards of glass explode into the room."

"It does what?"

Olympia takes one of the compacts and turns it to its side. "This button right here, if pressed, shards of glass and thorns so small they look like sparkles, will puff into the air. With your magic, I believe you can swirl this around to create an explosive device to cut into someone at a micro level, essentially shredding their skin."

Rue's eyes go wide as she takes the compacts from Olympia and gently (very gently) places them into her bag, wrapping an extra scarf around them for good measure.

"Wait, won't that hurt me too, if I use it?"

"Not if you trust your power. You decide where your wind blows, not the other way around. You just need to believe in your ability."

"I have no proper training!"

"You'll know when it's time. When you're ready. Trust your gut, remember." Olympia chuckles and turns back towards the open drawer of her desk. Bottles clink together as she moves them from side to side. Rue's eyes drop to her bag, nodding in agreement as if tricking herself into believing the words from Olympia's mouth.

She could do that. Her power is her own. The humans she would potentially use this against were in fact just that, human. Other than their fists, knives, and other blunt objects, there wasn't much they could do to counteract her magic. Yes, she could do it. She could use it, control it.

Rue rolls her eyes at herself for having to mentally prepare for a fight that may or may not happen. What a fucking coward. She would have made fun of another Smoke Runner for second guessing their abilities.

That's what gets you killed. A split second decision can cost you everything. And here she is, her first thought is that she isn't good enough to have a weapon like this. Annoyance rushes over her. Being in this part of town always makes her forget who she is now. It makes her weak, and warm, and fuzzy. Makes her remember too much of her life before the Smoke Runners.

"Did you say there were more than just these?" she barks, in a tone she wishes she can take back the second it leaves her lips.

Fuck, you are not Ghost right now, you are Rue. You are her Honey Bee. Be Rue.

"Sorry Oly, I just… I need to go soon," she says, rubbing a hand along her arm.

"Got to get back to that mysterious life. And here I was hoping we could share a meal together before you go," Olympia says searching through her desk. "I swore I put those blasted things in here. Where are—" She opens the bottom drawer. "Here! I knew I put them in here!"

Rue rolls her eyes. "Now I know where I get my organization skills from."

Olympia turns to face Rue, holding a drawstring, burlap pouch in her hands. "Oh, you. I knew exactly where it was." She walks over to her, cupping her hands and dumping the pouches contents out into it. Three metal tins, and four glass bottles fall into her hands.

"Are any of these going to explode?" Rue asks, wincing and looking away dramatically.

"No, of course not. These are poisons," she says pointing to the glass bottles. "Not able to be detected by human made machines. Use it sparingly. One of these vials could poison a dozen people or so. I added the spray nozzle so it would look like perfume."

"And what are these tins?"

"These are very special, prototypes really, of something I've been working on." Olympia takes one out of Rue's hand and opens it. A milky, cream colored paste is packed into the tin. The smell of mint fills her nose and burns a little. "Take a small bit and rub this on any wounds you might have out there. If you see an innocent hurt, this can cure almost any burn or cut."

"How big of a cut are we talking? Like a knife wound or paper cut?"

"If you can control the bleeding, and the person is still conscious, this will definitely cure a knife wound."

"Wow." Rue starts to laugh. "These all look so innocent but could be deadly in the wrong hands. And you trust me with all of this?"

"I made them specifically for you. My sly little fox, innocent until she isn't." Olympia winks at Rue.

"How did you come up with them, more dreams?"

Olympia grabs one of the glass perfume bottles and lifts it into the light. "Well, these are extracts from the roots of a Water Hemlock plant. They are naturally infused with a chemical called cicutoxin. It will have severe effects. Convulsions. Nausea. Death if the immune system isn't strong enough."

"And what if it is strong enough? Can someone survive this?"

"That's the best part! The poor soul who is misted with this, will have transient global amnesia, which means—"

"They won't remember?" Rue finishes her sentence. "Oly, that's incredible!"

"Just make sure you're pointing the vial in the right direction, or it could be you, and I wouldn't be able to live with myself."

"I know, I know," Rue says, rushing to put the items in her bag with the other compacts. "What is the glitter made of?"

"Glitter?"

"Yeah, the exploding glitter."

"Well, first of all it's not glitter, it's made of glass and thorns. The glass shards are just from the dump, and the thorns come from a new species of rose that I invented. I call it Aruelious Nightshade Rose. The flowers themselves are perfectly harmless, and breathtaking." She stops to look around the room, reaching down by the fireplace to grab a bushy, rose plant. "Ahh, here she is." The largest rose Rue has ever seen pop up out of deep green leaves.

Olympia continues, "The thorns are made of nightshade, which causes a lasting poisonous effect on those who touch them. I thought of you when I created them. The fiery red of the petals made me think of your lovely auburn hair. Hence the name *Aruelious* Nightshade. Oh, isn't it the most magnificent thing you've ever seen? It's perfect in every way, beautifully dangerous."

"You replaced me with a plant… you need to get out more," Rue jokes. "Please tell me you don't talk to it when no one is around. I get that it's your favorite, but do you really have to look at it like it's your own child?"

Olympia laughs as she pets the petals of the rose, placing the plant back down onto the only empty spot on the wood floor. "It's not my favorite, I don't have a favorite."

"Lies! You're a forest nymph, there is no way you don't have a favorite flower. Come on."

"I don't," she shrugs. "It would be rude to all the other species."

"Oh Gods," Rue says, rolling her eyes. "I'll leave you to romance your plants." She stands to leave, pulling her bag over one shoulder. "Thanks for the new equipment. I really appreciate it, Oly. I don't know what I would do without you," she admits, wishing she kept that last bit to herself.

No weaknesses. Weaknesses will kill you.

"I just want to be a part of your life, Honey Bee. If that means keeping you safe in the form of weapons, I'll do it. I wish I knew more but knowing you can protect yourself is enough."

Olympia moves close to Rue, holding out her arms to pull her into an embrace. The smell of jasmine and vanilla circle her nose and comfort Rue. The two hug for what feels like a century, Olympia not letting go of her grasp around Rue.

"Oly, I really need to go," Rue says with her head mushed into Olympia's neck, her Afro tickling her cheek.

"One more second. I don't know when I'll see you next, and my plants don't hug back."

The two giggle before letting go of each other. Olympia goes to pull a loose hair away from Rue's face when her demeanor changes, her hand covers her mouth.

"Aurelia, who did that to you?" Concern washes over her features as she lightly runs her thumb over the marks on the side of Rue's neck.

The bruises!

It slipped Rue's mind. She didn't cover up all her bruises from her and Diego's fight last night because she figured her hair, and hooded sweatshirt would cover enough.

Fuck! So stupid!

"It's nothing, I just got into a fight with this guy. It's fine. I'm fine," she lies, moving her own hand over the marks to cover them. She pulls her hood that has fallen back up. Her face stays indifferent for the sake of Olympia's stress level.

"Did a boyfriend do this?"

"A boyfriend? No, he didn't mean it. It was nothing honestly, I promise. It was a misunderstanding, I'm fine."

Rue looks at her fingers, running a thumb over her nail.

"I hope I taught you enough to know your worth. You don't deserve to be treated with this much disrespect," Olympia says in a harsh tone.

"It was nothing, okay! Can we leave it alone? Gods," Rue demands, getting angrier more at herself for being careless, than Olympia for prying.

"It's not nothing. That's not how you treat someone you care about. You deserve better. You deserve a life of love and safety."

"Love and safety? Have you seen the world we live in? What about dying of starvation, and being out on the streets tells you I can have love and safety? This place, this district is not a fairy tale."

"Well why can't we try and make it one?"

Rue's blood starts to boil, how can she not realize how cruel the world is?

"Because fairy tales aren't real. This isn't one of the stories you would tell me as a kid. This is our real, pathetic life. Fairy tales are believed by people who need to escape their terrible circumstances. I see mine very clearly.

"There is no happily ever after. There is never going to be knights in shining armor, whisking me away to live in their castles. It's just not real. Do you know what is real? Death? Death is the only thing I can believe in. Death is the only thing I know is coming for me. For all of us.

"Which is why I came here in the first place, to get your help with this poison formula, so we can escape death for a little while longer. And to make sure you're being careful." Rue motions her hands around the apartment. "This needs to stop, you are going to be killed for trying to help the same people who will turn you in to the marshals in a heartbeat. For once in your life, I need you to be selfish and look out for you above anyone else."

"Well, I choose to believe in the good. To trust my community, and my friends. Let's not forget that those people out there raised you too. They deserve your trust."

Rue shakes her head and runs a hand down her forehead. "Well, that's what makes us different then. You choose trust. I choose reality."

"I hope you're wrong."

Rue hesitates before answering, "I do too."

Before Olympia can respond, Rue is halfway out the door. Her heart races from being so reckless in her actions. Coming here in the first place is probably a mistake. Talking to Finny in the middle of the street, mistake. Asking Olympia to get more involved with this fucking poison and letting her see her bruises, the biggest mistake she could possibly make.

"Damn it," she says under her breath as she leaves Moon Child, swinging the door open with so much force the corner of the glass cracks. She promises to distance herself from this part of the borough for a while, needing things to calm down. *She* needs to calm down.

CHAPTER

IN Rue's opinion, The Lucky Clover Casino is the ugliest building in all of the High District. Not in the typical way a building could be ugly, no, there aren't cracks and exposed pipes. Ugly in the sense it hides its true nature from the rest of the world. From the outside, the glitzy, over the top, jewel encrusted building looks like the fanciest place a person could go. A place you felt rich just by walking in. It has the aura to make you feel more important than you actually are.

But, behind those doors, is a group of humans who are willing to do anything to see you fail. They will happily take your money, your car, your house, even your partner if they feel like they deserve it more than you. People leave and don't even realize the life has been sucked out of them. They have been swindled and lined up to slaughter one by one as if by fate.

Being in the line of business she is in; Rue understands the *practices* of The Lucky Clover. Card counting by undercover employees. Machines that are set to never win the jackpot, no matter how many times a person tries. Beautiful men and women hired by The Clover just to talk idiots into spending more money. Honesty is left at the door, along with the dignity of its patrons.

Lucky Clover is run by the Finnegan family. Also known in crime circles as the Fatal Finnegans, because of their reputation of killing people they no longer need. Rumor has it, they gave that real winner of a nickname to themselves, which always gives Rue second hand embarrassment every time she thinks about it. Nothing like giving yourself a nickname to try and prove you can fit in with the big shots.

The head of the beast is named Connor Finnegan. He is a larger than life, cigar smoking, wannabe celebrity of sorts. Taking over for his father after he suffered a brutal death at the hands of Diego's men a few years back. The newspapers called it a heart attack, which is technically true considering they stabbed him in the heart multiple times.

Under Connor are his brothers, the Goons as Rue likes to call them, sharing ten brain cells between the four of them. They each married into families with multiple siblings, who were recruited by force to join the ranks. The pyramid flows down from there. A group of men and women who are forced into this life is not what she would call a successful way to run a syndicate.

Their employee solstice party must be a blast.

Her heels click on the sidewalk with each step. She has been staking out the casino for weeks now, but tonight is the first night she is going in, undercover. Before this, the most she has done in person is go into the air ducts to survey the entrances and exits and hide supplies in inconspicuous places. Any good

Rogue should know at least three ways to get out of any given situation, Rue has five for this casino.

She adjusts the skirt of her Lucky Clover uniform, which is half way up her thighs, as she walks up to the employee entrance.

Bumping into a group of men leaving for the night, she squeaks in a voice that's not her own, "Oops! Oh my Gods, I'm so sorry!" She runs her hand up the chest of one of the men pretending to steady herself.

"That's all right, baby girl. If you wanted to get closer to me all you had to do was ask," the man smirks in a deep voice, leaning over the top of Rue causing her to stand within inches of him. She looks up at him through doe eyes and smiles.

Another one of the men leans in too, resting his elbow up on the shoulder of the man Rue ran into. "Now how have I never seen a pretty thing like you around here before?"

"Oh, I just started," she says, biting her bottom lip.

"When do you get off, want the five of us to show you a good time? Welcome you properly."

Rue lazily runs a finger down the part of her breast exposed from her strategically unbuttoned dress shirt. Just enough undone to still look somewhat professional yet give her easy access to her best weapon against neanderthals.

With a purr she asks, "All five of you?"

"You're into that aren't you, sweetheart? I bet you're a dirty girl," one of the men growls, walking up behind her to close her in.

"You have no idea," she says as seductively as she can, ignoring the sudden urge to throat punch at least three of them.

Alarm bells start to go off in her mind, reminding her that this needs to come to a close, so she can get into the building. She can feel the air around her start to shift into something hot, and predatory. The fine line of flirting and something more sinister is about to be crossed, and she needs to reel back control of the situation.

She picks up on one of the men's heart rates. His is much louder and faster than the others, which indicates to her his nerves have taken over. She can work with nerves.

She turns to him, brushes her hand up his torso, and stands on her tiptoes. Her lips hover over his ear and she whispers loud enough for the others to hear, "I get off at three. You can have me then if you want." Pushing him away with one final wink. "See you later boys."

In the glow of the building lights, Rue saunters into the casino, laughing to herself when she hears the whistles and explicit words come from behind her. She lifts her hand to look at the employee badge she just swiped from the poor fucker she initially ran into. The name Thoran Mezari stamped into the card makes her giggle.

Sweet, sweet Thoran. I hope you get in trouble for this, you absolute imbecile.

At the door, she buzzes herself in using the badge. She messes with her black wig, pretending to fix her bangs while she walks past the security desk. The Finnegans like to pretend they have the best of the best when it comes to security, but in reality, Rue wouldn't trust them to keep track of a roll of toilet paper, let alone a casino and it's staff.

Walking through the employee break room, Rue dumps the badge next to an overflowing trash can. The smell in here would make anyone with common sense quit on the spot, a horrid mix of dirty money, sweat, and cheap perfume. The fact that they can keep anyone employed is a mystery she will never understand.

She passes a table of twenty somethings snorting white powder off a woman's ass, fist bumping as they take turns. In another corner of the room is an STD soaked couch with two women going down on some guy with a mohawk. She can see the door to the main hall, and casually sprints to the exit. On her very graceful, very inconspicuous dash to leave, she clocks an ad for a roommate hanging on a bulletin board.

MALE (35) LOOKING FOR ROOMMATE
(FEMALE, AGE 18-22)
MUST BE OPEN TO STUDIO LIVING
MUST BE SINGLE
MUST BE ABLE TO COOK
MUST PAY HALF OF EVERYTHING
NO PETS

The class of the High District everyone.

It is at this exact moment Rue realizes she's getting a headache from rolling her eyes so much. This place is trash, Diego should have had a newbie do this intel run. These morons don't even realize a random woman just walked in with no issues.

Rue pushes through the door to the main hall like she has done it a thousand times. She grabs an empty black tray as she weaves in and out of the crowd, pretending to pick up empty glasses from patrons.

This main floor is so much louder than she anticipated, with sounds elevated because of her fae hearing. She closes her eyes and takes a deep breath in, calming her mind, reminding herself to focus.

The room is full of green and gold tables for card games, blinking slot machines, and giant crystal chandeliers that are so bright, Rue can't look directly at them. There are large wooden bars along the sides of the space that feel like they go on for miles.

The over the top feel doesn't end there. Women are hanging from ropes on the ceiling, doing aerial acts in bedazzled lingerie. Rue wants to laugh at the dramatics, or maybe puke from the fact that people pay real coins to be here, while her community is sick and suffering.

Time to focus. Step one is to count all security members, and see which areas are heavily guarded on the upper floors. If Rue's hunch is correct, the group is most likely meeting upstairs in one of the private suits. The less attention they attract the better. Even with all her recon, Rue was still unable to locate a private exit or entrance to this building. There are only the double doors for patrons, and the back door for employees. There must be something she isn't seeing.

On her initial scan of the room, Rue already knew this place was crawling with people she has personally fucked over. A man she conned into giving her inside information on his former company sat playing poker. Playing craps was a pair of brothers Rue once had to manipulate into giving her a safe combination of their boss. Threatening to kill their mother if they didn't comply. Over on the roulette table, sat the widow of a man she once seduced into admitting he was stealing from his clients, one of them being Diego himself.

Rue's eyes stop when she sees a group of men playing blackjack together. Business partners, who were contracted to take over all Metus owned buildings when Manny died.

Diego didn't approve of that idea, so he sent Rue to give them what they wanted in exchange for the rights to the properties.

"Whatever they want, Ghost. Your job is to do anything they ask."

Rue, trusting Diego like the idiot she is, agreed to the job. Little did she know at the time, what they wanted wasn't a *what* at all. It was a *who*. It was her.

Her body.

Diego knowingly sent her into a den of starving lions, ordering her to stay until they were done feasting.

That night still plays in her mind sometimes. Three, out of shape, wrinkling men, who demanded they all take turns getting off on her in whatever way they pleased. Calling her *whore*, and their *little dirty thing*. Using her like an object. After hours of lying like a dead body, cold and smelling like cigars and cum, her rage was overflowing into her veins. She held her composure, not for the sake of the job or for Diego, but for the fact that she needed to stay whole. Not let the words or actions of men break her.

She went home that night to find Diego at her apartment, ready to burn down the world. He pleaded with her that he didn't know what their intentions were until it was too late. He offered to kill them for her, but she insisted she was okay. The lie on her breath came easily, like all the other times her target's *intentions* were too far.

But don't worry, her sweet revenge came when a mysterious woman (looking nothing like Rue) snuck the men a potion that gave them symptoms of genital herpes, so severe they had to take off a layer of skin around the affected area. Funny how things work out.

The tray Rue is holding starts to wobble as she blinks back to reality. She forces back down the bile that is rising in her throat because of those men. She takes another deep breath, sinking the memory into the abyss.

We are here for a job. A simple job that doesn't involve talking to others. This is easy. This is what we are trained to do.

Rue's eyes survey around once more, and zeros in on a waitress walking in her direction with a full tray of champagne. Rue plasters a huge smile on her face, walks right up to her, and says in her perkiest voice, "There you are, the boss wants you. Like now!"

"James?" the girl asks in a mousy voice, her face pales.

"Yeah, he seemed pretty pissed. I would go quick."

"Shit, did he say why?"

"No. Sorry girl. Do you want me to take your tray for you? Where is it headed?" Rue asks, taking the tray of glasses from the girl's hands and replacing it with her empty one.

"Thanks. Over to table seven," she says, looking around frantically. Rue starts to walk away when she hears the girl call out to her, asking her name.

"Luna!" Rue says with her back still turned the opposite direction.

The steps to the second floor are close, she needs to move if this is going to work. The last thing she needs is the waitress coming to look for her after James did not in fact need her. She spots a bartender and moves swiftly towards her through the crowd.

"Hey, you got any champagne, someone wants a whole bottle?" she yells to her, clearly overwhelmed.

"Why aren't you using the back stash?" she questions, face scrunching up in annoyance.

Great question, why wasn't she using the back stash? "They were out, James said you might have some."

"Fine, here," she says, grabbing a bottle out of a mini fridge under the bar.

"Thanks, you're a lifesaver." Rue winks at the girl, hoping a friendly bond between gal pals will calm her icy stare. It doesn't.

"Whatever, just make sure you guys stock your own shit, stop using ours."

Rue nods and turns on her heels towards the steps. As quickly as she can, she climbs to the second floor, holding the tray next to her head to cover her face from the guests below. The black wig may be covering her red hair, but there is little she could do to hide her face, freckles, and golden eyes.

At the top, Rue is greeted by a large bodyguard with a no-bullshit facial expression. She shows off her biggest and brightest smile yet and tries to walk past him.

His hand comes out in front of her. Letting out a low laugh he asks, "And what the fuck are you doing? Waitstaff stay down on the main floor."

Panic wants to take over, but she holds it off. After a beat Rue looks up into his dark eyes, batting hers ever so subtly. "I know, but I was told to come up and bring this to one of the private rooms right away. So can I just—"

He stands in front of her as she tries to maneuver around. Rue glances at his name tag reading **JOE: SECURITY (SECOND SECTOR)** before smiling at him again, this time doing her best frazzled look.

"Joe, I really need to get past. I was told this was for an important group. I don't want to get in trouble. They said you'd know which room I need to go to."

"Who told you to come up here?" he asks, lifting his chin.

"James," she says with confidence.

"Figures. Fucking douche bag never follows the rules. And he has you come up here to take the fall."

"I know he's been up my ass all day," Rue says, shaking her head and covering a smirk from thoroughly throwing James under the bus tonight.

Joe looks down the hallway he is standing in front of. "Go ahead, babe. I won't tell, but next time have him come talk to me directly. Only one group here tonight, they're back in the last room, just go down the hall and make a left." He points towards the empty hall, but before Rue can pass, he grabs her by the arm lightly. "Between you and me, do your best not to linger in the room, they aren't the friendliest group."

"Joe, I could kiss you right now! Thanks for saving my ass," she whispers before heading down the corridor, thanking James in her head for being the worst manager a girl could ask for.

She is alone in the hallway now, only accompanied by strips of green lights at her feet along the edge of the wall. The carpet thankfully muffles her heeled footsteps so she can move about undetected. She turns a corner and can see the women's bathroom sign to the right. The golden door is silent as she opens it, walking into the blinding white light within.

Without saying a word, Rue lowers her head towards the floor, looking for people in the stalls. Lucky for her, the room is empty.

She dumps the drinks and bottle into the trash can, covers it with paper towels, and places the tray behind it. Under the cabinet of the sink, Rue pulls out a black canvas bag she hid behind some paper supplies on one of her recon missions. She races to the last stall, locking herself in.

Opening the drawstring, she pulls out its contents. Inside is her Smoke Runner uniform designed specifically for her and her skill set, so she can turn into Ghost. A suit made of lightweight material, great for climbing and squeezing in and out of places falls towards the floor in her hands. Black to blend into the shadows. A hood to cover her identity. The front of her shirt comes up to tie around her face like a mask.

After the shit show that was the President's Gala, Rue swore to herself she would never sneak around in a dress again.

Her boots fall to the floor, as does her daggers, making a piercing sound that echoes around the bathroom.

"Shit," she calls out in a whisper.

Within minutes, Rue has her new outfit on, and is tying up her boots when she hears the door to the bathroom open, and giggling women walk in. Their heels click against the marble tile.

Rue lifts her hood up, places her knives in their holsters, and picks up her belongings without making a sound. She perches herself on the toilet seat and prays that she doesn't have to kill anyone tonight. Her rising adrenaline does the opposite of bringing her stress, she uses it as fuel to focus on her job and getting herself out of this situation.

Through the crack in the door, Rue can see two women. One in a long, gold, beaded gown, the other in a short, white, silk cocktail dress. The two talk as they touch up their makeup in the mirror.

"Did you see the size of that man's dick? I almost let out a laugh," gold dress says.

"Ew, I know. We do not get paid enough to pretend that it's good. This job fucking sucks," laughs white dress.

"At least one of the guys was hot, too bad all he wanted was for me to piss on him."

"Gross no he didn't, really?" white dress chokes, stopping mid swipe of her lipstick.

"Yeah, the rich are fucking freaks."

Rue has to agree, although to each their own. What the hell was happening up on the second floor?

"Ugh, today has been the worst. I can't wait to get home and shower. My landlord promised the water would be back on by midnight. He better not be lying again," gold dress comments with a sigh.

"It's still not working? Does he know who you work for? Have Connor do something about it."

"Connor says I'm on my own, he's not my protector."

"No, he just wants the money we bring in. Sorry, you can use mine. It's at least working. I can't guarantee it's hot though."

Rue looks to her feet as the two women continue talking about their situation. Lowers. They're Lowers like her. Working for a powerful man, selling themselves for money they won't ever see.

"Did you see how shifty that guy was, walking into that back room?" gold dress asks her friend. "I practically popped my tits out in front of him, and he just looked away like I was disgusting. I paid too much money for these, for them to be ignored."

"Your tits are great, babe. His loss. He probably couldn't afford you anyway, did you see what he was wearing? A ratty old black sweatshirt. What a punk."

This perks Rue's interest. Black sweatshirt? No, they can't be that stupid. They weren't even trying to hide their identities. Rue's gut feeling jumps around in her stomach attacking her nerves. They are either very foolish, or very capable of tying up loose ends.

Rue needs to leave this bathroom immediately, but to do that with the least amount of blood on her hands means waiting for these two to leave. In a perfect world they will leave on their own without her being noticed, but Gods know how long that will take.

She looks down at her dagger resting in its sheath on her belt loop. She could scare them, but they might scream, causing attention she doesn't have the luxury to attract tonight. Maybe she could climb under the stalls and make her way towards the door? Although half way under the door wouldn't be a superb position to get caught in.

Fuck!

What would Diego want her to do?

Rue closes her eyes and leans her head towards the ceiling. She wishes she didn't know the answer, but unfortunately, she knows exactly what he would say. Eliminate any threat, innocent or not. Rue knows how to do it too. It is an easy maneuver. A quick slice across the neck, cutting into the artery supplying blood to the brain. She can have both women down in less than ten seconds.

She can do this. She has to do this, it's for a greater purpose. She hears Diego's voice in her head, *"There are always casualties in war, but we will not be one of them."*

She takes a silent breath in, calming her mind of the chaos within it. This isn't the first time she has killed someone, nor will it be her last, but for some reason her body is fighting the urge to move. She cannot physically reach for her knife and leave this stall.

These women are innocent. They are simply doing their job and came into this bathroom to have a moment to themselves. They are doing what they need to do to survive, just like Rue. And for that they shouldn't be punished. They may serve a different devil, but they are living the same life. Selling their souls to see another day.

Minutes go by that feel like centuries. The two women continue talking about meaningless things while Rue's legs go numb from squatting on the toilet seat. She is running out of time, so many loose ends running through her mind. Thoran's badge, James the manager, Joe at the top of the steps, all careless mistakes she's made in the name of getting to this point. And where did it get her? Locked in a bathroom stall waiting it out to save the lives of two paid prostitutes.

Weak. That is what Diego would call her if he could see her now. A weak child, who would rather get caught than hurt someone. A weak child, who doesn't deserve to call herself a Smoke Runner. Someone who doesn't deserve the name Ghost, if she can't simply kill and keep going in the shadows.

Fuck!

She can't afford to mess this up. Finding out who these assholes are is her only option, and she can't let anything, or anyone, get in her way.

She needs to be Ghost. She has to, it's the only way.

Be Ghost. Be Ghost. Be Ghost!

What else is she going to do? She is out of options really, backed into an inevitable corner, and has to do what she has to do.

She looks to her right at her dagger, pulling it out without a whisper of a noise. She says a silent prayer to the Gods to understand her situation but knows it will fall on deaf ears. The Gods are not on her side, and they never will be. She is on her own. This is her decision, and she must live with the consequences, no matter how dark. This will just be another tally mark on her ticket to the void.

The knife in her hand is burning a hole in her palm. This will never be easy, but she is ready. With an exhale, she takes a step off the toilet, placing a silent boot on the tile. Then the other. Holding her breath, she looks to the lock and moves her fingers to pull it open.

She peeks through the crack in the door, looking for a position to make this go quick, and slowly moves the stall door open an inch. Rue's eyes close with one more pep talk to herself before going further. She looks out at her targets, allowing the emotions to drain from her vision.

I am Ghost.

One more task.

"What the fuck are you doing in here?" a voice comes from beyond the door, familiar yet she can't place it. Rue stills, not daring to breathe. Did they mean her? There is no way any of them can see her from here. She closes the stall door before anyone notices her and waits to hear more. Maybe the Gods were on her side after all.

"You have paying customers waiting for you bitches, get your ass out here," he demands.

"Sorry, Connor Baby. We were just freshening up," gold dress says, looking into the mirror, unfazed by his harsh tone.

Connor? As in Connor Finnegan?

"I don't give a shit what you are doing. If I have to leave my own meetings to come find you worthless pieces of shit one more time, it will be the last day you work in this city. Do I make myself clear?" he spits, voice raspy and harsh. He doesn't wait for them to respond, before rushing in. A blur dressed in a black sweatshirt pulls them by their forearms, causing them to let out small whimpers from the jarring movement.

The hairs on Rue's body stand. Connor is here. Is he part of this? Is this all because of him? Her gut is screaming at her to find where they are meeting. She needs to know more. His voice makes this so much more real, an actual lead. Not a maybe, a definitely. This is important. She is meant to be here; she is meant to be the one to find these answers. She can feel it in her bones.

Her adrenaline returns in full force when she finds herself in the silence once more. Alone, in a bathroom, on the second floor of Lucky Clover, in the same building as the people responsible for trying to kill her. The scum responsible for so many kidnappings and deaths.

The heaviness of that reality pulls her down like a sinking ship. So much is riding on this information. It's up to her now. She knows she has to continue on. She is no longer a scared child, she is Ghost.

Rue opens the stall door to the bathroom, discarding her uniform and wig in the cabinet under the sink. Before rushing out, she ties her mask around her mouth and stares at her reflection in the mirror. Golden eyes sparkle in the light back at her, but no emotions show in them. Good. She is ready.

She readjusts her sheath, doing a once over of her outfit before striding to the golden door.

This is a vulnerable step she must take. She pokes her head out, one hand resting on the knife at her hip. With the push of the door, she slides into the hallway, planting herself against the wall. She coaxes the door closed with her left hand, as to not make a sound.

The end of the hallway is towards her right, and it seems to go on for a few more private rooms, then past an elevator, and a storage room before reaching the double doors on the back wall. After assessing the situation and finding blind spots to land where no one can see her, she moves towards her target.

Rue switches from one side of the hall to the other, zig zagging past doors, and plants, and random pieces of furniture she uses as cover. Luckily the hall is still deserted, making it easier for her to breathe the further she descends into it.

She is about to pass the elevator when she hears a sharp ding of certain death. As white light pours into the dark hall, she ducks into a doorway shielding her from the sight of the person exiting. A waiter by the look of their uniform, backs up into the center of the space, pulling a metal cart. It clinks as it's pushed towards the back room, drink glasses and plates of food hitting each other with every step. The sound echoes down the corridor.

Rue's hands start to tingle with anticipation. This is her chance. If this works (and Rue doesn't die) she might just admit to Olympia that the universe does always work out when you need it to.

With a deep breath in, she makes her move. She follows the waiter towards the double doors, using the sound of the cart to muffle her presence.

When the entrance to the back room opens, she gets a quick glance in before plastering herself against the wall on the outside. The doors close slowly, seeming to have some sort of soft close mechanism, which is perfect for what she needs to do. Now it's time to wait and pray no one else pops into the hallway.

When the server emerges moments later, Rue pulls her fingers towards the door, holding her dagger in the other hand. A soft breath out with her magic leaves the door open longer than normal, just a few extra seconds to slide in as it closes.

Before she has time for her heart to settle, she stops with the realization this might be a mistake.

THANKFULLY the room is dark, but that is where her luck ends.

Rue crouches down behind a half wall leading into the room, which looks like it's used for conferences. There is a long table in the middle, with green velvet chairs around it. She can see the table of food that has been stocked by the waiter against the wall.

At first glance, the room looks empty, but there is a light coming from somewhere she can't see, and muffled voices she picks up. She can't make out what any of them are saying in her current position and will most likely expose herself if she moves deeper into the room. Ahead of her is a wall of windows looking out onto the High District.

Rue sees the glow of the two moons being suffocated by the clouds of smog in the air. Lucky for her, this will keep her movements in the dark. If she can make her way to the other side of the conference table, and stay below eye sight, she might be able to see what's behind the wall blocking her view. But that is a serious *if*.

With a quick close of her eyes, Rue focuses on her surroundings. The smell of the carpet cleaner. The popping of the bubbles in the champagne on the table. The low pitch of the people talking. The thumping of their heartbeats. Six… no seven different rhythms. There are seven others in this room. Seven. She can take seven humans if she wants to.

Her next move will put her at risk. The unknowns of the space are something she didn't plan for, if you could call this a plan. It is more like a suicide mission, going in alone is never her first choice. In all her recon missions she has never once had access to the individual rooms on this floor, so this is a mistake if she's ever made one. But Olympia's voice rings in her ears about trusting her gut. Not that she would approve of this plan, but you need to get your motivation from somewhere.

Fuck it!

Without lifting herself up too much, Rue looks past the half wall. Shadows dance in the glow of a soft light still out of view. She moves towards the front window, using the desk chairs as cover. With her back towards the city outside, she silently shifts her position to get a better look.

The back of the space is deeper than she expected and connects to an adjacent room. The storage room she saw in the hallway, maybe. The light is coming from there, trickling out into the dark conference room.

Rue rounds the far corner of the table, assessing her path to the other room. Her only spots of defense are a faux palm plant, and a smaller side table in the corner. Not much to go with, but she's been in worse situations. She tugs her hood lower over her face, and sneaks towards the door frame.

A shadow pops into view, and walks into the darkened room, causing Rue to fall backwards and crawl under the table. She pushes herself in between two chairs and hugs her knees to make herself as little as possible. The tight grip of her hands threatens to release with the adrenaline pumping through her veins. She lets out a silent breath and a prayer to the Gods she was quick enough not to be seen.

She can hear the breathing of the person as they move to the food cart. It's unusual, not like any sound she recognizes. Motorized somehow, with a low and high pitch tone all at the same time. There is something unnatural about it.

The sound of glass crashing to the floor interrupts her thinking. Rue's body goes still. She may be camouflaged by the dark, but she is far from invisible. One long look at the black blob by the chairs and her cover is blown. Instinctively her shaking hand moves to the handle of her dagger, ready to fight for her life.

"What are you doing?" a voice calls from the other room. The sound of it is robotic and monotone, both masculine and feminine at the same time, similar to the breathing pattern of the first intruder.

Rue peeks through the chair legs to get a better look at the person speaking. They are wearing a mask, of course. That's it! That is why they all sound the same. That is why they could never be identified by survivors. Masks, with voice modifiers. Genius, even if Rue doesn't want to admit it.

"What? I can't see anything with this bullshit on my face and its fucking dark in here," says the person at the cart.

"Get back in here, we're waiting on your ass to get our assignments."

The person at the cart lets out an audible sigh, which echoes in the space thanks to the modifier. Rue can hear them wrestle around with the food for a moment longer before walking back into the illuminated side room, mumbling to themselves about *how the fuck* they got themselves into this situation.

Interesting.

Once she knows the coast is clear, she quietly steps towards the other room, slipping in behind the plant.

Deep breath in.

She keeps inching her way towards the voices against the open wall, wedging herself behind the door.

Deep breath out.

Through the crack in the door hinge, Rue assesses the room. It's small, only big enough for two emerald couches and a coffee table in the middle. A single floor lamp gives off the only light in the room, reflecting off the rich brown of the wood paneled walls.

She can make out the seven people. All dressed in the same black sweatshirt Connor had on in the bathroom, gloves, and a white face mask.

If they are going for anonymity, then congrats to them, it's a success. There is no way for her to know who is who, other than the fact that they are all different heights and two of them have breasts, these people could be anyone in the Southlands.

"He left me our assignments, new targets in different boroughs," one of them says to the group.

"How many this time?" someone questions.

"Four, you got a problem with that?"

"No, I—" they respond, but get cut off.

"Good, now you 75," pointing to the person who questioned them, "Will be in the Flats with 29 and 64. Your targets are on these papers." The leader (Rue assumes) hands the three members two small yellow papers. Rue's body goes numb. Her mind drifts to that back alley. Those blue eyes. The dead smile on his face. The drip, drip, drip of the foam in his mouth. She will remember that color yellow for as long as she lives. Her fate was once written down in blue ink, it may still be.

The leader continues, causing Rue to refocus. "24, you're with me. We are heading to Bridge Circle." 24 nods, and moves towards the leader, crossing their arms as they stand behind them.

"15, you are with 48, he wants you in North Peri." They step forward, handing a paper to the shortest member of the group who is sitting on one of the couch armrests.

15 takes one look at the paper and scoffs. "How is this supposed to happen, all we have is a last name?"

The leader steps even closer to 15, bunching their sweatshirt in a fist, "Do you want me to tell him that you don't want the assignment? Do you think that'll go in your favor?"

One of them pulls the leader off 15, pushing them back, stretching out their long arms separating the two. "Stop!"

"Tell that to her! The bitch can't just take direction like she's instructed to."

The member who got in the middle of the two, gets into the leader's face, "I'd think twice before you called her a bitch again."

"You'd like that wouldn't you? You're just waiting for a reason to take my post."

"29! He's not worth it," 15 comments.

"Yeah 29, listen to your fuck buddy," the leader laughs as his voice modifier cracks. His aura towers over 29 even though he is a few inches shorter than them. 29 shoves the leader back a few feet, getting into his face, ready for a fight.

This is a mess; I should have brought popcorn.

"Fuck guys! Let's just pass these out and get out of here. He's going to kill us all, if we are pissing around while we have assignments," 75 yells at the group.

Boo! Let them fight.

Rue is honestly taken back by the group dynamic. The chaotic team (if you want to call them a team) is so on edge she is surprised they haven't slipped up yet. This is too big of an operation for these members not to work well with others.

What am I missing? Who is HE?

The thick fog of testosterone that's filling the room starts to fade, and Rue watches as all seven members stand to leave. Her mind shoots to her position behind the door. An absolute worthless spot of cover after someone decides to close it. Her eyes dart around the room, if she can get behind the plant fast enough, she might have a fighting chance at staying hidden.

With her hand once again on her dagger in a death grip, she silently sneaks over to the palm, crouching down behind it.

She waits. And waits some more. But something is not right.

There are no sounds coming from the other room. She focuses on her environment but can only hear the hum of the air unit. Seven different heartbeats suddenly become nonexistent.

"What the fuck?" she whispers to herself. Quickly she paces the room, dagger out of its sheath, and peers around the corner. The room is empty.

Rushing inside she finds no trace of the people who occupied it just seconds before, like they vanished out of thin air. Rue spins around trying to locate an exit. She steps towards the couches and can feel a dip in the flooring. She looks down and steps again, a faint squeak comes from the carpet below her. She does it again, this time with more force, and the floor begins to move. A small square clicks open and pops up an inch from the rest. She squats down and lifts the hatch up with her fingers. Her heart is racing. Her hands begin to tremble, so she fists them closed. A secret door.

What is this, a spy novel?

Before she can second guess herself, Rue is climbing down the ladder. Half way she pauses to catch her breath, listening to the unknown darkness below her. Their voices. She can hear their voices, echoing off what sounds like metal.

At the bottom, she steps down to the ground without a noise. The landing isn't much bigger than the bathroom stall she was in earlier. Light trickles into the space by the door left open on the far end. Rue removes both knives, gripping them with force, and proceeds towards the mysterious escape route.

Beyond the door is a stark comparison to the room she just left. White. All white, and rust, and metal, and cold. Pipes on the ceiling go a million different directions. Air vents line the sides of the space every ten feet. All the walls and floor are made from some sort of cross hatch metal ore, which makes a sound with every step, even for a sly rogue like Rue. She is going to need to keep her distance if she wants to continue her pursuit.

She stills her body to listen for a direction to move. The sounds of steam coming from the left fall into the background of her mind when she picks up tapping sounds coming from the right. Footsteps.

The hallway is long and isn't much wider than her arms width. Faint drips can be heard from inside the walls, and the aroma of rust and mold linger in her nose. Clearly, this isn't used for mainstream use, if at all. It feels stagnant.

The hairs on Rue's arms stand up when she hears the voices getting louder, causing her to calm her movements.

Further down is a connection point to another hallway. She tiptoes towards it and peeks her head around the side. The group is walking down the left path, arguing about Gods know what.

She leans forward to get a better visual, but her knife scrapes against the pipe she is using as cover, making a clink sound not one of them can deny hearing. She sees them still, and quickly pulls herself against the wall, out of their sight.

Shit! Shit, shit, shit!

She closes her eyes from her own stupidity, but just for a moment.

"What the fuck was that?" she can hear one of them say.

"Go check it out 15," another says.

"Fuck you guys! Bunch of pussies," Rue hears what she assumes is 15. In different circumstances, she thinks the two of them would get along, maybe. If it weren't for the whole trying to kill her and other innocent people thing. 15 has guts, especially for the drastic size difference between her and the others.

Before she has time to panic, Rue is taking large silent steps towards the door leading back up to the conference room. The problem with that, is the door is too far away for the time she has to hide. Rue takes back everything she said about having luck tonight. Luck does not exist. This is a disaster. She hopes no one laughs at her funeral.

She can hear 15's footsteps growing louder. Rue's eyes dart around to find cover. A blank wall, obviously no. A large pipe running from the ground to the ceiling, maybe. An air vent, yes! An air vent.

She sprints towards it, using the blade of her knife to unscrew the metal plate. One stew out. Then the second. The sounds of boots on metal are ringing in her ears, screaming at her to hurry up. The adrenaline running through her veins is causing her fingers to sweat against the leather handle of her dagger.

Third screw out, but the fourth is jammed into the place so tight and won't budge.

Come on, come on, come on!

The sound coming from the other hall is now blaring in her eardrums.

Focus Rue, fucking focus!

15 slows as she rounds the corner, quieting her own steps to listen for those of someone else. She stops dead in her tracks when she sees the hallway is empty. Not a shadow of a person in sight. She spins around in a circle, looking to all the corners of the space for any sign of life.

A few steps away from her, Rue covers her masked mouth with both hands, trying to regulate her breathing. Curled into the fetal position in the air vent, she closes her eyes and leans back to the side wall.

15 moves deeper into the hallway, closing the distance. Rue can see her in between the slits of the grates, and she watches as she approaches the air vent.

"What the hell," 15 whispers to herself, voice of her modifier cracking with every breath. She shakes her head, and moves her hands to her mask, pulling it off. She inhales deeply, like this is her first breath after drowning. 15 lowers her hood, letting her bleached blonde hair fall down past her shoulders, running a hand through it.

Rue is taken aback. She sits in the dark, open-mouthed in shock. She isn't sure she has a heart anymore; it might have just exploded in her chest.

No, there's no way. No fucking way. Rocky!

Roxanne "Rocky" Bask, once a close friend, used to work for Diego after Rue recruited her. The two trained together for many years, growing into an inseparable pair. She was good. Really good, maybe even better than Rue, although Rue would never admit that to anyone. Rocky was like a chameleon. She could be anyone, play any part you needed her to. She has this way of manipulating people, conning them into false trust, false hope.

While Rue had perfected the short game, quick talking, sleight of hand, getting in before anyone saw her coming, Rocky played the long game. She would befriend you, be who you needed for months, get what she wanted, and vanish.

The two met at a bar in the Flats, Rue was working undercover, and Rocky was tending the bar. While Rue waited for her mark to show up, she watched as Rocky changed her personality for every single patron.

She observed while Rocky would convince people to buy top shelf liquor, and swipe watches and jewelers when exchanging coins. Quick. Witty. And so gorgeous no one would question the extra-long touch. All she had to do was bat her bright blue eyes, smile with her dimples and a person would be putty in her hands.

Long story short, Rue saw so much of herself in Rocky. She offered her a job. Rocky accepted. They trained together. Became friends. Even shared an apartment at one point. But at the end of the day, Rocky did what she does best, conned the Smoke Runners, and disappeared without a trace. Leaving Rue with a cracked heart to pick up the pieces of her mistakes.

Rue's eyes narrow at Rocky from behind the air vent. Part of her (most of her) wants to rush out and tackle her to the ground, strangle her into the void for making her endure what she did when Rocky left. The fire in her veins runs through her body like liquid rage.

Of course. Of course she would be here, on this team.

Her chest lifts with silent racing breaths. Without realizing it, Rue's hand is gripping her knives, ready to jump at the first sign of Rocky noticing her. But she doesn't. She just stands there, face to the ceiling, eyes closed.

She looks exhausted, like she hasn't slept in weeks. Her once sun kissed skin, now seems pale, and thin. Rocky lets out a deep breath, cursing to herself.

"What's taking so long 15?" a monotone voice comes from the other hallway.

"Noth—" she responds but quickly remembers her mask, placing it over her voice. "Nothing, it's empty. Probably just a rat or something." She readjusts herself, lifting her hood up and tucking her hair back into it.

Rue watches as her chest heaves like she can't breathe now that she's back in her role. Her mask faces the ground for seconds before she finally moves her boots, and retreats back to her group.

Rue sits, mouth open, rethinking everything she knows about the Organization.

CHAPTER

BACK at sinners, Rue is met with a rowdy crowd. It's Thursday, which means it's guys night. Men only. Women perform on raised platforms above the dance floor, twirling around and grinding on each other, while a sea of men whistle and shout from below.

"Show me them tits, girl!" yells one.

"Let me show you what I can do with that ass, baby!" screams another.

Rue wants to throw up but remembers that would be frowned upon. These women are beautiful, and talented, and shouldn't have to be degraded like this. She knows them. They are survivors like her. Some are parents. Some support their entire families. Some are paying off debts.

Most nights, the dancers are women and men, and they perform for a diverse group. They have routines and tell a story through their movements. But Thursdays, fucking Thursdays, they are thrown on stage and told to do whatever the crowd demanded of them. Practically having sex on the platform. If they don't comply, Diego fires them.

She walks past all the drooling males, weaving through the crowd. A sharp sting warms her ass as she walks by a table of twenty somethings, one of them slapping her. She stops for a moment, preparing to throw her fists in their face, but when she turns around to glare, they are so plastered she doesn't waste her time with fists or insults.

Lucky bastards.

Rue has to wiggle her way through chests and arms before getting to the steps. One of the dancers is on the bar, stripping for a group that is growing larger by the second.

She takes the metal steps two at a time and can finally breathe once above the masses. Maybe this is what it feels like to be the girls on stage, safe, like no one can touch you. The only people sharing your space are your friends. Everyone respects each other. A family of sorts. Rue pauses her ascent, smiling at the women on stage. Brave, confident girls, doing what they must to survive with one another by their sides.

That must be nice. To have friends.

At the top of the steps, Rue's expression drops when she is greeted with the very punchable face of Arrow, and Franky the bodyguard.

Franky moves to block her way, pulling her back with his massive biceps.

"Franky, as much as we both want it, it's not time for foreplay. I need to go talk with him." He chuckles, admiring her spunk, and opens his mouth to speak but gets interrupted by Arrow.

"ID number." He demands, towering over her more than a foot as he invades her personal space.

"I'd step back if I were you, Arrow. You know who the fuck I am. You don't need to see my number." She looks at him down the bridge of her nose, biting the inside of her cheek instead of biting off his head.

"It's protocol, Ghost. Don't want boss man thinking I'm not good at my job."

"Oh, don't worry, he already knows that."

"Well, we can't all fuck our way out of punishments, can we?"

"Are you insinuating I'm fuckable and you're not? Because I'm inclined to agree."

"Fuck you!" he shouts.

"Oh, baby you wish," Rue purrs.

Arrow moves in closer, glaring down at Rue with a tight jaw. Rue doesn't back down. She just looks up at him with a blank face. Someone is going to lose this staring contest and it sure as hell isn't going to be her.

"Guys, come on. He'd take us all out if he saw this shit in his club. People can see you, stop the pissing contest. Ghost, show us your arm. Arrow, don't let her get to you, that's what she wants."

"Yes *dad*," Rue responds, still not looking away from Arrow's gray eyes.

Arrow lets out a disgusted huff, shaking his head. "Whatever. Anyways he's in a meeting, we can't let you in there."

"He's going to want to hear what I have to stay, so fuck off." Rue scoffs, lifting her arm and pulling back her sleeve. "ID number 175774." She shoves her wrist into Arrow's face, showing off the black ink of her ID number, and lightly slaps his cheek twice before moving away. "Don't worry, I'll make sure to tell him how nice you were to me." Winking, she makes her way down the hallway, pulling down her sleeve and smoothing out her outfit.

When she opens the door, Rue is greeted with a scowl. Diego's eyes linger on hers then his expression softens, like he was expecting someone else. Meanwhile someone is talking to him on a communicator in a huffed tone. Without saying a word she walks in, sits on a chair across from him, and lifts her feet up on the desk. She picks at her navy nails pretending not to listen to the voice at the other end of the call, who continues to talk.

"We had a snag, sir. We believe someone was—"

"I'm going to have to call you back," Diego cuts them off, "My dinner just arrived, and I'd like to eat while it's still hot." His gaze drops, wandering down Rue's body, which sends a chill down her spine.

"Oh, okay, sir. It's just—"

Without answering Diego ends the call. He sits for a few moments, staring at Rue. His empty expression, which causes her to readjust in her chair and lower her feet, leaves her contemplating whether or not this was a good idea to barge in.

"Hey," she says as innocently as she can, like she didn't just interrupt a call from someone with no invitation, after being told multiple times he is busy.

He doesn't respond right away, instead his eyes narrow in on her, biting his bottom lip like he's thinking about how to handle her insubordination. The silence in the room is about as enjoyable as a punch to the gut. This is a mistake. The two still aren't on solid ground after her escape a few weeks ago. A punishment of ignoring her is apparently appropriate for her betrayal. After a deep exhale, Diego finally fills the silence.

"Come here," he growls.

The fuck?

She responds with a *make me* look in her eyes, lifting her brows.

He leans forward over his desk, looks her down the bridge of his nose and says, "Now."

It's a demand, one Rue knows she shouldn't find sexy, but she does. Warm heat fills her lower abdomen from his intense glare at her. Dirty thoughts fill her mind about what might happen to her if she doesn't listen.

Gods, I need help. Or at least to be touched.

She stands, slowly stepping towards him across the desk, then stops inches away. With a swift movement, Diego has Rue straddling him and is now rubbing her ass like he hasn't been pretending she doesn't exist. The two don't leave each other's gaze. Rue's body begs her for more connection, to be closer to him somehow. Her pride is arguing that she shouldn't give in, but the louder voice of her sexual needs (that desperate bitch) wants to melt into him and forget their fight even happened.

"I think I missed you," Rue admits before she can take it back, staring down at Diego's lips. She leans in against his mouth but wonders how he will take the statement. They don't tend to *miss* each other or at least not admit it, understanding the job responsibilities of one another take more precedence than a relationship. It might be too much. Too needy.

She told herself over the last few months nothing could continue emotionally between them, reminding herself he is her boss, and nothing more. He is no longer that carefree first love she always pictured him as. If sex is still happening, it will be just that, sex. Simply a primal urge to rip off his clothes and have him devour her until she can't walk straight. Casually of course. It means nothing. Just two attractive people, finding each other attractive.

Gods, he's attractive.

She can do this. No feeling. No wanting. Nothing emotional, she won't do that to herself again.

"Oh really?" he hums into her lips before kissing her, sending shocks directly in between her legs.

I can't do this.

A soft kiss, gentle and warm, maybe even *loving*. No, it can't be loving. She doesn't want loving. She wants, no needs, a purely professional relationship, with sex. If that's even possible. It has to be possible, for her own sanity and pride.

In between kissing her lips and neck Diego breathes into her skin, "You know, I should punish you for barging in like this."

Pride? Who values pride anyway?

Rue closes her eyes, tilting her neck into him. "I think you should too," she giggles.

With a squeeze of her ass, Diego's tender movements turn primal. His grip on her tightens and gentle kisses turn to bites. The warm feeling that fills her body, turns to goosebumps of passion. Ownership. That is the only word she could describe it as. He owns her in these intimate moments. And as much as she hates to admit it, it turns her on knowing she isn't the only one who feels this way. It makes the nerves between her thighs burn with need.

Rue starts to grind on him, working her hips slow and to the beat of an invisible song. How did he have this effect on her, and why was it so instant? She resents herself for being so drawn to him. All this man has to do is touch her, and her body abandons all sense of feminism. The feelings of being wanted overwhelms her. Her desperation to fill his desires is something she has no control over.

Why is she here again?

Oh, gods his lips.

What?

Fuck.

What is she supposed to be doing? Because it sure isn't trying to orgasm in Diego's office while Smoke Runners sit outside the door.

Fuck! Oh, that feels so good.

No! No, no stop this.

"Wait! We can't do this. Not now, not yet," she whispers, stilling her body against his. Every part of her brain is yelling at her to shut up and let him take her. Her chest rubs against his as their breathing calms. She's not denying she wants him, it's truly the only thing she wants in this exact moment, but she needs to keep her wits about her. Being this close to him is dangerous for her productivity.

"We can do whatever the hell we want, Beautiful." Diego continues to conquer more of her skin with his mouth, lips trailing the purple love bites already forming on her neck.

"No, no we really need to stop. I came here to talk about work." He kisses her mouth, pulling at her bottom lip. "The Lucky Clover." Another kiss. "You know, my job." Diego chooses to ignore her words, moving back to her neck, making a soft moan escape her lips. Rue dodges his next move and backs off his body.

This clear act of treachery causes Diego to growl at her, pulling her wrist back to him. The palm of his hand meets the back of her head, jerking her face to his. "Don't you dare deny me what's mine," he says through gritted teeth. The lust in his eyes turns to deep, dark anger.

Mine, that word again, haunting her every movement.

Something shifts in her vision, what was filled with sexual urge and warm heat seconds ago, now transforms into something else. Something hot and fiery.

How dare he, this separation of the two of them is on him. He is the one who has been making her sleep in the spare bedroom and ignoring her. She cannot continue to be an option of convenience for him to get his cock wet. All or nothing, she doesn't have time to wait around.

"Calm your dick. You're going to want to hear what I have to say, and who I saw."

She holds her ground, voice solid and steady. As much as she longed for sex with him, something about fighting with a man in charge, not falling to his every demand, is her favorite feeling. It empowers her in a way that her sex appeal never will.

"Calm my dick?" he scoffs.

"Yes, and fucking listen." She drags out the last word for dramatics. She steps back away from Diego, lifting herself to sit on his desk. Rue likes this angle a lot better, towering over him makes her feel like she is the one calling the shots, like the power dynamic changed.

Diego leans back in his chair, readjusting his visible hard on. He runs a hand over his mouth, face blank from emotion, and lifts his brows for her to continue.

"So," she begins, trying to recall the last few hours that somehow feels like a week of time. "I found where they meet. In a room on the second floor of Cover, but it's not a regular room." This piques his interest; he leans forward resting his elbows on his knees. Rue continues, "It has a secret hatch in the floor! Like some spy novel shit. And they have these numbers, ID's I think."

"Like ours?"

"No, like 24 and 15. They use them instead of names. And get this, everyone uses masks to alter their voices. I don't think they know who each other are. They definitely weren't a group who has been together long."

"What makes you say that?"

"They argue. About everything. Think Arrow and me but times seven. It didn't feel right. Like they didn't believe in the cause."

He looks off to the side, staring at nothing while he thinks. His pointer fingers tap on his upper lip. A lip Rue suddenly has the urge to suck on.

No! Stop you lunatic. Professional. We are being professional.

"And you know who one of them is? How could you tell if they had on masks?" Diego asks, pulling Rue back into the current moment and out of her fantasy of him sweeping everything off his desk to lean her back on...

Nope, I will not go there.

"I followed them. Down into the secret spy door thing. It led to a hallway, one of them heard me, and turned around to investigate."

"You got caught?" His voice raises a few decibels.

"Yes, they are holding me captive right now," Rue snaps back. "No, I crawled into an air vent, and watched who it was take off their mask and lower their hood."

"And?" An annoyed tone fills his words.

"*And* it was Rocky!" Rue's face can't hide the shock, still not believing that is who she saw. "I know it was. She's working for the Organization. They call her 15."

Silence fills the room once more. Diego looks around while thinking but doesn't give away his inner thoughts. Rue looks down her legs, swinging off the edge of the desk. Her hands grip tighter around the wood with every second that goes by with no reply. The lack of response makes her skin crawl.

Say something, anything.

"Okay I can't take it, talk please! Tell me you're shocked, or annoyed, or filled with rage. I can see the smoke coming from your ears."

"That bitch is still a pain in my ass. You never should have recruited her."

Rue's eyes shoot to his, "Don't you blame this on me! Just because you were jealous that she pulled me into her spell and away from you, doesn't mean her actions now have anything to do with me."

Her body stings with the insult. This is not on her, this was inevitable. Rocky was a rogue before she ever knew what one was. If it wasn't Rue who recruited her, it would have been someone else.

"I'm not jealous, especially of that low life. You're mine and she used that to wedge herself between us." His glare could cut through stone.

"Yeah, keep telling yourself that. We both got played and we need to live with that. It's over, what she does with her life now is not on us."

"But it is on us. She knows how we work, how *you* operate, your tics, your weaknesses. She knows you, which means she can get to you. Hell, she's probably the one who told that guy how to come after you." Rue looks away, she can hear the desperation in his voice when talking about her being in danger.

"I can handle myself. I took one out before, I can do it again."

"Yeah? Well, what if it isn't just one, huh? What if it's a whole fucking team? You're good, Rue, but you're not that good."

Rue rolls her eyes and looks down at her legs. What does he know? He has no fucking clue what she is capable of. The damage she can cause. She doesn't even know the limits she can reach with her abilities.

A chill runs down her, and what she swears is a faint smell of pine. She feels a cool invisible breeze brush her neck, which makes her unlock her nails that are leaving dents in the desk.

Deep breath, I have nothing to prove.

"I'll be fine."

Diego doesn't answer, he just stares at her. She wishes he wouldn't. The longer he looks, the less confident she feels in her abilities. Like he knows something she doesn't.

"So, what do we do? Do you want me to lead a team? Set up watch groups to follow them? It seems like things are progressing faster. I could—"

Diego cuts her off. "Lead? No, you're not a leader."

"What the hell is that supposed to mean, *not a leader*?" Rue's nails dig into her palms, and a cold sweat runs down her back. She can feel her face turning red.

"You know what I mean, Beautiful."

"No, please enlighten me." She raises her brows and crosses her arms. "Because it sounds like you don't believe in me. Even though you know I'm fucking capable of so much more."

"All right. All right. Calm down. No need to freak out over something you took wrong."

"No! You don't get to tell me to calm down."

Before she has time to blink, Diego is on her, gripping the back of her neck so tight she winces from the pain. His glare is deadly. "I'd be careful about how you talk to me." He loosens his grip, pushing a hair away from her face with no tenderness. "How about before you have a tantrum like a child, you listen for once."

Rue doesn't say anything, just lifts her chin.

"See, that's not so hard, is it?" He doesn't wait for her to respond. "If you had let me explain, I would have told you that I can't have you lead."

"Why?" she cuts in, not able to hold her tongue.

"You don't have it in you. You're a loner. Don't play well with others. You never have and you never will. And I mean that as a compliment, before you chew my head off."

She disagrees, she's never been given a chance to work with others, other than Diego when they were teens. She opens her mouth to rebuttal but gets interrupted.

"Besides, I can't let people know you are working on this. It'll put you in danger."

"Everything I am puts me in danger."

"And how do you think that makes me feel? That I'm the reason you aren't safe. All I want to do is protect you from these monsters. I can't just send you out there and sit back and wait for them to kill you."

"You're not even giving me a chance to prove that they won't."

Diego leans in, pulls Rue to him with both hands on her face. "You're not taking this on, end of discussion." His thumb runs up and down her lip, and she can see Adam's apple bob with a swallow. His eyes move to her neck, and he traces his fingers over the purple marks.

"It doesn't hurt, if that's what you're wondering," she whispers defeatedly, knowing she lost to him once again.

"Your body just doesn't want to get rid of me, does it? Holding on to these marks until I can make more. I was actually admiring them. It lets everyone know you belong to someone else."

"Or I just got in a fight," Rue snarks.

"You did. Just a little argument, but we worked it out. And now we're on the same page, aren't we?"

Rue's body stiffens, she never knows how to react to his sudden change in demeanor. He runs a finger down her neck, trailing lower to her breasts. Her body responds against her will, and her nipples harden under her shirt with his touch.

"That's right, it turns you on doesn't it, Beautiful?"

No, no it doesn't.

"You crave the chaos. What a dirty girl."

No, that's not true!

It would be easier to agree with her thoughts if her body wasn't currently betraying her and melting into a pathetic puddle on the floor. Rue knows this isn't right, knows that her feelings towards him are irrational, and makes her seem insane to someone looking from the outside in. But he is hers just as much as she is his. Their connection has grown through trust when they had no one else. She would follow him into the void if he asked her to. You don't abandon the people who care for you. You don't leave someone you see yourself in.

"What do you want me to do now?" she asks, barely audible, trying to focus on the problems they are facing, and not on the warm fingers flirting with the belt loop of her pants.

"Oh, so many things." His husky voice hums in her ears, sending tingles down to her thighs. A moan comes out of her mouth uninvited.

Pull yourself together woman!

She needs to reel him back in, get back to the conversation at hand. She needs to keep some form of professionalism. Rumors have started to spread since he asked her to live with him and has Smoke Runners standing guard outside his apartment. Clearly, they aren't hiding their, whatever this is, if Arrow is assuming she sleeps with him instead of getting backlash for her questionable actions. She does, but he doesn't need that confirmed.

"No, I mean what do you want me to do about the Organization?" She clears her throat and extends her arms in between them. This is not happening right now, and he needs to be okay with that.

He lets out a huff, "You're walking a thin line right now. I don't like to be told no."

"Give me my next assignment and you can have me all you want," she says, leaning in to brush a kiss against this neck. "Later. At home. In *our* bed," she adds. She hasn't slept with him in weeks, still exiled to the guest room, which if she's being honest is starting to get uncomfortable. And lonely.

"I knew you couldn't stay away for long. You're meant to be with me, you can't deny it," he mocks. His ego expands beyond the room itself. The half smile on his lips brings the warm heat back into her veins. Rue bites her cheek, trying to hide her own smirk from showing, vowing not to give him everything he wants.

But his face, his damn face. His midnight eyes, the unnatural arch of his nose that never healed right from a fight, the permanent crease in between his brows, and those lips. Lips that have explored every inch of her body more times than she can count. Gods, what she would do to have those running along her…

Nope! No, stop.

What is she doing? She needs to get out of here, clear her head, pull herself together, maybe throw herself into the bay for good measure.

His thumbs trailing back and forth over her inner thighs brings her back to her current predicament. "So," she says, clearing her throat. "My assignment. You were about to tell me what I can do with my time, so I don't go completely insane."

"Yeah, about that."

"I have an assignment, right? Diego, I better have an assignment."

"You do. A safe one."

"And that is what exactly?" Rue's eyes burn holes into him.

"I want you to tail Rocky for a few weeks. Find out where she hangs out, who she talks to, and what her patterns are. I heard she runs a shit hole in the Flats now."

"You're shitting me! Tail her? I'm not going to be a glorified babysitter, while there is so much more to do. You can get anyone else to do this. Why can't one of the new recruits do it?"

He leans into her again, pulling her back to him so her face is mere centimeters from his. "Because I asked you to do it," he says through gritted teeth, the huskiness of his tone overpowered with annoyance. "You want an assignment. This is that assignment. You are going to do it, because you work for me, and I am asking you to. Understood?"

A million thoughts run through Rue's mind, the first being what the fuck? Why is he acting this way? How come a new recruit can't do this meaningless task? What is so special about Rocky that deserves a two-week tail? Why her? Why continue to punish her, when she is capable of so much more than this?

She should be out there, finding who is behind this. Looking for connection to the different victims. Mapping their patterns. Going back to Lucky Clover.

"I asked you a question," he interrupts her internal freak out.

She doesn't have many options at this point. She can either do the job. Or she can do nothing. Have no purpose. Rot away in his cold apartment while the rest of the world moves forwards, for better or worse.

"Okay." She says it simply, and emotionless. There is no point in fighting, in the end what he says goes. The tightness in her shoulders lower, leaving her feeling limp and useless.

"Good." He closes the distance between them and kisses her forehead. "That's my girl."

Her eyes meet his, and she gives him a small smile, hoping he can't see the defeat in her eyes.

"Don't look at me like that," he laughs.

"Like what?"

"Like I just grounded you for a month. Quit the dramatics. I'm doing this to protect you. That's all." Well, there goes her trying to hide her disappointment. Asking this of her is like throwing a leash around her neck and telling her she can't run. She doesn't respond, only looks down at the red carpet. Diego moves to brush a hair away from her face.

"Wait for me at home, okay? I'll be a little late. I have some loose ends to tie up around here. When was the last time you ate? You want me to bring you home some food? I can have the guys in the kitchen make you some of those fries you like." He lifts her chin to look at him. What gives him the right to be sweet right now, after crushing her like this?

"Of course I want fries." The one decent thing this fucked up High District has is real food. Diego knows this is one of her weaknesses and uses it as an apology tactic often.

His smile is genuine, and gentle, and more charming than she wants to admit. "Why can't I stay mad at you? You're so annoying."

He kisses her one last time and says, "Because as hard as you try to hide it, I know you too well. And I know you love me."

Rue doesn't answer, she lets out a small huff and pushes him away playfully.

From the moment she closes the office door, until she reaches Diego's apartment on the east side of town, Rue can't help but feel a tingle of uneasiness. Her gut screams at her to be cautious, of what she isn't sure.

CHAPTER

RUE sits on a rooftop in West Harbor, the sun beating down on her as she watches Rocky grab her third bagel of the day. If there is one thing she has learned from tailing her the past week, it's that the girl has a serious obsession with bagels. It's all she ever eats.

Exhausted, bored out of her mind, and questioning her life choices, Rue looks to the sun that is peeking out behind a clouded sky, closing her eyes to let the rays fill her with vitamin D. The rainy spring weather is slowly being broken up into sunshine days and Rue is going to take in whatever warmth she can get.

When her job involves a lot of late nights and working under the light of the moons, being out on this hot as hell rooftop is a nice change of pace.

Most Lowers despise the heat. Heat equals danger. Less rain in the sky means less water for people, which leads to dehydration and infection related diseases from lack of proper hygiene. The higher temperatures also lead to hotter living conditions, which sadly cause a rise in heat related deaths amongst non-abled bodies and elders.

Not only that, but the sun brings the deadly smell of garbage, and decay, and reeking fish. Okay, Rue can agree with that one. The smells of the summer are not her favorite on this forgotten rock.

However, Rue loves the sun. She always runs cold, most likely from her Northlands heritage. So, the warm rays of golden heat are always her favorite clue to the change in seasons, even if the summer solstice is technically still weeks away.

Rue looks back down at Rocky just in time to see her go into a pawn shop. The same one she goes to every damn day. Rue knows she has about an hour to kill from watching her for so long. Every day she goes and gets a bagel at the corner stall, then walks into Harrison's Pawn Shop and talks to a guy working at the desk. The two sit there, flirting back and forth, ignoring the world on the other side of the glass.

In all the times she has spent watching the shop, not once has she seen a customer come in or out. Which is strange, but not enough for Rue to investigate it deeper. They could be selling drugs, or making weapons, or laundering money for all she cares. It wasn't her *assignment* to keep tabs on shady businesses in the Low District. Although it would probably be more exciting than what she is doing currently. Which is, oh that's right, absolutely nothing.

It would have raised a red flag if Rocky had ever come in or out with anything, but she never does. The first few days, Rue intensely watched, even went so far as to sneak in the back a few times to listen to their conversations. But you can only listen to two people talk about their plans for the weekend, and their most anticipated sexual endeavors with each other for so long, before the urge to vomit takes over.

This time Rue came prepared for the long hour wait. She unrolls the newspaper that is tucked into her bag and reads the front-page headline.

SAFE IN THE SOUTHLANDS? KIDNAPPINGS INCREATE BY 500% IN RECENT WEEKS

Wonderful, things are getting worse. She scans the article, searching for information she doesn't already know.

"...Statistics show that the number of those missing has increased from 30 in one month to 150 in the matter of two weeks. Citizens urge the Seven Presidents to take immediate action in this matter..."

Rue laughs at the thought of the Presidents doing anything to help the Lowers. When have they ever cared for them? The answer is never. That is why the Low District is the way it is.

If they keep Lowers starving and scared and uneducated, they can have all the control. They can set the wages, control the work, decide the rations, and the people will be so desperate for survival, they won't even understand they are being taken advantage of. The Presidents hide their neglect with yearly lotteries and "free" items each month in Generals around town.

Rue knows for a fact that the lotteries are rigged so no one ever wins. She worked an operation to take the money from one of the so-called *winners* after Diego got a whiff of foul play. After hours of torture, the winner confessed he was hired as propaganda by someone working in one of the President's offices, to sell the idea of free money and a new life to the Lowers.

As for the "free" items each month in Generals, from knowing Fiona, Rue can confirm that the store operators are responsible to front the cost of the times. The Presidents put out a newsletter each month explaining what the free times are, then make the store owners pay to get those items in their shops. If they don't stock them, they live in fear of riots in their businesses.

Nothing is ever free, no one is ever looking out for you.

Rue continues to scan the article.

"... So far, no word from the Presidents on their specific strategy to solve this troublesome issue. However, an anonymous insider to the President of Justice stated, "All seven of the Presidents are working tirelessly on this, and they will not rest until the kidnappers are brought to justice." They ask that all the citizens take the necessary precautions to keep themselves safe, and contact their local Marshal branch with any information..."

"Working tirelessly my ass," Rue mumbled to herself. "What a bunch of bullshit." She continues flipping through the paper skimming articles.

FIRE BURNS DOWN BANK IN NORTH PERI: FOUL PLAY CONFIRMED.

WATER TREATMENT PLANT HALTS CONSTRUCTION DUE TO RISING COSTS

PURPLE LIGHTNING PHENOMENON WORRIES WEATHER ENTHUSIASTS

FAE KILL SITE FOUND IN ABANDONED WAREHOUSE: CITIZENS REJOICE

Rue stops when she reads the last headline. Kill site. Her mind goes to that day by the docks. The alley. Those blue eyes. All the lands will be clean soon.

All the lands will be clean soon.

Is that what this was? Cleaning the Southlands of fae creatures? A chill runs down her spine and her skin goes cold, the heat of the sun doing nothing to warm the ice in her chest.

Her eyes regretfully scan the article, reading through so fast she barely has time to process what it's saying.

> *"…While two children were exploring an abandoned warehouse on the outskirts of The Flats, they stumbled upon what can only be described as a gruesome killing site. Multiple bodies of fae creatures were found stabbed to death, the tips of their ears cut off. This comes after numerous bodies have been found around the city, killed in a similar manner…"*

Rue's face goes pale, she has a sudden urge to puke over the ledge of this rooftop. Multiple fae folk. Brutally murdered for trying to seek refuge in this fucking city. How can people be so cruel to innocent lives? Rue is, and always will be, willing to hunt and hurt those who deserve it, but innocence is something worth protecting. She wipes at her mouth, trying to ignore the stinging pain in her chest.

> *"…Citizens around the warehouse applaud the mysterious vigilante for cleaning up the surrounding neighborhood. One citizen, Marjorie Lackland states, "It's about time they clean up the trash that lurks around our homes. I feel a little safer at night knowing those monsters can't hurt my family anymore." While the person responsible has yet to come forward, the Marshals assure us they will not be prosecuted for these crimes…"*

"Were not fucking monsters," Rue says, her jaw clenched, crumbling the paper into a ball and tossing it back into her bag.

The people in this city have no clue. Rue has never met another fae folk here who is a danger to society, other than herself maybe. But she isn't going to do anything to harm people, only those that deserve it. Sure, it sounds morbid to think this way, but she isn't doing this because she is fae, she's following the orders of a human. In fact, almost all the criminals in this city are human. The only ones they need to fear are themselves.

Rue runs her hands over her face, then to her neck. She pauses on the tiny braid in the underside of her hair, twirling it between two fingers.

After cooling her rage, Rue looks to the pawn shop once again. There is Rocky, still eye fucking the guy at the counter.

Before resting back into the arch of the roof, something catches her attention out of the corner of her eye. A black shadow. Two of them. Turning the corner on Main Street to some alley. Before they disappear, Rue gets a good look at the shadows and her face stills.

Black sweatshirts, with the hoods up.

Rue's gut is sounding the emergency alarms within her system to follow them. Without a second to process what her eyes are witnessing, she's on her feet, bag slung over her shoulder, climbing down the fire escape.

She doubles back around the corner, so Rocky doesn't notice her, and rushes to the alley the figures went down. It's empty. The breeze picks up around her, causing goosebumps to run down her arms. The alley creates a wind tunnel telling her to forget it, to turn back, to get back on the roof.

She can't, her curiosity is getting the best of her as it normally does. Plus, if she can stop someone else from being taken, gods forbid being killed, she is willing to risk her own safety. An innocent life is worth more than her own.

She quickly walks to a break in the cobblestone and peeks around the corner. A black shadow turns down another side street as soon as she spots them, almost as if they are waiting for her to catch up.

Those fuckers don't know who they are messing with.

If they want to play games, then let's play.

Rue jerks her bag to her front and pulls a small dagger out of a zipper pocket. She side steps against the wall towards the direction of her new friends, making sure to watch her six in case they try to come at her from a different angle.

Around the corner she can see two hooded figures running down the street and make a right turn. She is on her feet, chasing after them within seconds.

Rue takes her right hand and points it down towards her feet. Her eyes start to flicker with white sparkles. With a breath out, an invisible gust of wind blows her forward, doubling her strides with each step. Thankfully for her cover, the streets are deserted this close to the outskirts of town.

Rue takes the right turn too fast and slides, catching herself with her hand on the ground. She grunts with the pressure against her fingers, as clear wind blows up the dirt on the street around her. Another gust and she pushes off with her feet to keep running.

The two hooded people run straight into the tunnels that go under the bridge to the High District. Rue follows, using more air to push herself along. She slows at the entrance and readjusts her grip on her dagger before proceeding.

Thankfully it's morning, so the daylight trickles into the space. Taking light steps, Rue goes deeper into the maze of underpass tunnels.

There is an echo of something she can't place coming from the left. Two muffled voices, and a rattle, then a pressure sound of some sort. Rue continues towards the sounds, knife out in a ready position.

When she rounds the corner, she can finally see the two hooded figures, spraying something on a wall in front of them.

Light is coming from an exit she can't spot, washing over them as if it's a beacon. A breeze blows in her face, nudging her to retreat, but she ignores it.

With silent footsteps, Rue approaches the figures, holding her breath until she gets answers.

Before they have time to react, Rue has her arm around one of them, pulling her knife to their throat. He lets out a yelp, causing his partner to turn to face her. The partner backs up, tripping over his own spray paint can.

"You're going to tell me what the fuck you're doing, or I'm going to slit his throat. Then, before you have time to piss your pants and call for mommy, I'm going to slit yours too," Rue demands.

"Whoa, dude! Lady. Ma'am!" a wobbly voice comes out from the hooded figure on the ground. "We don't mean to piss you off, some guy paid us to tag here." The boy, practically a child, lowers his hood. His eyes are bulging out of his head, and he raises his hands in surrender. "He said you wouldn't hurt us!"

Rue's body freezes from the inside out.

"Who?" The two boys look at each other. Rue repeats herself, "Who? Tell me or my face will be the last thing you see."

The boy she's holding on to lets out a whimper, "Some guy!"

"You'll have to be more specific."

The boy on the ground clears his throat, hands shaking still raised above his head. "He didn't say, we were tagging an old building, and he rolled up in one of those fancy cenzium cars, gave us each a bronze to get you to follow us."

"What did he look like?" Rue orders.

"I don't know, white maybe."

"Is that supposed to be helpful? Give me something kid, or your buddy's blood is on your hands."

"Tell her dude!" gasps the boy Rue still has in a choke hold.

"He looked important; I don't know! I didn't see his face. He was wearing a suit; it was white and had these gold star buttons on it."

Rue rolls her eyes. "Okay, here is what's going to happen. I'm going to let your friend go, neither of you are going to run away from me because that will make me angry, and you don't want to see what I'm capable of doing when I'm angry. You two idiots are going to explain to me exactly what this mysterious, important looking, possibly white man said to you, and why he wanted me to follow you. Got it?" The two of them shake their heads in agreement. "Good boys."

Rue lets the kid go, and they both back up into the wall, not convinced Rue isn't going to hurt them anyway. Rue can see the panic in their eyes, and slowly moves her hands up, making a show of the dagger being placed back into her bag.

"See, no more weapons. Just a conversation. Now, tell me exactly what this guy asked you to do."

The boy Rue was holding, moves his hand over his throat, rubbing the now red skin. "He just pulled up in this black car, shiny, like… like it was brand new. Really sick, it had—"

"Focus!" Rue interrupts.

"Sorry." He moves his hands out in front of him. "He tossed us the bronze coins and told us to get your attention. He said you would follow us if we had these," pointing to his black sweatshirt. "But he said you wouldn't hurt us."

"Yeah, dude was wrong," the other one interrupts.

"You're still in one piece," Rue says, pointing to their perfectly intact bodies. "Continue."

"He said… He said to tag a message on the wall. He said you'd understand it."

Rue lowers her brows, knowing what is about to be displayed on the stone behind them. "What message?"

The boys look at each other, then slowly step away from the wall. Right there, in dripping red paint, are the words **ALL THE LANDS WILL BE CLEAN SOON.**

Rue rubs her hand along her mouth, trying to cover up her expression. The winds pick up around them, causing the unwelcome chill to return. Her body is still, but her mind is an explosion. It's running at approximately one hundred miles an hour currently with questions, and she isn't sure what she needs answered first.

Rue lets out a long exhale, "Where are you boys from? Do you have a home? Families?"

They look at each other again, speaking in a made-up language with their eyes, after a beat one of them says, "We're brothers, we just have each other. No home."

"Good, because I want you two to leave this borough, do not come back here. Whoever you met in the car, will be back for you. You're dealing with people who do not like loose ends. And you two are now liabilities."

The look of fear in the brothers' eyes pull at Rue's iron heart. Just two kids, trying to survive.

After a second of them sitting in shock, Rue breaks the silence, "Go! And do not come back. If I see you around here again, I will happily kill you myself." Panic rings with each footstep as they run off to the exit.

She runs a hand through her hair, pausing mid swipe when she sees more graffiti in the tunnel.

FAE WILL DIE.
7 PRESIDENTS = FAE.
WE STAND WITH FAE KILLER.
TAKE THE WEAK.

"Fuck," she says to herself, her voice echoing off the walls. This is becoming too big. The atmosphere of the city is leaning on the edge of pure chaos.

In the midst of her brain exploding with what's, and ifs, and who's, Rue realizes she left her post, and it wasn't a coincidence. How could she be so stupid?

Rue bolts out of the tunnel, kicking up dirt under her boots as she sprints back to the pawn shop. The muscles in her legs scream from the impact on the pavement. Her heart is leaping from her chest when she reaches the front door, then everything around her stops when she sees the note on the glass.

A yellow scrap of paper. Blue ink. Taunting her.

WE KNOW YOU. WE SEE YOU.

"Gods!" The words leave her lips with the confidence of immediate death. She does nothing to hide the fact that she is terrified. Not for her safety, but that Diego will have to know she messed up. She had one job to do, one she made a scene about being beneath her, and she couldn't even do that.

Maybe she can spin this. Maybe she can convince him she is on to something and can make him understand this is a move forward. She now has more information, she had the car description sort of, and the suit with the star buttons. Also, they are on to her, which to someone less experienced could mean trouble. But it makes Rue fill with smug happiness because they are afraid of her to some extent, or they wouldn't need her distracted.

Before she goes running to confess her sins to Diego, there are more questions that need answers. For one, it's now confirmed in her mind that Rocky is important in all of this. Why distract her from watching if there was nothing worth seeing? She will get to her in a day or so, but first there is still a question nagging in the back of Rue's brain.

Where is the poison from? If Olympia has figured out the breakdown of the poison, she may be able to get a lead as to where it's made and sold, which will snowball into who bought it. And Rue has a hunch it just might be the man in the white suit.

Rue runs her fingers through her braid, looking around at the now crowded city street. Whoever the man is, has no idea who he's messing with. Her mind may be human, and get caught up in conspiracies, but she has something no one expects. An ace up her sleeve. A secret weapon of sorts. A plot twist of the highest magnitude.

Magic.

CHAPTER

THE streets of West Harbor are busy at this time of night, Rue uses that chaos to her advantage as she weaves in and out of the crowds. Up to rooftops. Through abandoned apartment windows. Down fire escapes. Past vendors, where she swipes random hats and scarves, changing into one, then another. Layering and switching clothes to change who she is to the outside world.

Is it excessive? Maybe. But she has no idea who is watching, and probably failing, to follow her. A small smirk runs over her lips at the thought of pissing off someone trying to keep up. No one knows this part of the Low District like she does.

After three hours of randomly moving around the city, Rue jumps to the rooftop of her destination. She takes the ladder down and her boots clink against the metal of the fire escape.

Rue peeks into the window, and can see the yellow, floral wallpaper and second-hand furniture of her childhood home. She smiles at the sight of Olympia, safe, making tea on the stove.

Just as her knuckles move to knock on the glass, a vine sprouts out of an empty pot by her feet, climbing up the brick, and lifting the window in front of her open.

Rue's eyes dart to Olympia's, as she laughs into her steaming pot of water.

"I thought I told you no more windows."

Rue looks to her feet, "I couldn't risk anyone seeing me use the front door."

"That serious, huh?"

"It's that serious."

"I should have known something was up with you when I didn't see or hear from you on your Name Day. I'm glad it's for safety and not because you don't want me to be a part of your life. Happy twenty ninth cycle around the sun, Honey Bee."

Shit.

Her Name Day, how could Rue have forgotten about that? Every year on her Name Day Olympia makes her dinner and a cake complete with homemade candles. It has been a tradition since her first year in the Southlands.

She had promised to be around, and she ignored that promise. Although she wouldn't say ignored, more like forgot. With everything going on with this job, the state of the country, and her crumbling personal life, it completely slipped her mind. She is now twenty nine and didn't even realize it.

"Yeah, about that. I'm sorry. I've been so busy."

"No point in worrying about it now, we can use the candles next year for the big three zero. I'm just happy to see you."

Rue grins, but the emotions filling her make her wish she would crawl into a hole and never leave.

"Well, are you going to come inside, or do I have to talk to my window all night? Get in here." Olympia continues to make tea, keeping her focus on her task and not Rue.

"Yes, Ma'am."

Grabbing the frame, Rue hoists herself up and into the window, swinging her legs over the edge and into the kitchen sink below. Chunks of dirt fall into the basin from her shoes, and she winces.

Still focused on what she's doing, Olympia giggles under her breath. "It's not the first time dirt has been in that sink, you should know that, Honey Bee. Honestly, I'm surprised it still works with all the junk that gets put down there." Rue jumps down off the counter. "Come sit down Aruelia, we were just talking about you."

"We?"

"Fiona and Finny are here, we were about to have dinner. You hungry? It's not good, but it's something. I did make some of that homemade bread you always loved."

Just as Rue opens her mouth to politely decline, Fiona pops in from the living room. She takes one look at Rue and says, "Did your ears tell you we were talking about you? You always did have the best hearing out of any of us." Fiona moves around the table to get to her, wrapping her tiny arms around Rue's body.

"It's so nice to see you, Honey."

"I hope I'm not interrupting something," Rue jokes, giving Fiona the side eye. "Is this dinner, or *dinner*?"

"Gross, please don't or I'm gonna to regret coming." Finny comes into view, his iron eyes sparkling in the dim lights. "They already drool over each other more than my stomach can handle, I don't need you encouraging them, dude." He pulls

Rue into a tight embrace, leaving the scent of embers in his wake.

"Oh, you two!" Fiona chuckles. "It's just dinner between friends."

"Okay, because twin lights come in all shapes and sizes, I don't judge. It would be nice to see you two together, happy." Rue winks at Fiona while Finny pretends to gag. Fiona returns the gesture with a slight pink tint to her cheeks and rolls her eyes.

Maybe one day.

Rue moves around the kitchen with ease, like it's a well-rehearsed dance. She reheats the stove top with the remaining water in the kettle and picks some mint leaves from the pot hanging above her head to put into an empty mug. She reaches out a fingertip of magic to pull a sugar cube from its container into her cup without looking. Once steam is billowing out of the spout, she pours the water and spins a spoon with another flick of magic, stirring the comforting liquid.

Without realizing it, the smells of the apartment have lowered Rue's shoulders. The lingering scent of jasmine and bergamot reminds her of warm hugs, and quiet nights. Her jaw relaxes. The feel of steam and the taste of mint bring her back to cozy blankets and mesmerizing stories. The whites of her knuckles return to their normal pink. She takes her first deep breath in weeks.

She is safe. Thank the Gods they are all safe.

"So, to what do we own the pleasure, Honey Bee? I thought you were keeping your distance," Olympia says from the table behind Rue.

"I am keeping my distance. I'm not here right now. No one can know about this, it didn't happen." Olympia shifts in her chair, and Fiona stops mid sip of her tea. Rue can hear Finny's anxieties start to rise in his heart. She continues, "I came here to check on the status of that project I asked you to work on, and to make sure you're taking this threat of the Organization seriously." She turns to face the three of them, all expressing different emotions. "Which I see you are considering last time I was here, there was a full-blown forest where you are currently sitting."

"I have, we can discuss it later. And I am being safe. We all are. Has something changed since our last visit? Are they threatening you?" Olympia asks, with a maternal, protective tone in her question.

"One could say that," Rue admits. She takes a seat in the only available chair and continues to stir her tea. While her brain races to think of words that won't worry Olympia more, she takes a sip of the steaming liquid.

"They're—"

Before she can finish, the power in the apartment goes out. The four of them now sit in the dark, the only brightness coming from the light pollution of the city outside.

"Gods, this is the third time this week. Rue, Finny, go get the extra candles in the closet. I'll grab some matches."

"Yes, Ma'am." Finny stands, creating an ear melting squeak of his chair.

Rue does as she's told, shuffling behind Finny through the darkened apartment in search of candles in her old bedroom closet.

She's silently grateful for the poor visibility because if she saw her old room right now, full of blue and magenta fabrics and mementoes of her childhood, she would surely spiral into nostalgia. Great for warming the spirits, but not right now. Now she is at war, whether she wanted to be drafted or not. She needs to be a steel beam that cannot be bent into something soft.

It is for them.

Everything she is, is for them.

Her fingertips reach the cool glass of Olympia's homemade candle stash. She has been collecting old jars and containers since Rue was a little girl, and she uses them to create candles out of old oils, waxes, and things she trades other Lowers for. A useful skill for someone who lives in this area and loses power at least once a week. Rue herself has a stash back at her apartment.

"Got them, let's go."

She turns to leave, getting as far as one foot outside the threshold of the door, when Finny pulls her back into the room by her elbow. She can hear him close the door half way, making the sounds from the living space muffle behind the wood. The room darkens further into nothingness.

"What's going on?" she asks, truly intrigued by the secrecy.

"What's going on? You tell me. What do you know? Are we safe? Is this ending? Gods, I have so many questions for you, but I haven't seen you since that day outside of Moon Child. Fill me in. Things are shit out there. Those two won't tell me anything. Still acting like I'm some kid or whatever. I have been gettin' info from friends, but I'm losin' them so fast I can't keep up."

"Finny. FINNY!" she whispers. "Breathe. It's going to be okay. Take a breath."

"Dude, it's bad, isn't it?" he mumbles.

"Yeah. It's bad. But that doesn't mean we can't do something about it."

"Well, what can I do? I want to help. I've heard some things, seen some things myself. I'm… I'm valuable, they just don't see it."

Rue's heart warms. He wants to be useful, doesn't want to sit around and watch those he loves disappear or die. She can understand. She was already a Smoke Runner at his age, doing unfathomable things for bad people. If Finny wants to help and protect those he loves, who is she to deny him that right?

"I know you are. They know it too; they just feel the need to protect you. It's not that they don't see your value, they just can't lose you. I can't either so I need you to listen to me very carefully. Can you do that? We need to make this quick."

He nods, running a hand through his hair, and scoots in closer for her to reveal all her secrets. She wants to squeeze him out of pure admiration for his eagerness to do good, but she refrains, for their own embarrassment.

"They are getting bolder. I just got a lead about the person in charge. Someone has been driving around in a cenzium town car in the Low District, and I'm certain it's the head of the snake. If you ever see—"

"I have." Finny's eyes are big with the realization. "At least I think I have. Was it black?"

Rue blinks, not sure what else to do. "Yes. Finny where did you see it? And when?"

"Someone in a black cenzium four door was followin' me one morning on my way to the docks. It was early so it was still dark, but I know what I saw. It followed me down two streets before my senses told me to get to a rooftop. I lost it down a narrow alley and watched as it stopped for a few minutes before drivin' off towards the High District. Were they trying to take me?"

"I don't know for sure. It doesn't seem like the same MO as who takes the victims. Maybe it was a stake out. Did you get a good look at the driver, or any passengers?"

"No, the windows were tinted with this shiny metallic looking film." He runs his hand through his hair again, this time looking out into the darkened room in thought.

"What is it?" She can feel his heart ready to break through his chest.

"I just feel like we're missin' somethin'. How come more people aren't talking about a cenzium car seen in the Lowers? It seems so out of place you'd think it would have more buzz. I feel like some of my tagging buddies would know if someone came around driving something so valuable."

"Well, the lead I got was from someone who was paid off by the man in the car, maybe he's been paying off more than just that one person. What better way to keep yourself from getting caught, then to have kids in the neighborhood do your dirty work."

"Shit."

"Yeah. Well, my lead told me that the man in the car was white, wearing an expensive white suit with gold star buttons, anyone you know?"

"The only people who can afford to wear white suits are Highers. The gold buttons are interestin' though, the only person I can think of is the President of Currency, he likes to flaunt his gold."

Rue isn't sure, that seems like too much of an obvious connection for it to be a true lead. She will have to look into it herself, but maybe Finny is on to something.

Before she has time to voice her concerns, she can hear the agitated voice of Olympia, who is obviously getting annoyed by the dark conditions.

"We'll finish this another time, keep your eyes open. Your instincts won't fail you. You are a smart kid, keep yourself safe and your ear on the ground," Rue whispers.

Back in the kitchen, they make quick work of the candles, giving the whole apartment a warm glow. The smell of random herbs and flower petals mixed into the wax fill Rue's nose. She makes a mental note to ask Olympia for some spare petals to add to her own candles. Her dingy apartment could use some aromatherapy.

Rue's finger twirls around the rim of her mug while she waits for the others to get situated. She and Finny share a knowing look.

Olympia breaks the silence first. "Okay, so what is so important that you needed to sneak in here through the window under the cover of night like a rogue?"

Finny uses this exact moment to spit out his tea, coughing on air. Very subtle.

Her gaze locks on Olympia, which she returns with raised eyebrows. Rue opens her mouth to say words, but nothing comes out. She is mute. She has lost all knowledge of the Ethos language.

Does she know? Fuck, she knows. How does she know? No, she can't. Wait, does she?

"Don't be silly, Rue is not a rogue. She's a smart girl and knows when she needs to be extra careful that's all," Fiona adds.

Sweet, sweet, Fiona. Always looking for the good in everyone.

Olympia continues to glare at Rue, her expression changes from knowing, to something Rue swears is disappointment. She clears her throat before speaking.

"Actually," she pauses, not knowing if she can continue, but decides against stopping now. "That's exactly what I am. And I've been working on the disappearances as a job for my boss."

The room erupts in voices, none of which Rue can focus on.

Fiona gasps, "What? Really?"

At the same time Finny yells, "Sick, I knew it!"

While Olympia demands, "Who is your boss?"

Rue chooses to address Olympia first, afraid the now red flowers in her hair are an indication of the lava flowing through her veins. "It's best if I don't say. Plus, no matter what my answer is you won't approve. So, let's just say a powerful man, who is protecting me while I handle this problem for him."

Olympia scoffs, "This isn't stealing someone's wallet Aruelia, this is a group of humans taking people against their will. This isn't something you can fix on your own."

"I know that. No offense but you don't know what I'm capable of. I'm taking this very seriously, and that's why I'm here. That's why I've been visiting weird hours, and asking you random questions, and having you dissect a mysterious poison. So, I can get this taken care of, and we can all be safe."

"Wait, let's come back to mysterious poison," Finny butts in.

At the same time, Olympia and Rue both shout, "Not the time, Finny!"

Olympia waves her hands around the room. "I knew you were mixed into this somehow. All these years I sat back and said nothing. I did nothing. But this, this whole mess. This is bigger than all of us. This is not something we can stop from happening I'm afraid."

"Well instead of giving up, I'm choosing to fight back. To make this as difficult as it can be for them. I'm not just going to sit back, and watch humans get taken, and fae folk killed. They are killing us by the way. Cutting off our ears like we're trash." The emotion coming from her words hits Rue in her gut. Saying it out loud, the realization that this is real, terrifies her.

"You think I don't know that?" Olympia yells back, banging both hands down on the table. "Every day when I read those headlines, I stop breathing. Not a single speck of oxygen gets into my lungs until I know you are not one of the dead."

Tears form in her eyes, which causes Rue's stomach to fall to the floor.

"I didn't know," Rue admits.

"No, you don't because you are so worried about fixing the world for others, you forget that your life is important too. You forget that people care about you too. You are not alone. As much as you believe you are, we are all right here."

Fiona, sensing the tension rising to the ceiling, interrupts the argument. "Hey, hey. Let's all take a seat. And a deep breath. We will get the food out of the oven, drink this wonderful tea Olympia has made us, and share what we all know. Let's get everyone on the same page, so we can all do our part to protect our people. That's what we all want right? For our community to be safe."

"Right Mom," Finny adds to keep the peace, and his head.

Olympia moves her gaze to Fiona, who offers her a smile and nod. She lets out an audible sigh, and reluctantly agrees. "Okay, but just so we are clear, I do not like that you are mixed into all this."

Rue raises her hands in surrender, "I don't either. This wasn't my choice. I got thrown into it without a say."

"Why don't you tell us what has happened so far, Honey." Fiona reaches her hand over to Rue's, squeezing it a few times. "Let us understand your perspective, so maybe we can be helpful. While you do that, I'll get this food dished up."

Rue looks at her mug while Fiona gets up and moves to the oven. Her finger swirls around the spoon, allowing sparkles to dance along the rim pushing the handle around in a circle.

Just tell them the truth.

Breathe in. Breathe out.

"A few months ago, before this whole thing blew up to what it is now, I was attacked. The man followed me from your shop Oly, and he tried to kill me in an alley. He said the words…" She pauses to clear her mind of the visions that still haunt her from that day. "All the lands will be clean soon."

"He did what?" Olympia lifts a hand to her temples.

"Believe me when I say, he will not be a bother to anyone every again, and let's just leave it at that."

Fiona chimes in, facing away from the table, "What does he have to do with the Organization? No offense Honey, but if you work for someone dangerous, don't you think there will be people after you regardless?"

While Fiona drops plates of a meat and rice bake (what meat you may ask, no one knows) in front of all of them, Rue spends the next thirty minutes explaining the last few months of events, leaving out names and locations. If questioned in the future, the three of them will have no real information regarding this issue, just a vague understanding of the events that transpired. Rue dances between the whole truth, and the safe truth, so Olympia doesn't have a heart attack at this very table.

After explaining the two kids in the alley, and how she is being watched, she ends by saying, "So, this is probably going to be my last visit until this is all resolved, unless you need more time on the poison. I just came to see if it was finished up, and to ask you to spread the word of the magnitude of this. I know people understand what's going on, but they need reminders to put their safety in front of their wants. Also, you need to set up some sort of group willing to take in street kids, and someone better get Charlie to stay with them."

"Only the Mother herself can do that," Olympia jokes with her face in her mug.

"I know, but we have to try. I want the whole borough to be on lock down, well as much as we can. I understand this is people's livelihoods."

"You do realize how difficult this will be, to convince people to change their routines. Some of us need to be out late at night, it's the only way we make money." Fiona's eyes are wide. She looks to Olympia, then back at Rue.

"I understand that. And the last thing I want is for people to be suffering more than they already are, but this thing… This is bigger than all of us. I feel it in my bones. Every time I replay those words, all the lands, I can't help but feel like it's everywhere. Like we are all in trouble. I don't know how to explain it, I just feel it in my soul."

A hand moves over hers, which calms the trembles in her fingers she didn't realize were happening. "We will take care of West Harbor," Olympia reassures her.

"Yes, we will. Luckily people seem to love us," Fiona laughs.

Finny chimes in, "Yeah, and I can take care of the kids on the street. We have codes we tag when danger is near, and I'll start spreading the message."

Rue stands to start cleaning the mugs and plates from the table, disposing the herbs at the bottom of the mugs in Olympia's compost bin. Placing all the dishes in the sink, she turns the handle expecting water. Nothing comes out. She tries again, thinking air might be in the pipes, still nothing.

"Oly, how long has your water been out?" Rue moves her hand to pinch the bridge of her nose.

"Oh that. It's been a few days."

"What does the landlord say?"

"He can't do anything about it, it's a street wide problem. But it's all right, I'm managing. Fiona has been kind enough to lend me some water when she has it. And we're due for a nice rain storm any day now."

Rue turns to look at Olympia. "Your landlord is a prick with a God complex that uses your kindness as a form of weakness. He's still making you pay your water bill, isn't he?

This wouldn't be the first or second time Olympia's landlord made her pay utilities that were out of commission for a long stretch of time. One summer, when Rue was a girl, he demanded they pay for a whole month of electricity, even though they had power only three days out of the month. Rue put a Volt Fish (an electric snake looking menace from the bay) in his toilet in retaliation.

Olympia doesn't answer. She looks towards the living room. Rue's blood starts to boil. "You cannot keep letting him get away with this."

"He is just trying to make a living."

"At the expense of a kind old lady."

"Don't you dare do anything to that man, Aruelia! Do you hear me? I can see the schemes in your eyes. I don't want to hear about fish guts in his bed, or stolen coins, or gods forbid a missing limb. Promise me." Her eyes scream, *I mean it.*

"I promise no missing limbs."

Olympia walks up to Rue to put her hands on her cheeks, her olive green eyes staring into her soul. "I don't believe you, but I'll take your word for it."

"You were always too smart for my schemes," Rue smiles, trying to calm the tension of the evening.

"Well, I think we best get going, give you two a chance to talk," Fiona interrupts. "Finny has an early shift at the docks tomorrow anyway, and it's getting late."

"Oh, before you go…" Olympia moves away from Rue and into her bedroom. "You left this scarf here the last time we—" She stops herself and looks at Fiona like she just spilled a decade long secret. "The last time you were over for tea." She tries to play it off, but Rue knows the truth as soon as a rose color fills Fiona's cheeks.

Rue smirks but hides it behind her fingers. Fiona and Olympia have been dancing around being in love for as long as she can remember. A secret love, like a journal you hide under your pillow. One you don't dare share in fear of it being read out of context. Rue can see it in their eyes, and the way their touches linger just a bit longer than most.

The two of them are meant to be together. They will admit it to the rest of the world when they are ready, if they are ever ready. Sometimes two people are content to exist with their feelings without the comments of the community around them, and that's okay.

That's the kind of love Rue craves, glances from across the room, a magnetic pull to each other, someone you think of when you look at the natural beauty of the world.

"If you want, me and Finny can go so you guys can continue whatever happened with the scarf," Rue snickers, winking at Olympia and drawing an invisible heart with her fingers.

"As long as I can go, and never hear of this again." Finny says, folding over like he just got punched in the gut.

"No, I insist. I'll be over tomorrow, dear. Do you want me to bring anything from the shop?" Fiona leans in and kisses Olympia's cheek before hugging Rue one last time.

"No, it's okay. I'll see you tomorrow then." The look of disappointment flashes over Olympia's eyes before she masks it with contentment again.

Finny leans down to give Olympia and Rue a hug at the same time, Rue lingers a second longer welcoming his warmth. "Listen to those killer instincts, okay? And keep these two safe for me," she whispers in his ear.

He replies with a nod before walking over to the door, and starting down the steps, Fiona following. She waves as she leaves the apartment. Stopping in the doorway to get one last glance at Olympia, she smiles and closes the door softly. Rue's heart might disintegrate from it's lack of true love.

"You two are the cutest! Gods save some romance for the rest of us. You make my relationship look like a scab on someone's knee," Rue belts out after she hears their footsteps fade away.

Olympia doesn't respond, just gently presses a hand to Rue's cheek. She walks back to the stove, and starts cleaning up from the eventful evening, humming something pretty to herself.

Rue blows out a few of the candles to save them for another time, leaving the ones on the table lit so they can still see around the room.

"So, how is the formula going? Did you figure out what that weird natural agent is?"

"Yes, we need to talk about that." She stops what she is doing to turn to Rue. "I haven't seen this particular species in quite some time, almost five decades to be exact."

"So, what is it? Where could you buy it?" Rue leans back on the table, crossing her arms over her chest.

"Oh, you won't be able to find it on the island, it's from the mainland. It is an invasive species called Glowing Thistleroot, and it originates in the Northlands. Whomever made this poison, was an advanced alchemist. To understand how these ingredients work together, and to be able to access this species of Thistleroot... Aruelia, this was not human made. This was made by someone who has magic. And by that, I mean dark magic, shadow magic. The ingredients were bonded together at a micro level with traces of something I've never seen before. It attached to them as if it had a mind of its own."

"What does that mean, someone from the mainland is behind the Organization? Is this a sick attempt at killing off humans for good? The fae killings don't make sense then. None of this does." Rue rubs her thumb nail along her bottom lip while she thinks.

Olympia sighs, wiping her hands with a towel and flinging it over her shoulder. "If I was to make an educated guess, I'd say that someone with magic is behind it, or at least distributing it to a human who is behind it."

Rue's mind wanders to everything she knows, adding this half-developed clue to her jumbled list of random hunches. Shadow magic. It's so rare, Rue has always been convinced it was a myth, like a story to get kids to eat their dinner and brush their teeth. For some reason, the more she uncovers, the less she understands about this situation.

"I'm sorry it didn't clear anything up, I wish I could help more."

"No, what you uncovered is invaluable. I never would have figured that out on my own, so thank you. I really appreciate it." Rue gets up off the table and moves towards Olympia. "Do you want me to do anything before I go?" she asks.

Olympia pauses. "Stay. Just for tonight, so I know you're safe."

Rue sits on the countertop next to her. "You know I can't."

Olympia turns to her, "Worth a try." Worry fills her eyes as she looks Rue over, as if to memorize her features.

"I'm safe. I can take care of myself. You don't need to worry, you know."

"That's like telling me not to breathe air, Honey Bee." She runs hand over Rue's hair, stopping at the tiny braid poking through the rest, and tracing her fingers over the red strand. The two sit in the silence of the night for some time, neither wanting to say their goodbye just yet.

Rue looks around the room. "This whole thing is so fucked up." Her head slouches, staring at her feet dangling off the edge of the counter. The weight of it all pushes her to the tile below. She just wants to lay down and take a long rest. Ignore the world for a few moments of peace.

"It is," Olympia says in a breath. "But no one is expecting you to fix it all yourself. These types of situations pop up in history all the time. And the way we defeat the enemy, is as a collective. I'm going to tell you something my father used to tell me all the time when I was a girl. He used to say, *if you want to change the world, light a match.*"

Rue darts her gaze to Olympia. "Like set the world on fire?"

"Not exactly," she laughs. "But sometimes that works too. What he meant was, the light of one flame, can shine over many. Giving others the opportunity to find their own matches and become flames themselves. We win by empowering others."

A smile crosses Rue's lips, "I like that. Next time I'm rallying an army, I might steal it."

"He would have loved you, your drive, your spunk. I was a lot like you when I was a girl."

Their eyes meet, both wanting to say those three words, I love you, but neither speaks. They don't need to. Their bond is stronger than language. It's an understanding at the deepest level that they will be on each other's teams for the rest of their days. The bond between family. The bond between a mother and daughter, even if those words don't pertain to them.

"Well, if you don't plan on staying, you better get home. Take the rooftops for me, please." Olympia moves the kitchen towel back to her hands, wipes at nothing, and places it on the counter to distract herself from the goodbye.

Rue jumps down from the counter, wiping the back of her pants from leftover potting soil. "Can I use your window?" she jokes.

"Just this once, next time through the front door."

"Deal. Just as long as you and Fi get the word out, make sure people have a curfew if they can. And just trust that I'm doing everything I can to get these guys off the streets."

"We trust you, Honey Bee. We'll do our best. You do yours." Olympia reaches her hands out to Rue's, sandwiching it between her own. "So, this is goodbye for a while?"

Rue's unbothered expression fades. Her eyes drift towards the table as she says, "For now. But not forever. Promise." She hoists herself up, over the sink, jumping down on the fire escape.

"Oh, one last thing before I forget." Olympia pulls at Rue's hand to come back. "I am still working on The Blue Lady. She's a hard woman to find. Everyone who knows her whereabouts has either fled the city or is refusing to speak to me."

"Thanks for trying. It means a lot. If you find anything else out, you can tell me when we see each other next. Be safe, okay?"

"You too, I lo—" She stops herself, deciding against the forbidden words of attachment. "Just be safe."

Rue closes the window and starts her assent up the ladder. Before making it to the roof, she stops at the next floor, staring into the dark room beyond the glass. A wicked grin fills her face. Feeling a sudden urge to have a surprise visit with a certain landlord about a certain bill.

CHAPTER

RUE is sitting in front of a pile of clothes on her floor, back in her old apartment, trying to decide if a pair of cargo pants are clean enough to wear out. They aren't. It's not that she doesn't like clean clothes (she's not a psychopath), it's the act of cleaning them. Her building doesn't offer laundry, and the closest laundry house is a few boroughs away. Even if it was down the block, Rue would rather lay naked on a pile of rotting fish than have to sit in there, with strangers, while she waits for her panties to dry.

She usually tries to wash her clothes in her shower, filling a bucket she keeps under the sink with water and washing things by hand. Unfortunately, she hasn't had time since moving back in here.

It's been two weeks since Rue met with Olympia last, and one week since she talked Diego into letting her pack up her stuff to move back into her own place.

The daily commute from the High District into the Low was starting to take a toll on her, and it was wasting a huge chunk of her day attempting to cross the bridges without being detected. To her utter shock, Diego agreed. She spent three days double checking if he heard her correctly, and contemplating if she entered an alternate reality and didn't notice.

His only condition was to keep in touch with him weekly, debriefing over dinner at his apartment each Sunday. Simple terms, which she decided not to question and take at face value.

It's a good thing she did move back, because shortly after the bridge to the High District closed until further notice. Although this didn't exactly affect Rue, she knew ways around the bridge entrances. The Presidents decided, *for the safety of the people*, to close off access from one District to the other. What they didn't anticipate was the Lowers taking that as abandonment.

The act caused riots at the gates of the bridges, spearheaded by those in the community lucky enough to have jobs in the High District. Those bridges are the only route to their paychecks. No paycheck, no hope. And when you have a group of people with no hope in their leaders, things become chilling and unstable.

The energy of the Low District is scattered and overflowing with different opinions. While some are terrified and won't leave their homes, others are ready to burn the city to the ground. Then there is a third group, citizens who are just going about their day-to-day life like nothing is wrong. They scare Rue the most, those who are unwilling to admit something is unjust, and continue to go about their life with blinders on.

Rue's mind pops back into her reality after falling down a tragic rabbit hole that is *the future* of the Southlands. She holds up a pair of black jeans (with more holes than fabric at this point) and counts it as a win since there is no visible dirt on them.

"Better than nothing," she says to herself.

Pulling them up to her waist, she fastens the buttons on her jeans and pulls a black crop top over her head. It's too hot for her full Smoke Runner uniform tonight so she will have to go as herself. She might get farther into this plan if she is herself anyway. Tonight is for answers, and she is going to get them one way or another.

She stops in front of her entryway mirror before heading out, grabbing her backpack, and strapping a small pocket knife to herself under her shirt. Her eyes dart to her reflection and she takes a minute to look herself over.

Drained is the first word that comes to her mind. She can see it in her eyes, the way they don't open to their fullness. The purple undertones peeking out regardless of the amount of makeup she puts on. The paleness of her freckles. And the fact that her cheeks are starting to cave in a bit. That last one might be due to the fact that Rue cannot remember the last time she ate a full meal, but she's drained nevertheless.

"I'm okay, it's almost over." Rue isn't one for positive affirmations, but it feels right in the moment to remind herself. A tiny little pep talk before what she is positive will not be an easy night.

She leaves her apartment, locking the door behind her, and heads up the steps to the roof. The warm spring air hits her when she reaches the top. A safe welcome for an air magic wielder like herself. Not that she will be resorting to magic tonight, but it is reassuring to have it on her side as an option.

Rue can conjure air when she needs it, but when it comes naturally as wind, it works more efficiently. More pure in a way, like her magic is more refined. She doesn't have to concentrate so hard to manipulate it around objects.

Before she heads off on her journey, she sits for a moment, letting the breeze pull strands of hair out of her double braids. They tickle her face as they dance across her skin.

Somehow, high on this rooftop, in the middle of a chaotic city, Rue grounds herself in the wind. Letting it rush around her like a warm hug. She wonders if this is how Olympia feels when she places her hands in dirt. A euphoric feeling of bliss and power all at the same time. It makes her wish to fly into the wind, feel the rush of air blow past her as she swoops and dives her troubles away. Goosebumps form on her skin as a way to welcome her back to life, giving her the strength to continue on.

The blip in her gut wants her to go, she can feel it tugging towards the ocean. Knowing this is all leading up to something bigger than herself. She can feel it in her bones, the end is almost near, and then she will get off this rock, move herself and Olympia to the mainland where they belong. It's where her tether wants her to be.

With a deep inhale (one of which she ignores the smell of trash) Rue lets her lungs fill with oxygen. On her exhale, she stretches her back, reaching over her head with her arms.

Here we go.

Her original thought was to use the rooftops, but she finds herself walking on the street after realizing the sky bridges from building to building are overcrowded. The final straw was the absolute walnut of a man who nearly pushed her off the rickety wooden bridge. Solid cobblestone ground it is. It's unavoidable.

They say you find out who people really are in times of crisis, what Rue is learning is that crisis doesn't mean a whole lot to some people living in the Low District. The streets are packed with people. Along with the bridges closing last week to the High District, the Presidents have issued a suggestive curfew for all Lowers. Deeming the streets unsafe due to the high number of kidnappings.

Are they issuing statements on how they plan on *stopping* this from happening? No. Do they bulk up Marshals in the areas most targeted? Of course not. Does she think the Seven Presidents are allowing this to happen to distract from the quality of life issues throughout the District? Absolutely.

They are benefiting from this whole shit show more than anyone, in theory the people are too busy worrying about being taken, they don't have time to question why they haven't had drinking water in weeks.

In a perfect world, people wouldn't put themselves in harm's way. The streets would be ghost towns past dusk. But this isn't a perfect world. Nightlife is too important to the economy of the Southlands. People need to make money to keep their homes, and their families fed. There is no way around it.

Bars, strip clubs, and poker houses make the city money. Which means it also needs its trains and clinics open all night to deal with the patrons. As well as it needs its electricians and city workers out fixing the inevitable utility issues. So, with that vicious cycle in full effect, half the city is walking the streets after dark. The stone sidewalks look like they are at full capacity.

Rue passes a vendor shouting at passersby to buy his homemade baked goods. While he is talking to a couple about ingredients, Rue swipes a small biscuit off the corner of the table. Opening the cloth wrapper, she takes a bite. It's nothing special, a bland, dry biscuit with a slight hint of an unrecognizable fruity flavor. Similar, if not identical to the ones that come in Meal Bags.

The more she chews, the more she is convinced it *is* a biscuit from a Meal Bag. She isn't sure if she should be offended or impressed at his hustle.

She spits the contents from her mouth into an overflowing trash bin and discards the rest of the biscuit into the bin as well. She is hungry, but not that hungry.

The smell of ash and still smoking embers fill the streets with an eerie haze. In the late hours of the morning, word got out about some riots popping up around the district, Lowers targeting the Marshal stalls throughout the area. Homemade bombs were thrown into the windows, smoking out and injuring the Marshals, leaving the structures to be burnt to the ground.

Chaos ensued, leading most of the rioters, as well as innocent people passing by, to be detained and sent to the prison district outside of Alerious City, without the option for trial. It didn't end there though, now in the aftermath of the hostile situation, protesters raise their voices in solidarity with the innocent lives imprisoned.

Rue wishes she had time to join in the protests, remembering the empowering feeling of walking with Olympia in marches during her childhood. A sinking feeling in her gut keeps her moving forward and away from the protesters, knowing that if she were to get involved, she might be spotted by authorities herself, making this whole job irrelevant from prison.

Keep walking. You're doing this for them.

When she reaches the Flats, a smell of scum hits Rue's nose like a slap in the face. This strip of the Low District is full of slimy people, with bad intentions, praying on the weak. The energy is fun and upbeat to the naked eye, a drastic difference to the devastation a few blocks away. People are singing on the street, there is a small group gathered around two men fighting, and multiple street performers are trying to see who can play their designated instrument the loudest. Right in the middle of the chaos, is Rue's destination for the evening.

On The Rox is a small dive bar owned by the one and only, Roxanne Bask. Back when Rue first met Rocky, she was just a bartender in this establishment, but a few years ago she bought the place out right and renamed it On The Rox. She is a big reason this strip is as popular as it is, bringing back a lot of the clients after fixing up her bar.

Fixing up should be used loosely. The bar isn't nice. In fact, it's being held together with rusty nails and a prayer, but the locals love it. It's a popular place with fishermen because of the proximity to the fishing docks in the bay.

The stained-glass door is cracked open and there is some live music coming from the inside. Rue does her best to blend in with a group of men singing sea shanties as they enter, clearly already plastered. The bouncer at the door sees right through her ruse and grabs her by the bicep. This is either about to go really well, or Rue is going to be sore in the morning.

"Where do you think you're going, love?" His voice is rough, like his lungs are coated in black goo from smoking too much tobacco. He has a nice face though, dark features, green eyes, a jawline that could cut glass. He is towering over her, and his citrus scent takes up all the space around the two of them.

Rue jumps into action.

"Oh, I was just following my friend in. Is that a problem? Did you want to keep me company instead?" She looks up at him with huge doe eyes, tilting her head with a smirk. Her fingers trail a line down the middle of his chest. The man is carved from marble.

His hand on her arm tightens and she winces from the pain, dropping her flirty demeanor, eyes narrowing on his. She readjusts herself, pulling her arm out of his grip, and stands tall, looking up at him down the bridge of her nose.

"Do I look like an idiot to you?" he asks.

She crosses her arms and huffs, "Do you honestly want me to answer that?" She can feel the fire in his glare and smiles wider.

His nostrils are flaring at her unwillingness to be intimidated by his size, which makes her laugh. He picked the wrong redhead to mess with if that's what he wants.

"Boss doesn't like trash in her establishment."

"Yet here you are, working for her. Interesting. While we're on the subject of your boss, I'd like to speak with her."

A growl (an actual growl) comes out of this man's mouth. He leans into her, causing her to step backwards into a stone wall, but she doesn't back down.

"She'll want to see me. Tell her an old friend is here to catch up." She dares to wink at him, and in doing so can sense his heart rate starting to pick up from irritation.

"Tell her yourself."

He flips Rue over, so her chest is up against the wall of the building, face pushed into the cold stone. He pulls her hands behind her back and wraps a rope around them.

"Kinky, I usually wait to use handcuffs until the third date," she purrs.

His hands stop tying, trying to collect his wits, then he pulls tighter on her restraints.

Rocky needs a better bouncer, this man is so easy to rile up.

"Shut the fuck up."

"Oh, sorry. Did I confuse you? See sometimes, when two people really like each other, they go on dates. And if the date goes well, they end up in bed together. See the handcuffs can be used to—"

"I said shut. The fuck. Up." His breath on her neck is hot as he speaks into her ear. She can smell the tobacco as he exhales. Large hands pull at her hair, causing her to grunt, as he backs her up and walks her into the bar.

"Yes, officer," she mocks, getting in the last word.

She hides her excitement as they walk through the crowd to the back offices. This is going to be easier than she anticipated.

The last door on the left is locked, and Bouncer Man uses a key to get in. He swings the door open, and Rue looks into a tiny, dingy room with a wooden desk in the middle. A violet leather chair behind the desk is ripped in the corner, with what look like claw marks across the backrest. Across from it, sits a rickety wooden folding chair that looks like it could collapse from a strong breeze. Papers fill every inch of clean space on the desk, and the floor, and also the overflowing bookshelf.

"Charming," she mumbles under her breath. "Really love the stale beer smell, it adds a bit of romance to the space."

He pushes her into the office, shoving her down into the folding chair. It wobbles under her weight, and she tries not to take it personally. A strain on her shoulders burns into her skin as her arms get pulled back, and he ties the rope around her wrists to the chair itself. What he fails to do is tie up her legs. He most definitely is going to regret that decision.

While he is busy messing with the ropes, Rue somehow swipes some coins from his pocket without him noticing, gripping them in her hands. On the inside, she is laughing in his face for being completely useless to his boss.

"Wait here," he grunts.

"Yes, because I have so many other choices," she spits back, rolling her eyes at him.

He swears under his breath as he leaves, which makes her giggle.

"I'll miss you terribly!" she calls after him.

The door slams shut behind him, and Rue is left alone. She looks around for a way out, but there aren't any vents or other doors. The tension on her arms is starting to cause sharp pains in her wrists, something in the cheap rope he used is splintering into her skin. She tugs against her restraints, but nothing budges more than a few centimeters.

All her movements halt when the doorknob creaks as its turns. The wooden door flings open, hitting the adjacent wall. A chuckle comes from behind, one Rue knows all too well, and she assumes it's because of the shitty rope job of Bouncer Man, and certainly not her. As soon as she turns her head, her golden eyes lock on the turquoise of another.

Hello old friend.

Rocky enters the room like a snake, calm, slow, and with a face as cold as ice. Her bleached hair is straight, pulled back into a sleek ponytail, and her frosted eyes show no excitement to see who is sitting in front of her. She clearly doesn't think Rue's little charade at the front was as funny as she does.

Instead of walking towards her chair, Rocky steps in front of Rue, leaning back against her desk. Her arms cross over her body, and the look of pure hatred in her eyes burns into Rue's flesh. The two women sit in silence, not daring to be the first one to speak.

Something about Rocky's features makes Rue feel bad, like the misery in her eyes is slowly killing her from the inside out. The rage she is trying so hard to project, is a mask for the sleepless nights and demanding jobs that come with who she is. The purple undertones around her eyes match the ones Rue is sporting currently. She looks at her nails, which are chipping and red from nervous bites. Somewhere deep (extremely deep) within her heart, a small crack forms for the well-being of her once friend.

She wonders what their futures would hold in another life.

Rue opens her mouth after a minute, getting antsy from the quiet, and tries to speak. She gets interrupted with a slap across her face. The burn that follows is nothing short of painful, and she lets out a primal noise. The crack in her heart repairs itself miraculously for reasons unknown.

"Rocky, never a pleasure," Rue says between breaths.

"What the hell are you doing in my bar?"

"Just catching up with an old friend. I thought we could talk about boys and braid each other's hair."

With that, comes another slap to Rue's face. This one hitting harder than the last. With the force of the blow, Rue bites down on her cheek and blood is now pooling in her mouth. She leans to the side and spits right onto the carpet, turning back to Rocky with red stained teeth.

You draw blood, you get it all over your shit.

"What no warm welcome for your old roomie?"

"Cut the shit Rue, why are you here? Diego need something? I told him over and over again that I don't put up with his shit anymore. I'm done with you bastards." Her silvery voice bounces off the walls of the office.

Rue's mind travels back to the backlash she got from Diego when Rocky conned the Smoke Runners. She made off with thirty gold for herself and left the rest of the group in the dust. Rue has never seen him so angry, and all of it aimed at her, because to him, it was Rue's fault bringing Rocky in.

"I know about the Organization, and that you're a part of it."

Rue wishes she could live in this moment for the rest of her life, she'd spend all her money for someone to snap a picture of this exact scene. The look on Rocky's face is priceless. She's paralyzed. Her shoulders tense, hands gripping the desk. Beautiful blue eyes turn a pale shade of gray, as does her face.

"Close your mouth. It's not a good look." Rue leans back in her chair, pulling at her restraints. "Thought you were so sneaky didn't you. Creeping around the Lucky Clover in your cute little sweatshirt," she mocks. Rue's face is cold, and dark. "You're taking innocent people from their homes. Killing fae for no reason. Who is this for, Rocky? What's the end goal here?"

Rocky says nothing, biting down on her thumb nail as she looks away. Her arms cross over her body while she works through what Rue just said. "That was you, wasn't it? In the back tunnels."

Rue just nods. She raises her head to look her down the bridge of her nose, in the triumph of being better than Rocky.

"Fuck, I should have known."

"I'm disappointed." The look is plastered on Rue's face.

"Don't start acting like an upset mother," Rocky bites back.

"Oh no, I have no trouble believing you would swindle your way into something like this. What I'm disappointed in, is the handiwork of your bouncer. The man really needs to learn how to properly tie a knot."

As the last few words leave Rue's lips, her legs jolt out in front of her, kicking Rocky backwards. She somersaults over the desk, shouting some colorful curse words at Rue.

The ropes drop from Rue's wrists, and she jumps up from the chair. Adrenaline pumping within her, she grabs the folding chair and swings at Rocky, who is now on her feet again.

Rocky blocks the chair, causing it to fall to the ground with a crash and shatter.

Rue lunges at her, tackling her to the ground. Her fist gets one good punch in before being kicked off, flying into the bookshelf behind her. A sharp sting shoots up her back with the impact.

"You know," Rocky huffs. "You never really were one of us, were you? You care too much about the filth that roams the streets."

Rue wipes her lip and jumps to her feet. "I'm not the one mixed in with a group of kidnapping psychopaths."

With a groan, Rocky charges at Rue, taking a swing and connecting with Rue's cheek bone. Rue lets out a scream, "Fuck!"

Rocky argues behind her fists, "Don't act like you're some sort of angel, direct descendent of the Mother. You're trash. You will never be good, no matter how much you try to prove otherwise."

Rue spits red blood at her, landing on her shoe. Another punch from each woman causes both to back up and regroup. Breathing heavy, they both rub at sore spots on their faces.

"They're watching you. You know that, right?" Rocky spits.

Rue shoots her arms out to her sides as the two shuffle in a circle around each other. "Why Rocky! Why are you doing this? This isn't you. You steal possessions, not human beings."

"Some of us don't have a powerful set of balls to protect us from the real world. Some of us are just trying to survive."

She wipes blood from her mouth, then charges at Rue once again, kicking her in the chest. Rue flies back into the door, which rattles with the impact. She gets forced back into the wood with Rocky's forearm on her throat, grunting with gritted teeth.

"You want him, you can have him." Rue uses her knee to drive into Rocky's stomach, sinking her to the ground, yelling from the impact.

Rue stalks around her, wiping sweat from her temple.

From the ground, Rocky sneers, "Oh, trouble in paradise? And it wasn't even because of me." She lets out a cough, trying to find her breath again. Neither of the women are willing to admit they are in pain.

"You know him, there is no paradise."

"Oh, poor Rue. Save me the bullshit."

Before Rue can answer, Rocky swings her leg out, causing Rue to lose balance and fall to the ground, hitting her head on the desk.

Rocky jumps on top of her, using her weight to pin Rue to the ground. Her fist connects with Rue's face, and the impact pushes her to the side. In her blurred vision, she can see broken chair pieces just out of reach.

Rocky attempts to punch for a second time, but Rue moves her head out of the way, using her own body to flip Rocky over onto her back.

With Rue on top, she grabs a leg from the broken chair and presses it against Rocky's throat, pushing deeper and deeper until she is gasping for air.

"Enough! That's enough. Neither of us wants to kill the other. This is so fucking stupid," Rue yells. "Now, I'm going to remove this and you aren't going to hit me again. This is over. We're done."

Rocky's eyes lock on Rue's, defeat pours out of her. She nods in agreement, and Rue loosens her grip. Rocky begins to choke back her breaths, moving her hand to her neck.

As if all the adrenaline leaves her body at once, Rue slumps to the side, and lays down with her back against the carpet. She tosses the chair leg across the room, hearing it crash into the bookshelf which is in shambles from the fight.

The two lie there for a moment, listening to the muffled sounds of the bar outside. Their breaths create a hectic beat, only interrupted by the occasional moan from pain.

"This isn't as fun as when we were eighteen," Rocky admits, which causes the tension in Rue's body to soften.

Before she can stop herself, Rue is laughing. A genuine, full body laugh she finds within her soul. One that is killing her ribs slowly, but she doesn't stop. She's not necessarily happy, but if she doesn't laugh at her situation, she might just replace it with crying. And that will not be happening today, or any day.

Rocky joins her, and the two of them fall into a beautiful moment between friends, and not two enemies lying on the dingy carpet.

"When did getting hit once make me want to crawl into a hole and die?" Rocky asks.

"I don't know, but I just kept thinking about our sparring matches when we'd train together, and how we used to be able to go ten rounds."

Rocky coughs and admits, "I think we're old."

"Nah, we're still young… just've gone through a lot of shit and are tired from it all."

"Amen to that."

Rue looks over to her, and confesses, "Honestly, you've gotten good."

Still out of breath, Rocky says, "So have you, that move at the end, when you flipped me over to get the upper hand. I'm impressed."

Rue turns to the side and gets to her feet, reaching out a hand to Rocky. "Truce?"

Rocky looks to her hand, "For today," she answers honestly, taking Rue's offer of peace and letting her help her up.

"Thank the Gods, I don't have it in me to go again."

Once Rocky is standing, Rue takes a few steps back. She may have offered up a truce, but Rue isn't going to take another chance of getting hit.

Rocky sits back down on her desk, wiping away some dried blood from her lip. "Why are you asking about the Organization anyway? What's in it for you?"

Rue takes a second before answering, trying to piece together a response that's truthful, yet doesn't give away too much. At the end of the day, Rocky is one of them, how deep Rue isn't sure, but she needs to be tactful.

"I've been trying to ignore what they, *you*, are doing. But it's personal now, I was attacked. Clearly, they didn't finish the job, or I wouldn't be here right now. I know the Organization is behind it. It started as a nuisance, but hundreds of people are either missing or dead."

Rue clears her throat before continuing. "This is turning into something much worse than anyone anticipated. And I think you know that, Rox. I saw you in that tunnel. You looked exhausted. Over it all. What I can't understand is why? You're on your own now. No contracts. No debts. Free. Why would you put yourself back in this situation again?"

Rocky's silence is deafening. Her downcast face places another piece of the puzzle together for Rue.

"It wasn't your choice, was it?" She asks the question but knows the answer already. Rocky looks directly into Rue's eyes and nods. A sharp pain pulls at her temples, and the feeling of being hit resurfaces.

"I was told if I didn't comply, my bar would be nothing but rubble and ash. It almost was, thankfully I was here late that night to put it out. Every night after, the head of one of my regulars was left at my door." Rocky looks to the ground as she speaks, her voice breaks when she continues. "If you can't burn down a girl's dreams, make it so all of her customers are rotting in graves. After I was tossing the fourth head into the bay, I decided—" She stops, swallowing down her heartbreak.

When she looks back at Rue, her eyes are glossy, like she might sob at any moment. "This bar is all I have. It's everything to me. I couldn't just let them take it away. This place—" She motions around the room, "It's the only family I got."

"Who do you work for?" Rue asks softly.

"No one knows. They're experts at keeping things from us. I know it's a man, because my advisor uses those pronouns, but that's as much as I know. We don't even know each other's assignments. They always shift us around, so we never work with the same person twice. I swear to you, I didn't know you were someone's assignment."

She puts a hand to her chest and with desperation in her voice whispers, "I swear." Rocky opens her mouth to admit something else, spill more secrets, but decides against it. "I'm sorry, but I can't say anything more. I shouldn't have even told you that. It'll be my head next if someone finds out we were talking, so unless you want me to haunt you every second you have left in this world, I'd keep your mouth shut."

"It's not too late to make things right. You have a choice."

Rocky looks away, crossing her arms, and sighs, "We aren't all that lucky. It's too late for me to be anyone other than this. Someone needs to stay in the trenches."

Rue nods her head slowly. "Then you need to live with your choice." She pauses. "I'll leave now, and I won't come back. But next time I find you in that mask, I can't promise to ignore it. We're on opposite sides of this."

She stands to leave cautiously but Rocky doesn't move to protest her exit, just continues to stare down at the carpet. At the door, Rue turns back to her old friend. Once so close they shared a life together, yet now she looks at her like a stranger.

She opens her mouth to say something, to beg her to come with her, to help stop this, but no words come out. Rocky's hope is lost, and Rue asking her to fight against an anonymous force isn't going to bring it back.

"Good luck out there, Rox."

Before she has time to hear a goodbye, she is walking towards the back door, and into the night.

CHAPTER

RUE walks into the chill of the night. The back alley behind On The Rox is empty except for a dumpster and a few miscellaneous crates and boxes. It's a small space, only about four feet wide, and backs up into an old warehouse turned apartment complex. Neon lights flicker from the main streets around her, casting a red and purple glow down the alley.

The smell of garbage, and what she is refusing to admit is probably vomit, fight for dominance in her nose, both trying their very best to make her gag first. She steps around puddles from the early morning rain, and watches as a rat runs under an old metal crate, carrying a piece of bread in its mouth.

"Lovely."

Ahead of her is the main street into The Flats, and she can see the busyness of the night has not slowed since being in the bar. People are filling the sidewalks, laughing and talking to one another like there aren't kidnappers out there waiting for a chance to snatch them up.

"Hey, Rue!" a voice calls out from behind her.

She turns to see Rocky jogging to catch up with papers in her hands.

She rests a palm on Rue's shoulder, causing Rue to tense with the touch, still sore from the fight.

"Let's preface this by saying, this is not me trying to be a good person. I just have no use for these anymore, that's all. Don't read into it too much. I just don't want them to be linked back to me if they fall into the wrong hands," Rocky says, with a knowing look in her eye. A look of trust, even if she doesn't want to admit it out loud.

In her hand is a file folder, stuffed with papers. She passes it to Rue and takes a step back, waiting for her to look through it.

"What is this?" Rue asks as she opens the folder. Her answer comes without needing words to explain it.

Inside is stuffed with yellow paper after yellow paper of victims, each one clipped to a file. Who they are, where they live, their job, their family members, everyone they come in contact with, when and where they were taken, and what port they were shipped off from.

There are probably thirty plus victims just in this folder alone. As Rue sifts through them, her questions double with every new name.

"Look in the back," Rocky instructs her, taking the folder and flipping to the last few pages. She pulls out a white sheet of paper, with an obscure letterhead, like nothing Rue has ever seen.

The words **WHITE RAVEN** are pressed into the top in an unusual script. Something swirly, and dainty, unlike the thick black lettering used in most common prints from the Southlands.

In the top right corner, there is an insignia that catches her eye. Not large, no bigger than a few inches, but the image has her puzzled.

A bird, wings out, made of tiny swirls and curves in all directions. It has an ancient look to it, something Rue can't place with any other insignia of a group in the Southlands. Her mind runs through all of the different syndicates in the area and comes up short as to who it belongs to.

Behind the bird, is a hexagon border, made out of tiny dots and lines in an ancient language she doesn't understand, like controlled chaos. It mimics the ancient symbols of the elemental magics.

Rue rubs her finger over the symbol and takes note of the indentation it makes in the paper, as if it was pressed with a stamp of some sort. Gold flecks mix into the black ink. She wonders if it's real gold or a composite.

The special papers each come with a single line of instructions.

Next Target: (Person's Name)

Destroy at all costs, so all the lands will be clean soon.

Below the phrase that Rue has come to know so intimately, is a signature. The letters LM swipe across the page with grace, sending a chill down her body.

LM? Who is LM?

Rue's fingers begin to sweat, the weight of the paper feeling like a cinder block.

"Before you ask, I don't know who LM is, just that they send me names of people to kill. Once I finish one job, I get another assignment."

"Is it the same person who gives you instructions on who to take? Did I read that right; you ship them off to the mainland?" Rue asks, looking up from the file for the first time.

Rocky's focus darts to the street from the eye contact, she shakes her head. "Yeah. We hold them and ship them off in batches."

"These people are not animals!" Rue urges.

Rocky pulls her back, deeper into the alley. "You think I don't know that!" she whispers through gritted teeth. "Why do you think I keep files on all of them? You're not the only one who knows this is bordering on a point of no return. And I refuse to go down with a ship I didn't ask to be on."

She pulls the files from Rue's hands and turns the page from the first raven letterhead. Behind the kill notice is a file like the ones before. A write out of all the information one could get on a victim. Names, acquaintances, places they visit, everything like the others.

"So, you write these, they don't give you this information?" Rue asks, flipping from one to another.

"What can I say, I'm thorough," she jokes, but quickly tenses up again. "This wasn't how it was pitched to me, you know. I was told this was for the greater good of the human population. These people aren't innocent. You'll soon discover some got what was coming for them, as for the others… Guilty by association." Her eyes sweep the area. "You need to look at these names. I mean really look at them. It will make things clearer."

Rocky looks out into the street beyond Rue. Her arms cross over her body, and she shakes in the chill.

"I have to go. This never happened. You were never here." She pauses, thinking about her next words carefully, but decides against speaking further, and turns to walk away.

A feeling of longing rushes over Rue. This might be a final goodbye. Like this friendship that never was, is actually over. Things are about to change.

"Rox?" Rue calls out to her.

Rocky turns back to Rue, with her hand on the back door.

Rue takes a step closer. "It wasn't all bad, me and you."

Rocky shakes her head in agreement. "No, it wasn't." She opens the door and just as she's about to enter, she adds, "But if you tell anyone I said that I will murder you in your sleep."

Rue laughs, "Like I'd admit that to anyone."

"Good luck, Rue. If anyone has the balls to end this, it's your psycho ass." Rocky gives her a second of a smile before entering the bar and closing the door behind her.

Rue looks down at the stack of papers in her hands and lets out an exhale she didn't realize she has been holding in.

"Time for some light reading."

Rue jerks her apartment door open, pushing with her shoulder to get the usual jam unstuck. She tosses her keys on the table by the door, turns on a lamp that starts to flicker immediately, and kicks off her boots. Stepping over a pile of clothes she didn't feel like folding, she drops the file folder on her mattress.

On top of her dresser, she unlocks the wooden box that holds her savings and tosses in the coins she picked off of the bouncer. Not much, but any money is good money when it means getting off this island.

In the dresser, she pulls out an old black sweater and some white cotton shorts, taking them with her to the bathroom to shower.

Her muscles scold her for getting herself into a fight earlier, and she wishes nothing more than to wash the pain away in a hot shower. She drops her clothes on the sink and shuffles herself to the shower faucet. Before turning the knob, she says a little prayer for hot water.

The prayer goes unanswered.

There's no hot water, no water at all in fact.

"Fuck me!" She grunts into the ceiling, shoving the green tiles.

After letting out a few choice words to the Gods, she stomps into the kitchen for her emergency stash of water under the sink. Pulling out a jug, she pours what she can into her antique kettle on the stove.

While the water starts to boil, she grabs one of the bottles of wine she swiped from Diego's apartment and pulls out the cork with her teeth. Three swigs in, and the kettle is already whistling. There are some perks of having a stove top that only gives all or nothing.

The water from the kettle gets mixed with room temperature water, and she brings a bowl of it into the bathroom along with her wine.

As she wipes her body down using the makeshift bath water, she recoils into herself with the pressure of the cloth. Getting thrown into a wooden shelf, and almost choked to death takes a toll on a girl.

She cups the water in the bowl and splashes it over her face, cleaning off the traces of blood still on her skin. In the mirror she stares at her reflection.

Looking rough girl.

The idea of a break sounds nice, a moment of stillness in the mayhem, after this is all over and she can breathe. Maybe once this is done, she can get out of here and go somewhere warm, with life, and trees, and animals, and peace.

Peace, yes peace sounds nice.

After fighting to untangle her braids, Rue runs her fingers through her hair, massaging her sore scalp with the release of the tension, and pulls it into a loose bun on top of her head. She welcomes the comfort of clean clothes while she ties the strings to her shorts, allowing the sweater to fall over them almost completely. Relaxing in the warmth and softness.

She grabs the file folder from her bed, making sure to bring the half empty wine bottle with her for emotional support as she locks her door and heads to the roof. Something about the cool air helps her focus. And she needs to focus more than ever right now.

Once in her chair, she takes another sip of wine, before diving straight into the profiles of the victims kidnapped and sent to the mainland. She is still trying to wrap her head around that fact. The mainland. They are being shipped off to do Gods know what. They must be so terrified.

From what it looks like to Rue, most of Rocky's marks were located in the Flats, the Falls, West Harbor, and North Peri. Which makes sense considering that's where she grew up, to have her find people in those boroughs would be beneficial to the leader. Rocky knows the area, the streets, the shops, and the people.

What isn't connecting is the backgrounds of the people taken. A shopkeeper who owns a shoe repair business in the Falls. A newspaper delivery man who works for the Low District Press. A deckhand for a crab boat. A club dancer from the Flats. An unemployed father of a teenage boy.

All these people, with nothing in common. Something doesn't add up. Maybe Rocky was giving her too much credit for her abilities to understand how reading these is going to *make things clearer.*

Looking over the kidnapped victims lasts all of two minutes before her curious mind draws her to the back of the folder. The White Raven files. The insignia. The bird. Rue has never seen a raven in real life, but Olympia had taught her about them, and she can only assume this bird is one.

The only thing she keeps coming back to, is the shape of the hexagon. Her first though was that it was another form of magic, matching the ancient symbols that represent all of the bright and dark magics. But this one is made up of words, or runes maybe.

All seven of the presidents have an identical shaped crest to represent their respective positions. But theirs are more polished. Clean lines. No abnormal script making up the shape of the hexagon.

And the way the bird is designed is so much more detailed than the images on the President's crests. It gives her the impression this is an ancient crest of someone whose family has been around for millennia. Unlike anything Rue has ever seen come from the Southlands.

She switches her focus onto the names at hand. Sadly, these victims are different from the ones on yellow paper. They are all now dead, and a revelation hits her like a train.

After a moment of denial, Rue accepts the fact that they are all fae folk. They are victims of the hate crimes the city has come to be so desensitized to. The slashing. Their ears. All part of a tactic to assassinate the fae folk hiding in plain sight.

One is a druid who was hiding in the flats as a bartender. She flips the page to see a dwarf who did home repairs. The next is a nymph who cleaned chimneys for homes in West Harbor. After her, is a teenage elf who worked at a printing press on the weekends. The same printing press that produces the Low District Press.

That's odd?

Rue flips back to the human victims.

Tobias Cromwell. Kidnapped the first week of spring. Left behind by his wife Angela and son Bennett. Occupation, Low District Press pickup and delivery.

This man would have been picking up the newspapers from the printing press every morning for distribution. The exact same company this kid was working for.

It's a strange coincidence, but that is all it is, a coincidence. *Is it?*

The next file is of a human man who lives in West Harbor, Jerico Florian. Occupation, crab fisherman. Rue can't find any connections other than to the other fisherman, but there are a handful of them in her pile, it is a very common job. That is until she dives deeper into the chimney sweep nymph, Estell Ripley.

Rue sends a silent thank you to Rocky for being so thorough, because she is now going over a whole list of clients of Estell's over the past year. She almost misses it, but Jerico was a client of hers, paying for five clean outs in the last four season changes. Rue didn't know much about Chimney maintenance, but she knew enough to understand that five is excessive.

She continues flipping through people's profiles, making notes when things tie together, wishing she brought a pen to write her thoughts down.

Soon the rooftop is covered in piles of profiles with relations to one another. Rue stands back, assessing the situation that has unfolded at her feet. Running her thumb nail along her bottom lip, deep in thought, she finally connects the dots like a mysterious constellation.

"It makes sense. It all makes sense," she whispers to herself. All these humans knew fae folk. Cleaning the lands means eradicating fae folk from the Southlands, and all those who keep their secrets safe.

In the same moment of feeling euphoric for uncovering something important, Rue can't help but feel confusion in the back of her mind. With one question answered, three more pop up to take its place.

"Fuck," she draws out, running a hand through wispy pieces of hair across her face.

She needs sleep. Good, deep sleep. To clear her head and look at this tomorrow with fresh eyes.

Rue bends down to start collecting her papers before heading downstairs. Her eyes focus on the file on top, with the raven insignia. A feeling scratches her mind deep into the depths of her memory. A feeling like she should know who it belongs to. Like the answers are written within her consciousness, but they are written in a different language.

Her mind is still on the raven, when she pushes open her unlocked door with ease. She looks deeply into the ancient text around the bird's wings as she steps into her dimly lit apartment.

There is a shooting pain in the back of her neck.

And everything goes dark.

CHAPTER

...I'm stuck...

...Those eyes...

...His shadow...

Suddenly I'm pinned down, ice wrapped around my hands like a pair of handcuffs. He laughs, a slow, deep, gravelly laugh. The voice doesn't match the man from the alley, but it's familiar. A voice of a man I know, but don't.

Black smoke starts radiating from him, engulfing the two of us within it. A tornado of darkness swirls around us as he stands above me.

The shadow of Blue Eyes looks at his knife. He runs a finger over the blade, which is dripping a crimson liquid. I taste blood in my mouth. Oh Gods, I'm choking on it. I'm drowning in it. My lungs are full of red death as he watches me. My vision starts to go, coming in and out of focus, while I choke on my own blood.

He raises me into the air with one cold hand. Ice forms around my throat. Crystalizing into my veins. The frigid feeling creeps its way up my neck and into my mouth. It's frozen shut. I have no voice. No magic. No power.

I try to jerk out of his grasp but fail. My hands are still covered in ice, tied behind my back. I can't move.

Water splashes on my face, an angry wave pulling me to my surroundings. A boat. I'm now on a boat. In the middle of a rough sea.

Waves violently smack into the deck. Endless gray clouds cover the sky, moving in closer and closer to suffocate me to my end.

My once ember filled night dress is now soaked, sticking to my skin as it blows in the gusts of wind, causing me to shiver with every spray of sea water.

I look down and try to scream, but it's silent. Below my feet is nothing. This shadow of a man is holding me out over the edge, ready to drop me to my demise. My future is in his hands, and an overwhelming sense of dread washes over me when I realize, this is it. This is the end.

I'm not ready.

Please no. Let me live. I'm begging.

I want to live.

The grip around my neck tightens, causing me to thrash for breath. I whip and sway as much as I can, but nothing works. He is too strong. Tears fall from my eyes, not wanting to surrender. The darkness is in the corners of my vision, stalking me. Waiting for me with terrifyingly open arms. The black of the end is here, and it's here for me.

Just as my vision fades for the last time, a white blur darts out of the shadows of the ship and sinks its teeth into the shadow man. Not a blur, a wolf. A white wolf.

The force of the bite causes the shadow man to lose grip on my neck. I can inhale again, but before I can focus on anything, I'm being flung to my death.

It's as if time slows. I fall feet first into bitterly cold water, arms still tied behind my back. Bubbles rush up my body with the impact. I pull my arms, twist my torso, and try to kick myself up to the surface, but it's no use. I'm being pulled down to the bottom by invisible hands.

Once again, the darkness welcomes me. This time for good I'm afraid. My last few moments are filled with nothing but regrets.

I'm jolted out of the water by a warm glow.

I'm on a beach. In the early morning sun.

But it's not the sun, it's a figure. Glowing. Warmth and safety radiating off of them.

"Wake up Sweetheart, you gotta keep moving," they whisper into my ear. The voice is unlike any I've heard before, but I trust it.

Water is pouring out of my lungs in a cough, giving me the chance to breathe again.

"Please, give me one more try," they say, cupping one hand on the back of my head, and rubbing my cheek with the other in small circles. They are so gentle with me at this moment, like I am some sort of priceless gem they need to preserve.

A faint memory of a man standing before me rushes to the front of my thoughts. I can't see his features, but he's there. To rescue me. To protect me.

I try to concentrate on his face, one I should know. One that pulls me toward it with the smoky tone of his voice. I know him.

I reach out to touch him, feel his warmth, but I'm interrupted.

A sound comes from behind him. A shriek that fills my ears and makes me feel like my eardrums will rupture.

"Don't worry, just wake up." He turns to look at what is causing the bellow. I look too and see a bird. A white bird with black eyes, cawing at me.

When the golden figure turns back around towards me, he is no longer safe. He is no longer him.

It's a demon.

A white feathered face, with a bird's beak, and endless black eyes. Cawing at me. Screaming at me to wake up…

…Wake up!…

…Wake up!…

"Rue, wake the fuck up! Please!"

Rue is startled awake with a deep inhale, begging for oxygen. She is back in her own apartment, fully clothed, laying down in the shower. Freezing cold water rushes over her, shocking her shaking body. Going from one nightmare to the next before the darkness takes her once again.

CHAPTER

RUE'S eyes flutter in and out of consciousness. The taste of copper coats her dry mouth. A migraine welcomes her into its toxic clutches from the bright light in the room. Her body is still numb from whatever trance she has been in.

She doesn't remember much.

The feeling of warm hands against her frigid shower water.

A white mask.

A dark figure pulling off her soaked clothes in exchange for dry ones.

Being lifted into the air.

The hardness of a chair.

The tight restraints.

A white mask being taken off.

"You. It's you," she wants to say, but her throat is too sore to speak. "Don't leave me…" is the only thing she can breathe out before drifting back into the void.

One more.

What she hears are muffled whispers.

The distant sound of a train car passing by.

The laugh of a person on the street.

The cracking of old wood against footsteps foreign to her.

Her eyes blur every color together. A mesh of black, and green, and brown, and specs of yellow, and white, and red all swirl around her vision. Her brain deceives her thoughts, unable to comprehend what it's looking at.

She tries to move, but her body is cemented to the chair, unable to part from it.

The colors soon turn to darkness, as she lets the abyss take her once again.

One more day.

This time when she wakes, Rue has control. She attempts to move her wrists, which are tied behind her back, but does so with no avail. The memories come flooding back into her mind, smashing into her system with realization.

The walk down to her apartment.

Her door was unlocked.

Getting knocked out.

Someone begging her to wake up.

The white mask, the Organization.

She's in her apartment now, sitting in a chair in her kitchen that is facing the rest of the room. She decides against opening her eyes right away, wanting to listen first. Issak's wise words come to her, *"You'd be surprised how much people are willing to admit, when they think you're passed out."*

Let's see what these assholes admit.

Rue keeps her head lolled to one side, hair pooling over her face to hide an accidental facial expression. She slows her breathing, concentrating on the sounds around her, and not her splitting headache.

She can feel five heartbeats, all human. Two faster than the rest, which tells her two of them are nervous, or excited to kill her. Hopefully it's not the latter. If (when) she figures out a way to get out of these restraints, she is going to make every single one of them wish they were never born.

Slowly she pulls at her wrists, feeling around to see what her restraints are made of, shrinking a little after realizing they are metal handcuffs.

"I don't know what we're gonna do! They haven't given us any orders, just to keep her here," a low voice says from across the room, their voice muffled into a motorized tone.

"What the hell was in that syringe? She's been out for three days," a robotic feminine voice whispers back.

"The fuck I know!"

"Well, if she dies before she is supposed to, we're all fucked. You better pray to the Gods she wakes up."

"Shut up the two of ya," a third voice, much closer to Rue, speaks up. She can hear their footsteps walking towards her bathroom, intruding into the conversation. "We have orders. We are following them. End of discussion."

Across the room, in the opposite corner someone spits, "This bitch isn't worth the time sitting around this dump. Just slit her throat. Higher ups don't fucking know shit! She's just a Lower whore, no way she's important to the cause."

A crackling sound comes from behind his voice modifier, like his mask is malfunctioning. Rue can hear him take it off and slam it against something. He repeats it a few times and yells out, "Fuck these fucking things! Why does it matter who sees my face anyway?" before tossing it against the brick wall.

"51!" comes a low, authoritative voice from behind Rue. This one is close, so close they could probably reach her where she sits. "Put the mask back on, now."

"But what does it—"

"I said put the fucking mask on!" The voice gets louder, which Rue isn't convinced is possible. "Our company just woke up."

Rue stills. A cold sweat forms on her neck, and some part of her wishes she had the power to be invisible.

Shit!

She takes a deep breath, trying to channel all her Ghost energy. She allows the anger that lives in her soul to surface, letting it bleed into her veins like fire. Taking over her body like a shield made from spite and wrath.

Her eyes dart open, and is surprised when the room is almost dark, the sun halfway over the horizon. Thankfully it's easy for her pupils to adjust to the light, and she looks directly into 51's muddy eyes. His pale, almost translucent skin. And his black scruffy beard that hides his gaunt features.

He puts his mask on, and readjusts his sweatshirt, taking steps towards Rue. He's not tall, maybe an inch or two taller than her 5'8" frame. Scrawny, and jumpy as he approaches, like he isn't sure how to intimidate someone.

Rue has seen his type before, hot heads who think they are big shots, but freeze when it comes to actually doing the job.

Her eyes don't leave his, a small smirk forms on her lips, and she can't keep her laughter in. This is going to be fun.

"What's so funny, whore?"

Rue leans back in her chair, allowing her hair to fall away from her face as she looks at him down the bridge of her nose. The tension in his shoulders and movement of his jaw tell her everything she needs to know about how easy this will be to get under his skin. Cracks crumble even the strongest of buildings.

She clears her throat. "Oh, nothing. It's just so hard to find loyal help these days. I'm sure your boss would love to hear how little respect you have for their authority." Her voice comes out hoarse, but she gains her honey tone back by the end of it.

Within seconds, 51 flips out his knife, and lunges towards Rue. The cold blade brushes her cheek, but she doesn't wince. She just smiles and says, "Is that a knife? Sir, it's inappropriate to flirt with me like this in front of your little work friends." She gives him a wink, just to be an ass.

What she doesn't expect is the sting from a slap across her cheek. Rue lets out a grunt as her body moves with the blow. Déjà vu laughs at her luck this week with being slapped. She looks back up at him, and spits right in his face.

"Be careful how you speak to me, whore," he says, wiping away the wetness with his shirt.

"Really, whore? Got anything more original? It's a weak insult really," Rue fires back, rubbing at her cheek with her shoulder.

"I call em' like I see em'."

"Don't be jealous that I'm hotter than you, it's not a good look for a big scary bad guy."

His eyes shrink into slits as he takes a step back. "Don't flatter yourself girl, you're not my type."

"Oh, that stings. I'm crushed, truly." Rue lets out a small chuckle. "Sorry to break it to you, but I saw your face earlier and I think my tubes tied themselves. How about you tell me which of the other assholes is in charge, because it's clearly not you."

"You're not the one running the show, we are. And I'm not going to stand here and be told what to do. Tell us what you know about us, and where you got this information." He turns to the counter and pulls out the file folder that Rocky gave her.

Rue lets out a long sigh. It's not fun being a smart ass to someone this idiotic. She sinks back into the chair, slouching as much as she can with how little movement her arms give. Her eyes gloss over with complete boredom.

"I know nothing. I'm just a whore remember?" She can see his hands form fists. "Are we done here? You clearly have something to prove. So just beat me up, fuck me, kill me, whatever you need to do to prove to these strangers, that you've amounted to more than what your daddy ever told you, you would."

He lets out another annoyed grunt, before his fits connect with her gut. The pain is excruciating, but this is not her first time being interrogated, and it certainly won't be her last.

She is pissing him off, which is what she wants. Chaos. She needs chaos for their plans to be railroaded by rage and annoyance.

"Wow, what a punch. You really swung with the power of eleven cockroaches, didn't you? I see why they wanted you on the team. A real asset." She can hear someone behind him chuckle, but she stays focused on 51. "Now, are we done with this little dance so you can finally point me in the direction of the guy who bosses you around? Or should I keep going on about your daddy issues? Your choice."

51 moves into her space with speed she isn't expecting. His hand pulls at her hair, and the knife in his hand cuts into the

side of her neck, leaving a small trail of blood running onto her shirt.

Rue's breathing accelerates as she tries to push her pain aside. The burning sensation is beginning to irritate her to the point of trying to pull herself away, but she won't give him the satisfaction. She glares at him, trying to find his eyes behind the mask.

Through gritted teeth she says, "If you get one drop of blood on my floors, I will kill you. Very slowly."

"Is that what you want your last words to be?"

"No, I'd rather spend my time kicking you in the balls, but I don't know if I'd find them in time before you slit my throat. So, this will have to do." Rue smirks. "Now tell me who is in charge, so I can have a conversation with an actual adult, and get myself out of this situation. Please run along and fetch them for me, will you?"

He turns around and takes a few rushed steps back, lacing his fingers behind his head. His hands connect with the counter top, and he lets out a primal growl, he lowers his head down past his shoulder blades.

She jumps for joy inside when she sees his chest raise and lower a few times while he collects what little dignity he has left. She can feel his heart race for its life to keep him composed.

The two members standing to the left, by the bathroom, lean against the bricks with arms crossed, hiding their masked faces. Giggling to themselves in his pathetic attempt to threaten Rue.

Hope you're enjoying the show, you're next.

There is another person, taller, with a stocky frame, who isn't paying attention and is searching through Rue's dresser drawers. The hairs on Rue's neck stand up when they reach into the top drawer and pull out the letter from her mother.

Without much interest, it gets tossed on top of the dresser, along with a few other mementos from her childhood, before continuing the search in the drawers.

Enjoy my socks with too many holes and lingerie.

"The drawers are clean," they call over to the group, a crack comes from their modifier.

Rue still isn't able to see the Organization member who is sitting behind her in the kitchen, but she can feel their eyes on her. Watching her every move. Waiting to see what will happen next. Listening to how she answers. It's eating at her to not have eyes on them. They are allowing this moron to make a fool of themselves, which she appreciates though.

She takes a dramatic exhale, looking up towards the ceiling. "So, you came into my apartment. Are going through my stuff. Have me tied to a fucking chair. For what? To scare me? Really? Aren't you guys supposed to be badass vigilantes cleaning the streets of gross, disgusting fae folk?" Rue twitches slightly as her words leave her lips, but she says it with so much confidence she hopes they don't notice her tone change in the lie.

"I'm just a Lower thief. Nothing special. No secrets to the universe in my home. No threats to your little club. It's cute by the way, the matching outfits. The masks. Adorable. It really gives off—"

"Don't you ever shut the fuck up? Gods!" 51 blurts out. His hands are white knuckled fists by his sides again, which makes Rue smirk.

Poor little guy.

"We know you know something; the evidence doesn't lie. What were you doing with this information?" he asks, holding up the file from Rocky. "Only someone with inside information would know these details, who gave this to you?"

"The evidence doesn't lie," she mocks him. "Very Marshal of you."

"Answer the fucking question!" he spits.

"As we have so aggressively established, I'm nothing but a Lower thief whore who is the fungus of the Southlands. I wasn't given that from anyone, I stole it, from where I can't remember. I take a lot of useless shit. Now the real question I want answered, is why is someone so important like yourself, doing the dirty work of those above you? Or do you like people above you? I don't judge." She looks at him through her lashes, biting the inside of her cheek to hold in a smile.

"I'm sick of your shit! You're in this situation because we want you to be. We are the ones in charge, not you. And as soon as you wear yourself out, we will get what we want. But in the meantime, I'm not going to sit here and listen to your whiny ass voice talk about shit she doesn't understand. You are not the tough shit you think you are."

Rue leans forward towards him and whispers, "You're doing great sweetie, really tough speech. Love the part about my whiny voice, really got me where it hurts. I bet if you keep this up, they will finally let you sit with them at lunch." With a wink, she is back in her slumped position, stealthily pulling at her restraints. Rue sneaks a flicker of sparkles in her irises to catch him off guard.

He doesn't notice, or at least isn't showing it, which makes Rue a little sad.

Well, this is boring.

He walks up to her chair, and leans in. "You can't manipulate me, bitch."

"You know, I'd be able to take you seriously if your fly wasn't down this entire time." Rue's grin grows with his panic.

He steps back frantically, checking to see if his pants are in fact unzipped. They aren't.

"What was that about manipulation… Bitch." Her predatorily laugh echoes throughout her apartment. "Gods, you make it too easy."

With that, 51 charges at her with a roar. The full force of his fist connects with her ribs, pushing the chair back with the impact. Another blow comes with his other hand to her jaw, pushing her face to the side. Rue lets out a cough, before sitting back up tall. She will not let this scum of a human take her dignity from her.

"Is that all you got?" she says with a wheezing breath, trying to turn her body, so he doesn't punch her in the same spot. "Come on, show them how tough you are. Beat up a girl who is defenseless and tied up. Show them the real man you are."

He doesn't take her bait, and throws another gab into her chest, this time directly into her gut, forcing her to fold over. The pain flows through her body like lightning. Shocking her system with a jolt of torturous throbbing.

A guttural noise escapes her lips. She coughs up air as her body begs to fill back up with oxygen. The trembling comes at a cost to her ego, shrinking it with her unwillingness to get back up. Centering herself seems like a liable option, unfortunately her center has been punched into different directions, and she can't focus on each of them enough to pull herself together.

Breathe Rue. Just breathe. Everything bad ends. The feelings will end.

Another strike comes to her face, throwing her to the side and almost knocking over the chair. Blood and spit pour from her mouth onto her tile floors. Holding on to what self-worth she can reach right now, she lets out a huff that burns her muscles. "What did I say about the blood on my floors?"

Just as he raises his fist to punch her again, the voice behind her speaks up. "Enough!"

51 stops in his tracks, stumbles back, cupping his bloody knuckles in his sweatshirt pocket. He looks behind Rue's line of sight, and demands, "What the fuck? She was about to break."

False.

"You have a lot to learn 51, this one is feisty," the voice jokes. Behind her the sound of shoes stalking towards her ring in her ears. A cold hand runs over her shoulder, sending a shiver down her back. Their fingers tighten on her arm, squeezing into her sore muscles before they show themselves. Rue bites down on her cheek to stop herself from flinching from the pain. Their hand doesn't move off of Rue, instead they run their fingers from her arm, up her shoulder, and grip around her neck.

"Such a pretty face under all that blood. You'll have to excuse my colleague; he doesn't know how to treat a lady."

Rue glares up at their face, thrashing herself out of their grip. The hairs on the back of her neck are in the front of her mind. Without breaking eye contact, she pools the blood in her mouth, and spits once more at 51.

"Finally, you seem to be the man in charge, or woman? I really can't tell with those voice modifiers."

"I'm all man," he says simply, running a finger over her bottom lip to clean off the blood. His gloves feel like ice against her red skin as he moves up her face, to cup her cheek.

"I'm sure you are," she deadpans. Rue's throat fills with vomit. She hates forced intimacy. It causes her to lose focus. Visions of her feeling like a man's property rush into her thoughts. Feeling like she doesn't have a choice, like if she screamed for help right now, it would be silent.

She moves her head away from him, but there isn't anywhere for her to go. He grabs the back of her head, pulling at her hair. His white mask gets inches away from her and he says, "Watch it beautiful girl, or I'll think you don't like me."

Beautiful. Usually, she loves when Diego calls her that, but now it holds a different reaction, ruined forever. *Beautiful.* The feel of acid burning away her skin.

"What gave it away?"

He laughs. "Oh, I like you. You're gonna be so fun to break, Rue Kylexi."

CHAPTER

"LET'S try this one more time shall we, Rue? Admit to what you know, who you got this information from, and we can move on. You have knowledge we do not want you to have. You give up your source, you live. It's as simple as that."

Rue lies limp against the chair in her kitchen, puddles of blood and other liquids form around her feet from the torture she has endured. Her muscles spasm like she is under a curse. She's positive her ribs are broken. She can barely breathe. And her vision is blurred from blood.

But she is still alive.

The five of them have spent the last few hours taking turns trying to break her. Trying to bend her spirit to the point of no return. 51 continues to use the blunt force of his fists and shallow cuts from his pocket knife to scare her into submission. Creating splatter paintings around her kitchen from the blood.

One more try.

Another, which she learns is named 88, uses more needles to cause pain of a different kind, internal. After the second needle, she feels like bugs are crawling through her veins, breaking through her skin, leaving welts the size of coins in their wake. It gives her visions of shadows and monsters she cannot name, circling around her, biting at her body.

One more try.

A woman they call 32 prefers waterboarding as her form of torture. Leaning Rue's head back and covering her with a towel, freezing cold water fills her mouth, ears, and nose. Unable to breathe, Rue thrashes against her chair, banging her arms alongside the wood.

One more try.

There is one masked member who opts out of the torture, just watches her from the across the room. Their stare lingers in the background of her thoughts, observing as she takes all of it without breaking.

At some point they move around the room, looking through her things, tossing objects on the floor, breaking furniture, ripping clothes. Showing there was a struggle when they inevitably shatter her to her demise.

But none of them are the one who makes her want to break. Their leader, 5, does that all on his own. His movements are slow, methodical, like a cat stalking his prey. His smell of tobacco and pepper fill her nose with an uneasy feeling. There is no world where this is the first time he has used forced intimacy as a torture tactic.

"I've heard things about you, Ghost. You're somewhat of a legend. A woman of the night. A sly fox. In and out before they even clean up their cum."

His hands move around her body, pinching, and rubbing, and grabbing what isn't his. Slowly, he pulls out a knife from his back pocket, one she realizes is her own. Using someone else's knife is as big of an insult as you can have in the crime world. Your dagger is as unique and personal as your own fingerprints.

His fingers linger around her breasts as he cuts her t-shirt down the middle, exposing her bra to the room. His palms dig into her bruised ribs as he rubs her, smearing blood and sweat around her abdomen, circling around her tattoos and scars from previous fights. He laughs, making her feel more exposed and pathetic. She looks away, she can't witness this and have the memory burned into her mind.

A slap across her face forces her eyes open, and he pulls her head down to watch. She does.

"I think I want to see what all the fuss is about with this pretty little cunt."

His hand moves down her body, onto her sex, then to her hips to pull her closer to the edge of the chair. Her dagger breaks the fabric of her pants with ease, exposing her lace underwear to him and the rest of the group.

"Well, aren't those pretty," he hums, rubbing the tip of the knife in between her legs. "I think we're going to have some fun."

Rue's heart stops beating. This is not how it goes. She is not here. This is not real.

He leans into her ear, pulling at her hair so her neck is exposed to him. "I'm going to fuck you over and over again until you can't remember any other part of your pathetic life. He did warn us not to kill you, but he's not here, and I'm extremely interested to see how close to death a ghost can get." The smell of his stale breath lingers longer, imprinting into her memory.

With that, his hand slinks its way down her torso, playing with the hem of the lace. The chill of his gloves make her back up, but all it does is urge him further, ripping the delicate fabric in half.

The tremors are back, the curse over her own body refusing to leave her. She looks anywhere but at what is happening.

"You really are a whore aren't you, Rue? It's almost as if you *like* being tortured, not giving up your source so I can play with you all I want. You opened your legs for me so easy. I bet Diego loves these legs."

Somehow it feels like the bugs in her veins are back, making her tense and shake at the same time. Like something slimy is twisting around her limbs, sucking the life out of her and all she can do is sit and die slowly.

She wants to scream, to thrash from his touch, to bite, and spit, and curse, and hit, and kill. And kill. And kill. But her body is frozen ice, refusing to melt with her rage.

"Fuck you," she manages to whisper.

One more try. Let's try one more time.

He moves his hand to his belt; the sound of the metal leaves her ears to bleed with unwelcome anticipation.

All she can focus on is her legs. Her shaking legs. She wants to cry, but the tears aren't there. She needs to yell in agony, make any sound of resistance, but no sounds form in her throat. A blanket of fear swirls around her mind, which she is actively trying to fight off. To stay strong. To keep fighting for her life. But what's the point? These humans aren't going to spare her life.

This is it.

Is this how her life ends?

One more try. One more, please.

The feel of his hands on her inner thigh causes her to squirm. Her entire body lights up in goosebumps. A little whimper leaves her lips with his touch. Her body is crawling. She wants to run. To burn. To forget. Wants to melt away into the abyss with the rest of her self-worth.

A million feelings run into her mind. The hands of other men before him. Brutal. Selfish. Taking what they want and leaving a shell behind for her to piece back together. Never truly whole again. Just the product of assault, entitlement, and evil.

Of all the ways to go, this is not one she expected. Her body is supposed to be hers. She is the only one who should be in charge of it. Yet, here she sits, exposed to these strangers, on the edge of a chair, preparing herself mentally for what is to come next when his hand isn't enough for him anymore. The inevitable. The final crack he knows will break her completely.

No. It will not be today. One more day.

Rue runs her handcuffs against the wood once more. Trying to force an inch of movement so she can try her best to fight back. A primal shriek comes from her core as she thrashes in his grip. She collects all her courage off the floor of her soul, and spits red into his mask, causing him to fall back.

A direct hit. The once white mask turns scarlet, dripping pieces of her down the front of it.

Her heart is shocked back to life. Her nails dig into her palms. Time to fight back. She has to fight back. She has always fought back.

"You fucking cunt!" he yells. Stumbling to his feet, he takes off his mask to clear out his eyes, but turns before she can see what face is hiding behind it.

Coward.

When he turns around, he is moving with so much determination, she doesn't have time to react. He growls and forces two hands around her neck.

Rue does her best to push away, but with her restraints it's impossible. He is too strong. He lowers his hand down to her panties once again, ripping them further for easy access.

She finds her voice amongst the shrapnel of her being. "Stop!" she screams over and over again. He refuses to listen.

"Don't pretend you don't want this."

Rue tries to look around the room for someone to stop him. To tell him he's gone too far. To help her. To be a decent person. But she is alone. They all stand back, looking at one another, then back at her.

With a last-ditch effort to save herself, her legs shoot closed. She uses all her strength to keep him out. He hurls a slap across her face that momentarily loosens her muscles, but it doesn't last long, and they are back tightly together in the matter of a second. He tries to pry her open, not giving in to her at all.

The force of his body is overwhelming. She can hardly breathe. Her muscles are shaking. She is about to give up.

She might have to give up.

Rue shuts off her mind, closes her eyes, and can feel him overpowering her. She has no choice but to accept her fate, as he forces his way in. Pain so sharp, like she is being electrocuted, invades every muscle, every vein, every part of her. The sound of his belt against the chair tattoos itself to her consciousness. An empty darkness fills her, holding her close, shielding her from the truth of what is happening.

She focuses on colors. And her favorite flower. And the sound of the waves against the rocky shore. And Olympia brewing her tea at the kitchen table.

Peace.

She searches for peace, but she can't find it. This world has no peace.

Her eyes well with tears, but she doesn't allow them to fall. Her mind hides her behind dark nothingness for minutes, or hours, or days. She isn't sure.

But she is ripped from her search to the feel of the burning sensation suddenly halting, and the cold of the apartment taking its place. The feel of, or rather lack thereof, a male body on top of her.

5 is pulled back with the force of a hurricane wind, tossed onto Rue's mattress by the member who wasn't part of the torture.

"The fuck are you doing? We need her to give up information before you go and fucking destroy her!" the modified voice calls out. His height over top of the others makes him dominate the room. He walks over to the mattress on the floor and shoves 5 back down when he stands.

"You're supposed to be in charge, not whatever the fuck this is! He wants her alive."

5 stands, pushes down his sweatshirt, and puffs out his chest, invading the member who is challenging him.

"Do you have a problem with how I run my crew, 29?"

29? If her mind hadn't been so scrambled from the last few moments, maybe she would be able to process this whole mess, but all she can do now is try and stay alive.

Before 29 can answer, 5 nods in the direction of the hot head from earlier. 51 comes out of nowhere and throws a punch at Rue, hitting her in the jaw. "See what you're doing to us, cut the shit and talk you fucking cunt."

Punch. "Tell us what you know!"

Another hit. "Come on, we know you know too much."

A hit to her gut makes her fall to the side and beg for air.

"Talk, just fucking talk!" He is screaming in her ears. The ringing echoes off her brain, causing her to recoil. The pain of it all crushing her.

With the next blow, Rue is at her end. She wants to be able to take more, but she can't. She physically can't.

The smell of pine fills her nose with comfort and safety.

Try one more time.

Suddenly she can see clear.

I need you to be brave.

She can remember who she is.

I'm right here. You can try one more time.

A cool breeze lifts her chin to stand tall. Something within her relights her flame.

One more day.

One more task.

One more try, my brave little fox.

"Fine!" she spits out. Her heavy breaths cause her hair to sway with each exhale. She coughs through her surrender.

"What was that? Say it again for us."

"Fine!" she yells again. "I'll tell you what I know. Then please… Please let me go." She looks up to him. "Please."

"See, obedience can have its benefits." 51 gives her one more strike across the face before pulling her up by a fist full of hair to address the room.

Rue looks at all of them, making sure to connect with each of their eyes. The look of worry plastered on her face. Her breathing is loud and heavy. Body shaking. She can barely lift her head when she says, "I only know one thing."

"Well, spit it out, girl."

Rue pauses a moment. Clears her throat.

"I know I'm winning," she taunts.

The room falls silent.

The only sound comes from Rue trying to catch her breath. Her innocent, terrified face turns to stone in an instant. She lifts her head at 5. The golds of her eyes burn into his mask with a glare that could kill.

"Pff, and how is that exactly?" 51 gawks, taking a step back.

Rue slowly leans back into her chair, pulling at her cuffs, masking the pain it causes to her body with an attempt at confidence. Picking up her missing pieces off the floor, she reconnects her soul. Survive. She will survive this.

"If your boss wanted me dead, which you have expressed to me multiple times is not the case, I'd be dead already. I'm very familiar with all of your work now, and I don't doubt you could each kill me ten times over."

She wheezes under her breath with another tug on the handcuffs. "Yet oh, here I sit. Isn't it strange, they put all of you in charge of babysitting one random girl from the Falls? If you are all so important to your cause, then why do I get the sense that my life is more valuable than yours? Maybe it's you they want dead and not me. Just a thought, and again that's all I know."

"Fucking bullshit!" 51 calls out, pointing to Rue. "Don't let her speak."

A voice comes from behind the men in front of her. "He does want her alive. Why?" 32 steps forward, tilting her head. "Why her?"

51 chimes in, "How should we know? Maybe he wants to fuck her. Look, no one is going to miss her if she disappears. We can make it look like an accident."

"Gods man!" 29 add. "You fucking psychopath."

"Don't pretend like you're so innocent," he fires back.

"Enough!" yells 5. He walks up to Rue, grabbing her by the chin. "Maybe we kill her. Tell him it was her own doing."

Rue laughs while she tries to catch her breath. "But there are only five of you."

"Is that a problem, should I call for backup?" He pulls her face towards him. The feel of him back on her makes her stomach churn, but she shakes it off.

I am the one in control.

"It's just not enough to kill me." Rue smirks at him, pulling herself out of his grip. She grimaces with the twist of her muscles.

5 looks back at the other members of his crew. 51 starts to laugh. The others look confused. 29 is once again not paying attention and searching through Rue's stuff.

Rue grits her teeth. "Just so we're all on the same page here, I am going to kill each and every one of you, and no one is ever going to know what happened. By the time I'm done, there will just be piles of unrecognizable flesh on the ground. I wish people would appreciate my talents more, I'm often underestimated."

5 scoffs in her face, turning around to look at 88 who has been sitting back and watching this all unfold, "Tie up that godsdamn mouth."

88 nods and does as he's told. He stalks into her kitchen and pulls the towel off her oven handle, shreds it down the middle, and ties it around her mouth. Forcing her to bite down on the terry cloth material.

Rue grunts at him and tries to resist but can't. She thrashes a few times in her chair, once more trying to pull apart her cuffs.

Her vision is drawn to 29. The backpack in his hands. The purple scarf full of Olympia's potions falls to the floor as he dumps it out. The glass bottles and compacts catch his eye, and it makes Rue's heart skip a beat.

Pick it up.

He grabs a tube of lipstick and opens it to reveal a red tint. Tossing it behind him, he grabs one of the poison perfume bottles. Rue can't peel her eyes away, her chest heaves with anticipation. The other four voices, arguing about how to make her death look like an accident, fade into the back of her mind.

Come on.

29 locks eyes on the compact, looking at it up close.

Come on. Come on! COME ON!

The moment he opens it, glittery glass shards explode around him, and the room erupts into chaos.

29 screams a blood curdling scream, as the glass cuts through his eyes and skin, shredding the fabric of his sweatshirt and pants.

The others turn to inspect him but not before Rue emerges off her chair. The old handcuffs finally breaking against the pressure of her wrists and wood. The cuffs now dangle from her bruised wrists like bracelets.

She pulls the cloth from her mouth and uses all her strength to channel her magic. Sticking out a hand, she blows out, extending her arm with white sparkles. The other compacts lift into the air and rush across the room into her grasp. While 29 is curled up into a ball, howling in pain, the others follow the floating objects to Rue.

She holds up the compacts in her hand and laughs. "I told you five wasn't going to be enough. Who's next?"

51 lunges towards her, recklessly swinging at nothing as she pushes him away using her powers. His back is bashed into the kitchen cabinets with a crack, and a scream. His body falls to the floor, but he is still breathing.

Arms extended out; she lifts him into the air and uses him as a battering ram to knock out the other Organization members. He whips across the room, knocking over 88 and 32 with his fall against the brick.

Rue screams with rage. The flames around her spirit lick at her skin, wanting to be freed. The winds inside of her pray to be let out. To destroy.

5 looks at her with his arms out, trying to surrender, but that is not happening. He will pay for what he did to her. What she is sure he has done to others in the past. No one will ever be violated by this man again.

She fights to hold control over her body, the trembles are back, making her want to collapse with how much power she is draining.

Rue looks to the compacts, then to 5 who is standing inches away from the others. Her breathing is quick and rough, the fire in her veins is ignited with the gusts that swarm around her mind, longing to burn the world to the ground.

Without looking away she allows her eyes to turn solid white and throws both compacts towards him. They break on impact at his feet and more glitter explodes into the room.

Rue takes a slow step towards her captors and opens her palms. Her hair and ripped clothes whip around her as wind enters the apartment. A swirl of it collects at her feet, lifting her into the air so she towers over the others, who are struggling to see with the explosion.

With a deep exhale, her magic grows around them. The glass glitter starts to swirl around the five of them like a tornado. The air in her apartment spins around with such force, it picks up loose papers, clothes, even furniture.

The screams of all five of them bring Rue her first moment of peace. The power that is flowing through her is enough to bring any human to their death. The glass shreds their clothes, and skin, and eyes, and all of it fuels her. It gives her strength. A deep darkness steals her soul, making her want more. More power. More suffering. She craves it.

She tries to move forward, trying to harness this feeling. Her feet find the floor again. Her hands start to curl inward. Her arms want to give in, to fall to her sides from the stinging pain coming from her palms. The sheer force of her magic is taking her with it, slowly draining her. It burns, like she really is set aflame from the inside. But she presses on.

Rue screams with her whole voice as anger pours from her towards them.

Another step forward, and she lifts their bodies up into the center of the storm she has created.

The strength of her powers are almost fully depleted. She falls to her knees with a grunt, still holding the magic, shaking with fury.

A sharp sting on the back of her neck threatens to disconnect her from her powers. It runs up her spine and into her skull like a shock collar, demanding she stop before there is no return.

Something is pulling her back, a warm light trying to bring her back to reality. She ignores the feeling. She isn't done and pushes her body against the restraints. She pays no attention to the fact that they are no longer screaming for their lives.

They are no longer alive.

She will stay here as long as she wants. She will torture them like these monsters did to her, and she will never allow them to hurt anyone else ever again. They deserve this pain. They deserve this death.

A trace of a voice comes to Rue's consciousness. *"It's okay. It's over,"* it whispers, almost silent to hear. She swears there is a hand on her shoulder.

The black spots are blinked out of her eyes. Her arms lower, and so does her magic. The bodies fall to the ground, a mess of sliced flesh, and blood, and bone, and the remains of cloth. So mutilated, she doesn't know one from the other.

She tries to catch what little breath she has left, pushing out one last scream of agony from her lips.

Rue is kneeling before a massacre of her own doing, shivering, and about to pass out.

Soon the darkness takes her in its embrace, falling to the floor from exhaustion, but not before hearing her front door creak open.

CHAPTER

…I'm on a boat…

…Waves splashing into my face…

…The wolf…

…The fall…

…Bubbles rush up my body with the impact. I pull my arms, twist my torso, and try to kick myself up to the surface, but it's no use. I'm being pulled down to the bottom.

Suddenly, something is pulling at my arm, sharp fangs grip my skin, but not strong enough to hurt. Just pressure. Pressure pulling me to the surface.

I break out of the ocean, filling my lungs with air I thought I'd never get again. My arm is slung around the fur of the white wolf. She jumped in after me. Her body pushes us to the shore. I try kicking but I don't have the strength, so she carries me to the stones that meet the waves.

I'm trying to warm myself up, rubbing my hands up and down my arms, hoping the friction is enough to keep me from turning to ice.

Salvation comes when a beam of sunlight breaks the cloud covered sky above. The warm amber light fills my body with the heat that I've lost. Suddenly I find myself shivering a little less, covered in rays of golden life, and the soft fur of the white wolf. She has curled herself around me to form a fur blanket of sorts.

My hands. Once covered in ice and frost, now turn the shade of pink I am used to. My palms and fingers drip water that sparkles in the light. My entire body glitters against the reflection of the rays in a way that makes it look like I'm glowing.

A warm sensation covers my back, and I look to the sky to see something on fire. A beautiful being soaring through the sky with bright orange wings made of flames. A fiery silhouette eclipses the sun covering me in shaded safety.

As they fly, their wings stream embers behind them, creating a trail of mesmerizing sparks swirling into the wind. They cross over the ocean, swooping past the beach, and disappear behind the pine trees in the distance.

I stand to follow them home, but my eyes are drawn to a green butterfly fluttering along a large piece of driftwood. It dances across the dried wood until it reaches the end and falls to the rocks below. It rests on a white pebble that is a stark contrast to the black rocks that fill the beach.

My linen dress, that is now dry, blows in the breeze, leaving goosebumps on my skin as I walk over to the stones. My feet are now covered in mud and sand and somehow causing wild flowers to peek through the pebbles. Colors of blue, white, and yellow fill my shadow.

The butterfly flutters over to a white daisy that popped out of the wooded log as I pass. It rests it's delicate wings in the sunshine while I observe. The wings open and clothes as if to say hello.

I hope she'll come with me. I could use a friend. I reach my hand out to touch her, and she places her dainty legs on my finger, letting me carry her to our next adventure.

When I stand to start the journey home, my eyes lock on the fox. She is standing on the edge of the forest, where the trees meet the stones. She's red again, doing her little happy dance, which makes me giggle.

"Go to her. Find the light," a voice sings over my shoulder, winds pushing me towards the trees.

When I take a step towards her, the butterfly lifts off my finger, returning to the shore. I turn to get her back in my hand, so she can stay safe with me, but she flutters too far out of my grip.

My lips part when I see the white wolf still on the beach. She looks kind, her eyes a clear turquoise that reminds me of icicles. Her fur blows in the breeze while we stand and talk without words. Understanding each other's journey. The butterfly lands on the wolf's ear in silence, and I know what I must do, but don't want to.

She bows her head, giving me the okay to leave. She will hold onto my friend until I am ready to return. Her aqua eyes never leave mine.

When I turn back to the fox, she is walking into the woods. The pine trees blow in every direction from the winds. It's beautiful. I want to be afraid of the unknown, but I think I might be okay. Something feels familiar. Feels like home. Like I've been here before. A sense of belonging fills my mind and gives my heart a boost of adrenaline.

My body moves towards the tree line with a fluid motion. The pebbles under my toes feel like bubbles with each step.

Before I trek into the darkened forest, I look back to my friends once more. A smile washes over my face knowing I can come back for them, once I've found my way. They are safe on this beach with my flaming guardian protecting them while I'm gone.

"Go. Find her," the voice whispers, reminding me of my journey.

With each step into the woods, the pine needles under my feet grow colder and colder. Soon the trees are covered in white powdered snow and it's once again winter.

A heated glow radiates off my body in warm armor, swirling around my skin with sparkles in a milky mist. My dress is filled with fiery embers, fraying the fabric. The wildflowers under my steps are turning to frost as I walk away.

The fox has stayed a few feet in front of me on this journey through the seasons. She runs ahead through the brush, only to wait for me to get closer to her, eager to show me the treasure we are searching for.

I can't help but feel at peace in this forest. Like I remember all of these great pines, and they remember me. They move, and flow, and show me the right direction. My heart calms with each step deeper into them.

Up ahead I can see a change in vegetation, less trees, more rocks. The fox stops at the foot of a rocky cliff. Her paws do their little jig in the snow beneath her. She's excited. We've made it. The only problem is, I'm not sure where we are.

Towering above me is a jagged stone cliff, covered in ice, snow, and crumbling mineral deposits. On the side of it, about fifty feet up, a rock formation protrudes out. An overhang covers the top to form a cave-like structure.

I try to survey the area, but my eyes lock on the tree growing out of the side. One I've never seen before. With small, pale green leaves, on long, skinny branches. It hangs low over the cave entrance, swaying in the breeze. Each individual branch is coated in a layer of ice, making the tree look like shiny glass. Specks of light reflect in all directions off the sun, blinding me if I stare too long. However, I can't look away.

I hear the faint siren of the voice that follows me, "Go to her. Find the light. Now, Aruelia!"

I do as I'm told and follow the fox who is now climbing up the cliff side, making sure to dodge the pebbles that fall from her steps.

Up on this ridge, my peaceful heart starts to worry. Something isn't right. Someone is here, someone that shouldn't be. I am not alone. I need to hurry.

My hands finally reach the top of the bluff, and I gather my dress in my hands before hoisting myself up, rolling over onto my back to catch my breath. The ground beneath me hums. It welcomes me home, but a part of me knows I need to move quickly, so those who aren't welcome cannot find me.

A branch cracking reverberates off the rock and into my ears.

Movement that isn't mine.

"Quick, find her! He's coming!"

I know I must move, but I don't know where. I'm stranded on the side of a cliff with no weapon, no direction, and no clue who Her is.

"Move, Aruelia, come on. She needs you to get to the light!"

"What light?" I call out, begging for guidance, but my thoughts are soundless.

The branches of the ice tree sway, clinking together making eerie music with the wind. Another crack of a branch, and I see movement within the tree out of the corner of my eye.

My gut tells me no, but I'm drawn to the sound, curious who is with me. I slowly step to the tree, grabbing a fallen rock as a weapon, cautious to keep the upper hand. This disturbance isn't right. The balance of the cave is off. The energy here is very wrong.

This is my home. I know it is. This is where my soul lies to recharge, to find peace. But I cannot find my peace if I do not know who lives here with me.

"Who's there?" I shout. "Show yourself, I am not afraid!"

Under the tree is notably colder than the rest of the cliff's edge, the ringing from the branches hitting one another fills my ears.

Above my head, a branch breaks and falls next to me, causing me to let out a scream. I look up to see a bird. Small in size but takes up the whole tree with its presence. I see white feathers, dipped in an oily ooze on the ends. Black beady eyes stare back at me. The longer I look, the deeper into them I fall. It caws at me to come closer to it. To touch it. To give it myself.

Against my will, my hand reaches out to it. My heart is racing, and I am suddenly trying to turn but I can't. Those eyes. The black fills my vision with dark thoughts. Death. Frozen over lands. Destruction. The void.

I see the void.

I can't escape it. It's here. It's coming for me.

Gods help me.

I'm jolted back with a pull at my dress. I blink myself back to the tree, the ice, the rocky cliff. I'm being dragged back out of the glass branches. The fox, she's here, pulling at the ripped cloth, burning her mouth from the embers that are now dripping black ooze.

"Go! Now, Aruelia. Find her, you're running out of time!" the voice demands, terror filling every word.

I turn to run, but there is nowhere to go.

The cave! I can go to the cave.

I fly past the branches, jump over rocks, listening to the screech of the bird behind me. I don't dare look back in case it draws me in again. Panic fills my veins. It's flying over me, casting a misty black shadow over my golden one.

Another screech.

My feet keep moving, resisting the black oil trying to slow me down. Was this cave always so far away? Was it this hard to find the entrance?

I hear a yip come from ahead. The fox. My sweet little fox. Always showing me the right way.

My legs start to burn from pounding on the stone path. My feet and fingertips are covered in the same black oil.

Keep moving. I have to keep moving.

The cave entrance is only big enough for my body to squeeze through, scrapping my arms and legs against the rock. I use all my strength to push a boulder in front of the opening so I can't be followed.

After a few seconds of screeching, the bird gives up. I'm alone again, safe, with my fox. She paws at my legs, wanting to be lifted. I sink to the ground and cuddle her in an embrace. Her soft fur warms me, finally able to touch her after all this time.

She is safe. We are safe. Yet, I still feel uneasy. Like this journey isn't complete.

Ahead of me in a glow.

A faint light.

It's getting brighter, filling more of the space around me.

...It's...

...It's a being...

...Oh gods it's...

CHAPTER

RUE'S eyes open in a hazy fog. The sunlight of the morning fills her apartment with twinkling specs of dust. She's staring up at the ceiling, lying flat on her back against the mattress, trying to make sense of reality. Unfortunately, it's not coming easy at the moment. Was it all a dream? Is she in a dream now?

Rue is drowning in memories of white masks, and torture, and being violated. She can picture getting herself free and using the compacts as weapons to keep herself alive, but the rest is a blur.

What happened to them? To me? Wasn't I in the kitchen?

She blinks her eyes a few times, trying to clear the smoke and remember it all, but she can't. What happened after she got free? And where did she go when she was sleeping? A tree? A cave? Rue has never seen a tree like that in her life, or a cave for that matter. But it was so vivid, like it was happening in real time.

She exhales and closes her eyes, moving to rub her lids with her freezing palms. When she does, the pain that rips through her is so excruciating, she yells out a guttural moan.

"Fuck!" she cries out. Gods, it is painful. Every part of her wants to be sedated for the rest of her life, never move a muscle again. Her ribs feel like they are being held together by string and a prayer. Like if she moves too fast, they will crumble to dust.

Slowly, as to not fracture herself in two, Rue sits up in her bed. Even the simple movement of resting her elbows on the mattress for support breaks her into a cold sweat. Her lungs barely move to refill oxygen into them, and even that makes her wish she was dead.

Opening her swollen eyes slowly, afraid if she does so too fast, they will detach, she takes a look at her apartment. The cold sweat turns to ice.

It's clean.

Like someone came in and reorganized the whole space while she was out. Someone had to have cleaned up the evidence. The last thing she remembers, there were five bodies being cut to shreds by a tornado of glass shards. Blood had been splattered around the room, on the windows, and in the cracks of the brick. But now, it looks as if it never happened.

Did it even happen?

She looks towards the kitchen, which causes a sharp stabbing to shoot up her neck. "Gods! It definitely happened," she whispers to herself, hoping to convince her mind it's real by the enormous amount of pain she is in.

The kitchen looks spotless, no chair, no blood, no water spilled on the floor. The cabinets have been wiped clean, pink roses left on the counter, and the towel (now sewn back together) hanging from the oven handle.

Her apartment smells of bleach and sandalwood.

"What is happening?"

She moves her arms to sit up more and stops at the sound of metal clinking together. Her eyes meet the cold silver of an old pair of handcuffs, now hanging off her wrists.

When she looks down, she is still in the same bloody clothes as the night before. Like whoever cleaned the apartment, didn't care enough about her to show her the same courtesy.

Her t-shirt is ripped down the middle, covered in sweat, spit, and dried blood. The once yellow lace of her bra is now a shade of dark reddish brown. Her clothes are a stark contrast to the blue and purple tones of her abdomen and wrists. Her gaze lingers down to her pants, shredded with her own blade. Equally as dirty, but for a much more disturbing reason.

Her mind flashes to 5, and his leather gloves, and the parts of her that are now his, along with the men before him.

Rue wants to stay calm, but she can't, it's impossible. The images of his hands haunt her mind, going places that were never meant for him. The feel of him lingers on her skin in a way she desperately needs to burn off. She wishes to cauterize the parts of her memory that hold his face.

"*I want to see what all the fuss is about with this pretty little cunt.*"

She rubs her arms to comfort herself, shaking her head to try and erase his voice.

"*Don't pretend you don't want this.*"

If her ribs weren't in so much pain right now, she would remove her clothes. Wash herself of *him*. She smells like *him*.

"*We're going to have some fun.*"

"Stop. Stop! STOP!" she cries out, forcing her hands to squeeze the reminders away.

Scream. She forces herself to scream. There is simply nothing else to do but scream.

She claws at her pants, ignoring the throbbing of her body. With a few grunts in agony, she manages to discard the cotton material, throwing them across the room. Doing her best not to allow the tears to fall from her eyes, she looks to the ceiling.

He will not be the reason for her grief. He is nothing. He will not be her demise.

"You're going to be so fun to break."

He did not break her.

She needs to get up and get the hell out of this apartment. She can't look around at this perfectly clean space and only see torture.

With the burning sting of a thousand suns attacking her muscles, Rue manages to stand. Each movement brings her to the edge of passing out. Breathing is too difficult at full capacity, so she is forced to take short, shallow breaths. Every part of her trembles, even her teeth are chattering from the exertion.

Rue crawls her way over to the kitchen and opens a cabinet to find a glass for some water.

Please Gods, give me water. Don't mess with me today.

The sink turns on and the sweet, clear liquid life comes pouring out into her glass. She says a little thank you to Cyra, the Goddess of Water, before searching through drawers and cabinets for something to take the pain away.

In the back of a stuffed drawer of junk, she finds the blue vials she saves for rainy days. A concoction from Olympia to help heal bruising and internal damage from blunt force hits to the body.

This little miracle has come in handy many times over the years, so much so that Rue taught herself to make it when she finds time, so as to not worry Olympia with how often she needs it. In the same drawer, she grabs an ear elixir for herself. Not sure how many days have passed since her last dose; she realizes it's better to be safe than sorry.

Over the sink, she fills her cup once more, and downs the ear elixir, ignoring the warning not to use it until her ear points have returned. She doesn't have time to wait around for that. She tosses the vial in the sink and takes another chug of water. Plugging her nose, she drinks the blue healing potion. The sour taste burns her sinuses going down.

While the potions do their magic, working to heal her battered body, Rue stands above the sink, looking out onto the city below. Her eyes immediately focus on a little red pebble on her windowsill. Issak! He has information.

How long has this stone been here? Gods only know, but if this is another opportunity to gather more intel to take these fuckers down, she will do it. All she hopes is that it's worth the trip to the homeless community today, and the price of a bagel and coffee.

With whoever cleaned her apartment last night taking the liberties to put stuff where they see fit, Rue can now find absolutely nothing in her space. Her pile of clean work pants are now gone off the pink chair. Her favorite combat boots are nowhere to be seen. And most importantly, her lucky bra has been wiped off the face of the planet.

Searching through her drawers she huffs in frustration. "Where the hell is all my stuff?" She pulls out a folded tank top, and some jeans shorts before slamming it shut.

The top drawer, which she usually keeps for mementoes and dirty clothes (dirty clothes being a great level of protection for important things) is now full of neatly folded bras and underwear.

"No! No, no, no!" She whispers in a panic. Where is it? Where is her mother's letter?

It's not here. Her most important possession is gone and there is no way of replacing it. It has to be in the room somewhere, who would take a letter?

Rue gulps down her anxieties at another possible scenario. They read the letter and now know her secret. They know she's…

Nope, no, no, no. NO!

Rue falls to her knees, which hurt a little less due to the healing potion kicking in. She searches under chairs, behind her curtains, under the mattress, and her heart stops when she spots a small, crumbled shred of paper, wedged between her dresser leg and the wall.

"Please no."

With slow shaking hands, she pulls out the almost forgotten parchment. It is the letter, but only a part of it. It's mangled, and torn to pieces, and rips more when she tries to pull it out. The folded edges are now gone and left in its place is nothing. The void itself, taunting her for her foolishness in thinking she deserved to keep it.

The small sliver of her true self, one that has kept her going all these years, is gone. Destroyed, like the rest of the meaningful things in her life. And it's because of her. Her rage. Her untrained magic.

What little was left of her mother's memory is lost forever, probably blowing around, forgotten in the dump by now. Like her legacy doesn't mean anything.

That was it. Her letter was the last spec of her mother she would ever hold. That and the opal necklace which she can't find the strength to go and check at this moment.

Rue curls into a ball in the corner of her apartment, running her finger on the frayed edge of the delicate paper. What has she done?

This can't be happening.

It's not fair.

Water blurs her vision, but Rue wipes it away before it can fall in defeat. Her heart shakes, and cracks, and something in her wants to give up, to turn herself in.

How much more is she willing to lose?

She's running out of reasons to keep going. She's just one person, and it seems like the weight of this tragedy is starting to trap her in its clutches.

She hits her head on the back of the wall, closing her eyes in the hope that when she opens them, it will have all been a dream. A nightmare she is begging the universe to let her wake up from. The pain she's constantly bearing is too much, its slipping through her arms like trying to hold water. She's ready for it to be over now.

She wishes her mother was here, alive, rubbing a hand on her back and telling her this isn't her fault. That she will be okay. Reminding her that you can move forward after a part of you is taken. That those who try to break you only succeed if you let them. She doesn't want to let them succeed, but how does she save herself when there is no one here to help her to her feet.

On an exhale, she gingerly flattens out the parchment against her chest. The dainty penmanship of her mother's handwriting draws her in, to the part of her she has left.

Sometimes you must make extraordinary sacrifices for the ones you love.

Rue has read this line over and over again, memorizing the swirls and lines of her mother's writing. She looks down at the inside of her bicep, where the same text in the same writing is inked, *extraordinary sacrifices*, along with the date of her mother's passing. The date she left on that ship, and her life changed forever.

She runs a finger over the tattoo, and it fills her with light and strength. That is what she's doing here after all. Sacrificing herself or those who cannot.

She closes her eyes and imagines the rest of her mother's letter of love and sacrifice, pictures the whole message word for word.

Hold on to your determination, it will keep you going after you've been knocked down.

Be the light, my love.

Have faith in yourself.

You are good.

You are good. The words were written so simply, with invisible lies weaving into the ink. Rue pulls the letter to her chest, wishing for it to be whole again.

The path she has taken in this world is not one her mother would have chosen, but it is the one she's been dealt. The life of a rogue, a thief in the night, shady, and untrustworthy, and manipulative. The life that leads to being taken advantage of in the name of information and loot. A life on your own, where others are kept at an arm's length away. A life of solitude. Of loneliness.

She blows the loose hairs out of her face, not allowing herself to stew in the sadness for too long. She sits in the numbness, knowing at any second her emotions will surface. She can crumble then. But not in the present moment.

What has happened, happened, and there is nothing she can do about it now. She has to keep moving forward. Forward is the unknown, and it can't get much worse than where she has already been.

It's time to go. One more try. One more day.

She stands up, her pain almost nonexistent. The bruises have withered away to faint blue marks, and her swollen face is now its normal, freckled self.

Before she leaves for under the bridge, she grabs the red stone from the windowsill, and places it in her pocket. Out of her very depleted savings box, she takes a few coils for Issak's bagel and coffee payment before she leaves. The moment the door closes behind her, and the horrendous events are locked away behind the wood, Rue welcomes oxygen into her lungs.

She has to keep going.

She has no other choice.

With payment for services in hand, Rue rounds the corner of the homeless community. The tents line both sides of the bridge, creating a tunnel of unhoused individuals and families. As she walks, she takes note of the vacant, forgotten homes. Shredded tarps blow in the wind, and let her peek into the unoccupied shelters, raided down to the rusty studs of reclaimed wood beams.

Rue stops on the corner of the community and the abandoned scrap yard.

At the end of the row sits a deserted spot where Issak's tent has sat for decades. The cement on the ground is a lighter shade of gray from years of protection from the elements. A square of dirt outlays the square footage of his makeshift home.

Rue looks around with furrowed brows. She is positive this is where he lives, she's been coming to this spot for years. Was the abuse so serious that she would forget something so ingrained into her brain?

To the right of his spot, is an a-frame tent made of old wood planks and mismatched tarp pieces nailed to it. Standing outside is Gayle Kennedy. She's an elderly woman in her mid-eighties, with sun damaged, olive skin and white, curly hair down to her shoulders tucked into a hand knit, brown flat cap. She is wearing three different jackets ignoring the hot, muggy late spring weather.

Gayle is another one of the residents who has been around since the beginning of the community. Forty five years ago, she was one of the founding members who protested for the community's right to live here.

She worked on getting the Highers to agree to a contract with the citizens, who were allowed to build homes around the bridges for free in exchange for keeping them out of sight of the Highers up above. Which is the reason all the residents of the community build their shelters under the bridge itself.

Rue approaches with caution, keeping in mind Gayle's hearing has deteriorated over the past few decades, and tries not to startle her.

"Miss Gayle?" Rue says, making sure to use her full voice, and places a hand gently on her shoulder.

Gayle stops mid movement, jumping from the sudden contact, but calms once she sees who is invading her space.

"Red! What are you doin' here?" Her soft voice calms the stress fueling Rue's body and she forces a smile. Gayle was always one of her favorite neighbors. "Not movin' back to this dump, I hope."

"No, not that. And it's not a dump, I see you got new tarps."

"Well Issak hit the jackpot at the casino a few weeks back and came back to camp with fifty coppers. Can you believe it?"

Rue rolls her eyes. "Oh, I'm sure he did." Looking around she can see the good he did with his gift, and it makes a hint of warmth brush over her.

"He spent all the money on each of us, gettin' supplies and what not. We all came together to split it up. I bet Jynx that she couldn't beat me in cards for an extra tarp, and I smoked her ass."

Rue has to force her smile a little less. For an old woman, no one can out-bluff Gayle. "I wouldn't expect anything less. Speaking of Issak, where is he? Am I losing my mind, or is this where his tent normally is?"

Gayle rolls a part of her tarp up and tacks it to a wooden plank with a nail as she speaks. "Oh, he moved down into the scrapyard. He was sayin' somethin' about not feelin' safe, didn't want to be by the crowds. And you know what I always say, safety in numbers. You know things ain't gettin' accomplished if you ain't got a community backin' ya up. There was this one time I wa—"

"Gayle! Gayle," Rue says with the tiny amount of patience she has at her disposal. "Can you point me to where he is staying now, please?"

"Oh, sorry dear! I was ramblin' again, wasn't I? He moved just down there," she says, pointing towards a dirt path leading to piles of scrap. "Past the ol' tunnel entrance and between those two piles of ol' vehicle parts. He posted up his tent up against that far corner. I ain't seen him yet this mornin', so he's prolly still home."

Rue nods her thanks, and pats Gayle gently on the shoulder.

She turns to go meet with her old friend, but not before Gayle gives her a care package for coming to visit her. Two day old biscuits, and a one of a kind, gaudy, knit hat now sit comfortably in Rue's bag as she walks down the dirt path.

She watches each step, trying not to roll her ankle from the trail being so eroded away. Alerious City has been hit with quite a few storms in the past few weeks, and it shows in the quality of roads deteriorating in the Low District.

The dirt road soon turns to wooden planks and warped metal as she approaches the scrapyard. If Issak wanted seclusion, this is a perfect place to hide away.

The scrapyard is more of a graveyard of past inventions. Metal motors, old steering mechanisms, and so many tires all mixed into the piles with scraps and shards of past ideas.

With the wall to the High District right next to this once empty space, the Presidents of Environment and Technology gathered with their cabinets to form a plan for waste produced by city advancement research.

Their brilliant idea was to haul scraps and failed creations off the edge of the wall and into the Low District. Originally advertised to the citizens as a utopia of free building materials for all, quickly turned into a second bump for the Highers. They truly live by the motto, out of sight out of mind.

While Rue scales piles of trash, trying not to cut herself on a raw piece of metal, she keeps her eyes on the destination.

Issak's shack sits nestled into the corner of the bridge and surrounding stone, using the two corners as braces for his lean-to metal roof, and tarp walls. The bottoms blow in the wind as she approaches.

The surrounding area is quiet, other than a few pigeons cooing to each other on random piles of scrap, and the sounds of flies buzzing around her head. The whole place smells of burnt metal, and decay. Rue isn't sure why anyone would willingly choose to live here.

"I come bearing gifts!" she yells at the tent. "I almost got an infection for you, climbing over these piles."

The scraping sound of iron and tin echo off the surrounding walls with each of her steps. Rue swats as flies buzzing around her face, hitting them with the bagel bag.

"Issak, it's Red. I got your message."

Silence. Nothing but silence.

This doesn't feel right.

Rue approaches the shelter slowly. "Issak, you home?"

Pulling back the tarp door, dozens of flies hover around her face. She swats them all away and freezes at the sight that greets her inside Issak's home.

"Oh Gods!"

CHAPTER

"ISSAK!" Rue screams, rushing into the tent. The bagel and coffee fall to the floor as she reaches her arms out to Issak, who is lying lifeless on the ground.

"Oh Gods! Fuck! Um… I can fix this. Issak, it's going to be okay. Oh Gods!" She runs her fingers through her hair trying to figure out what to do, and what happened, and who she has to kill, and why him.

Why him?

He is good, was good. So good.

This isn't supposed to happen to good people.

Pacing back and forth, Rue tries to calm her shallow breaths, shaking out her hands that are now numb. She puts her palms over her mouth and kneels down to him. Tears form in her eyes, but she doesn't allow them to fall. Her mind pushed down all the hurt and emptiness she's feeling into a nice, neat box to handle later. Grief will come later. Right now, she needs to keep herself composed. This is not the time to panic, Issak needs her not to panic.

Trembles fill her body, hesitant to touch him. Her fingers shake as she taps his cheek to wake him up, ignoring the fact that no one who has lost this much blood could have survived.

"Issak, don't let this be the end. This isn't how it's supposed to end," she whispers into his ear. The smell of copper and the end of life fill her nose against her will, coating her senses with hopelessness. This is not real. This cannot be real.

There is so much blood. Gashes fill his torso, tearing through tattoos and flesh as if it was nothing. Red gore pools under him, soaking through his flannel and onto the rug covering the floor. She cradles his head in her hands and pushes his hair back, covering his severed ears so he won't have to listen to this cruel world any longer.

She runs her quivering thumbs over his temples, trying to ease his spirit, and allow him to rest.

He didn't deserve this. He deserved safety and protection from these animals who thought having powers and a different appearance meant you were dangerous. The idea that someone has this stereotype and thinks this gentle, kind man could have been anything but that, drives a nail straight through her heart of stone.

To murder him based on his lineage and ignore his character makes them the real monsters. He was a healer. He saved people's lives. He saved her. He spent decades of his too short life protecting the very same species of people who did this to him.

Rue leans over, giving her friend a hug, knowing once she lets go, he will really be gone.

"I'm so sorry. I will get whoever did this to you, I promise." She holds her forehead against his, reminding him that she is here, and she will never forget him.

With a gentle kiss on his forehead, she rests him against the ground, sitting there for a moment. Her eyes are full, hands bloody, mind blank.

She leans back on her feet, wiping her running nose with the back of her hand, and lifts her head to the skies above. "Mom, if you're listening, meet him in the meadow for me. Make sure he is taken care of. He deserves a rest."

Rue sits in the silence, paralyzed. Her mind races around in circles, trying to figure out what to do now. She looks around the room for a blanket or something to wrap him in, and her eyes catch a frayed piece of fabric hanging crooked off a nail in the limestone wall. Lines of red drip down onto the floor, but she can't make out what it is. Curiosity consumes her, and she leaves his side to investigate.

The fabric, which was once a sack from imported produce, is now a deteriorating form of insulation against the cold, damp wall.

Rue's red stained fingers peel back the material, revealing a message of warning. It's them. It's always them. She can't escape them.

THE ORGANIZATION WILL ALWAYS PREVAIL- ALL THE LANDS WILL BE CLEAN SOON.

Her eyes lock on the dripping paint from the sprayer being held in one spot for too long.

Those bastards took their time. Rushing wasn't a worry for them. They could sit, allow the paint to drip, while he was taking his last breath in fear. Alone.

The pigment trails down, through cracks in the wall, bringing Rue's eyes down with it.

But there is more to this tag than the others. A small smudge is displayed at the bottom, like a finger painting from hell. She kneels down to inspect it, and can barely make out the words, running her finger over the letters that spell out **DON'T** and **TRUST**.

Don't trust who?

The third word is started, but got smeared over, wiped away with water. It might start with a P? Or an R? Or even an L for all she knows. Hell, it could be half the letters of the common alphabet.

She ponders the idea, the man behind the curtain of this whole mess. The *Him* she has seen so many people grow to fear so intensely. Is it someone she knows? Someone she has walked past on the street? Sat next to on the train? It's someone. Someone out there is walking around with all the answers.

Issak had answers, and that got him killed. Although, she brought him into this mess, so she got him killed.

Guilt fills her. It replaces the blood in her veins, with more black ink of the ones who have died because of her. Slowly draining her existence and substituting it with regrets and shame.

She looks back at Issak, needing to know who he was trying to protect her from, even in his last moments in this world. Don't trust who? What could he have seen? Or heard?

Don't trust… Don't trust… Gods who the fuck is it?

She lets out a loud exhale, feeling helpless, and useless, and responsible. The feelings eat at her, taking large chunks of her to fuel their laughter. The feelings torment her mercifully.

Pressure pulls at Rue's head when she stands, dizzy from the remorse of her fallen friend. She looks to him, laying on the cold ground, and comes to the conclusion she needs to give him a proper burial. She respects him too much to leave him here to rot.

Rue wraps him in his blanket, placing his ears in his hands to pass on with him, and covers his face from this disgusting world. She reaches into her pocket and pulls out the red stone from their exchanges, rubbing it between her fingers.

"You would have told me to let you rot. To let you be picked over by birds and allowed them to have a meal. You would be barking orders, telling me to divide your stuff up for the others." Rue places the red stone on top of his protected body.

"But I guess I need to make my own decisions, because I'm the one that's still here. It should be me being covered and saying goodbye to, not the other way around." Her voice breaks.

Rue lowers her head, closes her eyes and continues on, "I know it wasn't your time. And I know that it's all my fault you were dragged into this mess. I will carry that guilt with me until we meet in the meadow. I also know I will carry your spirit with me while I'm still here. I will never forget your kindness, and your grace, and your ability to make anyone feel safe." Rue looks up to the tin roof, trying to push her tears away.

"I'm going to miss you, Issak. Not just as an informant, but as my friend. I don't think I'd be here without you, so thank you. Thank you for every single thing you've done for me throughout my life. I hope you're at peace now, you deserve peace."

Rue kisses two of her fingers, and places them on his blanketed body. She blinks away more water from her eyes, then stands up. In her bag, she pulls out her lighter. Hands shaking, she kneels back down over him and hesitates before lighting the blanket on fire.

It is custom in elven culture to burn the bodies of their fallen elders. It is said to send them to the afterlife in a peaceful way through the smoke of the fire, lifting them up into the next life. Issak was so important to so many people, she can't bring herself to leave him alone in death.

On her way out of the shelter, she closes the door, lowers her head and whispers, "I'll never forget you. I hope you're resting now. I hope you're sitting in the golden light of the meadow with good coffee and a warm bagel. I'm going to figure this out, Issak."

On a pile of scrap metal a few feet away, Rue sits and says a final prayer to him, watching the flames light up the wood and fabrics of his shack. Her eyes trail up with the smoke, knowing he is going home.

Walking back up the dirt path, the cloud of black smoke can be seen from behind her, pouring into the space of the sky. A few of the community members stand and watch in worry, wondering what is on fire, and if it was intentional.

Rue's eyes meet Gayle's, and she can tell she knows. Her eyes are filled with pain and tears.

"Someone got to him ain't they?" she mumbles to Rue, pulling her to the side where there aren't listening ears.

Rue moves a hand to her chest, trying to force herself to breathe. As if she's been hit in the gut, all the emotions she has been trying to keep contained, explode out of her mouth. Between gulps of air she says, "The Organization… They… They killed him… He knew… He knew something… and they killed him for it."

She bends at the waist, resting her hands on her knees, trying to catch her breath. So much has happened within the last few days that she isn't sure is even real, and yet here she is, smelling the burning body of one of her closest allies. She is just one person. One person who can't stop this from happening. It's just going to keep happening.

I can't… I can't stop this…. I can't do anything right.

"Now, how do ya know it was them, Red?"

"What?" She shakes her head, forgetting Gayle is still here.

"How you know it's them Organization scum?"

"I'm the one he was giving the information to. It's my fault." Rue's panic is breaking the surface again. Her chest heaves with rushed breaths and she tries to stop it, but she can't. She can't get herself under control.

Gayle huffs, rubbing a hand on Rue's back. "Breath for me, Red. In and out." Rue does as she's told. "That's it. Good job. In and out. You can get through this."

The panic subsides (at least for the moment) and Rue manages to get a faint *thank you* out.

"Now, how the hell is this your fault? Did ya kill 'em yourself?"

"Well, no but I—"

"But nothin', this ain't your fault. He knew the risks. You were more important to 'em than those idiots in masks."

"I don't know what to do. I'm just one person. I can't fix this for everyone." She turns to lock eyes with Gayle. "I don't think I can fix this."

"No one is askin' you to. I may not have all the info Issak did, but I sure as hell know we just what ya to be safe. He wouldn't want ya to worry 'bout him, or us, or anyone in this city. Worry 'bout yourself."

Rue ignores Gayle's urges for self-preservation and conjures her Ghost courage, changing the subject. "You guys can't stay here." She swallows. "They'll come back. They don't like loose ends. You have to leave, especially the elders and children."

Gayle looks around brows furrowed, nodding in disagreement. "Easier said than done, I'm afraid."

Rue continues, "At least equip yourselves with protection. I know how important Issak's abilities are... *were* to the community."

"Well, it ain't as simple as askin' around for another elven healer, but we'll survive. We always do."

"There is someone you can trust in West Harbor; she runs Moon Child Apothecary on Artisan Row. Ask for Olympia. Tell her I sent you. Her *talents*, are similar to Issak's." She looks around at the state of the community. "And if you're really planning on staying here, set up a neighborhood watch. I would also move everyone in closer. The space between tents is nice for privacy, but you said it yourself, there is safety in numbers. Now is not the time to be on your own."

Gayle chuckles under her breath. "There's our girl. Ya always were a natural leader; I see you've grown into your own powers now. Thank ya for worrying 'bout us after all these years, Red." She moves to grab Rue's face with both hands. "I know he meant a lot to ya. He'd want ya to continue on, not lookin' back at him. I'll handle things here. Stay safe out there, sweet girl."

"You too," Rue murmurs, closing her eyes.

Gayle leans in, placing her forehead on Rue's. The feeling calms her for the first time in what feels like months.

After their goodbyes, Rue takes off towards the tunnels. She stops before entering to say one final farewell to Issak, blowing out some of her magic to push him to his afterlife faster. She hopes he can feel her trying and feel her apology.

Standing in the shadows of the concrete, Rue's eyes wander to the unknown of her future. Wondering what to do now. Wondering who she can trust, and who she cannot.

A sense of overwhelm washes over her. The feeling breaks down her barriers of bravery, shattering them into an abyss size doubt she now carries on her back. She is truly just one being. And she somehow has to take down a group of an unknown size to save her people, by herself.

Who am I kidding? This might be the beginning of the end.

CHAPTER

RUE can smell the spices as she walks up to the entrance of Olive Leaf, an "authentic" Westlands cuisine restaurant in the High District.

The humor is not lost on her that they have restaurants specializing in food from countries humans are too afraid to visit. She finds it ironic that they claim to be the most authentic Westlands food in all of the Southlands, when no one in this whole city has ever ventured off this rock, let alone into the West.

It's an easy claim when the market is so unbelievably naive. It plays into the notion that the South is living in peace and harmony with each of the other countries, when in reality they are their greatest enemies.

The smell of paprika and turmeric fill her senses with comfort. Whether it is authentic or not, it is one of Rue's favorite types of food, if only she had the stomach for it today.

She enters the front door with the confidence of a mediocre man, strutting into the venue one heel after another like she owns the building. Her thin gold dress hugs her hips and hangs low off her chest, exposing just enough to be scandalous to the prudes that patron this establishment.

If there is one thing the Highers hate more than the Lowers, it's a woman with confidence. Higher women are to be seen and not heard. They are accessories. They are meant to be good little girls and listen to their male counterparts. Obedience is ingrained into these women from the moment they are born. Too bad for them, Rue was raised to be an independent bitch.

She wonders who she should talk to about the fact that every set of male eyes in her general vicinity is on her right now, it doesn't seem very "High District" of them to be drooling over her like she's their last meal.

Hypocrisy at its best.

Not even a week ago, this attention would have fueled her confidence, but a growing black hole in her gut has her wondering who of these people would be the most dangerous to her. Which set of eyes are attached to a man who could overpower her if she was caught off guard?

"You really are a whore."

Rue tightens her grip around her bag to stop her fingers from trembling.

Tonight is not the night to allow his voice to get to her. She has to choose to continue on, she needs to be Ghost. The cracked emotions that make up her mind right now will not be the ones that show. They are trapped in their box just out of reach, shaking the lock desperate to get out.

Be Ghost. Be Ghost.

I. Am. Ghost.

She is Ghost, she made Ghost. Stone cold. Refusing to bend for anyone, especially a man. She is strong, and brave, and she has to show that to the world. She can do this.

Rue tosses a lock of blonde hair off her shoulder as she scans the tables for her company for the evening.

The space fits thirty tables comfortably, with white tablecloths and red velvet chairs, spread out over an exotic looking interior. Rue is convinced this is a much gaudier version of what the West actually looks like. There is no way the Westlands are covered in this much terracotta, candelabras, and swirly iron bars. The dim lit dining area is accompanied by a stage with its own set of red velvet chairs, ready for entertainment.

Tonight, the patrons are serenaded by a live band, made up of a few fiddles, or guitars, or some kind of string instrument. It's not Rue's area of expertise. They pluck to a beat that isn't quite synced while a harp player moves her fingers at an incredible speed. She finds this style of music devastatingly boring and pretentious.

The hostess stands straight up, readjusting her tie. "Excuse me miss, I'm sorry but we are reservations only. If you want to give me a name I can put you on the list, maybe get you in another day. We don't allow just *anyone* to walk in off the street." Her eyes shift down to Rue's dress, arching an overly plucked eyebrow.

Rue looks at her, scrunches her nose, and flashes her brightest smile. "You're cute. Of course I know that. I'm looking for someone, you may know him. Diego Metus. He's a regular at your little restaurant. I hope you don't greet all his closest friends like that. What a shame that would be if it got around."

Bitch.

The girl's eyes go wide. Of course she knows who Diego is, he has only been coming to this establishment every Thursday night for years. It's not a coincidence that Rue just happened to stumble into the door to find him.

The girl mumbles something about taking a message for him, but Rue ignores her. In the crowd she can see his tattooed hands, grasping a newspaper. His family's M symbol is inked into his knuckle, along with other symbols for ranks he has surpassed in the syndicate.

"Oh, there he is," she points. Without listening to the stuck up hostess, Rue struts onto the floor of the restaurant, weaving in and out of tables to get to his.

Heads turn with her when she walks, getting side eyed glances from other patrons with their conservative necklines and pastel color palettes. Something as shiny as gold isn't necessarily a favorite shade for Highers, they prefer white and taupe, which is why she chose this flashy dress. Anything she can do to make them uncomfortable.

In the back corner of the floor, he sits at a small circular table for two, his back to the wall, that way no one can ambush him from behind. Perched in the shadows of the kitchen, Rue spots two Runners keeping watch. She winks at them, blowing kisses in their direction with a smirk.

"Is this seat taken?" she purrs as she stands across from Diego.

Without lowering the paper he groans, "Not the time or place, Ghost."

She sits down anyway, grabbing his water glass from his side of the table and taking a sip. A red lipstick stain stays with the glass as she places it back down.

The newspaper finally lowers, revealing dark eyes under even darker lashes, and a stubbled, clenched jaw. Diego's vision lingers down her body before returning to her face, giving her goosebumps down her arms. The act usually sends heat straight to her core, but tonight it covers her in a cold sweat.

His eyes wander at her crossed legs peeking out the side of the table.

"I bet Diego loves these legs."

She readjusts herself so they are hidden under the tablecloth, hiding the fact that they are shaking from the attention of his gaze.

The sight of him always used to make her feel safe in a weird, twisted way, like the monster across from her wasn't as scary as the rest in the world. A beast she has spent so much of her life with, she has learned all the secrets to tame him. But tonight is another story, no one makes her feel safe now, not him, not even herself.

He folds his paper into fourths and places it on the table, leaning back in his chair with one arm over the back. The white button down he has on tightens around his muscles, revealing his tattooed forearms peeking out under rolled up sleeves.

Feelings of self-protection come to the surface in her head, scooting back in her chair to gain a little more distance between the two of them.

Run.

The word rings in her ears, but she shoos it away. It's just Diego. Diego is safe.

Usually, his muscles and tattoos were a weakness of hers, wanting nothing more than to bite into them, but tonight is different. The feel of 5 lingers on her skin like a bad rash. As much as she wants to itch, and scratch, and scrub it clean, it remains. A part of her she is ashamed to let anyone else touch, in fear of them knowing how dirty she is now.

"Why the hell are you here?"

Rue scoffs, she can't believe what she's hearing. "Why the hell am I here? I've been fighting for my fucking life. Alone. They found me, Diego. They know where I live. I was knocked out and tortured in ways you could only imagine." She crosses her arms and looks away. Under her breath she mumbles, "Why the hell are you here?"

Diego leans forwards, and without looking angry whispers, "And you thought this was the right venue to talk? Rue people are staring at us. At you! Why do you do this to yourself? You could have come to my apartment."

"Well, I'm so sorry for just escaping not even twenty four hours ago, and not having much time to prepare for my miraculous return into your life. Did you even hear me? They had me. I almost died. Doesn't that matter to you?"

He looks down at the table, reaching for her hand. His warm grip covers her trembling fingers, and she lets go of the breath she has been holding in.

"Of course it matters. I've been driving myself insane trying to find you. When you missed our Sunday dinner, I knew something was off, and I came looking for you. When I tried to find you at your apartment it was locked, and the fucking landlord saw me trying to break in. He wouldn't let me in. Said he hadn't seen or heard anything from you in days."

Rue tries to pull her hand away, needing her own space as memories of her apartment flood her brain, but Diego's grip on her hand tightens, and she is trapped.

"I wanted to kill him for not letting me in, but I couldn't go around killing the landlord, there were too many witnesses. I figured you were just mad or some shit like you always get, but I know you'd come around, so I gave you space."

Give me space now and don't touch me.

"If I had known for one second you were being tortured in there, I would have burned down the whole fucking block to get to you. You have to know that."

Rue looks in his eyes for a lie but doesn't find one. His features are relaxed, and his squeeze is more comforting than dominating.

He is safe. Diego is safe.

He continues, "I have a reputation to uphold. I couldn't spend all my time looking for a ghost. I hope you can understand. I had to go about my daily business like nothing was wrong because no one could know about the work you're doing. I had to put all my trust in you to keep yourself safe and I was right, you did. How could you think I didn't care enough to worry?"

Rue's stomach drops. Her ability to keep herself safe was almost not enough. If it wasn't for her powers, she would be dead.

She opens her mouth to apologize and explain the situation, when she gets interrupted.

"Can I get you anything this evening, miss?" a waiter asks to her right, pulling a notepad out of his apron.

The idea of eating anything makes Rue want to vomit right on the "authentic" terracotta floors. She hasn't had an appetite since the incident in her apartment, only eating a meal bag protein bar when she was about to pass out.

After returning from the homeless community, she stumbled into the kitchen to find something to eat, scarfing down the bar only to vomit it back up minutes later. Her head becomes light with the vision of Issak lying dead in his shelter.

The smell of burning flesh makes her queasy. She moves a hand to her stomach.

No, this isn't happening here. Not now.

"Miss?" the waiter repeats himself, looking to Diego for guidance.

Rue shakes her shoulders, fighting off the chill that surrounds her. Her hands are numb by her sides, and a sick feeling starts creeping up her throat. "No, sorry I'm not—"

"She'll have the eggplant with red sauce, and a glass of whatever wine the chef recommends as a pairing," Diego interrupts.

"Oh, no I'm really not—"

"That's what she'll have." Diego makes eye contact with the waiter, lifting his chin at him to challenge who he is going to listen to.

The poor kid clears his throat. "Yes, of course, sir. It's a lovely option."

Diego holds Rue in a chokehold stare. With a smirk, he says, "It's her favorite."

The boy scurries off, not daring to look back at the man who holds such power over people.

In a faint voice Rue admits, "I'm not hungry." A flicker of annoyance fills her soul with how well he knows her, how he remembers her favorite foods. She wonders if he remembers the times she would stop for it after a job, the two of them sitting on the rooftops watching the city live on below, eating and talking like they were invincible.

Diego is safe.

He is safe.

He leans back into his chair, picking up his glass to take a sip. "You need food. Plus, I have a feeling that there is a lot to this little adventure of yours, so we might be here a while."

Little adventure to hell and back.

Rue manages to keep down five bites of her dinner before abandoning it. She spends the rest of the time moving it around on her plate to look like she's eating, while she explains everything that has transpired over the last week.

She breaks down the formula of the poison of the man that attacked her, explaining that they are getting the main ingredient from the Northlands. She goes into detail about finding the connections between fae folk and humans without giving away Rocky. She describes what happened to her when she was ambushed and the types of torture she endured (leaving out the part about magical powers and it all being mysteriously cleaned up after), and even chokes her way through Issak's killing.

When she finishes spilling all the information out like vomit, Diego's brows are furrowed, looking off at nothing in thought. She says a silent prayer of relief knowing she managed to keep her tears from falling.

His face is unreadable, only the veins in his hands showing his anger boiling beneath the surface. After a long while he says, "Do you have any proof of this?"

Of all the things to take away from the words I just spoke.

"No," she says, lowering her head. "I had proof, but when I was knocked out, they must have taken it. When I woke up it was gone."

"What exactly can you remember from those files? Names? Locations?"

Rue thinks back to the files on the victims, which feels like something she uncovered months ago. Unfortunately, she can't remember specifics, but something does jump out at her.

"There was this symbol. It was all over the papers from the leader, it was like nothing I've ever seen before."

"Well, plan on sharing that with me, Beautiful? I can't help if you don't tell me what you know."

"Watch it, beautiful girl."

"Um…" She clears her throat. "It was a bird, I think a raven, though I'm not sure. It was made of swirls, and around the outside were these markings, like ancient words in a different language. It felt so familiar, but different, like the President's crests almost. I don't know how to explain it, but I felt like I should have known who it belonged to, like I've seen it before."

Diego ponders that description for a moment, his face looking towards his newspaper. "Hold on one second."

Flipping through the papers, he comes to a page in the center and folds it over, so an article is on the top. Tapping to a picture of two men he asks, "Is this what you're talking about?"

Rue's spirit drops into the pit of her stomach, suddenly her dinner is making its way to the surface. She covers her mouth, staring down at an image of Lex Macellarius, the President of Currency, shaking hands with a pale, rich looking man, posing for a photo op. The article expresses congratulations to Lex and his cabinet for leading the Southlands to expand their trading route with the mainland. In his hands is a treaty with the raven crest on it.

Flashes of page after page of instructions to kill fly by Rue consciousness.

LM. Lex Macellarius. Why didn't I fucking put that together?

"Could it be this? I mean I know it's a blurred image, but that's pretty fucking close to what you just described to me."

Rue doesn't know what to say, or how to act at this moment. Nothing makes sense to her right now. "But I don't understand his motives. How does it all come together? It doesn't make sense to me?"

"It makes perfect sense to me. If you look at the article," he picks up the paper and reads, "It says they grew their workforce by three hundred percent to make this possible. Where do you think they got those people? Doesn't it make sense now why they are being shipped off to the mainland? Forced labor, Rue."

"Yes, that part I understand, but what is he getting out of it personally? Why him?"

Diego runs a hand over his chin, leaning on the table with his elbows. "Someone told me some information a while back that makes more sense now. I had a contact that was keeping tabs on him for some tax fraud digging we were contracted to do, and they had a suspicion he was working with someone who is fae. We never got hard proof, but what if it's that simple, a partnership. They do this trade deal, the fae get humans to do their dirty work, he gets a cut of the profits. He uses the hatred they have for humans for his own advantage."

More dots connect in her mind. "Glowing Thistleroot," she says under her breath.

"Glowing what?"

"The main ingredient of the poison. I wasn't able to detect it properly because the main ingredient is native to the Northlands. I had no idea it even existed, I needed to get a specialist to figure it out. But if he's working with someone from the mainland, that's where he must be getting the suicide poison."

Diego watches her rub her thumb nail over her bottom lip while she thinks, giving her space to continue her fox-like curiosity, and make connections where he can't.

"Something still doesn't add up. It doesn't feel right." She looks off towards the wall, mind flowing with thoughts about how this has been happening for so long, without anyone stepping in. How far does it go up in the chain of command? It is just Lex, or is it all of them?

Her body tenses at the thought of him, remembering the night in his office, with his gloating story of his closeness to the Master President. She shakes her head, trying to talk herself out of the blame for letting him live that night. So many people would have been saved if she had ended him then.

As if he can tell what she's thinking, Diego grabs her hands once more. "This isn't your fault. You got dragged into something that was never meant for you to be a part of. Don't blame yourself for this happening. Someone manipulated you into thinking they are someone they aren't, let it be and move on."

"I was in his office. I had him. I could have stopped this whole thing from happening."

Diego pauses before answering, he pulls at her arm to get her attention, waiting for her eyes to meet his before he speaks.

"You still can."

"How? I'm one person. I can't stop an entire army. If anything, you should do something. You have the power behind you. I don't."

"Rue, how do you kill a snake?" She doesn't answer him, just looks at his brown eyes with exhaustion. "You cut off the head."

"What if we're wrong?"

"What if we aren't? What if he keeps doing this until there are no Lowers left. Not one of these Highers are going to do anything about this. They see it as a good thing, cleaning up the city. I'm doing everything I can behind the scenes, but if it gets traced back to me, there goes our whole way of living. That would be it for you and me. We'd be on the run for the rest of our lives."

Rue sighs, "Then let's run. Let's get the hell of this rock, and travel north. What's left for us here anyway? Let's leave, like we always talked about."

Diego pulls away from her, running a hand down his face in frustration. "We've done this dance before Rue. It's not an option for me anymore. Him being eliminated is our best bet at coming out of this on the other side. Then we move on. We make legal deals. Focus on my legit businesses. We make a good life. Together. You're mine, and I'm yours. That's what we need to focus on. Are you okay with that?"

Rue takes a deep breath, filling her soul with the oxygen it's lacking. "Yes," she lies. "Do you have any ideas? I'm not sure the best way to assassinate a president. But how hard can it be." She says it with so much sarcasm, she almost believes it. She runs her thumb over her bottom lip again, thinking through all the ways this could get her killed.

There are too many to count.

He flips over the newspaper showing her the article. "They are having some white tie thing for him in a few days to celebrate the trade deal. We have until then to come up with a plan. In the meantime, come home with me and we'll worry about this tomorrow. Take your head out of work for one night. Let's make up for the time we lost. I missed you, Beautiful."

"Beautiful Girl."

Rue's hands start to go numb again, shaking under the tablecloth. Her initial instinct is to say no, to be alone, but the idea of going back to that apartment to sleep fills her with dread. Having to lay on her mattress, staring up at the ceiling, knowing what happened feet away in her kitchen, is too much to bear.

"Um, okay. I have to go home to get a few of my things first."

"No," he says with such demand it stops her racing heart.

She looks at him with a scrunched face. "Why not?"

"I have everything you need at my place. Plus, I like you better in my clothes, or none at all." His face goes from stone cold to something mischievous, dirty thoughts going through his head and straight to his cock.

No. I'm not ready. I'll never be ready again.

"Don't get any ideas. After what happened in my apartment…" She stops talking, trying to push away visions of 5's hands on her body.

You're with Diego.

This is your Diego, he is safe.

"After what he did to me, I just can't. Not for a while," she chokes out.

"Well, I'm not him," he says simply, and motions to the waiter for the check like this is the end of the conversation.

As if being assaulted in your own home isn't that big of a deal. Like 5 didn't alter her body's chemistry with his touch, leaving her to feel like the trash they toss in the dump.

CHAPTER

AFTER the check is paid, they stand to leave. Diego walks beside Rue with his palm on her lower back, and even that feels like a violation. Her body tenses with his warm touch, and chills run down her spine. A prickly sensation fills her fingers that she tries to shake out through subtle fists.

In the back of the car, she slides in first, the cold leather rubs against her bare legs. She smiles to the driver in the rear-view mirror, who is staring back at her with dead, unamused eyes. Diego slides in besides her and puts his arm around her.

As they drive, Rue tries to keep her own space free from his touch, pretending to look at the city lights outside so she can scoot closer to the window. Unfortunately, every time she inches away, he pulls her back into his chest.

She focuses her view on a Temple of the Gods as they pass it, looking at the roof to move closer to her side of the back seat.

She hopes she's playing off the awe-struck-tourist look enough to make him believe it. In reality, this city disgusts her. The modern stone buildings, with their bright and happy colors, and lush greenery (although factory derived) falling out windows and balconies like there isn't a food desert and homelessness blocks away in the Low District.

Diego's hand lowers from her shoulder to her arm, running his fingers slowly back and forth. The movement makes her want to jump out of her own skin and run away, or burst into flames, or maybe a combination of both. She doesn't know how to feel, every touch makes her emotions skyrocket into an endless sky of torture. She takes a deep breath, trying to stop herself from the convulsions that have taken over since her capture.

He is not 5. He is not 5. He is not 5.
You are safe now. It's not him.

Anger comes and goes within her, one part of her brain telling her to suck it up and get over it, it wasn't the first time unwanted hands were on her body. The other half reminds her this was different, she was always in control of her body the other times. Before 5, she was mentally prepared to be with someone, able to separate herself from her job and her body in those moments.

This was different.

This was by force.

She was helpless, tied up, and begging him to stop.

"I think I want to see what all the fuss is about…"

"So I can play with you all I want."

She swears she can smell a toxic mix of leather gloves and stale breath. Air gets stuck in her throat; her chest starts to ache with the rushed movements of trying to calm herself. This dress feels like it is burning her skin, she needs to scratch and rip it off so she can breathe. She can't breathe.

Calm down. Calm down. This is not your fault. Not. Your. Fault.

Diego grabs her chin, pulling her out of the spiral she was plummeting towards. "Where did you just go?" he asks, gently running this thumb over her cheek.

Rue takes a trembling breath trying to catch up with the oxygen she's lost, desperately trying to forget about the heat of 5's body. With a fake smile she mumbles, "Nowhere, just looking outside. I'm fine."

Lies.

"You're safe with me, Beautiful. I'm gonna take care of you always. Promise." He pulls her forehead to his, as movement to show he's with her. "Let me shows you how much you mean to me."

Without her consent, he starts to move his hand (that is now on her leg) up her inner thigh. The movement against her skin feels like being sliced with knives. She twitches under his touch, trying to shrink herself away. Trying to find a place to breathe. A place that is only hers.

He doesn't take the hint and follows her movement, leaning himself on top of her against the back of the seat. His lips meet her neck with soft, playful kisses and bites.

She manages to get a hand in between them, trying to push him away, but he doesn't budge. She pushes harder, he pushes back, moving his lips to her collarbone and trying to work his way to her breasts. This time she uses both hands to shove him back into the seat next to her.

"Stop," she whispers, eyes full of hurt.

"Come on, Beautiful. This will make you feel better, get him out of your system," he growls, leaning back into her.

Rue's arms come out in time to catch him, and she manages to twist herself away. Her eyes meet the stormy gray ones of the driver, an act that makes him immediately switch his focus back on the road.

Diego sits up. "What, you afraid of a little show? It's never bothered you before."

"Well, its bothering me now!" She expresses herself in a way he can understand, by shoving him off of her and moving as far away as she can. "I'm not fucking you with an audience. The answer is no." Rue pulls at her dress, which he has managed to lower past her breasts and readjusts herself back inside.

Instead of stopping like she hoped, Diego just leans back towards her with a devilish grin. His hand runs over his shaved head, glaring at her down the bride of his nose. "You don't want to deny me, I can make you feel better."

He leans into her, this time slowly, cupping her face in his hands. In her ear he whispers, "I can make you forget about him, about anyone who's ever touched you. It's just me and you right now, and you know I care more about you than anyone else does. They don't know you like I do. No one knows what you need and how you like to be touched like I do." His hands lower to her neck, massaging her throat with his thumbs.

Looking into her eyes he says, "The safest place for you is with me. Let me remind you of that. Let me erase his touch."

His eyes melt into hers, leaving her feeling warm for the first time in days. He doesn't move, doesn't pry, just sits and waits for her, allowing this to be her decision.

Diego doesn't want to hurt or scare her. He has only ever wanted to be with her. The only man to ever want her for her, not the persona she pretends to be.

When she hesitates still, he says, "I don't want this to be forced. I want you to want to be with me as much as I want to be with you. I need you to give me the okay." His lips meet hers for a quick peck, holding her in his hands. "Tell me you want this."

"Don't pretend you don't want this."

Fuck. 5's voice engulfs her mind, taking over like a plague. *He is not 5. He is not 5. He is not 5.*

"Do you want this, Beautiful?"

Did she want this? Rue pauses, playing through her options in her head. On one hand, she can say yes. Let him fuck her in his car, hopefully erasing any feel of 5 off of her body. It wouldn't take long, just until they got back to his apartment. She could sacrifice herself to make him happy, it would be the easiest answer for her.

On the other hand, she can say no, listen to her gut screaming at her to not let another man touch her for as long as she lives. However, she isn't sure how he would react if she denied him again. Would he let her say no? Would he yell? Tell her she is overreacting? Or would he get pissed off, and kick her out of the car to walk home alone with no weapons to protect herself?

She starts to shift in her seat, ringing her fingers together. Her eyes don't meet his as she thinks.

"Make up your mind, Beautiful. The car ride isn't long. I'm only suggesting this for your benefit. To help you get over whatever internal crisis this is. You have to understand that everything I do is for you. So, if you don't want to give me anything in return, I understand. I'll just drop you off at your apartment and that will be the end of it."

Rue's mind flashes to her home, which is no longer that. It may be cleaned of their presence, but it will always hold their spirits, trapped into the walls with the last of her soul. The idea of going back there to sit in the dark by herself is worse than anything Diego would do to her in this moment.

"No!" She closes her eyes, and tires to stop the panic painting her skin.

"No, you don't want to be with me?"

Rue blinks over at him, forcing herself back into the present. "No, I can't go… I don't want… I… Don't drop me off at my place. I want to be with you."

Well, there is her answer. She looks down at her own body, then blinks to his. Rue moves slowly into his lap, looking over every inch of his face to brand it into her mind as someone she trusts. A safe place.

"Please let me be with you."

This is what she wants. What she needs right now. She needs to get over the initial shock of another person's hands on her, and then it will be easier. It will make sense. It won't make her feel like she's drowning. And this is Diego, he is familiar, his touch shouldn't make her feel this way. He is her person, always by her side when no one else is. She is the most important thing in his life, he wouldn't try and hurt her.

Right? Right.

"Let me take care of you." His eyes darken with need gazing down at her body, and she can feel him harden against her thigh. "Gods, that dress is so pretty. I'd hate to ruin it."

"Such a pretty face under all that blood."

This is what I want. This is what I need.

She shifts her mind into who he needs her to be, lets go of the pain, and opens herself up to him. A sly smile fills her face, and she purrs his favorite words, "I'm yours."

In an instant his hands are on her hips, rubbing her against the length of him. He lets go briefly to press a button besides him, lowering a privacy screen separating the front and the back of the vehicle. Rue turns her head to see if it's completely closed, but he forces her back to him.

"Is that better?" She nods. "Good. Just focus on me. It's about you and me right now. No one else matters."

With that she smiles, a little part of her anxiety disappearing into the wind. She pulls him into her with a fist full of his shirt, rocking her hips back and forth, trying to remind herself what it feels like to want sex.

He runs a hand down her hips, peeling up her dress so she is exposed from the waist down. With a smack on her ass, Rue's mouth opens, and he uses that as a way to explore her with his tongue.

They move in unison, both knowing exactly how the other likes to be kissed. They go until there is no more air in their lungs, only pulling away to stay alive. He sucks on her bottom lip, pulling on it before letting go, revealing a bright smile of white teeth.

"There's my girl. You gonna be good for me?"

Out of breath, Rue answers, "Yes, so good."

Lies.

"Let me see that perfect ass of yours."

Without hesitation, Rue turns, maneuvering herself on all fours in the back seat. She pulls the wig off her head, allowing her red hair to fall around her face. She shakes it out, before leaning back to him and slowly rocking her hips from side to side. She spreads her hips as wide as she can, giving him the show he wants.

I want this too. This is for me too. I want this.

She can hear him unbuckle his belt, and her perfect fantasy of fucking Diego is ripped from her hands. The metal sound. 5's belt hitting the chair. A cold knife between her legs. Rue grips the seat, repeating to herself that he is not 5.

Another smack to her ass has her back with Diego. His voice, this time low and husky, growls, "Play with yourself, get that little cunt ready for me. I want to see how wet you get for me."

Rue licks her shaking fingers, moves her hand between her legs, and rests her face against the seat. She finds her entrance and hesitates for only second before doing what he asks. She rubs slowly at first, trying to warm herself up, circling her clit, and feels… Nothing.

No. No. No. I want this. This is good. I'm safe, and I want this to happen.

She moves two fingers in and out of her core, ignoring the soreness, searching and praying for that blissful feeling. The warm, tingling sensation that makes her legs go numb and her eyes see stars. She will find it; it's just going to take a minute. She needs to ground herself, let her body come out of its fight or flight mode.

"Mhmm, that's it. Show me how you fuck yourself. Get your pretty little pussy ready for this cock."

His voice pushes behind her, reminder her that she's not alone. She is putting on a show. Rue closes her eyes to concentrate on the motion of her fingers, moving in and out of her, touching all the spots that usually drive her wild.

A muffled curse and the sound of him spitting into his hand, then rubbing himself ignites something in her she is afraid she almost lost.

Oh, thank god.

Her hips loosen with his loud moans. Wetness finally coats her fingers with a feeling of need, wanting him to be inside of her. Trusting him and giving in to be the reason for his pleasure.

Her fingers pump faster into her, her flat palm hitting up against her clit in just the right spot to make her knees start to shake. A breathy "Fuck" comes from her lips, and she bites down on the leather seat. The sound of wet flesh, and short breaths fill the space. Rue breathes a silent sigh of relief with the return of her libido. Grateful for the comfort of her own touch. For a moment she forgets Diego is sitting behind her, watching her finger herself.

"Fuck, Beautiful. Make yourself come so I can fuck that soaked pussy."

She looks back and can see him fisting himself out of the corner of her eye. His large cock twitches in his hand, red and throbbing with each stroke. His eyes go from watching her fuck herself, to looking up at the ceiling in his own pleasure. He reaches over with a smack, then lingers on her ass, massaging her.

Before she knows what is happening, his licked finger is pressing into her along with her own. The pressure fills her whole body, stretching her so much she can barely hold herself together.

This is what I want.

"Come for me like this. I want to feel you tighten around our fingers."

Rue's eyes squeeze shut as she tries to focus. She wants to give him what he wants. What she wants, she reminds herself. She tries to position her hand and hips in just the right spot to make something happen.

She can feel the glorious pressure start to build within her, attempting to reach the surface and allow her to be fueled with ecstasy. Unfortunately for her, Diego repositions his hand, causing her to skydive into her own thoughts again. The foreign hand of another person pulls her from her pleasure. She huffs, getting frustrated with herself.

She wonders if he notices her losing her spark, or if he feels her tightening around him in a way to push him out. She hopes he doesn't get upset at her weakness. She needs to fix this, fake it so they can move on.

This wouldn't be her first time faking an orgasm, she just needs to get this part over with so they can move on.

I swear I want this. This is what I want. I am safe.

With a flick of her wrist, she arches her back into him. Opening her mouth wide and covers it with the seat. An almost silent moan comes from her lips. Her hips shift back towards him, and her muscles tense almost as if to fool herself into thinking she really is having an orgasm.

She comes down off her fake high, breathing into the side of the seat. Her heart calms for only a second before his cock is filling her, stuffing her with its size. He smacks her ass again while he works himself in and out. The motions start slow but accelerate once she adjusts to his girth.

Rue's focus moves off the pleasure and into the action itself. She pushes her ass into him while he thrusts, making their connection rougher.

I want this.

"That's it, ride my cock. Let me fuck this perfect cunt over and over again."

"I'm going to fuck you over and over again until you can't remember any other part of your pathetic life."

A flash of a white mask fills her vision. She shakes it away and look back at Diego. He is behind her, not 5. It's just Diego with her now, she doesn't need to be thinking about 5 while she is fucking her boyfriend.

Her mind returns back to the car with the sting of another slap, Diego kneading her while he thrusts. He mumbles curses to himself, although she doesn't pay attention.

She focuses on finding the pleasure in his touch. This is good. She is safe and this is good.

This is what I want. What I need to get over this.

But when he grabs her arms and pulls them behind her back, she loses her control. The feeling of cold metal against her wrists replaces the satisfaction of being fucked by someone she trusts. Her muscles tense with the feeling of being trapped. A cold sweat covers her body like frost, and she has an overwhelming urge to vomit. Suddenly she can't breathe, or think, or even speak to ask him to stop.

She is frozen in time, reliving a horrible scenario over and over again. Her mind leaves her body, trying to escape the torturous feel of being given to a man to use as he sees fit.

The black of the leather looks dull now, old and run down. She focuses on the stitching of the seat in front of her, fraying in one spot. The lights of the city passing them dance around the car while she lies face down, wondering if it will ever end.

She pictures mint tea. And sunrises against the ocean. And the sounds of piano music playing in the streets on a Friday night.

She wonders if the meadow is warm, and if you can see the two moons and every constellation at night. Does the afterlife have night? Who will greet her? Who will take her hand and tell her that the pain is over?

A single tear runs down her face and onto the seat beneath her. She doesn't notice, her numbness looks into the abyss trying to remind herself that horrible things end.

This will end.

Later that night in Diego's apartment, after being fucked again in his bed, Rue lies awake. Diego lightly snores behind her with his arms wrapped around her, fully blinded by his own needs to notice how little interest she had in the act. The sounds of the city mock her from the street, blue and purple lights alternating in the space with a cold glow.

She feels him suffocating her with his warmth. His arms around her waist somehow feel like five hundred pounds pushing her into the mattress. She needs space. She needs to get away.

Away. Away. Away.

Slowly, as to not wake him, she lifts his arm over her, resting it against his leg. He shifts but doesn't wake, turning back over to his side of the bed. She flips the covers off of her and stands in complete silence.

Tiptoeing around discarded clothes, she makes her way out of his room and into the rest of the apartment. Once the door is closed behind her, she finally takes a breath.

Walking into the spare room, she closed that door too and locks herself in the attached bathroom. Finally safe.

Her eyes catch herself in the mirror, and the sight makes her sick. She rushes to the toilet, right as she spills her guts into it. The motion hurts her muscles as the contents of her dinner spill into the bowl.

For what feels like a lifetime of pretending, Rue finally decides to stop. She is not okay. She hasn't been for some time. Her life is a mess. She doesn't know how she can move forward without posing as someone else, putting on an act is the only way she knows how to exist. How is she supposed to heal from this, when she doesn't even know who she is without the hurt?

She allows her mind to empty as she stands up, flushing the evidence of her fear down the drain. She lifts her arms up over her head, taking Diego's shirt off with them. The cold air hits her naked body and feels like sharp icicles pelting her.

She turns the shower on, moving the handle all the way to the left so there is only hot water, and allows the bathroom to fill up with steam before stepping in.

The feel of hot liquid hurts. It burns her cold hands and feet, but she welcomes it. She wants the pain so she can remember she is still alive.

She doesn't feel alive. She feels like a ghost.

Rue slowly sits down on the tile of the shower, letting the burning of the water clean her of any prints left behind. She tucks her knees into her chest, holding on to them for dear life. With her head against the wall, wet hair on her face, she lets go of all feelings.

Her mind is empty.

She is alone.

CHAPTER

THE merriment from the party downstairs echoes through the halls of the offices. Rue is silent as she maneuvers around motion sensor points and keeps herself hidden in the shadows of office furniture and doorways.

Looking for the men that monitor the upper floors of the building, Rue hides in the darkness of a file cabinet. As if on cue, two men walk past her through an adjacent hallway leading to conference rooms. She sucks in a breath and plasters herself against the metal cabinet. A bright light coming from their flashlights spill down the hallway, which pushes her farther into the wall and out of sight.

"Did you hear something?" one of them questions.

Rue's heart rings in her ear as it attempts to kill her with the sheer force of its beats.

"Nah man, no one's coming up here tonight. You're just hearing things."

The sounds of their footsteps grow quieter the further they get, allowing her to release the air in her chest.

To the right of her, twenty feet away, is a wooden door she needs to pick. In her back pocket she pulls out a lock picking tool that's hidden in a sided compartment of her key ring. Perfect for disguising her tools in plain sight, right next to her hot pepper powder hidden in a disco ball (courtesy of Olympia), and a tiny, crocheted fox keychain for good luck.

The keys jingle for a split second before she grabs them in her hand, pulling them to her chest.

That's nice Rue, ring the bell and call them to your location, really spectacular rogue work. Your mentors would be proud.

She closes her eyes to focus on the sounds around her. The hum of tech. The haunting echo of string music from the ballroom. Her heart drumming away with anxiety in her chest. No sounds of boots against stone floors.

Thank fuck.

Tonight is not the night to make mistakes. She's been making too many careless mistakes lately, and the constant visions of her previous attack isn't helping her stability. Ever since that night in her apartment, being a rogue is no longer natural to her. But that stops tonight.

Her goals are simple. She will not fail.

This will all be over tonight.

One more task.

Darting from where she crouches, Rue makes it to the dark wooden door. For how modern the rest of the building is, this door is easily a century old. The wood has cracked under the pressure of screws holding it in place.

Where is this from, because it sure as hell isn't the Southlands?

The glow of the city lights outside cast a spotlight on the door, the carvings on the wood almost illuminating, pulling her curiosity into them.

She runs her fingers over the swirls and markings that paint a history she doesn't understand. The divots curl around her fingertips, luring her into a trans of a past life. Energy forms in front of her, and without realizing it her eyes start to sparkle. A dark warmth surrounds her, snaking its way up her body, wrapping the feeling around her shoulders and head.

It's calling to her from afar. Whispering in her ear to trace the markings, rewrite the runes.

Watching her hand like it's an out of body experience and she has no control over her movements, her fingers begin to trace the first markings. A burning sensation pricks the back of her head and the nape of her neck, a foreign current zapping her, causing her to let go of the door.

In the same instance of the pain overwhelming her, it disappears. She moves her hand to comfort her neck, but there is no bump, or scratch, or any remnant of whatever is causing her discomfort.

Before she has a moment to comprehend what just came over her, the ding of the elevator reverberates through the office floor. Struggling, she continues picking the lock and has only moments before being spotted.

With a click, Rue is in. She softly closes the door behind her and relocks it from the inside. Peeking out the small office window, she can see two figures advancing towards the room she's currently in.

She walks in the middle, only lit by a hazy glow of the moons through the clouds, sits down on what she believes is a sofa, and waits impatiently for an overdue reunion.

The doorknob shakes as it's unlocked, and two voices are muffled but clear enough for her to roll her eyes.

"You know Robert and I go way back."

"Oh, really? That's incredible."

"Wanna know a secret? Sometimes we even…" the man trails off as the door swings open and the lights come on. Standing in the doorway is Lex Macellarius, eyes wide, and disgust painted on his stupid face.

Rue looks up at him through her lashes as she lowers her mask. A checkmate smirk on her lips causes him to sweat. She crosses her legs where she leans and gives him a little wave with her fingers.

Without addressing Rue, Lex turns around and ushers the woman out of his office. He grabs her by her slender shoulders and turns her to walk away before she sees Rue, closing the door behind him.

From the hallway, she can hear him say, "You know what, Gorgeous, I just forgot I am about to give a speech downstairs. They are probably looking for me, and I'd hate to leave you unsatisfied if our time gets cut short."

Rue makes a gagging face. This man couldn't satisfy a woman if she was giving him step by step directions and handed him a map. Even then, he probably wouldn't listen to her, and believe he knew more than she did… you know about her own body.

"Oh, well I guess that's what happens where you're a powerful man." The woman responds with a timid, flowery voice.

Come on girl! You can do better than this bag of wet garbage!

"It comes with the job I'm afraid. But hey, someone's got to save the world."

Barf.

Rue listens as he escorts her to the elevator and tells her he will be right down. He makes up the excuse that he left his speech notes on his desk and wouldn't be but a moment. The ringing of the elevator door opening and closing repeats down the hall, followed by furious footsteps.

Once again, Rue is met with Lex in his office. He slams the door behind him and grunts in frustration, running a hand through his slicked back hair.

"I should kill you for what you did to me."

"I might do the honors myself after having to listen to your insufferable pickup lines again. I had to stop myself from vomiting all over your floor."

"Why the hell are you in my office, ruining my night?"

Rue rests her hands on the arm of the sofa against her thighs, letting out an audible sigh. "What? Did I leave you unsatisfied last time, Lex? Hurt your little ego, did I?"

Her eyes flicker to his white knuckles forming fists by his sides. "Be careful there, your true nature is showing," she purrs, standing up to look at her nails. "Wouldn't want any of your supporters knowing you love to beat up women. Violence isn't a good look for your image, Lex?"

"You and I both know the public would side with me over believing a disgusting whore like your—" His words get cut off by a dagger flying through the air, and landing in the wood of the door, inches from his head.

"You really are a whore aren't you."

"Call me whore one more time, I dare you." Rue's hand moves to the dagger on her other thigh holster. She hovers there, waiting for him to make the next move. A single twitch of her fingers is all the anger she shares with the outside world, but inside she's a windy inferno of lava and seething hatred.

Lex slowly turns to the left, eyeing the knife sticking out of the dark wood target behind him. He must realize who the blade belonged to by the runes on the side, because his surprise is everything she hopes it would be.

That's right. I know you hired Blue Eyes to kill me, you son of a bitch. But guess what? I won.

A slimy smile forms across his face, and his hands go up in surrender. The laugh that leaves his lips sends chills down Rue's body. A dark, guttural snicker sound comes for her, like it's pulling the void up with it.

"You got spunk, I'll give you that. But I'd think twice before threatening me, girl."

He laughs again, which makes him sound more confident than what his body is showing. His hands, still up by his head, twitch with uncertainty. His eyes shift from Rue's to her hand by her weapon.

Like a fox hunting its prey, she stalks towards him, gaze shooting arrows into his soul. Once she's mere inches away, she smiles up at him, a small, entertained giggle comes out of her. "You know, last time we were in this office together, you were a lot nicer to me." The words come out like velvet. "Is it me? I bet it's me, you're not a fan of red hair, huh? Oh well, nothing much I can do about that."

His hand comes around to grab her, but she anticipates it and has her dagger pointed at him seconds before he makes contact. "Ah, ah, ah. Not so fast. It's not very gentleman like to touch a woman without her permission." A vein on his forehead starts to bulge to the surface. "Come have a seat Lex, we have a lot to chat about. You've been a very bad boy."

Before she turns to walk away, she runs the dagger down the side of his face, slicing into him at the very last second, just enough for it to sting.

With her back towards him, she can feel him release a breath. His charging footsteps don't surprise her, in fact she would be shocked if he had listened to her degrading demands with no pushback.

His hands connect with her shoulders, and Rue reaches back to grab the back of his head, falling to her knees. With all her body weight pulling forward, she flips Lex onto his ass, pulling his left arm behind his head, which is now in a chokehold.

"You're so predictable it's sad." Rue pulls back on his arm, causing him to scream out in pain. "Now, are you going to be good, or would you like to be outmaneuvered by a whore again?"

Her arm squeezes tighter around his neck, and he coughs from the lack of oxygen. He uses his other hand to tap out and yield. Rue squeezes one more time before releasing him to the ground, then stands to tower over his pathetic body.

He keels over, pulling at his neck tie for some sort of release. With both hands on the ground, he spits out between breaths, "Why are you here? What do you want from me? Is it money? I'll give you whatever you want."

"You think I want your money? Is that all you fucking care about? Don't insult my intelligence by pretending to be some innocent bystander in this mess like the rest of us. I know about your little plan, trying to pull one over on all the people you swore to protect. You're the head of the snake, the man behind the curtain if you will. I know that the Organization is under your control. I know that the blood of every life lost is dripping off your hands."

Instead of denying her accusations, his face turns from worried to something darker and more sinister. His hazel eyes lose their shine, and the mask he uses in the public lifts from his face. Somehow, he looks older and more tired, like trying to parade around pretending is aging him at double the speed.

"There you are motherfucker. You ready to have a conversation?"

Lex laughs and says, "I'm not the person you are searching for," which makes Rue's blood boil. Her boot meets his gut with a swift kick, causing him to fall back down in the fetal position. He lifts himself up on one arm, holding his stomach with the other.

Rue steps on his hand, twisting her foot with enough pressure to make anyone cave. "You're really boring me, Lex. You make hurting you so easy. How about you tell me what purpose the mainland has with the humans you are shipping there, and I'll tell you the mistakes you made in your little plan. Like a fun little game of show and tell. You go first, help me understand."

Lex continues to mock her with his laughter. "If you think I'll tell you anything, you're less perceptive than I originally thought. Nothing you could do to me will stop the inevitable. You're too late. The plan is already in motion, stupid girl. You lose."

With a grunt, Rue grabs him by the collar of his shirt and pushes him on his back. As her knee digs into his chest, she leans in close, gripping him by the tie and pulling him towards her. The movement sinks her knee farther into his body.

Finally, he submits to the pain and lets out a howl, scrunching his face with a clenched jaw.

"Listen you absolute fungus, let's be civil about this. You explain to me what your motives are, why you're working with someone in the fae countries, and I'll decide if the answer is worth saving your life. If it is, you can walk out that door a living breathing man with some sort of dignity left. Or, and the better option in my opinion, I kill you right here on this floor and disappear without anyone knowing I was ever here. You'll be nothing but a news story in tomorrow's paper."

The first moment of weakness is expressed in his eyes, and he looks around the room for an escape of some kind. In a desperate attempt to break out of her clutches, he puts his hands on her. He manages to shift his body weight to flip her over onto her back, pulling himself on top of her. However, his attempt is short lived, as she kicks him up over her, flipping him once again onto his back.

"Stupid idea asshole," she mocks, kicking up to her feet and turning towards him.

Lex shuffles back until he is up against his desk, one hand on his chest, one out in front of him. He struggles to catch his breath in panic.

"You know it wasn't supposed to go this far, at least to my knowledge," he admits, voice hoarse between a chuckle that makes Rue see red.

The statement catches her off guard. "What part exactly was too far for you Lex? Because it seems I'm a little behind on whatever the fuck you think is so funny. Was it ripping people from their homes that was too far, or was that part okay?" Rue takes another step towards him, ready to pounce and slit his disgusting throat.

"Oh, I know, it was killing innocent fae folk for simply existing." She lifts her finger to tap her chin. "No, that couldn't have been it, fae folk are disgusting to you people."

He sits, pondering her words for a few moments, looking around at nothing in particular. "Interesting choice of words."

Annoyed with the amount of time that has passed with no solid answers coming from Lex, Rue takes another step towards him, grabbing at her dagger in its holster.

As cool and comfortable as one can be, he raises his hands once more and admits, "I'm not that different from you in this situation. I too had no other choice but to get involved. My friends across the pond had some pretty *interesting* information on me that would be foolish to deny. They leveraged that and in exchange for their silence about my little side business, I would finance their projects."

He licks his lips and smiles at her, it makes Rue want to jump into a pit of acid. "What would the information against you have shown?"

"Oh, you know, the usual corrupt political jargon. Stealing money from the country's current trade deals with the mainland, causing both parties to lose money, and I profit the difference. Turns out they did the mathematics, and now I owe them a debt. It's an incredible deal on my end. I continue profiting off the Southlands side of things. They get the money they rightfully deserve from the deals, and we exchange silence for workers." Rue sneers at him. "Oh, don't look at me like that, it's a common thing in my line of work. And the money, gods the money, you'd do the same thing to get out of that dump beyond our walls."

"It's only a dump because those in charge want it to be. Those people did nothing to deserve this fate."

"Those people? You seriously are going to look me in the eyes and tell me they aren't the scum of the world. When this plan came together, and we decided those in the Low District would be targeted, I was ecstatic. They are doing us a favor really, cleaning the streets of their appalling filth. I would happily part with every single one of them in exchange for what wealth I'm gaining from this deal."

Rue's jaw drops. "Do the other Presidents know *your* stupidity is the reason their people are disappearing? I'm not sure that would go over well in the next election. That is unless they are a part of this sick game too."

He doesn't answer her.

Rue paces around the room, the anger growing in her chest begging to be released.

"You know the worst part of this whole thing is that people trust you," she yells. "But I guess that's why it works so well." She stops in front of him. "You men all think you're so invincible. You take advantage of those you believe are beneath you to fuel your ego, when in reality, those same people are the reason you got to where you are now. They believed in you. Trusted you to take care of them!"

"Trust is not how this world was built, Gorgeous," he laughs. "I think our time here is done, there isn't a whole lot more for me to say."

Rue pulls him to his feet by his shirt, he is frail in her arms and winces in her grasp. With a lowered voice she demands, "We are done, when I say we are done. Now tell me the names of those involved, human and fae. My patience is running very thin."

The laugh that comes out of Lex's mouth has her seconds away from slicing him open and stringing him up on a flagpole. It's slow, and croaky, and nothing short of insulting.

He looks her dead in the eyes, a gleam washing over him, like the last piece of a puzzle was just found, and he won.

"You really have no clue, do you? That's rich. All this time, I thought you had the upper hand, when in fact you know nothing of importance. Admitting who my partners are would be a death sentence. And if you think I'm going to let a mere child get that out of me, you're sadly mistaken. Oh, I hope I can be there when you figure it out, it might just finally shut that mouth of yours up."

Rue growls in his face, before kicking him in the balls and letting his body fall to the ground.

With her hands behind her back, Rue says, "Let's try another question, shall we? Tell me what happens to these people once you ship them off to the mainland."

Down on his knees, Lex mumbles through gritted teeth, "For the last time, I am not the one you're looking for to get these answers. I have simply been brought into this like you have, Aruelia." The last word rolls off his tongue with such confidence she almost misses it.

A shock flows through Rue's body, she turns to lock eyes with him, a line appearing between her brows.

"What did you just call me?"

Through his lashes, Lex Macellarius's eyes turn dark and all knowing. "Well, that is your birth name, is it not? Aurelia Kylexi of the North. Half fae daughter of a whore mother. Bastard of a human father. It's a shame you didn't get any of her powers, or this conversation wouldn't end well for me. Tragic what happened to them. I knew your father, knew him well, but sadly you never will. Nor will anyone else on this island since I had your entire bloodline exterminated."

Rue's mouth is dry. Her body is numb. Her eyes search his face for a lie, but she doesn't find one. Panic sets in as she takes a step away from him.

"Why? How do you know who I am? How do you know my father?"

He sits back against the desk, calmer and more casual than before. "I'll admit, I didn't at first. I knew those siren eyes from somewhere but couldn't put my finger on it. Then I put some hunched together after seeing you on my security cameras. I figured out who you worked for, and everything started to fall into place. You needed to be eliminated for the good of the

Organization, and we both know how that ended." He rolls his eyes, pointing to the dagger in the door. "As for my relationship with your father, he was simply in the wrong place, with the wrong people, at the perfect time. Funny, isn't it? That's what happened to you at sixteen as well. Like father, like daughter."

Rue goes pale, control slipping out of her grasp with each word.

"But see the part that really surprises me, is how little you truly know about yourself." Lex rubs two fingers together, holding something small in his hand.

Rue walks towards him, keeping her eyes on his fingers. Cautiously she says, "I don't care what you think you know about me, but I'm very aware of who I am."

"You know who you've become, but not who you are."

"Just shut the fuck up and give that to me. Don't be a coward."

He looks down at his left hand, running his thumb over a white capsule, so small Rue almost didn't notice it. He holds it up to the light, twisting it between two fingers. Rue inches closer. With a laugh he says, "If you think you are safe, if you think he won't find out you're still alive, then you are sadly mistaken. He probably already knows."

Rue takes another step, aware enough to not make any sudden movements.

"He knows everything. He knows everyone. No one is safe. All the lands will be clean soon."

Before Lex has even moved his arm to swallow the capsule, Rue is on top of him swatting the pill away. It flies through the air, hitting the ground and rolls under a file cabinet.

He tries to get out of her grip, but she is too strong for him to escape. She holds him immobile and threatens, "You will not die at your own hand, it's my turn."

With a quick breath in, Rue ignites into a glittering mist. Her arm shoots back and the dagger, still stuck in the door, is hurled through the air and into her hand. With no hesitation, she drives it into his chest, pushing straight through his heart and buries it into the desk behind him.

"That is for every single person in this city you failed."

With blood pooling in his mouth, Lex manages to whisper, "He is unbeatable. He is… the White Raven. All the… lands…"

She leans forward, planting a cold kiss against his forehead. When she pulls away, a deep crimson red mark is left in the shape of her lips as a mark of triumph.

His last breath is spent trying to pull her off of himself. Rue's eyes don't leave his until she is sure he is dead. The one spec of peace she can get, is knowing that the last thing this man saw was her face. It doesn't bring any justice to those that have suffered from his hand, but at least now she knows there will be no more.

The only way to stop evil from continuing, is to burn down the bridge it takes to reach its victims. And Rue just plunged their bridge into the desk as if he was a thumb tack.

She can finally rest.

It's over.

Rue is feet away from her apartment when she notices Finny running down the opposite side of the cobblestone, swaying his arms over his head and yelling something in her direction.

The streets are busy with nightlife, so she can't quite make out what he's saying, but his eyes make her stop dead in her tracks. They are practically bulging out of his head.

Her body goes tight, and a cold sweat drenches her in worry. He doesn't have to say anything for her to understand something is wrong, very wrong. Finny would never leave West Harbor alone in the middle of the night. He is covered in sweat, like he's been running for miles.

Did he run all the way here?

Her heart races with the appending storm. The voice in her head screams at her to go to him and prepares her for disaster.

She races over, meeting him half way down the street. "What is it, Finny?" she asks out of breath, already planning for the worst.

"Rue it's so bad," he admits, practically in tears. He lowers his head, shaking in disbelief.

"What is it? Tell me!" she begs, fingers twitching. She puts one hand on his shoulder and lowers her face to his view. "Finny, what's wrong? Who's hurt?"

He starts to cry. "We didn't know what was happening. We just heard screams."

Rue is starting to panic now, searching his face for unanswered questions. "What happened? Who's screaming?" she shouts, desperate to know what the fuck is going on.

"We would have helped," he whimpers. "If we had known, we would have helped."

She grabs his face to make eye contact. "Who, Finny? Fiona? The homeless again? Who?"

His eyes well up, as if realizing the magnitude of the situation and mumbles, "Olympia."

The world stops.

Rue can't breathe, her lungs stop working. Her vision blurs. She puts a hand on her heart to stop herself from hyperventilating. Her whole body is shaking as she looks around the crowded street.

"Where?" she tries to say, but it comes out almost silent.

"Her shop," he sobs, and lowers himself to his knees, crying into his hands.

She looks around once, then crouches down to Finny, handing him her apartment key in her shivering hands. "Go inside, lock the door behind you, and wait for me, okay? I'm going to go figure this out. It's going to be okay. She'll be okay," she lies. "Do not let anyone in except for me. It's not safe out here." She does her best to seem brave, but inside she's seconds from death.

Before she has his answer, she's up and running. Racing towards Olympia. Lungs burning. Legs about to give out. Heart gone.

Rue was preparing herself for the worst. However, this is not the worst, there is no magic in the world that can change this outcome. No, this is catastrophic.

CHAPTER

RIPPING her way through the street, Rue halts at the front steps of Moon Child Apothecary. The door is broken apart from its hinges with force. The glass from the front window crunches under her boots as she enters.

"Olympia?" she cries in her bravest voice.

Please don't be here.

"Olympia, it's Rue!"

Don't you dare be here.

The shop is in complete disarray. Shelves are on the ground, bottles scattered across the floor, display cases demolished into rubble. Dirt, smoke, and dust fill the air, making it hard to see or even breathe. Her hands tremble and she swears her heart is going to break through her chest.

Please don't be here. Please be safe.

Using what little strength she has at the moment, Rue pushes a cabinet, once holding miscellaneous books, back up towards the wall.

She looks around in overwhelming dread. This place, once a safe haven of her childhood, is now crumbled to dust and ashes.

"Olympia!" she calls out, scanning the debris for any sign of life.

Before she can search any further, a cough behind the counter breaks her heart in two. Rushing towards the back, she jumps over a broken table of crystals and the remainders of a plant from a smashed pot. The front desk is leaning against the back wall. Underneath it, is a hand. Her delicate hand, covered in blood and dust.

"Olympia!" she gasps with a broken voice, letting out a yell as she uses her whole body to push the counter up right, and shoving away the broken wood and papers from Olympia's body.

There she lies, coughing, holding on to her last few moments in this world.

This isn't real. This can't be real.

Rue drops to her knees, moving towards the only person who ever truly cared for her, cradling her head in her lap. She brushes back her beautiful curls, still holding onto flowers, even though they are full of dust and drying out. Olympia's stomach is full of gashes, her ears have been cut, and blood is pooled around her.

"No Oly, please no. Don't leave me like this."

Another cough comes from her almost lifeless body. "My Honey Bee."

Rue's eyes dart to hers, those perfect olive irises staring back at her with the gentlest gaze. Hands shaking, she brushes

Olympia's cheek as soft as she can, but still gets met with a wince in return.

Tears fall from Rue's face. Real tears, for the first time in years.

"I'm sorry. I should have been here. I should have known they would find you. It's all my fault. I'm so sorry," she begs.

"Everyone takes a turn leaving this world one way or another. No one is safe from death, my sweet girl."

"No! I can get you to a clinic, a healer. I can get help."

"There is nothing to be done Little Bee. My time spent here is coming to an end. Soon I'll step into the wildflowers with my fellow fairy… My pain will be gone. I can see them… reaching out their hands for me," Olympia says, letting out a few more coughs. Her hands move off her bloody abdomen, and rest in Rue's.

"No, you can't. I need you still. I need you here with me," Rue admits through tears.

"I'll always be with you. Every time… every time you…" She trails off, looking into Rue's eyes. "You may have your father's hair and eyes, but you are so much like your mother."

"Wh… What?" Rue whispers. Her breathing stops. Panic starts to flood her features.

"I would have gone to the ends of Ethos for you my Little Honey Bee. You were my purpose… My reason to stay here. Aura and Cillian would be so proud of the woman you became."

"Oly, you're not making any sense. Just rest, everything is going to be okay. It has to be okay," Rue says, wiping tears from Olympia's face.

"You are my greatest achievement. You are my favorite flower. My brave little fox." Olympia smiles, coughing up blood.

"Please don't go. Please." Rue doesn't know what else to do but beg. She moves Olympia's hand to her cheek, hugging it in the hopes of some sort of miracle. "Please."

"Oh, but I must, you have a very important journey ahead of you."

No, this can't be happening. This isn't real.

"Please," she pleads. "Please stay with me."

"My Aruelia," Olympia says with a sincere smile. "Our last hope. The blend of Twin Light. Salvation will come when Aruelia returns to the North."

"Just rest. It will all be okay; I'll go get help."

"No, my child. The wildflowers are calling for me… I can see them. I can see their… their hands. Please plant me with the flowers when I pass."

No, that is not going to happen. You can't die.

Rue scans her face, there is no hope. None. Nothing she can do to save her. All she can do is sit with her and make sure she isn't alone.

Alone. Always alone.

She runs a hand down Olympia's cheek once more, wiping away tears.

Instead of arguing, Rue just smiles and says, "Yes Ma'am, I'll do whatever you want me to do."

"That's my girl." Olympia reaches up and wipes a tear from Rue's eye, palming her face to comfort her. "Did I ever tell you the story of how I got to this… godsforsaken city?"

Water streams down Rue's face faster than a waterfall. "No, I don't think you have."

"Well, it all started with a quest… for answers," she mumbles between coughs. "I was tasked with finding a… someone…" another cough, "…someone to…" She closes her eyes.

Rue leans her body over Olympia's head and shoulders and pulls her up towards herself, cradling her from the cold floor. She cries to the Gods and prays to whoever will listen to take her pain away.

"Aruelia, be brave," she whispers as she lets out her last breath. Olympia lies motionless in Rue's arms, pain leaving her body with her last heartbeat.

Her spirit lifts to her afterlife.

To walk with the wildflowers in the meadow.

"No! No, no, no, please no." Rue's stomach churns as she tries to ignore this new reality, one when her memories are all she has left of Olympia. She has to force them back down, deep into her soul, so she won't have to come to terms with this unsolvable heartbreak.

Her body fills with fire so cold she can scream, and it makes its way up into her eyes. Sobs, uncontrollable sobs come out of her frozen, shell of a body, finally allowing the grief and fear of what's happened to wash over her.

Rue sits up, pulling Olympia with her as she pets her head. She can't look at her clearly, bloodshot eyes blurring her view, or maybe it's her mind trying to protect her from who's in front of her. She isn't sure anymore.

Olympia, the only person who welcomed her with open arms as an orphaned child. Olympia, who's embrace once made her feel safe and loved. Her passion for helping others made Rue wish she followed in her footsteps.

The only mother she could remember. The one who taught her strength, and resilience. The one who always reminded her to trust her gut. The only person she ever truly loved, is now lifeless in her arms. And it is all her fault.

The girl who would not be broken, just shattered into a million different pieces.

Rue emerges from the shop holding Olympia's body in her arms, cradling her against her own. The glass crunches under her feet with each step. Eyes slack. Face numb. Reason to continue on, now floating in the meadow with Olympia.

Hope does not exist. She questions if it ever truly did. What's the point of it? Why have hope in a world that is so careless about who it loses? She had so much more life to live. So much more wisdom, and love, and change to bring to her community. And in the matter of one day, it was taken away.

Evil won.

Evil took her from Rue, and she will never get her back.

Time slows, each step feels like an eternity. A brutal, painful reality sets in and Rue feels like she will never be whole again. Never stop drowning. She is wading through never ending mud, pulling her back five feet with each inch forward.

She is met outside the shop by most of the neighbors, even at this late hour. Rose has her arms around Fiona, who is sobbing into her hands. She whispers something into Fiona's ear to make her look at Rue. Charlie is standing by a group of people with his head low, holding his hat against his chest. Shop owners are huddled around, waiting for the news they are all dreading to receive.

Not a single sound can be heard, as if the city itself is in mourning.

Rue doesn't make eye contact with anyone. She just gazes down at Olympia, arms quivering from the lingering adrenaline.

"There has to be something we can do! We have to take her to a clinic to see a healer or something," she pleads. "Please, help me! Please."

Her tears are back, running down her face and onto Olympia's clothes, pooling on her dirt covered sweater.

"Help! Help me!" She is screaming now, a silent scream no one seems to respond to. She needs someone. Anyone. "Help!… HELP ME!"

She sinks to her knees, holding Olympia tight against herself, weeping. "Please, Gods, bring her back. I need her back. She has to come back."

Fiona's mouth parts, she thrashes out of Rose's grip and runs to Rue. Throwing herself over top of both of them she cries, "I know." She's sobbing. "I know, Honey. Shh. Shh. Shh. I know. I know." Running her hand over Rue's hair, she tries to calm her. Her touch is the first sign of warmth Rue feels.

The two of them hold Olympia's lifeless body in their arms for what feels like years, crying and rocking back and forth. Neither of them say anything while a crowd forms around them.

Rue doesn't stop crying until she feels a hand on her shoulder. Her vision is blurred as she stares at the fuzzy figure.

Charlie stands above her with bloodshot eyes. His hand rubs along her shoulder blades. "We are all with you, Rue. You are not alone in this pain. Let's lay her to rest, she is in the meadow now, sweet girl."

"I can't," she cries out, lowering her head to Olympia. "She can't leave."

Fiona's eyes fall to Rue, wiping away tears from her own cheeks. "She will always be with you, Honey. With all of us."

"Let's lay her body to rest, so her spirit can live on," Charlie says softly. Rue doesn't answer, just nods, and lets Fiona and Charlie lift her to her feet, Olympia still in her arms.

Her mind is empty. No thoughts. No sadness. No anger. No pain. Nothing. Absolute nothingness. She is just a shell, a shell of a woman who didn't realize what she had until it was too late.

This can't be real. This can't possibly be how this was supposed to end. Her life deserved a safer ending.

Rue looks up from the woman in her arms for the first time, and she is taken back. The crowd around her is astonishing. Her mouth opens and she looks around confused. The street is lined with people, some she knows, most she doesn't. Most of them are holding flowers and plants, shovels and other tools. Candles fill the alcove with a warm light. People from all over the district, there to help her bury her dearest friend.

"We are all here with you, sweet girl. You are not alone," Charlie whispers into her ear.

Rue starts to cry again. *Alone.* She wants to believe she isn't alone, but the emptiness in her chest says otherwise. She is alone, the last of her happiness gone when the void itself killed Olympia.

"None of us can bring her back to you, Honey," Fiona sniffles through tears. "But let us help you. You do not have to do this on your own. We are with you."

Rue looks to her, all life gone from her gaze. She can't think, can't bring herself to make a decision. Her eyes physically hurt from crying. Her only strength left is gripping tight on Olympia.

"Show us the way. We will follow," Charlie says, rubbing her back.

Rue's eyes shift from Fiona, to Charlie, to the group of mourners around her. A warm breeze pushes her forward gently, dragging her consciousness to the coast. To their tree. The oak tree by the sea.

As if some spiritual force takes over, Rue's body starts to walk towards the shoreline. She isn't sure how she has the power to move, yet she is. Like the Mother herself is holding her hand in this journey through grief.

The crowd in front of her parts to make room for them. People line both sides of the sidewalk, bending down on one knee as she passes.

Bowing in respect for the fallen angel who lived amongst them.

Thanking her even in death for keeping them hidden, and alive.

Somehow, the mass of people never calms. Every street. Every turn. Every alleyway they take to get to the ocean is lined in candlelight and heartache. They form a barrier for her to walk in peace to her final resting place. The golden glow warms Rue, thawing the ice that covers her iron heart. Those that knew Olympia best, follow Rue, taking turns holding her arms to keep her moving forward.

When Rue turns the corner to see their tree, she stops.

Movement. Life. Energy. They all leave her body. Nothing can make Rue take another step. A step forward will mean it's over. And now Rue will have to continue on, while Olympia will not. A step forward will mean the memory of her will live longer than the time she spent with her. That doesn't seem fair. None of this is.

The water filling Rue's eyes reflects off the glow of the candles. The street grows quiet. No one moves. No one pushes her to continue. This is her decision, and she just isn't ready to make it yet. She studies Olympia's face wanting to burn her features into her memory and leans her forehead to touch hers. It's cold to the touch, the color on her cheeks has faded, she really is gone. Rue silently sobs into her, until she hears a soft voice from behind.

"She doesn't blame you, Honey," Fiona says. "She would not want you continuing thinking for one second this was your fault. Right now, she needs you to be brave. We both do. We need to be brave without her now, okay?"

Her mother's words ring through her mind.

You are my brave little fox, and now I need you to be brave without me.

Olympia's last words to her, *be brave.* Rue looks to Fiona, eyes barely open, and nods.

She gazes out onto the oak tree and takes one step. Then another.

After all her tears had dried, the last kind words were said, and everyone had stepped away from the stone of her fallen angel, did Rue finally let oxygen into her lungs. The walk back to the shop had been a long one. Each step took years of her life away. The pain that filled her limbs was something she was positive would keep her company forever.

And now she stands here, staring into a dark building, her legs refusing to enter.

I need you to be brave without me.

Rue starts to move.

Be brave without me.

Another step.

Be brave.

She enters into the shadows of what used to be a peaceful place but is now stained with death.

With every crunch of glass under Rue's boots, a flash of a bloodied body fills her mind. *Crunch.* Her red hands. *Crunch.* The dried blood splattered in her hair. *Crunch.* The tips of her ears lying on the ground next to her.

No, no, no. This isn't happening.

This is a nightmare. A devastating nightmare she will wake up from any second. It has to be. She can't possibly still be on this planet when someone so pure is gone.

It should have been me.

It should have been me.

Me.

The memories from the last few hours come and go as Rue moves around Moon Child Apothecary. The dirt from digging under the oak tree stains her fingers, darkening them like her heart. This is all so fresh.

It should have been me.

She feels the need to clean up, to get the shop ready for Olympia to open with the sunrise but falls to the ground with the realization that won't happen. Her back slides down a cabinet that was tipped onto its side during the assault. The dim light from the streetlamp barely reaches her as it flickers on and off.

The world is silent, not daring to make a sound. Not willing to admit that there is life, and time, and a future for those that survive. It's too soon. The darkness of the night suffocates her in its embrace.

It should have been me.

Rue tilts her head back, closing her eyes, and lets out all her feelings in a scream. A sound so loud it reaches the High District. The mainland. The afterlife. A call for help, a signal to those suffering that there is another amongst them. An SOS that will never be answered.

She cradles herself in her arms, wrapping them tightly around her legs, and begins to rock back and forth, trying to push all the pain out so it can be over. Would it ever truly be over? Would this loss fade, allow her to move on and find peace?

Or would it stay with her? Melt her into nothing until she has no choice but to slip away.

Another wail of pure agony comes from her throat, staining the room with the sounds of misery. Rue yells curses to the space like it's the building's fault this happened.

It should have been me.

When she can't find the strength to continue screaming, she sits. Sits in the silence of the dark morning, trying to find a reason to get up. But this time, there isn't one.

In the quiet, throughout the corners of her spirit, a part of herself whispers, *"It's time to get up. One more time."*

Let's try one more time.

Rue lifts her head, hoping to find someone to tell her what to do now. Where to go. Who to be. Anything. Unfortunately for her, motivation isn't something she has access to at the moment.

She looks around the room for some direction and stops on the stairs leading up to Olympia's apartment. She thinks about the strength it will take to see her home one last time.

Her mind drifts to the yellow kitchen wallpaper covered in flowers. Visions play in her mind, like when they would sit around the table, making homemade cookies from ingredients traded for medicines. Or when she would read on the couch until she fell asleep and found herself tucked in her bed in the morning. Or the two of them searching through the fog to see glimpses of the moons out on the fire escape.

Dreaming. So much dreaming happened up those steps. Always about where they would live on the mainland, or what jobs they would do for money. Olympia would share her life in stories, and Rue would happily crawl into her lap and soak up all the adventures.

Rue wipes away a stream of tears from her eyes, remembering the life that was lived up those steps. The happiness and safety that once was, is now just memories.

She looks at her legs, curled up into her chest, and wonders how much energy she has to move. She has to find something within herself. Olympia would want her to continue on.

Olympia.

Gods, how she wishes she didn't have to think about her in the past tense. This cannot be real. She wants so badly for her to walk down that empty stairwell. To stride right to her and ask, *"What are you doing sitting here, when you could be out living your life?"*

The answer is simply. Rue doesn't have meaning in her life without Olympia in it. Everything good that has ever happened to her, she owes to that woman. The only happiness she has ever lived was up those steps. She only wishes she realized it sooner.

She is staring off into the abyss, mind blank, when her spirit tells her to move again.

Try one more time.

The draft in the building from the broken glass door picks up, causing her hair to blow in her face.

A gentle pull to the steps.

Rue closes her eyes, lifts her head, and speaks. "Okay," she whispers, almost voiceless.

"Okay."

CHAPTER

ON a deep inhale she lifts to her feet, shaking from the shock still lingering in her system. Taking one step at a time, she tries to move around the room, stepping over broken glass, papers, and plants. Stopping at the demolished front desk, she runs her hand over the worn out wood. The dust collects on her shivering fingers, holding on to her like a tattoo.

To her left, the tapestry of the realm pools on the ground, ripped from its hooks on the wall. Olympia loved that tapestry; it was one of the only items she brought with her from the mainland.

Rue shuffles over to it, grabbing the fabric in her hand, and examines the craftsmanship. Her fingers trail over the stitching of the Eastlands, where a white heart is sewn on top of the original, representing Olympia's village back home.

She moves over to the Westlands, drawing over the Great Falls that bring water to all the villages in the West. Then she outlines the path to the North, the home that is part of her, but she doesn't truly know. Up her fingers go, past the evergreen forests and the Dioden Mountains.

Rue stops moving at the northern woods, where legends talk of North Witches, said now to be extinct. This part of the fabric feels off, stiffer than the rest.

In what little light is filtering in from the horizon, Rue pulls the cloth closer to her face, wanting to examine the weird stitching on one part of the woods. It's almost as if someone cut it open, and resewed it with a similar thread, although this is thicker.

"The Tree of Life has all the answers you will ever need weaved into it. Never forget that, Honey Bee."

Rue looks to her thigh, quickly pulling out the dagger from its holster. With steadiness she didn't realize she still has, she carefully cuts the newer thread, leaving a square flap in the fabric.

The stiff part of the tapestry isn't fabric at all, it's a small, square package wedged in between the two sides of the piece. Rue's brows scrunch together with curiosity.

She pulls the small bundle out, biting down on it while she puts the tapestry back up on the hooks. After haphazardly smoothing back out the fabric, Rue lets go of the paper package and opens it up, making sure to not rip the corners.

Wrapped in a torn out page of a book, is a golden key.

Confusion is an understatement. Rue isn't sure what to make of this new found treasure hunt only hours after burying her. Questions roll through her mind faster than she can process them. Who left this? Who is it for? What does it open? Why is it hidden? Why did she have to find it? Why can't she leave anything alone? Why is she the way she is?

Rue runs a hand through her hair, overwhelm takes control. This is too much for her right now. She doesn't have the capacity to take on any other mysteries at this time.

This is too much. It's too much, I'm just one person.

The tingling in her hands can no longer be ignored, and panic settles into the pit of her stomach, making its way into her thoughts.

I can't do this.

She can't catch her breath. She moves a hand to her chest, closes her eyes, and tries her best to block the emotions attempting to flood into her body. Sharp pains push at her temples, wanting release in oxygen but she can't breathe.

She just can't breathe.

What am I going to do? I can't. I can't…. I… I'm just one person.
This is too much. It's too much. Too much.

The restriction from her clothes cuts off her limbs. She can't feel her body, just little needles digging deeper and deeper into her skin. She wants to shred her clothes off so she can be free, and move, and think. She can't think. She can't focus on anything, or sit still, or think, or focus, or move. She can't move. She can't breathe.

I can't do this. This isn't happening.

She sees spots in her vision, trying her best to scoop up oxygen with every inhale, and emptying her fears with each exhale. In and out.

I can't do this.

In and out.

I'm just one person.

In and out.

I can't save everyone.

Breathe in.

I can't.

And out.

In and out.

In.

Out.

With her breathing somewhat under control, Rue can feel her hands again. The key, still burning a hole in her palm, brings her back to where she is. It's old, centuries maybe by the look of the metal. She runs her fingertip over the ridges, two lumps at the end like an old skeleton key from the pirate stories Olympia would tell her as a child. The top is made up of two swirls that come to a point, and there is a tiny, engraved dot on the side.

Rue holds the golden key up to the light, flickering in from the street. Her mouth opens with the realization that the engraved dot isn't a dot at all, it's a little bee.

She searches for the paper packaging, needing more clues. Pickup it up off the floor, she steps back into the light, and with shaking hands the words register. Words she once had memorized as a child, the beginning page of her favorite book growing up.

Adventures of the Elemental Seven.

The story of how the Gods came to be.

This is not a random key. This was left for her to find.

Teardrops fall on the page, running down and soaking into the old parchment. Rue's gut is in knots at the thought of Olympia not only keeping a page from this book but going to the lengths she did to hide it. Why did she hide it? What does it open? Why is it for her?

Rue loses her battle with trying to keep her eyes from crying and lets out a sob, sinking to the floor on her knees. The key is heavy in her hand, and she pulls it to her chest. Some part of her hopes she can feel Olympia within the key itself. It's true purpose is unknown to her, but the attachment she has to it already outweighs any other reason to keep it.

It's her. It holds Olympia in its aura.

Leaning forward she cries into her lap, holding herself tight. Silent tears stream down and soak her pants. Her stomach muscles burn from contracting through the pain. Hopelessness fills the room. A swirl of heaviness takes her in its embrace, leaving nothing left of her.

Can grief really hurt this much?

She lifts herself up, sniffling and trying to stop her heart from racing. With the back of her hand, she wipes the water from her face, making a sad attempt at composing herself. The only thing keeping her from throwing in the towel, is the idea that Olympia wanted her to find this key. Some part of her knew Rue couldn't resist investigating when something was off.

She holds the key up to the light, hoping for another clue as to what it opens. Her eyes wander around the room at the old chests, cupboards, and display cases. And before she realizes it, she's up and moving, legs striding across the space with another boost of adrenaline. She will play this game, even if it's a desperate attempt to hold on to any single part of Olympia. If it means Olympia's spirit stays a little longer, Rue will do it, that's all she cares about.

As if there is a time limit on how long she can search, Rue flies around the room. She tries every lock the store has to offer her, but nothing is right. Her hands quiver with each attempt, trying to shove the key into places it doesn't belong.

"Fuck!" she yells out, tossing a small chest to the ground when it doesn't open.

She shuffles things around, lifting up fallen cabinets to search for hidden compartments, frantically trying to find answers. With another scan of the shop, her eyes lock on the steps to the apartment. Of course! How could she be so stupid?

Taking the steps two at a time, Rue climbs to the second floor. She pulls the spare key out of the loose floorboard under the mat and opens the door to the apartment. Only, the door won't budge, something is blocking it.

With all her body weight, Rue slams herself into the door. An inch of movement is all she gets. Well, that and the sharp pain reverberating throughout her left forearm from the impact. She tries again, still not budging.

She looks down the hall in both directions, double checking for signs of life. Confident she is alone, Rue places both palms on the door. Swiftly, she blows out a deep exhale and pushes the door open with her powers. Cloudy, white sparkles bleed from her hands, forcing the door open against its will with a loud snap.

Inside the apartment, Rue is greeted with an overgrown forest. Vines and branches outgrowing their pots cover the walls, creating a cocoon around the space. The orange light of the sunrise trickles in between leaves and limbs of plants. It's as if they knew Olympia wouldn't be returning and were protecting themselves from the cruel environment on the other side of the brick.

Rue runs her hand along a twisted branch covering the kitchen wallpaper. Leaves fall as she brushes past them, helping her understand that they too are dying. With Olympia's magic the only force keeping them here, they now are on their own. What was once a green, lush mini forest, is not brown and shriveled, pots grasping at their roots to hold on, to stay alive.

In the midst of the decay, sits a small, yellow mug with a wooden spoon in it, filled with tea that has been left behind. Rue runs her finger over the rim, imagining Olympia sitting at her table, enjoying a quiet evening by herself. In peace.

She picks up the cup, thinking about how things fell into chaos so fast. The idea of Olympia being tricked into going downstairs, and brutally murdered, brings all her rage back to the surface.

It should have been me.

The indentation of Rue's name in the side of the mug makes her want to vomit. If Olympia had never found Rue on that beach, if she had never willingly taken her in and raised her, none of this would have happened. She would have gone on living her life, helping humans until she moved on to another calling.

Rue stares into the cracks in the pottery, filling her mind with darkened thoughts. Pictures of Olympia happy with Fiona, and Charlie, and Finny pass in her mind. Dreaming of how simple her life would have been without Rue in it. No fights. No getting hurt. More money. Less worry.

Easier.

Lighter.

Better.

An electric shock runs through Rue as the cup crashes to the ground, shattering across the floorboards at her feet. Liquid and pieces of clay ricochet everywhere.

"No! Shit, no." She bends down to collect the remains, soaking her pants in the process. Pieces of the past are cupped in her hands, tea shaking out and soaking the ground like blood. A lump forms in Rue's throat, one she has no control over, and she begins to weep.

Bent over, she pulls what's left of the mug to her chest. An agonizing cry comes up from her soul and fills the room.

"I'm sorry," she cries out. "I'm so sorry. This should never have happened. It wasn't supposed to go this way. It should have been me; it was always meant to be me."

She tries to inhale but can't. She tries to stop herself from crying but can't do that either. She has lost all control over herself. Her future is now in the hands of the Mother, or whoever is out there watching over her. Rue isn't sure if they even exist anymore. How can someone so powerful, loving, and nurturing be so careless? How can a higher power sit back and watch as good beings die? She wants desperately for it all to make sense, but right now nothing does.

"Fuck!" she screams towards the ceiling, throwing a broken piece of the mug against the kitchen cabinets. Rue folds herself forwards, slamming her fists into the ground, causing a gust of white magic to escape. When she lifts them, two identical dents are left in their wake.

The sound of the metal key dropping out of her shirt pocket rings in her ears, as if no other noise exists. Simmering her rage for the time being, her curiosity takes over again, wanting so desperately to understand the secrets held by the little key.

Rue sits up, dries her angry tears with the back of her hand, and studies the key. Her mind runs through scenarios on what it could open, and where that lock might be in the apartment. When she finally stands, her legs are weak from exhaustion. The invisible weight of guilt she holds on her back makes them want to give out and give up.

Olympia. This is for Olympia.

She repeats those words over and over again as she starts her search. She prowls from room to room, checking every drawer, and every cabinet she can find. She searches closets, under couches, and behind bookshelves. She rummages through medicine cabinets, and behind hutches, and peels up rugs for something out of place.

When she gets to the last room, one she is hesitant to enter, the shaking in her hands returns. Her old bedroom. The feelings of the past creep into her mind, reliving memories of her childhood. The disconnect she feels now is gods awful.

The girl that lived in this room is not standing here now. That girl had dreams, and ideas, and the belief she would be something great. That girl's innocent mind would not be able to comprehend who she turned into. A sneaky, conniving, terrible rogue. Someone who isn't deserving of the love and kindness that little girl was so willing to give to others.

That little girl would be so disappointed. Rue knows only because she feels it herself. Disappointment. Shame. Disgust.

This room, hell this whole house represents everything Rue should have been, but never will be.

Crossing the threshold into the blue and magenta room feels like a knife to the heart. Somehow it feels different to be in here without Olympia around to ground her.

She moves into the space, looking around for obvious places a key would go. The dresser drawers show her no insight as to where it could be. The closet reveals the same, nothing but old blankets, candles, and backup items for emergencies.

Rue continues her search, rummaging through old treasures she had displayed on shelves. There is a bookcase in the corner that gets destroyed in her frenzy. The nightstand, next to her homemade canopy bed, is tipped on its side to check for hidden compartments with none to be found.

Rue falls to her knees, searching for chests under her bed. She is about to stand back up in defeat, when she sees a floorboard that is lifted up in the corner, a small detail someone else would have brushed off as an old house with old materials.

On her knees she attempts to push the iron bed frame to the side of the room. With her weakened muscles and everything that has been going on, her strength isn't enough to move it. She takes a deep inhale and places her hands on the side of the frame. With all her energy focused on this one movement, the bed flies across the room, white sparkles trailing behind.

After every use of her magic, Rue can feel her exhaustion building. Her hands, that normally cover with a galaxy looking cloud, now only hold power in her palms. Never in her life has she used it so much in such a short amount of time. Olympia would warn her about energy limits, but she never paid attention. The only other time this much of her power has been used, she passed out after shredding the five Organization members who captured her.

"It's almost as if you like being tortured, not giving up your source so I can play with you all I want."

Rue shakes the magic from her hands, tossing that dark memory out with it.

Focus.

Now that the bed is gone, Rue gets a better look at the wooden board. The corner looks like it has been pried up with a crowbar, ripped from the nails holding it in place. There is only room for a few of her fingers which makes it hard to grab ahold of, but she manages to pull up and loosen the wood, removing it from the floor.

Her mouth dries, and a lump forms in her throat. There, sitting between two floor joists, is an old metal box with a golden bee on top.

Rue quickly shimmies a few of the surrounding floorboards loose, creating a large enough hole to lift the box from its hiding place. She cleans off the dust with a blow of magic, feeling her lungs retract at another use of power.

In the kitchen she places it on the counter and paces back and forth. Her mind shifts from needing to open it, and not being sure she is ready to see what Olympia left behind for her. Why her? What if she can't handle what's inside? What if it spirals her deeper into the void? What if it's nothing? An empty box full of what-could-have-beens.

Rue looks to the ceiling for answers that will never be replied to. The key in her hand warms as she rubs it between her fingers, fidgeting her anxieties out into something tangible.

"I'll be okay," she lies to herself in the empty room.

Ever so slowly, Rue inserts the honey bee key into the lock, a small part of her hoping for it not to work, so she can move on and forget about Olympia's faith in her. Looking at what is left in this box, means Olympia is gone. Really gone.

The key turns with a click. A shock of goosebumps form along Rue's arms and neck.

As she opens the top of the lid, she mumbles to herself, "Please be nothing. Please, please be nothing."

She looks down into the velvet lined box and her eyes fill with tears, blurring her vision of its contents. She doesn't need to see clearly to understand what this is. It's a memory box of Rue's childhood, filled with items from a simpler time.

With shaking hands, she pulls out the first item, a soft, yet overly loved red fox. Phoenix. The little arms still hold on with a few stitches, and there is stuffing coming out along the seam of the tail. Rue pulls it to her chest, a musty smell masking the usual scent of dried mint jammed into the stuffing, something Olympia added to help Rue calm down after nightmares.

Phoenix looks up at her, all withered away and fragile, and Rue can't stop her bottom lip from quivering. This fox was made to help keep her calm, and now all she wants to do is hold it tight and disappear forever.

Setting Phoenix gently on the table next to the box, Rue braves what else it has to share with her. She pulls out some loose papers, full of drawings she did as a child. Images of what she imagined the mainland to be like cover the pages in crayon. Treehouses with waterfalls as backdrops. Islands full of bright colorful flowers and seashells. Desert landscapes with imaginary sand creatures. Wintery hills with snowmen lining the pine trees.

A tear drops onto one of the pieces, running down a stick figure Rue, holding hands with a stick figure Olympia with flowers in her hair. All of these images have that in common, a happy, smiling Rue, being led into all these adventures by her protector, Olympia.

Rue closes her eyes and lets the tears soak her cheeks. Her heart cracks a little deeper, emptying its hope a little more into the void.

Under the drawings are more shattering moments of her life. She picks up three colorful, woven bracelets she gifted to her. Rue would make them while Olympia ran the store. She'd sit on top of the counter, asking random customers to help hold the string, while she tied knots. Olympia would tell her they held magic and promise to never take them off.

Half melted, homemade name day candles Olympia would surprise Rue with, sit in the metal box waiting to be used again. The mix of different materials all squished together, in the form of numbers for each year, brings back memories of quiet nights around the table in late spring. Olympia and Fiona would make things out of Meal Bag biscuits, place the candles in the middle, and Rue (and eventually Finny) would laugh at the warped shapes. The four of them would sit by the table, sing songs from the mainland, and play guessing games.

Rue can't stop the shaking of her chest while she cries into the memories. The candles tremble in her grasp. She looks at them through a cloudy layer of water that coats her eyes, wishing for the hurt to stop.

Continuing into the box, Rue pulls out a metal tin, spins the top off, and almost drops it when she realizes what it holds. Inside are little pieces of her auburn hair from haircuts long ago, tied in red ribbon. Along with that are teeth she lost, glued to scrap paper with dates on them and how they fell out. Little one-line stories of her life, written by the woman who loved her most.

Rue looks at the ribbons of hair and closes her eyes to sob. Olympia cared, she always cherished everything. Rue's memories growing up are not just her own, each one is also Olympia's to hold onto and take with her to the Meadow.

Loneliness fills Rue's lungs, replacing the oxygen. Parts of her soul crumble into darkness once again, pulling her away from the happy memories and into the realization that those are over. There will never be any more.

When she thinks the box has given her all it can, she is surprised to find a cloth covering something on the bottom. Rue pulls up on the dark, forest green cloth, and opens it up against the sun rays coming through the branches. As if it was painted by hand, the crest of Olympia's family stains the green linen with yellow ink. Lines of branches border the cloth and create a circle matching the one hanging over the fireplace.

She folds up the cloth and puts it in her pack, looking back into the box. A golden dagger lays perfectly in the middle, so shiny it's almost glowing. The hilt is made from emerald leather, tied together with twigs and dried vines. When she picks it up, she can see the pommel has the same family crest on it, in the middle of the diamond shape.

She realizes the magnitude of this gesture. This dagger, which was once Olympia's, now belongs to Rue, its rightful heir.

She holds the weight of it in her hands, allowing her sniffles and shaking breaths to fill the room's silence. Slowly, without looking away, like if she does it will disappear from her hands, Rue removes her old knife from its sheath, replacing it with her new one. Amazingly, it fits, like this holster was always meant for this knife. Like it's been waiting for this golden heirloom to be returned home for decades.

"Thank you, Oly." Even in death, Olympia is here protecting Rue when she cannot. Giving her this dagger is like giving her an extra life, one she does not deserve, but will carry with her with pride.

Rue turns to close the lid of the small chest, praying for no more memories, or surprises, or agony. She almost gets it closed when she spots a piece of paper at the bottom, so tucked into the shadows of the metal, she almost missed it.

It's an envelope addressed to her, with a letter inside. She loses her composure as soon as she reads the swirly handwriting of Olympia that fills the page.

My Dearest Honey Bee.

"No," Rue sobs into her hands.

CHAPTER

THROWING the envelope and the letter to the ground before she can get through the first line, Rue screams out in frustration. Her tears feel like thorns in her eyes, and she truly cannot fathom being able to move on from this torture. Everything she has ever endured, being lost, beaten, violated, used, none of it will ever compare to the pain of losing Olympia.

"No!" she screams out, wrapping her arms around herself. She can't see anything from her waterlogged eyes, but she can feel. She feels too much. Too much of every single emotion you can feel when you're lost, and alone.

Forever alone.

It should have been me.

Rue's exhaustion and sadness turns to adrenaline fueled rampage. With a long grunt, she swipes at the metal box, causing it to crash against a flower pot. The clay shatters against the impact, dirt and roots spreading across the floor.

With eyes turning the color of snowfall, a whirlwind picks up, blowing her hair and clothes around with the force. Her mind becomes something else, something charged by the darkness she keeps at bay. Large orbs of air swirl around her fists, as her magic gives one last push before being completely depleted. The usual translucent sparkles of her power, now covers her hands in solid white clouds, thick with the ability to destroy what she wants.

One of her hands shoots out towards a plant on the counter, and a rush of air pushes it off, along with four others. The sound of her heartbreak forms in her throat as agonizing grunts, filling the room with its devastating melody accompanied by the echoes of smashed pottery against the kitchen walls. A strong smell of the ground hits Rue's nose, which makes her want to smash more.

Olympia is gone. She's gone, and no one is here anymore. These plants are just reminders of what used to be, and Rue is sick of it. She is so tired of caring for someone and them being taken from her.

Another shriek comes from her throat with a rush of air towards the kitchen table. She flips it on its side and smashes it against the door frame to the living room. Wood shards go flying through the air, hitting everything, even Rue.

As more and more pots smash, and furniture is left in ruin, Rue's power is almost at its limit.

She's weeping now, arms to her sides shaking from the power that is keeping her upright. Her eyes are like rushing rivers. Her whole being crushed, and unable to accept this new reality.

She falls to her knees, when the last of her magic is released into the air. With her powers now depleted, Rue finally feels the pain. There is physical pain from using so much of her energy. Her arms feel bruised, her lungs ache with each inhale in, and her mouth dries out from breathing so heavily.

There is nothing left of her.

Rue sits in the silence, head low, staring at her fingertips. She tries to make something flicker in them to give her strength, but she is empty.

The sound of paper flickers through her consciousness, and she looks up to see the letter floating back down after being caught in the wind. It lands peacefully in front of her as if by its own magic.

She can't. She can't find the strength to look at it. To read that letter, is to read it in the past tense and Rue doesn't think she can bear it.

But as much as this is going to kill her physically and emotionally, she knows she has to.

She sighs, then reaches out for the parchment, hand hovering above it before grabbing on.

Olympia's handwriting is beautiful, dainty, and magical. Rue runs her pointer finger over the words, hoping to scoop up as much of Olympia's soul as she can. Her tears return, which shocks her because Rue is sure there was none left to fall.

Through mournful eyes, and trembling hands, Rue begins to read.

> *My Dearest Honey Bee,*
>
> *I do not have all the answers to the questions you seek. But I think it is about time I share what I know. Share the things I had to keep from you all these years, until you were ready to hear them.*

Unfortunately, this letter will have to do in my absence. I knew you would be clever enough to find it.

I was not meant to be here forever. That was never my destiny, but you, Aruelia of the North, you will do great things. You will move mountains. You will change lives. Most importantly, you will show this world what it means to be fae. You will rise up from the shadows you protect your spirit in, learn your purpose, and restore the world as The Mother herself once did long ago.

Purpose is a strange concept. My purpose, as you know, was once to come to the Southlands in search of answers. A way to unite the realm. Sometimes, what you think you were meant to do, is just a stepping stone on your path. A decision you make that leads you to your greatness. My greatness, my purpose, was always going to be raising you.

The Mother, the Gods, the Universe, whomever you choose to believe in, has a plan for each of us. And I believe with all my heart that yours is going to change history. Because you are not just a lost girl in a city of strangers, you are one of the last of your kind. Pure Bright Magic. The product of love and light. You are a beacon that all of us can turn to in our time of need. Someone to remind us of what hope feels like running through our veins. To pull us out of our own darkness.

You know the story of my life, and the path I took to get to our life together. But there are parts of my story I kept from you to protect you. Protect your progress, and your ability to become who you truly are, instead of becoming who you thought you needed to be for others.

I knew your mother, Aura. I worked in the infirmary of her estate for many years when she was a girl. Helping cure soldiers and teaching her potions for herself. You are so much like her, in your sense of curiosity and need to know the unknown. You two share the urge to create for yourself and find solutions to the problems you face.

She came to me one night, begging me to leave and go as far away from the castle as I could. She said I needed to be safe from the shadows that were coming for us all. I needed to protect the prophecy. See, Honey Bee, your mother had visions, like the ones I believe you have at night. Visions of her future, and the future of all of those living on Ethos.

So, I listened when she demanded I leave. I chose to believe and went south looking for the blend of twin light, a brave warrior to fight for our lives. Leaving her was like leaving my own child. A heartbreaking reality I had to face in the name of the greater good.

Your mother wrote to me over the years. I saved them in a box in my potions desk. They are yours, if you want them. They are filled with stories of her life. Retellings of her growing into a powerful air magic welder, and how she was forced to marry a man she didn't love, and what led her to finding her true twin light.

That leads me to your father. His name was Cillian Kylexi. A human working for your stepfather. He was originally from the Low District, growing up not far from where you did. I looked for family members for you, I truly did, but there were none. They disappeared when your father left the Southland.

They planned on running away to the South together, raising you as human, and creating a life for the three of you. Unfortunately, as you know, that was not their fate.

I received a letter from her a week before I saved you on that beach, telling me she would be sending you to me to protect. Asking me to keep things from you, to keep your identity safe from the outside world. With that letter was the one you still hold on to today, and the pendant you wear around your neck. She trusted me with her purpose, and in that you became mine.

Your mother once asked you to be brave without her, now I must ask you to do the same. Show this world who you truly are, Aruelia, be the hope everyone prays for each night. It is time for you to move on from this city, nothing but pain awaits you here.

There is something dark coming for us all. I believe it is already here. It was created like you were, but instead of pure bright,

I'm afraid it is pure shadows. Go to the Northlands. Stop the shadows from spreading. Give this realm peace once again. Your visions will show you the way. Listen to your fox, she has always been your guide.

I know this is a lot on your shoulders, and that it may seem like you are just one being in a sea of millions. But always remember, if you want to change the world, light a match.

Do not make this journey alone, find your tribe. Find those who believe in you, as much as I do. Allow them to help you believe in yourself. You do not have to carry this weight alone.

Aruelia, I always tried to live in the sunshine. Thank you for helping me see there is beauty in the moons. There is beauty in suffering and darkness, it has the power to show us who we are at our core, what we are made of. It can point us in the direction of our destiny.

What I accomplished in this lifetime was worth any suffering I may receive in death. I did my best to raise you the way your mother would have. She was an incredible woman, and so are you. Her and your father are so proud of you. We will all be reunited once again, but you have work to do first. The three of us will be walking with you. You will never be alone. Never.

Whatever the outcome, whoever you choose to be, and wherever you end up, just know I am always going to be proud of you. I would have chosen to raise you in every lifetime. You are so beautiful Honey Bee, but that is not all you have to offer this world. Your possibilities are endless. Your potential is endless. Your love, and kindness, and intelligence are endless. Aruelia, you are strong. You are a fighter. You are hope.

You are the greatest gift. I love you.

Oly

PS: Enclosed with this letter is one more answer to one of your millions of questions. Use it.

Rue slams the letter down on her lap, tears rushing from her eyes, but she doesn't have time to wipe them away.

The envelope, where is the godsdamn envelope?

She tossed it to the ground in her rage, but there are so many plants smashed around her, it could have dropped anywhere. She throws herself to the ground, frantically searching through the dirt. The memories of the oak tree splinter her mind in two, but she continues on.

Another answer? What other answer could it possibly be? This letter gives answers to questions I didn't even know I had.

Under a pot behind her, buried in the dirt is the envelope at last. Rue wipes it on her chest, brushing the soil off onto her shirt. Inside of it… is nothing.

She is about to give up when she sees scribbles on the inside of the envelope itself. Handwriting. Olympia's handwriting.

There, written in green ink, is a map and a name she has been searching for.

Without giving herself much time to think things through, Rue is on her feet, pacing around the destroyed apartment, collecting things that can't be left behind. She grabs Olympia's potion book, and the stack of letters from her mother tucked away in the back of a drawer (which she decides are best left unread for now), her stuffed fox, and a few other mementoes.

After shoving the random things into her pack, Rue is out the door and flying down the steps.

Before leaving this shop for what will be the last time, Rue searches for things to bring with her. Medicines, meal replacements, extra coins, she grabs anything that was meant for Olympia before looters get to it.

She pulls the tapestry down off the wall, welcomes the familiar scent of patchouli and bergamot, then rolls it up and shoves it in her bag. The thought of leaving this behind is too devastating to think about. Rue pictures it swaying in the wind from broken windows, as looters empty shelves and cabinets. None of them would see the beauty in the world they grew up fearing. She can't stand the idea of a piece so special to Olympia being lost and left behind.

There are shelves of different salves still intact by the window, Rue dumps what she can into her bag. If her mind wasn't so foggy right now, maybe she would be more strategic about what to take, but there is no time.

She runs to the front desk, but the register isn't there. Dropping to her knees to search underneath it, sharp pains shoot up her legs with the contact of the cold ground.

There it is!

Pulling off broken pieces of wood and wiping away the dust, Rue opens the register. All the coins from the day before are still accounted for. She pockets the lot, leaving nothing behind, and places the box back under the desk.

As she moves to stand, something catches her eye in the morning light that makes Rue stop in her tracks. She kicks the shiny metal object with her foot, uncovering it from the rubble hiding it. Bending down to pick up the mysterious object, her mind ignores the fact that she knows what it is. It's a knife. *The* knife, with red traces of her still coating it. Rue balls up the bottom of her shirt to clean off the blood, and notices something that makes her heart stop beating.

This knife. The knife that is responsible for killing Olympia, just gave away the killer. And as soon as she has the strength to move, she will destroy them.

Because Rue knows exactly who it belongs to.

CHAPTER

ALL Rue can see is red. Pure anger, and rage, and determination to burn the whole world down. They will pay for what they did to her. Every single person who ever breathed in the same room as them, will regret ever stepping foot in this city.

The ledge Rue is balancing on is starting to wobble, and she is no longer afraid to drop into the deep pit of darkness below. In fact, she wants it. She wants to cause pain. To kill. The voices in her head, that usually tell her to stay strong when her anger surfaces, are now screaming at her for revenge.

The plan leading up to this point was an easy one. It came to her as if by fate. She ran home, prepared herself for what's to come, and now found herself outside the business of the person responsible for shattering her.

Rue walks up the steps, her black heels clicking with each foot closer to the end. She looks down at the bottle of Lucky Clover whiskey in her hand and reassures herself this will work.

The neon lights outside the building are blinding her as she approaches. The front entrance is empty, the place shutting down for the night an hour ago. Lucky for her, she knows exactly how to enter. Inside is business as usual, too late to be busy, which she was counting on. The tables are empty, but the staff is still here cleaning up from tonight's crowd.

She weaves in and out of furniture to make it to the bar, grabbing two glasses as she passes. Her face is stone cold as she makes her way up to the second floor, hips swaying with the beat of the music still playing from the night before. None of it reaches her ears thought, the thumping of her battered heart is all consuming.

She walks past the bodyguards, flashing the mark on her wrist as if it was any other day. She winks at the tiny woman glaring at her and bows mockingly at the man towering above her.

Staring at the red door, her world goes into slow motion. The walk to the killer seems to expand further away with each step she takes. She inhales, but with all this built up adrenaline in her veins, she can't exhale. Not yet.

With her chin tilted up, head high, and a bright smile on her red lips, she pushes the door to his office open. Her feet stop in the doorway to study the man down the bridge of her nose.

"Franky, can you give us a second? I need to talk to Diego alone about a little *project* I just finished for him," Rue moans, slowly stepping into the office, the red carpet under her heels feeling like shattered glass.

This is it. No going back. This is for Olympia.

Franky glances at Diego with furrowed brows, waiting for his boss to answer and tell her to leave. But he doesn't. Diego's eyes wander down Rue's body, burning into her for seconds that feel like hours. His gaze stops on her corset that is exposing her breasts just the right amount. The leather of her pants hugs her curves like they were made for her specifically.

A flash of realization crosses through his mind, showing Rue he remembers what this outfit is from. This very outfit *was* made for her, the first time he sent her into a room with men to get information. The first time he willingly sent her into a room where the only intention was for her spirit to die. For her body to be violated.

Diego designed it himself. He explained that men wouldn't be able to resist her in it, and she would be able to manipulate them however she wanted. He told her it gave her the power in the situation, told her everything they did was giving her the upper hand. Well, here's to hoping he's correct.

Because this time she will have power. He will be the one who is violated. He will be the one begging her to live. His spirit will be so far gone, it will never recognize him in its return. She will break him. Destroy him like he has been doing to her most of her life. This is her turn. She will be the villain. She will sit and watch as he questions why he saved her all those years ago.

"Leave Franky, Ghost and I have some stuff to work on. The rest of you can go home," he smirks.

Good.

She wants him to feel comfortable, feel like this is a hook up not an assassination. Her face definitely says it is. The siren eyes, biting her bottom lip, the slow movement up and down her arm, they all mask the glow of her anger ready to turn him to stone. She crosses her legs, arching her back a little against the doorframe.

Diego runs his finger over his bottom lip, trying to hide a smirk. He always loved when he could see how bad she wanted him, watch her squirming for his touch. So, she will give him the show he craves, be who he wants her to be.

"Leave. We might be here a while," he orders.

Never breaking eye contact Rue purrs, "All night probably." The hum of her voice makes Diego bite his bottom lip.

"I'll close up, tell everyone to go. And no one better fucking interrupt. It's business."

"Just business," Rue whispers, smirking at Diego.

Franky looks in between the two of them, rubbing a hand on the back of his neck. "Sure thing Boss, see you two tomorrow." He raises a brow as he passes Rue, questions on his mind he doesn't dare speak. As she closes the door behind him, she winks.

She wishes she could explain it to him, tell him to run while he still can. Rue has always liked Franky, he never caused any problems and was always there to have her back, but this can't involve him. She is here for one purpose and one purpose only, and he is currently sitting in his final resting place. Morbid really, thinking about death with such excitement.

I guess that's what happens when you create a monster, it bites you when you corner it.

Rue saunters over to Diego, stopping at the edge of the desk, leaning over it to get closer to his face. The golds of her irises dance with the void itself.

"Hi," she whispers. "I have a problem I need some assistance with." The glasses clank as she sets them down on the desk.

"Is that so? Pretty bold of you to storm in here, wearing that, expecting me to drop everything for a quick fuck. That is of course, if that's what you need me for, Beautiful. By the way you keep twitching those fucking hips, I assume that's why."

"Oh, I promise it won't be quick." She winks at him. "And don't lie to me and tell me you don't want to fuck me right here, right now. If I was a betting woman, I'd bet you're hard right now just thinking about all the filthy things I'm about to do to you." Rue leans further over the wooden desk, pushing her breasts into his face, running her tongue slowly over her top lip.

He clears his throat and readjusts his pants, which makes Rue use every ounce of self-control not to roll her eyes. Diego stands up from his chair, moves around the room, and pulls her hips into his. His hard bulge rubs against her ass, which sends shivers down her spine in celebration.

I am once again screaming from the rooftops that all men are the same.

He moves a hand around her throat, lifting her toward him so her back is to his chest. With a deep inhale of her scent, he greets her neck with his lips. "I'd never lie to you, Beautiful. You know exactly what you do to me. You can feel it can't you?"

Rue wiggles herself around so she is facing Diego, wrapping her arms around his neck. His hands slide down her back and cup her ass. With a grunt of approval from the tight leather hugging her, he goes in for a kiss. Rue turns away at the last second, looking back at the whiskey that is still on the desk.

"I brought that so we could celebrate." She smiles up at him, switching her siren eyes for those of an innocent doe.

"And what are we celebrating exactly?" he asks, brows snapping together.

"I took care of our problem. Lex won't be bothering us anymore."

"You did now? All by yourself?" His smirk widens to show all his teeth from pride. Pride for the ruthless creature he has created within her. She nods slowly, allowing a small glimmer to be seen in her eyes. "That's my girl."

Rue turns to the whiskey, taking the top off with her teeth, and pouring the amber liquid into the glasses. She turns back around, leaning into his chest and looks up in her sweetest expression. "Cheers to cleaning up loose ends," she says, handing him the glass and taking a sip of her own.

Diego smirks, downing the entire glass of whiskey without breaking eye contact. This used to be an act that would turn Rue on, the constant connection to him. Light touches when no one is looking. Longing stares from across the room. The heat between the two of them. All of it, every single thing, was a way to get her to do what he wanted, to dominate her. None of it was ever real.

Rue grabs the whiskey bottle, refilling his glass. "Is this too much?"

His eyes slowly wander down her body before admitting, "It's perfect."

"Good, I'd hate for you to miss what's coming next." Her smile turns into something more devilish. Rue's hands are starting to tingle, and she regulates her breathing as inconspicuously as she can. "Why don't we move to the couch."

"What if I want to take you here?" he asks, pointing his glass towards his desk.

"We're going to do what I want today."

"I think you have that backwards Ghost, you do what I want. That pussy is mine, remember? Every part of you is mine."

She laughs at the use of the name Ghost. She was never Ghost. Rue leans in closer, moving her hand to his cock, rubbing over his jeans with slow movements. The friction causes him to twitch with need. Diego lets out a silent breath and leans his head back.

"See, you're like putty in my hands. I can stroke, and pull, and make you forget everything but my touch."

"Fuck," he says in a long, drawn out voice. The siren is back, and her magic is working.

"You, Diego Metus, are a very easy man to control, if you know how to do it. And, oh do I know how to do it. I know all your secrets. All your spots of weakness." Rue licks her lips, leaning into Diego's ear. She kisses his neck, licking and nipping at his skin with a moan. She teases, "Sit on the couch for me. Let me show you exactly what I plan to do with you."

Rue grabs Diego's hand and leads him to the couch, pushing him down to straddle his lap. She lets out a giggle when he smacks her ass, causing her to warm from the heat.

An electric shock runs down her body, but not with lust, with the notion that he is falling right into her trap. Men. So simple minded. So full of their own worth, they forget others can take away their desires. Rue can admit, he did teach her that. He taught her the reality that men, oftentimes, look to women as objects, things placed around a room to add to their own value. Women are simply products for them to use up and toss aside when something new comes along. It's all a fantasy.

So, she can thank him for showing her exactly what to do with his ego tonight. She knows what to say, and how to act, and how to feed his need for power.

"Rock your hips. Look at them under your lashes. Lick those perfect lips of yours. Show them how wet you are, without them needing to touch you to find out. Then, when you have them in a vulnerable position, slit their throat and take what's ours."

He really did know what he was talking about. He taught her well, maybe even too well. Because what Diego was failing to see at this moment, is that he just let a sly fox into his space. And this fox has nothing to lose.

The smile that runs over Rue is anything but innocent. Her head tilts to one side as she examines her prey, almost giddy with anticipation for what happens next.

"You're so godsdamn sexy after a kill. I fucking love you," he mumbles, leaning in for a kiss. Rue allows it, kissing him back and sticking her tongue down his throat like he wants it. She leans into his touch when his hands run over her body, squeezing her ass as she bites his bottom lip.

Without a word, she moves her hands to his shirt, pulling it over his head like she's done countless times before. She moves her mouth to his neck, leaving a trail of red from her lipstick, making her way around all his favorite spots, and ends back at his lips.

The pricks in her fingertips have now moved into her arms, her head feeling light from the pressure.

One more task.

Rue stops her sensual movements, the coldness filling her veins takes over. Sitting up straight in his lap she smirks and lets out a menacing laugh.

"Love me? That's interesting. You know, you've shown me so much, how to fuck, how to become invisible, how to steal whatever I wanted, be whoever the targets wanted me to be, even how to spare a life, but love—" She pauses to run a finger over his lips. "Love was never one of those things."

Before he can protest from the sudden change in her demeanor, she kisses him once more. A deep, passionate kiss, pulling on the nape of his neck to push him closer to her.

With the realization of what she just admitted, Diego pushes Rue off of himself, causing her to fall to the floor. She laughs, pushing away the hair that is covering her face, and moves to sit on her knees.

Diego tries to stand up but loses his balance and falls back on the couch. He moves a hand to his chest, letting out a cough when suddenly his eyes dart to hers. "What the fuck is wrong with you? What's going on, Rue?" He coughs again, rubbing his hands over his eyes and blinking before looking down at his body, which is slowly failing him.

"What's wrong, Diego? Not feeling well? Is it the numbness in your hands, or the fogginess of your vision that is more annoying? See, for me it's the numbness, but being poisoned can be a different experience for everyone." Rue looks him down the bridge of her nose in triumph.

His expression drops, along with his mouth. Horror fills his eyes, which causes Rue to grin. Without looking away, she reaches into her corset in between her breasts and pulls out a small vial of magenta liquid. She slowly undoes the cork, and tips her head back, taking it like a shot.

"You know the antidote is a little too floral for my taste but hey, at least I'll live."

She stands to her feet, which is easier said than done due to the poison still running through her veins. A small price to pay for the outcome she wants. After all, she has the antidote Olympia created. She will be okay. The poison mixture she concocted is unpredictable, and untested. An enhanced version of the lipstick Olympia made for her all those months ago. The outcome left to the Gods above, hopefully in her favor.

Rue brushes off the invisible dust on her leather pants. "Well," she exhales dramatically. "I'm feeling much better, aren't you?" She looks at him, raising her eyebrows for him to respond. He just gazes at her with confusion still plastered on his face, trying to put pieces of the puzzle together.

"Oh, that's right. Sorry, I would have shared that with you." She tosses the bottle behind her. "But I don't want to."

"What the fuck, Rue?" Diego gets out between coughs. He tries to readjust on the crouch, but his body is becoming harder and harder to control. The heaviness from the poison in his bloodstream takes dominance in his brain.

"I can see you're still trying to wrap your pretty little head around this. I understand. Let's see, where were we?"

Rue rests her hand on her chin, tapping her lips with her pointer finger, pacing back and forth in front of him. "I walked in, seduced you without a problem, tricked you into kissing me… what's next? Oh yeah! I poison you and make you wish you never met me. Doesn't that sound like fun?"

"You did what!" Diego yells behind gritted teeth, trying to get up.

"I wouldn't move too much if I were you, the faster the blood moves through your body the worse it's going to feel."

Rue steps forward, pushing him back down with her palm, jolting him with a tiny spark of her magic. In her eyes, shines a glow of white sparkles, ones she's never let him see before. She doesn't care to hide from him anymore, pretending she isn't half fae. She is done concealing her true identity.

"Fuck you!"

"Fuck me? No, not today unfortunately. Wasn't it you who once told me fucking is a privilege?" She leans in to whisper, "And you haven't been very good to me, have you?"

Rue moves on top of him again. Letting herself sink into his lap, she runs her hands down his chest, then back up to his neck. She lazily traces a finger across his cheek, smiling at him and moaning at the thought of the sex they've had. "Gods, it was good though. At least I got that out of it. It's a shame we won't be able to continue fucking."

"It doesn't have to be like this, Rue," Diego pleads with her.

Rue sits for a moment. No, it didn't have to be like this. He didn't have to betray her. He didn't have to lie to her and make her believe this was somehow her fault. And most importantly, he didn't have to kill Olympia. He didn't have to do any of it.

Bile wants to rise in Rue's throat with a vision of Olympia's lifeless body hanging over her arms. Her anger makes her skin as hot as a flame. So many years of torture, disguised as love.

"Betrayal is a bitch," she says in a seething whisper. Her heart is about to explode out of her chest. There is so much she wants to do, so much pain she wants to cause this man.

"The fuck did you do to me?" He moans in agony, probably because the poison is making its way to his *more important* body parts. Sweat coats his skin as the chemicals do their magic, making Rue grin at her handiwork.

"Don't you recognize it?" she asks, puckering her lips at him. "You must remember, it's how this whole shit show started!" Rue moves her hands over her body, feeling for something. "I poisoned you with my lipstick. You see it activates with alcohol. The more you ingest, the stronger the effects. It's a more potent version of the one I used on our dear friend, Lex." She looks around her. "Where the hell did I put that?"

She turns to face his desk, still straddling him, and says, "Oh! There it is, it's so hard to keep track of." Rue takes a deep breath out and motions her fingers over to the bottle. The sparkles in her eyes return as a white, glittery cloud pours from her hands. Her magic grabs the lipstick tube that she *accidentally* dropped earlier, returning it to her.

She spins back to Diego, who's eyes burn with horror, and laughs at him. "You know, I've known you for a long time, and this is the first I've ever seen you truly terrified. I like that it's because of me."

"You're... You're..." He can't speak, partly because of his current state, partly because he can't believe he didn't know *what* she truly is.

"Oh, I'm sorry. This must be a lot to take in. I never told you, but my Mother comes from the Northlands, and I share her abilities." She leans in close, face stone cold when she says, "That's right, Diego. Your girlfriend is half fae."

CHAPTER

"**HE** never said you had powers!" Diego grits his teeth as he speaks, unable to move his body.

Rue scoffs. Of course Lex, or his father, or whoever the fuck he is talking about didn't know. "Why in the world would I have told anyone that? It's my little secret. Gives me an edge, don't ya think?"

Diego's eyes turn black, staining his face with anger, and realization.

Rue leans into him. "I can see this is all a lot for your tiny human brain, so let's just get past it and move on to something more interesting. I don't have a lot of time. Oh, wait." She pauses to run a hand down his face, lifting his chin to her. "That's you."

He goes rigid, the only movement he makes is with his rushed breaths. The joy this brings Rue would be concerning if her mind was in the right place, but now is not the time to be rational. Her whole life with him has been filled with nothing but chaos. Now is the time to do what she wants. To be who she wants, and not who he assumes she is. No more hiding behind the mask. She is Aruelia Kylexi of the Northlands, and she will not allow this human man to take any more of her.

She lets out a dramatic sigh, slapping herself on the thighs before lifting off of him to stride around the room.

"It's a shame really, you almost had me. That would have been very embarrassing, not knowing my own boyfriend killed my grandmother. Being oblivious to the monster in my sheets with me. Being so naive that I didn't notice the man I called mine, was willing and responsible for killing the only person I actually cared about. The only person who ever loved me." Her voice cracks with her last sentence.

Her words sting. As if he suddenly gets movement of his body again, he inches forward and spits, "I loved you!"

She lunges for him, stopping inches away from his face. Pointing a finger at him she demands, "Don't you dare say that! Don't you dare say you loved me. *That* wasn't love. It was never love, just control. That's all I ever was to you. A toy to fuck and manipulate into what you wanted."

He doesn't answer, just blinks at her in disgust. Rue can see the veins in his arms, the muscles tightening in his chest. His face is flushed as he tries to win back control over his own body.

"It's not fun when your body doesn't feel like your own, is it?"

She moves her arms behind her back and begins to pace back and forth again, making sure to keep her eyes locked on his. "Let's go over the facts, shall we? You, Diego Metus, were the one to bring me into this shit show the night of the Presidential Gala. Making me believe I was in Lex's office for tax documents. Clever of you to leave the Organization file right there, loose in a cabinet for me to find. Knowing me so well, you knew I wouldn't miss discrepancies like that. Understanding my need to know more. Followed by that same night, after fucking my brains out of course, you played dumb when I asked about it."

He mumbles something she doesn't catch. "What was that? Say something worth sharing with the rest of the class?"

"You were never meant to find that file," he repeats himself, voice soft for the first time tonight. His head drops to his lap. "Lex should have shredded it but kept it as collateral in case things went south."

"Well, you could say they've gone south. I guess that's what you get for working with unreliable people."

He looks up at her under his lashes and begins to say something, but Rue speaks over him.

"Then, when I came to you after someone attempted to *kill me*, suddenly you were involved, and you had a whole team of people working on it. Was I allowed to join this mysterious team of crime fighters, of course not. It wasn't safe for me; you know with them threatening my life and all. I brushed it off as you wanting to protect me. I thought, how sweet, he finally cares about my wellbeing. And yes, sure that is on me for believing in you."

"I did... I do care about you," he utters under his breath, cutting her off. "Why do you think I let you stay with me? I tried to bring you in, and he wanted me to take you out for knowing too much." His voice is husky, yet annoyed like she is finally getting under his skin.

Rue's hand goes up. "That's enough! Let's not sit here and pretend this was all a misunderstanding. Bottom line, is that you sat there, making me believe you were just as much in the dark as I was. You let me believe we were on the same team. We never were. Not a single day in our lives."

His muscles soften, and he goes limp where he is sitting. A line forms in between his brows. "That's not true and you know it."

"Again, with the lies. Cut the shit. Your little scheme is done. I don't understand why you're still trying to fabricate a different reality for us." Rue is yelling now, exhausted from this game of pretend. "You knew what you were doing. You sent me into that casino knowing who spent money there, knowing the men I would see. When I gave you information about Rocky being one of them, you had me tail her like a fucking child to waste my time. Waiting for me to get bored and come crawling back to your bed in defeat. I know it was you who paid those kids to make me lose her, what you underestimated was my ability to continue on."

His brows lower over his eyes, like he is trying to recall all the events of the last few months. "I never—" But he cuts himself off. A calm darkness covers his features as if he is turning into someone else. "Rocky was... unexpected." He tries to shift where he sits, but all he manages to do is crack his neck to the side.

"Her involvement was just for my benefit, to get her under me again where that bitch belongs. But sadly, she won't be a part of our group anymore."

Her soul sinks lower into the void that consumes it. "You didn't," she breathes, tears of fury collect in her eyes.

"I had been waiting for her to fuck up. Thankfully, she failed once again by giving you that information. So, I took care of it like I always do. Sad when a building collapses with patrons and the owner inside. What a tragedy."

She blinks her anger away, not wanting to give him the satisfaction. A monster sits in front of her, desperate to be in charge even though she has him immobile. His words sting. More black ink fills her veins. Is there even any blood left in her at this point? Or is she just the black ooze of others who sacrificed their own lives for her?

Ignoring his confession, she continues. "Now, let's talk about my informant. His name was Issak. Although, I'm sure you already knew that. You're the one who killed him after all. You had to have done it. I have been going crazy trying to wrap my brain around who woke me up in the shower after being drugged. Trying to remember who was begging me to wake up. It was you."

Rue steps a little closer. "You woke me up, just to be tortured by them. You could have let me die, but instead you let me be ripped apart from the inside out. Did you know what they were doing to me? Did you know and do nothing?" Her breath catches in her throat, trying to stop the quiver of her bottom lip as tears fill her vision. "I bet you didn't expect for me to kill all five of them, that must have put a wrench in your plans. Must have been a shock, knowing I'm more powerful than you ever thought I could be."

His gaze is strong, yet uninterested. His body shakes with what she knows is a very strong amount of poison running through it. Sweat is dripping down his forehead and arms. His attempt at hiding the pain is almost amusing, stubborn until the very end, she will give him that.

"Issak saw you that morning when you were cleaning up my mess didn't he? When he was leaving the red rock in my window, he saw you, and knew what you did, and who you were. The writing on his wall, in his own fucking blood, was outing you. Don't. Trust. Diego. The warning was about you." She whispers the last word, not wanting to believe it herself.

"That's not even the worst part of it all. Your twisted game went too far when you killed Olympia." Rue's voice cracks at the use of her name. She pulls her emotions back into her chest and stops her shaking body before continuing.

Memories of having to wash off her blood in the shower whip past her mind against her will. The red of her blood mixing into the water and swirling down the drain will be in her mind forever, taunting her with grief when she least expects it. There is nothing left of Olympia in this world other than the memories of losing her. The trembles in her fists don't stop, causing her to break skin in her palms from her nails.

"She was nothing. Didn't even put up a fight." He says it with so much anger it makes her want to rip him limb from limb.

"She was innocent!" she screams. "An innocent woman who was just trying to help people. She did nothing wrong, and you treated her like she was an animal. Cutting off her ears as if slashing her wasn't enough." Rue turns away to hide the water pouring from her eyes, but quickly turns back around, not afraid of what version of herself he sees any longer.

"You humans are the savage ones. Killing other beings with no regard for who they are or what they do for *your community*. Just because they are different from you."

The void in his eyes locks onto her, clawing into her with need, wanting to rip her to shreds and leave nothing behind.

"Oh, I didn't kill her because she was fae. I killed that monster because seeing her dead would break you. It's your fault they're all dead. You did this to yourself. You just had to go around getting into other people's business. Coming to me like a fucking lost dog offering up information in exchange for affection. You're pathetic. That's why I saved you all those years ago, I couldn't watch such a pathetic bitch die a heroic death."

Her anger is now lodged in her throat. She is swimming in rage. She wants to throw things, and scream, and cry, and smash his face into a table. She wants him to beg her for an ounce of forgiveness while she cuts him apart piece by piece.

The darkness inside of her bubbles to the surface, whispering in her mind to end him. It entices her to feel his warm blood on her fingers as she destroys his flesh and rips out his heart.

But that is what he wants. He wants to die a noble death for his cause. And as much as she wishes she could be the one to ruin him, she has another plan in mind. One that leaves her conscious cleaner than Diego's will ever be.

Rue's stare meets his once again. He sits helpless on the couch, waiting for her reaction to his devilish attacks. He is still trying to seem calm and collected, like the poison isn't currently shutting down his organs. Maybe, he is hoping if he sits long enough, the poison will take over for good, making this all end in a peaceful passing for him.

Brave. He would be sadly mistaken, but what a brave idea.

This poison won't kill him, paralyze, burn, take him to the edge of death, oh yes, but not kill.

Rue lets out a little moan, time to make him sweat more. Arching her eyebrow she purrs, "Aren't you dying to know how I pulled it all together? With my tiny pathetic girl brain?"

He turns his head away from her as much as he can, which isn't much. She stalks forward, swinging her hips like she's done over and over again for his pleasure. Leaning down, she jerks his jaw back towards her. His eyes slam shut, and his breath becomes jagged. "You will look away when I say you can look away. You are not in charge here. I am. Now, I asked you a question."

Still squeezing his chin between her sharp finger nails Diego chokes out, "Fuck you."

Rue climbs on his lap again. His body is tense under her, trembling against his will. "See you made one little mistake. Just one. You thought you were invincible and could use something personal to kill her. But that was your fatal mistake, you got cocky, and I caught you."

Against her thigh, in her dagger holster, Rue pulls out the murder weapon. A small knife, with the letter M on the pommel. She holds it up to his face, laughing in her victory.

"If we hadn't ever slept together, I probably wouldn't have made the connection. But this silly little M marking on this one of a kind knife, matches the one right there on your chest. The same M you wear around your finger." Rue pushes the dagger into his chest, right above where his tattoo is inked, just enough to break skin. She twirls it around in her hand, causing him to scream out in pain. A trail of blood starts to drip down his abdomen.

She puts the knife between her teeth as she lifts his hand, and slowly pulls the platinum ring off his pointer finger. In the same movement, she places it on her own, admiring it on her hand.

Once back in her grip, Rue uses the knife to taunt Diego's body, sending more shivers down his skin, light brushes back and forth over his collarbone, then his abs.

"The only thing I just can't seem to understand is the why. Why come after me? I'm no threat to you. Why not just let me in on your tiny," she kisses his lips. "Little," another kiss. "Secret?"

Rue takes her free hand and deepens her kiss with Diego. She runs her tongue along the inside of his mouth, and he doesn't fight it. The sick bastard, needing her touch even after being betrayed. She guesses she could say the same about herself. She wants to murder him, yet her lust for him leaves her feeling sadistic and twisted with wanting.

She lets go, letting cool air fill her lips. Both of their pulses race to keep up.

"Gods, I think I'm actually going to miss kissing you," Rue moans. "But alas, I have bigger issues to deal with than worrying about why my boyfriend doesn't like me anymore. I'm leaving this fucking shit hole of an island. I'm going to find the man that killed my parents, and I'm going to make him wish he never let me get away. And as for you, by the time they find you, I'll be long gone."

Rue stands to leave, readjusting her breasts in her top, still holding the knife.

Diego's gruff voice fills the room with hatred. "I'm the only reason you're still alive."

Rue looks at him, rolling her eyes at the thought.

Imagine being so delusional, trying to kill your girlfriend and failing, makes you believe you're the one keeping her alive.

She laughs, resting her arms on his shoulders to get close to his face. She whispers into his ear, "Well, I hope you realize how stupid that is now, considering the position it got you in." The smile plastered across her face is probably making him want to strangle her.

Rue stands to look him over, admiring every inch of tattooed muscle. "Hey, we had a good run." She shrugs her shoulders, flinging the knife around loosely in front of his face. "Well, we had a run. Too bad it had to end like this, I'm heartbroken."

Her finger runs over the edge of the blade, admiring the craftsmanship. She lifts it up towards her lips, running the cool metal across them, leaving a trail of red behind.

"Please!" he spits out in a last rush of desperation. "You don't have to do this. You're better than this, better than me."

"Oh, please. We both know I'm so much worse," she scoffs.

With one swift motion, Rue digs the knife into Diego's thigh, just a few inches from his cock. He wails in agony, unable to move his body to remove the blade from his leg, which is now starting to pool a glorious crimson color.

Rue grabs his discarded shirt and wipes the rest of her lipstick off onto it, tossing it on his wounded leg.

"I want you to know I could have killed you with one exhale. I could have thrown myself into this room and destroyed you without even breaking a sweat. But that wouldn't be fun. I want to go on living my life knowing you're in constant suffering. I want to close my eyes at night with the knowledge that you're only breathing because of me. Because I let you. That's what we do after all, isn't it? We spare each other's lives." She looks him dead in the eyes, as he struggles to keep them open. "Well, this is me, returning the favor. A life for a life."

As Rue turns to leave, her magic shoots out of her left hand, grabbing the whiskey bottle and bringing it towards her lips. She takes a swig as she walks towards the door.

Before she crosses the threshold, she turns to look down on him one last time. With all her anger ready to burst out as tears stream down her face, she warns, "Find me again, in this town or in any other, and I won't be so sweet. I no longer belong to you; my debts are paid."

CHAPTER

RUE opens the door to her apartment. The burning smell of disinfectant hits her nose with force, but she doesn't flinch. If she reacts, that will mean this is all real, and that is not something she is ready to admit to herself. The numbness has returned, all her adrenaline and anger left behind in Sinners. Now she just feels exhausted.

The hazy glow of the sun behind the smog filters in through her windows, in different circumstances it might make her smile. Seeing the determination of the sun is a powerful thing, cutting through the gross chemical sky the humans use as a shield to keep out anything natural, anything they can't control.

Rue's silent exhale somehow fills the space with sound. She looks around the room that is no longer hers, traces of hatred and deceit paint the walls in invisible ink. Her simple mattress on the floor is not a place to rest, it is now where she was manipulated to care for a man that was never honest. The kitchen is no longer for cooking, it holds the grime of pain and suffering at the hands of a white masked devil. The bathroom across from her will never wash her clean again, it only holds the memories of nightmare dreams and the shock of water waking her up into a new one.

No part of her life is hers and hers alone. Which is why she must go. Olympia is—*was,* she reminds herself—right. The only thing left for this city to give her is pain.

She steps up close to the window, looking out the glass at the streets below. She loathes the innate ability of humans to pretend everything is okay and keep going, when the world around them is falling apart. She watches as they continue on in their daily chores and meaningless jobs, ignoring the fact that their numbers are dwindling. Their neighbors and friends are being taken from them, yet they still hang clothes to dry and try to sell day old goods for full price.

These are not her people. They were never her people. Rue belongs with those who are willing to fight. It may have taken twenty nine years to realize this, but now she is more sure than ever. She was never meant to be a rogue, good at it yes, but it was never meant to represent who she is.

She looks up into the clouds, and questions who *is* she meant to be? It isn't a thief, but it certainly isn't some sort of *beacon of hope* Olympia thinks she is.

The only true sense she has is the idea that it is time for her to go.

Her mind shifts to the people she is about to leave behind. Fiona, Charlie, and Finny will be left with questions, but she doesn't have time on her side. She needs to leave now, because her enemies will return for her. That much she is certain. It will be safer for all of them if she disappears.

That thought alone is keeping her moving as she starts to pack her bag. The quicker she can get off this rock, the better it will be for everyone else.

She reaches into a small closet in the bathroom and pulls out her largest pack. It's a two strap bag made of old green canvas, with leather straps and zippers, big enough to hold a few days' worth of supplies. Rue decides its best to save space during travel, and lift what she needs off others along her journey.

On her bed, she shoves some old t-shirts, pants, and other clothes she imagines will be comfortable for traveling into the pack. Random toiletries she can easily carry get tossed on top with no real rhyme or reason. She empties the contents of her smaller bag out onto her mattress, transferring the items she took from Olympia's into the new, bigger space.

She holds the pack of letters from her mother to Olympia, running her hand over the lavender, silk ribbon keeping them together. Someday, she thinks, someday she will read them. Not yet, she needs to heal the hurt trapped in her heart first. She takes the green cloth with Olympia's family crest on it, and blankets it around the letters, keeping them safe, and tucks them into a side pocket of her bag.

At her dresser, Rue collects all the coins she has been saving from her wooden box. In her kitchen drawers, she pulls out every potion she has hoarded over the years, things for healing, sleeping, and even illusions. She picks up one of the sparkling pink liquid vials of Ear Elixir and decides against bringing them. For the first time in her life, she won't have to hide who she really is. That thought sends a shiver down her spine, but Rue can't name the emotion. Whatever it is, it brings her one small step closer to feeling alive again.

On top of the essentials, Rue stuffs the remaining space with Phoenix the Fox, a few of the bracelets Olympia wanted her to have, and the rolled up Tree of Life tapestry.

Before she closes the pack and leaves for good, she searches for the remains of her mother's letter to her, and the one from Olympia. With a burst of sparkles from her hand, she guides the notes from their spot on her pink chair, stopping a moment to read them over before sticking them into the side zipper with the others.

A little prayer of faith in The Mother leaves her lips, hoping she never has to receive another letter from someone she lost again. Two is far too many.

She lifts the bag up onto her shoulders, lighter than she expects, and walks into her bathroom. Behind the mirror, Rue grabs her mother's opal necklace off the hook and clasps it around her neck. She brushes the rough, diamond shaped stone between her fingers, watching as it shines in the reflection of the glass. After years of hanging on a hook, this heirloom of her past finally gets to be worn again.

Rue has only one more trick up her sleeve, to make sure people stop their search for her. She examines the studio apartment and starts conjuring her magic into her hands. Her body aches from how much she has been using over the past few weeks. She isn't as strong as she would like, but there is enough in her soul to get through the next couple minutes.

Pulling strength from her diaphragm, she starts to exhale as a wind forms around the space. She casts her sparkles into the few pieces of furniture she has and throws them across the room. The old, wooden end table splinters against the kitchen cabinets. Her mattress is tossed onto its side, knocking over the only lamp she has. Glass, plates, and cookware fly out of the cupboards and onto the floor, shattering with loud cracks against the kitchen tile.

She reaches for her dagger, putting it up to the palm of her hand, and slicing into herself. The pain is stronger than anticipated, which brings her a sense of calm knowing she can still feel and isn't actually numb. Wiping the blade against a blanket, she places it back in the holster, as blood starts to drip onto the carpet. Lifting her hand to her mouth, she begins to blow out magic, which takes the blood with it, creating horrific spatter art on the walls.

Soon the whole room looks like a gruesome murder scene, and Rue knows it's time to go. She wraps her hand in a cloth soaked in a healing potion. Within a few moments, the wound is gone, and she is no longer in physical pain.

As she's leaving, she catches a glimpse of herself in a broken mirror. Her eyes are red, and her skin is pale. The vibrancy of her auburn hair looks faded, and she feels defeated. She tucks a lock of hair behind her ear, exposing the small braid that hides by the nape of her neck. Her thumb and pointer finger smooth it between them.

In a few hours she will be gone. Leaving no trace of herself behind that she doesn't want others to find. She finally understands what it means to be Ghost.

She has no concrete plan, only one goal. The same one she has had since she was a young girl. Kill the man that made her life this living hell. Kill the man responsible for taking her parents away from her, her last and longest vendetta.

Rue is going to go to the mainland. Make it to the Northlands. And slit Lord Magnus's throat.

But first she has one final goodbye, one she is dreading to have to say.

The waves crash onto the shore as Rue walks by, stones crunching under her boots. In front of her is the oak tree, and she does her best to keep her composure.

As she approaches, the sign of wildflowers growing up the trunk helps slow her heartbeat. Just knowing Olympia continues to create beauty in death, is enough to help her continue on. Beautiful pops of blue, yellow, and white wrap their way up green vines, hugging the trunk in an embrace of familiarity. At the base of the tree, where less than two days ago was soft loose dirt, is now a flower patch of magic. On an island that cannot produce natural things, a spot of wonder sits in its chaos.

Rue kneels down in front of Olympia's grave, letting her legs and pack rest in the stones of the beach. Tears pool in her eyes, and she allows them to fall, not wanting to keep the emotions at bay when it comes to her. Her hands tremble in front of her while she fidgets with two white stones. Gently, she places them at the base of the tree, tucked into the flowers for protection.

One for Issak. One for Rocky.

Protect them Oly, especially Rocky. She was so lost. She needs someone to care about her. Protect her like you did me.

Rue sits and watches, not willing to say the words goodbye yet. She isn't sure how to handle this. This empty feeling in her gut won't leave her. It doesn't quite feel real yet. Like she's still caught in another nightmare.

"I'm sorry."

Her voice comes out hoarse and breathy. Unable to keep her eyes up, she lowers them to her hands. A wave of emotions washes over her, and she sits in the heaviness of death. It's so final. So permanent. Nothing can change the outcome once it's happened, and now she has to learn how to move on. She wonders if that is even possible for her, if the hurt will fade, or if she will stay in this universe of pain forever.

"I hope you can forgive me. Please forgive me. I need to know… I need to know you'll still watch over me, protect me like you always have," she says, voice small and so unlike her.

"I'm sorry I couldn't kill him. I wanted to. I still do, but I looked at his face and knew you wouldn't want me to. A part of me sat there, and knew I had to let him live, even though he took you from me." She wipes fallen tears from her chin.

"I don't think I can be everything you want me to be. I will try my best to live in the light, but that seems impossible without you."

Rue lifts her heat to the branches of the oak. "I understand why you kept things from me, I wasn't ready to hear them. Even now I don't know if I am, but I'm glad I know the truth.

"I think it took losing you, to make me realize why I have to keep going. Why I want to live. Thank you for that gift. Thank you for my life, and the only happy memories I have. I understand love, and beauty, and gentleness because of you, Oly. You've changed my life in the best way. You taught me to survive. I am going to survive. I hope that makes you proud."

Before she loses the last little spark of strength she has, Rue stands to her feet. With heavy eyes and an even heavier heart, she walks up to the oak tree. Both her hands connect with its rough exterior, and she leans her forehead on it. Tears get lost in the empty feeling filling her soul. They seep into the bark, watering the tree with sadness. She closes her eyes and sobs, prolonging her final goodbye.

"I don't know how I'm going to do this. I think I'm afraid, Oly."

The words leave her lips without fully processing them. Afraid is not a word she attaches to herself often, yet it is how she feels. For most of her life, even when she wanted to be alone, she always had Olympia. As much as she ran away, and ignored the pull to family, Olympia welcomed her back every single time.

For years Rue told herself she was alone, believing the lie that she had no one to her core. Now, standing over Olympia's grave, she truly is alone, and she is terrified.

A fragile, feathery sensation hums on Rue's hand. She lifts her head and is frozen in place when she sees what has perched itself on her. A beautiful, green and white butterfly is using Rue's hand as a spot of rest. It flutters its wings, opening and closing them to match Rue's heartbeat. She takes a step back, holding it out in front of her, and begins to sniffle her tears dry. The shock of what she's looking at takes over her body.

Under the delicate wings, a trail of golden glitter drips down and evaporates in thin air like an illusion.

Is this an illusion?

She was always told spirits aren't strong enough to be seen in the Southlands. Yet here sits a butterfly with green and white wings, Olympia's spirit animal. A sign from beyond, from Olympia. She is with her; how could Rue ever doubt that?

The initial shock wears off, and tears begin to drop down Rue's face once again. Tears of relief this time, instead of pain. Olympia would never let her down. Never leave her alone when she needed someone. Her face is soaked by the time she stops, making her question how much emotion she has within her after all these years of not allowing it to surface.

After a few moments of peace, the butterfly flutters off her hand and lands on the tree, resting on a blue forget me not flower.

"I want to stay with you, Olympia, but it's time for me to go now. This is no goodbye. When my time comes, I can't wait to see you again in the meadow."

Rue reluctantly turns to walk away. After a few steps down the beach, she stops to turn around, wanting one last look at the tree.

To her surprise, the butterfly is now gone, and all that is left is the mighty oak and its flowery vines sitting over Olympia, watching over her while her body rests below the dirt. The petals and branches sway as a gust of wind blows up the beach off the ocean behind her.

She attempts to smile, but realizes she isn't ready for happiness yet. She will get there, she has hope of that, but for now she is allowing herself to be heartbroken.

CHAPTER

RUE walks along the cobblestone streets of the fish market as the sun starts to make its descent into the ocean, her bag slouched over one shoulder. The smell of mold, piss, and rotting fish fill her nose, but she doesn't care tonight.

She strides with purpose as a few of the drunken sailors start to cat call her for a quick fuck, while they lay out against the dumpsters. Rue uses that as a reason to pick up her pace, lifting her black hood up over her head to hide her features.

The rusting, metal bridge onto the fishing docks scratches against the stone as she crosses. Once she reaches the other side, and her boots hit the wooden planks, she lets herself breathe. She is officially not on Southland soil any longer, the farthest she has ever gotten in escaping this hell hole.

She reaches into her pocket as she surveys the boats in the marina. Rows and rows of colorful (yet warn from the ocean) fishing boats fill all the spaces. Some new, most very old. Her eyes are drawn to one in particular, a green boat on the end. It looks as though it was a pirate ship at one point in its life, like one from the stories Olympia would tell Rue as a child. The pirate sails have been replaced with fishing nets and cranes for easy unloading.

Her eyes shift to the piece of paper in her hand, the envelope from Olympia. She reads over the words written in green ink, ingrained into her head with hope.

"The Blue Lady"
Dock Number 77.
Fishing Charter.
Leaves at Dusk.
The captain will be expecting you.

The mysterious woman who was responsible for rescuing fae folk in danger and sending them to the mainland, is just a simple fishing boat. The name **LADY JOVANNA** is painted on the side of the green ship in bright blue letters, hiding in plain sight.

She can feel the blip in her gut pulling her tether to the boat and she welcomes it, knowing deep in her bones this is the right decision for her. She looks back only once to the island, feeling content knowing nothing is there for her anymore.

The wood creaks beneath her steps as she passes boats. Men yell terms she doesn't understand, as crates and nets of fish are offloaded from the day's catch. Others fill ships back up with supplies for their next departures. The energy is chaotic, yet these men seem to have systems in place like a choreographed routine, ways of doing things that make their crews run like well-oiled machines.

She lowers her head as she walks, making sure to conceal her face in the shadow of her hood. Not that she thinks anyone is paying attention to her, but the last thing she needs is for someone to come around asking questions, and one of these men remembering the woman with red hair leaving on a fishing boat, and not returning.

At the end of the harbor, she reaches the dock of Lady Jovanna. Now getting a closer look at the ship itself, she can see that the original wooden exterior has been painted this emerald green. Ropes and nets hang off the side, with bright colored buoys tied to the railing. The wheelhouse is towards the back of the boat, still a beautiful golden wood color, although it has seen better days.

Rue is interested to see this ship in the daylight, wondering if the darkened skies are making it appear younger than it is. She wonders what the ship was like in its glory days, before weather and time held it in their grasp, causing it to become tired.

She can relate. She is tired too. So tired.

She knows nothing about ships. Nothing about the ocean. In fact, all she knows is that if you fall into the bay, you have a better chance at getting eaten alive, then making it back up to the surface. She isn't sure if the entirety of the sea is the same, or if like most of this volatile island, the waters surrounding it are also cursed.

Her mind shifts against her will. Can she do this? Can she safely cross this sea, into a new world she knows dangerously little about how to navigate? Maybe this is a bad idea. Maybe she should turn around and hide out for a bit while the search for her dies down. What if she leaves and it's worse than here? What if fae folk hate half fae? What if she can't do it? What if she's not enough?

She wasn't enough for Olympia. She watched as she spoke her last breath and did nothing. It's all her fault. The blood. So much blood on her hands. It will never be washed away; part of her soul will always be covered in the darkness of death. Surrounding her. Suffocating her hope until she has no choice but to surrender to the pain.

Rue gets brought back to the harbor when someone clears their throat in her direction, and she realizes she's been standing there like a psychopath staring at the boat with dead eyes.

Pull yourself together.

Thoughts of Olympia lying in her arms fill her mind, and she can't stop the tremors. White masks, and blood, and dried flowers, and letters, and metal handcuffs attack her thoughts.

Breathe Rue, breathe.

Rue realizes her eyes are closed, and when they open to meet those of another, her breath finally releases from her lungs in a quick gust. Standing down the dock a few feet away is a tall, broad shouldered man, with arm tattoos covering his olive skin, peeking out of his rolled sleeves. His curly black hair is long but tied up into a bun in the back of his head, a few loose pieces fall down, sticking to his sweaty face. He stares at her like she is about to commit a crime he will ultimately have to clean up.

He says nothing.

Feeling the awkwardness in her bones, she has the urge to break this eternal silence

Say something. He's expecting you to say something. You need to be allowed on this boat. For the love of every single God pull your head out of the void.

"Hi," she says softly, clearing her throat and shaking the pins and needles out of her hands. "Are you the captain?"

Did your question really have to come out so desperate?

Again, he says nothing.

His only movement comes from the crate of live fish sloshing around in front of him. The veins in his arms pop out like he might crush the wood with his bare hands. She can see the muscles of his jaw twitch under his facial hair.

This is going to be a long trip if I can't pull myself together.

Rue inhales deeply to center herself. She packs all her sorrow and grief into its box in the back of her mind. Securing it with a lock she doesn't have the combination to, and hiding it in the darkness of her soul. Praying that she never has to open it back up.

She repeats her question now, this time a little louder, with a little more confidence in her tone. When he still chooses not to answer her, her annoyance steps forward in her mind, and she feels the rush of her old self again. Rue huffs with her arms in the air and gives him a look that says *"are you going to answer me asshole"* walking up to him.

He is almost a foot taller than her, maybe more, but she holds her ground, glaring up at him. There is a heat coming off of him, and she doesn't know if she is imagining it, or if it's just muggy and he is currently sweating. Her heartbeat rings in her ears, but she doesn't look away. He smells of fish, for obvious reasons, and under that stench sits a hint of wood and smoke.

She gets caught off guard by the color of his eyes. It's as if they are made of charcoal half way from being burned. A deep gray with flecks of silver, and when his stare intensifies, she swears she can see burning embers within them.

A feeling pulls at her mind, like she has met him before. Has she hustled him in a card game before? Or was he one of the men working at Lucky Clover?

Whatever it is, best not to bring it up. This is my only ticket out of here.

"Can I speak to the captain? Or do you need me to recite some sort of sea shanty to enter?" She welcomes her wit back with open arms, relieved that she can break out of this helpless fawn curse of being sad, at least for the time being.

His lip twitches, but that's all the response she gets for her question. Instead of actual words leaving his mouth, he motions his big, rude head towards an older man behind him, farther down the docks counting crates of fish with a clipboard.

"Thank you. Your willingness to be helpful will be studied for generations I'm sure," she sneers, and moves around him without another look.

Walking up to the captain her mood shifts, the ringing in her ear subsides as does her heart rate. His eyes are kind, smiling at her with wrinkles framing his face. He's wearing an open button down shirt, covered in oil and guts from fishing. His gray hair is wiry and disheveled, as is his mustache. He looks like his ship, weathered yet still going strong.

"Are you the captain?"

He places his clipboard under his arm and wipes his hands against his shirt before reaching out to shake hers. "Why yes, I do believe that's me. Captain Sebastian Crowley, at your service. Nice to meet you—" He pauses so she can insert her name.

"Rue," she says with a small smile, taking his hand to shake. She can feel the rough calluses in his palms, but his grip is warm and reassuring against her cold fingers.

"Well, nice to see you, Rue. How may I be of service this evening? Not many women want to be deckhands these days."

"I was told by Olympia Tutrice that you did *fishing charters*, you know, to the *mainland*." Rue nods in the direction of the ocean.

His eyes scrunch up for a moment, before realization hits him and he reaches out towards her, second guessing his movements when she winces away from the idea of contact. "Are you Aruelia? *The* Aruelia? Your grandmother told me so much about you."

He pauses to lower his head and put a hand to his heart. "I'm deeply sorry for your loss. She was a great woman. I was there that night. We all were." He nods his head towards the man she just passed. When she turns, his charcoal eyes are locked on her with so much intensity, her composure is threatened to crack in half.

Crowley continues, "Watching you walk through that city; thought you might just be the bravest kid I'd ever seen."

Rue looks to the sky, not wanting her first interaction with his man to be one where she blubbers like a baby. When she meets his gaze again, she admits, "She was like no other."

He stands there in a peaceful silence, not speaking in fear of saying the wrong thing.

When Rue can't take it anymore, feeling like she is being suffocated from this interaction, she asks, "So… Can I get on the boat? I'm kind of hoping to leave tonight."

"Of course, Kiddo. I already have one other stow away, so what's one more!" Crowley points to the ship, where there is another person sitting against the side. A lanky looking kid, maybe eighteen to twenty, with dark skin, short, white tipped locs pulled to one side, and round rimmed glass. He is hunched over with his knees to his chest and his head in a notebook, like he doesn't want to be seen over the side of the ship.

From this distance, she can't make out his features, but she gets a sense he might be scared. She can feel it in the beating of his heart, and there is a pulse running through him, almost as if he will burst if provoked. She can relate to his uneasiness. If he is willing to make this trip alone, at such a young age, something is chasing him, whether that be someone else or himself.

"I can always use another set of hands. Oh, and call me Cap, all the boys do," Crowley, Cap, chimes in when she looks back at him.

"Thank you." Rue says those two words with so much sincerity that she might just burst herself. This is the first night in a long time she feels safe, like her problems will be gone once the lights of the city cannot reach her anymore.

Cap winks at her and nods his understanding. He hands her a crate of dead fish, which she politely accepts (and definitely does not make a face), and he ushers her onto the ship, showing her where to set it down. She takes a seat in the front as she watches two deckhands load up for the trip.

Other than the stone wall who refused to speak, there is another worker too. He is just as tall, but half the width as the first. His dark skin shines against the light of the city, showing her his striking face, and an even more breathtaking smile. His energy is electric. He sings and talks to himself as he moves crates and buckets to and from the dock. He seems to have a way with the first guy, because he actually responds when he speaks to him, as if the two are friends.

Her curiosity is interested to see how the dynamic works. How does he get him to engage? She wants to continue watching and observing, and does so through side glances until she meets the big boulder's eyes again. She quickly redirects her sight to the wood beam above her head.

Maybe if I'm lucky and I pray hard enough, it will fall on me and knock me out.

Rue vows to keep her eyes to herself for the remainder of the trip. Settling in, she pulls the tree of life tapestry out of her bag, wrapping it around herself like a blanket. The smell of the shop consumes her, letting her release calm breathes.

The sun is now hiding, and the night is filled with a clouded sky. The light pollution bleeding off the building mixes with the darkness to make an eerie glow of red and yellow against the clouds.

She looks forward to the quiet. She craves the idea of stillness on the water, where no one is shouting, or fighting. There is no honking, or music blasting into her eardrums.

Yes, that will be nice.

After what feels like hours of anticipation, the boat is pulling away from the shore. Rue walks to the back of the ship to watch Alerious City fade away. A shiver crawls down her spine as the unknown of her future takes her mind in it's hands. The wind whips around, causing the ropes and hooks to sway back and forth.

As the city gets smaller and smaller, she views it from a new perspective, more concrete in her way of thinking perhaps is a better word. From the water, she can see the lopsided wealth in full effect, out in the open with no smoke and mirrors trying to hide it. The bright, white lights of the High District tower over the dim, and flickering lights of the Low District.

Stunning stone towers overshadow the makeshift, reused shacks that surround them. She has never seen something so disgusting. Her eyes wander to the stone wall separating the two districts, and she vows to come back some day and demand justice for those who cannot. She makes a note in her soul to never forget this place. Never forget the struggle it takes to survive here.

But that day is not today. Today she begins her fight for herself. Today she focuses on her future. Her purpose.

The Southlands are now a part of her past. A part of her story that will be reread as sadness, and loss, and betrayal, and loneliness. But as she looks out on the water, gazing at the twinkling lights reflecting off the surface, she chooses to remember the good. A time when her family was one she made herself. Not the Smoke Runners, not Diego, but the people of West Harbor, her people.

Fiona, Charlie, Finny, Issak, and especially Olympia. For they will be in her soul, traveling with her while she discovers her origin. Avenge her parents' death. And mend a tiny part of the iron stone she has as a heart.

She has to believe that. It is all the hope she has left to carry her.

Her hair sweeps around her face as a gust of wind blows through her, pulling her into its warmth. She embraces the tapestry around her arms tighter.

She is alive. She made it.

I am still alive. I did it. I survived them.

The breeze replenishes the energy she desperately needs to keep going. In the back of her mind, her senses pick up a smell she often experiences with wind off the coast. It fills her with comfort, but this time it is not just the smell of pine from her mother. This time it is mixed perfectly with hints of mint, an aroma she will forever know as Olympia.

I am still alive.

Rue closes her eyes and allows the tears to fall down her cheeks, the current swallowing her up. Her life will continue on because she did not allow herself to be broken by broken people.

I survived.

Her mother is with her. Olympia is with her. And she is alive.

I am alive, and I am free.

EPILOGUE

... She lied to me; our whole relationship was built on lies. She could have killed my father that day, all those years ago. She could have killed us all. She was a monster. A fucking fae monster who had no business being in the Southlands. Yet, she stayed. She hid who she was from everyone. From me. She obeyed every order for the most part. She did everything I asked of her until this fucking mess.

She was never supposed to be involved. I was supposed to protect her, Metus men protect what is theirs. She was mine. She was fae, but she was mine. Mine and only mine. The enemy was sleeping in my bed, working for me, and she belonged to me. I loved her, but she didn't care. I could only clean up her mistakes for so long.

And she made this happen. She betrayed me after I protected her over myself.

I loved and lost a monster...

Diego jerks awake. The sun's rays are blinding as he opens his eyes. His vision is blurred, and he can't recall where he is.

The last thing he remembers is Rue. Her anger. Her hatred towards him. His leg. She stabbed him in the fucking leg.

He deserved it, he was supposed to protect her, but instead he betrayed her. A lump forms in his throat. He was responsible for killing someone she cared for, someone she loved more than him. The jealousy bubbles up in his chest, causing fists to form in his hands. He loved her, and not once did she say it back.

I protected that disgusting beast.

His body tenses immediately, making him wince in pain. So much pain. He tries to focus but his vision is still foggy.

Where am I?

There is a ringing in his ear—no, a beeping sound. He slowly moves an arm to his face, rubbing his eyes, moaning in agony as each muscle stretches. He is so fucking sore. There are tubes coming out of his arms, and he does his best to focus his mind. Where is he?

"The President of Currency dies of mysterious causes, Lipstick Killer at large! Such a ridiculous headline. What a shame that old Lex died on us, is it not?"

NO! That voice. It can't be that voice. That man. No, it's not possible.

The man laughs and sets down the newspaper he is reading on Diego's bed. "I see you are trying to make sense of this, dear boy. You have been in a clinic for three days, in critical condition after ingesting enough poison that should have killed you. You are also suffering from a severe infection on your leg due to a knife wound in your upper thigh. That little bitch did a number on you it seems. She was not delighted when she found out you killed her precious Nymph, was she?"

"Magnus," Diego breathes through coughs. He hardly has a voice, dried out from the clinic air. "What are you doing here?"

"Oh, just visiting a friend in his time of need. Making my rounds. Looking at all of our progress. Tying up loose ends if you will."

That last line causes Diego's stomach to churn.

Magnus continues in his throaty voice. "The worthless girl did us a favor by killing him really, he was beginning to get power hungry. And I do not appreciate when my *companions* get their own ideas. It makes for messy work, and distractions. Do you agree?"

Diego's vision starts to clear, and he can finally see the demon posing as a man in front of him. There he is, sitting in a clinic chair, in a white suit not even a president could afford, unbuttoning a golden star button on his suit jacket.

His icy blue eyes make Diego go stiff. His stark white hair blends into his pale features, with a perfectly trimmed beard to match. His face shares no insight as to what he's thinking. No emotions other than disgust are painted in his expression. Lord Magnus of the Northlands, here, sitting in the High District because Diego fucked up.

"So, are you going to enlighten me? Explain how you ended up here instead of her?"

"I did everything you asked of me," Diego whispers, still not able to move his body. "She's gone. On a ship to the mainland as we speak. She won't be a problem for us anymore."

Magnus lowers his brows and stares deeper into Diego, moving a hand over his beard. "You naive boy, she's more of a threat off this godsdamned island than on it. On it, we could control her. On it, she could be watched and manipulated."

Somehow Diego manages a laugh. "There is no controlling that woman."

Magnus shoots up out of his chair and gets within inches of Diego. He spits, "Maybe if you thought with your brain instead of your cock for one second, you could have."

"Did you know she has magic? She's not fucking human! She can move air around with her breath. She's fucking fae! How was I supposed to manipulate a beast like that?"

Magnus freezes, his eyes go wide as the words reach his understanding. This makes Diego smirk, knowing something he didn't, making him uncomfortable for once in their four year partnership. He laughs again. "You didn't know."

Magnus stands up, taking a few steps back, running a hand through his perfectly styled crew cut. "How is that possible, she is not even fully fae? She had shown zero signs as a child."

The hairs on Diego's arms stand up, he plays those words back in his head, *as a child*. "What? You knew her as a child? Who the hell is she to you?"

Magnus swallows, body tensing up. "She is my biggest liability; one I should have taken care of when she was four and I threw her off that damned ship."

Diego coughs, trying to make sense of this all. "So, this whole thing, getting rid of her was what? Some personal vendetta? Some sick, twisted rivalry between the two of you?"

"No, boy! She has the power to be my demise, and you let her get away. Which makes *you* a new liability. You could not kill her when you had the chance, letting some pretty eyes and nice tits get in the way of the job you were contracted to do."

He moves closer to Diego, towering over him as he stands by his bedside. His smile is the most evil thing Diego has ever seen. Nothing but the void radiates off this man.

"My people won't let you leave this building if you touch me."

Magnus laughs. "Your people? You are a foolish child who thought having me kill your father for you, would in some way make you man enough to run his business. Be better than Daddy in every way. You honestly thought just because I gave you his dynasty, that you would be in charge of the people around you? You are weak. A pathetic excuse for a leader. They were never your people; they were always mine. They listen to me, because I was the one strong enough to kill him. You did nothing but agree to terms you did not understand. Everything you have is because of me. All I asked you to do in return was one simple thing in exchange for your power, and that was to execute that redheaded nightmare. And this is how you repay me, allowing her to get away? Oh, I think not."

"You won't get away with this," Diego breathes.

"Oh, but I already have," he wickedly admits, his half smirk growing wider. "I have no use for the South any longer. I have what I came for, and soon I will be untouchable by all of you beneath me. And as for you, our contract is hereby voided. You are no longer an asset to the Organization."

Magnus reaches into his suit jacket and pulls out a vial of pearlescent liquid, glowing in the light of the sun. "You see, our dear friend Rue is not the only one who can create potions, or *poisons* as you pathetic humans would call them. In fact, I am quite skilled at it myself. This exquisite little bottle is made from Glowing Thistleroot. It is an invasive species on the mainland, growing in my territory, the North. When ground into a paste, added to Spittlebug larvae and Jimsom Weed, my research found it to be very effective at separating souls from their bodies. However, when you add that mixture to a few drops from the Forbidden Waters in the Northlands, this vial is unlike any before it. Lethal to the human body at any dose."

Diego goes cold but uses what strength he has left to show no fear. He won't give Magnus the satisfaction.

Magnus adds, "As thrilling as that all sounds, that is not even the best part. You humans are so laughably unintelligent, no one will ever be able to detect it in your blood after you die. And know it will be painful, boy, but quick. I am no monster."

He moves to Diego's IV bag hanging off a hook next to his bed. Pulling a syringe out of his pocket, withdrawing the glowing liquid into it, and injecting it into the IV, Magnus laughs in his victory.

He puts a finger onto the puncture hole from the needle and a small swirl of black smoke melts from his hands. He mumbles words in another tongue Diego doesn't understand, and when he moves away, the hole is gone. Black ooze drips from Magnus's fingers which he cleans with a handkerchief from his pocket. The fae monster gently folds it back up to stick in his suit, like the action is common. Diego can smell the darkness radiating off of him, burning his nostrils and plunging the smell of death into his brain.

"Any minute now, you will be reunited with dear old Daddy, and your mother who was taken too soon. A pretty thing she was, tragic what happened to her really. But you know all about that. After all, you are the reason she is dead."

Diego's breath becomes rapid. His eyes go dark with rage.

Magnus continues, "And I am sure you will be seeing your love soon too. I am going to end her."

Magnus lets out a hoarse laugh, making Diego want to throw up the acid filling his lungs. His skin starts to burn with a stinging agony more powerful than he has ever felt, like being thrown in a fire and freezing to death at the same time. Sweat streams down his face, his lungs feeling like they might explode. Through gritted teeth Diego whispers, "I can't wait for her to fucking destroy you."

"I look forward to the day I get to see her try, and I can finally slit that pretty. Little. Throat." With every word, Magnus moves closer and closer to Diego's face, dominating every part of the situation.

Diego lets out a laugh through the overwhelming torture, foam starting to drip from his lips while he smiles. With eyes fighting to stay open, so his words reach into Magnus's empty soul, Diego spits, "She will win you know."

"And why is that?"

Diego's body starts to shake violently, his vitals drop, and he uses his last breath to whisper, "Because we made her."

Magnus watches as he fades away, spirit dropping to the depths of the void. The machines he is hooked up to start to beep, and two human clinic assistants rush in. One of them holding a white coat matching the other surgical healers in the building.

Magnus looks at her and she nods with a nervous smile. "Please, my lord, put this on. We need to get you out of here." The two of them leave and as they exit the room, a marshal clinic guard follows close behind. The floor erupts into chaos behind them, with more clinic assistants and healers rushing in to try and save Diego's life.

With a face as cold and dead as ice, Magnus storms out of the clinic, leaving the woman assistant at the door ushering him out. The guard follows right behind, and as if waiting for this exact moment, a black cenzium vehicle pulls up in front of him. Without stopping his stride, Magnus jumps into the back seat, followed by the marshal. The car speeds away as if it was never there.

Inside, Magnus runs his hands through his hair, slamming a fist into the leather seat.

"Fuck!" he yells.

He looks around, trying to come up with a solution for this festering problem that is Aruelia Kylexi.

"Franky!" he screams to the driver.

"Yes, My Lord?" Franky, the bodyguard from Sinners, allows the outdated title to roll off his tongue. His eyes focus on the road, but his heart is beating out of his chest.

"We need to go to the ships, now!"

"Of course, Sir." Franky's eyes are wide with worry when he answers, but he doesn't flinch his movements, or he could be next.

"I will not sit idle and allow that prophecy to proceed any further than it already has."

Magnus looks out the window, fists right against his sides. "That Half Witch can never make it back to the North."

A Note From The Teller

Dear Traveler,

True bravery comes when everything around you is pulling you into the depths of defeat, yet you continue on.

Until we cross paths again, I wish for you to continue on.

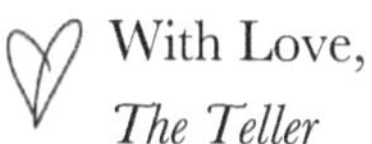 With Love,
The Teller

A Note From Me, The Author

I've always been fascinated with the idea of morally gray men, and the fact that in fiction those men are the ones we readers swoon over. The concept of someone being so bad to the world, yet still comes home to the main character and shows them affection like no other, makes my body melt just like the next girl. The big reveal that the morally gray heart throb would quite literally burn the world down to make the MC happy, makes me levitate into another plane of existence.

But, during my day dreams of being picked up, tossed over a tattooed shoulder, and carried off into the only bed left in the inn, my mind sometimes drifts to- *what if it doesn't end like that?*

Now this may be my own personal trauma talking (I'll have to ask my therapist), but what if the line these types of characters are teetering on, good vs bad, pulls them into the darkness instead of the light? What if they aren't good in the end? What if it's all a mask?

Not only that, but what if the MC can't see that for themselves right away? What if they are holding on to the memories that are like sunshine, so they won't have to admit that they are not going to save their morally gray love?

I know this is fiction, but that doesn't mean questions of morality shouldn't be discussed in the real world. I worry that sometimes, fiction can give us a false hope that love and respect could be found in anyone if you wait long enough, when sometimes that's not the case.

Sometimes you put your vulnerability in someone's hands in the hope of them protecting it, and instead they burn it to ash.

Now I know that's not what readers want to see in the end, I'll be the first to admit it's depressing as hell. But it's real. And it's an idea I have always wanted to write about, because I need there to be a perspective of someone who moves on after that. I need to know that you can go through hell and make it out on the other side as a whole person still.

So, I apologize if you went into this hoping for a different outcome. Wanting the *love* Diego had for Rue to be real and him help her take down the Organization like a badass spy couple. That is just not the story I wanted to tell.

I do need you to understand Rue is not a victim in this part of her story. She is a survivor. Victims sadly do not win against their monsters. Rue did, over and over again. Granted she used some dark measures, ones I DO NOT encourage using in the real world, but she freed herself of the chains the only way she knew how.

Those of you who are fortunate enough to never experience something like Rue does, I hope you understand how hard it is to pull yourself out of the only world you know, and not allow it to break your spirit. But I hope that you also see that it is possible, despite the difficulty.

I dedicated this book to those who survived the darkness and wear their scars like armor, because I needed to remind myself that it's possible.

Some of us have seen firsthand what darkness in a person's soul can look like, whether that be a partner, a parent, a friend, or even a complete stranger. There is a group of us who have gone years just trying to survive, while glass is shattering by our feet and time stands still.

It is not simple. It is not safe. And it does not always end in a happily ever after. It takes guts, and bravery, and determination to free yourself from that darkness. Survivors of any form of abuse are the strongest amongst us.

If that is you, I hope this story gives you hope. Hope that it will end, and you will get out, and you will have peace. It is not going to be easy, or beautiful, or fun, but it will get better, because you will not give up. You are not broken. I hope you can see that you are so brave. You are a survivor. And this is not your fault.

Your story is not your trauma, it is how you choose to continue living. The same can be said for Rue. She does continue, and her story does get better as she finds herself, meets her found family, and learns what real, honest, safe love looks like. Over this entire series, my only goal is to show what it looks like to pull yourself away from giving in to your monsters.

I hope and pray to all the Gods, the universe, even The Mother, that you can find that for yourself. You deserve a good life. And I hope the story of Aruelia Kylexi, Half Witch of the Northlands, and the other members of The Elemental 6 who you will meet very soon, can hug your soul when you feel alone. Because none of us are.

You are not alone.

And your story matters.

You are alive and you are free.

Keep holding hope!
  With Love,
  K.H.B.

Trigger Warning Chapter Guide

Blood
-Chapter 5
-Chapter 8
-Chapter 12
-Chapter 22
-Chapter 23
-Chapter 24
-Chapter 30
-Chapter 31
-Chapter 35
-Chapter 36

Death
-Chapter 3 (off page)
-Chapter 4 (off page)
-Chapter 8
-Chapter 24
-Chapter 27
-Chapter 30
-Chapter 31
-Epilogue

Depression/ Thoughts of Suicide
-Chapter 22
-Chapter 24
-Chapter 29
-Chapter 31

-Chapter 32
-Chapter 33

Drug Use
-Chapter 15 (Just witnesses)

Emotional Abuse
-Chapter 4
-Chapter 11
-Chapter 24
-Chapter 28
-Chapter 29
-Chapter 34
-Chapter 35

Physical Abuse
-Chapter 4
-Chapter 11
-Chapter 23
-Chapter 24

Poisoning
-Chapter 1
-Chapter 8
-Chapter 34
-Chapter 35
-Epilogue

PTSD/ Flashbacks
-Chapter 14
-Chapter 26

-Chapter 28
-Chapter 29
-Chapter 32
-Chapter 35
-Chapter 37

Rape/Sexual Assault
-Chapter 24
-Chapter 29

Sexual Harassment
-Chapter 1
-Chapter 6
-Chapter 9
-Chapter 17
-Chapter 23
-Chapter 34
-Chapter 35

Torture
-Chapter 3
-Chapter 10 (off page)
-Chapter 22
-Chapter 23
-Chapter 24
-Chapter 34
-Chapter 35
-Epilogue

Songs of The Southlands
AKA Tropes and My Hopes (and dreams)

Toxic Relationships
Born To Die by Lana Del Rey
Power by Isak Danielson
My Tears Ricochet (Long Pond) by Taylor Swift

Dystopian Fantasy
Soldier by Fleurie, Tommee Profitt
Gangster by Labrinth (inspired The High District)
Angry by Paravi

She's A Criminal
Secrets and Lies by Ruelle
Who's Afraid of Little Old Me? by Taylor Swift
Maneater by Nelly Furtado

Loss
The Truth by Fernando Velázquez (inspired the entire book)
Don't Leave, Don't Go by Deyaz
Moving On by Michael Giacchino

Continuing On
Angel By The Wings by Sia (inspired chapters 31-33)
Castles by Freya Ridings
Tessa by London Music Works (inspired Aruelia Kylexi)

Head to Spotify to get special character soundtracks for The Rogue Of The South and a complete playlist of songs that inspired life in the Southlands.

Acknowledgements

I'm humble enough to say this was not a one woman show. You know that phrase, it takes a village? Yeah, that was this book. It was a long process of trial and error, and more trials and one hundred more errors. But it's here! And it's done! And you are reading it, which is still wild to me.

What I want to do is write a ten page thesis about how important every single individual is on this list, but you don't want to read that, and this book is long enough. What I will do is take a quick second to thank as many as I can, before that dreadful music from award shows starts playing and they pull me away from my keyboard.

Ryan: Thank you for pulling me out of the dark and reminding me that I am allowed to be whole. I am so honored to be able to go through life with you. I hope you're proud of me. I'll be your eyes forever.

My Honey Bees: Thank you for being my reason to continue on. Being your mom is the greatest privilege of my life. I love you two more than anything else. Also, thank you for leaving me alone in my basement gremlin hole to finish writing this, and by *alone,* I mean the two minute intervals in between questions "only mom can answer." Never stop following your dreams.

Loren, Jackie, Kelly, Jordan, and Michelle: Thank you all for listening to me ramble about plot holes and taking the time to read my shitty drafts. This story wouldn't be what it is without you. I wouldn't be who I am without you. Love you tons.

Dad and Amy: Thank you for teaching me to dream. Also, thank you for only reading the redacted version of this book, Dad.

Alex: Thank you for helping me heal my soul so I could write this story. Also, I promise I'm okay.

My High School English Teachers: Thank you for not giving up on that sad, quiet girl. You reminded her that writing could be beautiful and therapeutic, and reading could comfort her in a way her world couldn't.

TikTok and My Writing Community of Strangers: Thank you for inspiring me to keep going and making me feel like I wasn't alone.

Decaf Coffee: Thank you for cosplaying as the real thing to get me through those long nights of editing.

The Others: I'd also like to take a second to thank everyone in my life that didn't have faith in me when I said I was going to write this book. I almost believed you. I'm glad I didn't.

About The Author

 Karissa H. B. is an independent author based in Cleveland, Ohio. The Rogue of The South is her debut novel which began as a prompt from a therapist to write out her trauma, and snowballed into a full length, six part series because her brain couldn't let it go. When she isn't writing, you'll find her dancing in the living room with her kids, sketching, or contemplating if one more chapter of her current read is worth the sleep loss. (The answer is always yes.) Throughout every phase of her life, writing has been an anchor. Her work is always based on the idea that every emotion we experience as humans, even the ones we try to hide away, can be viewed as beautiful.

CONNECT WITH KARISSA H. B. ONLINE
Tiktok @karissahb
Instagram @karissah.b.books

www.ingramcontent.com/pod-product-compliance
Lightning Source LLC
Chambersburg PA
CBHW022014300726
48970CB00003B/888